Praise for Patricia Snodgrass's
Mercer's Bayou

"The reader is hanging on by her fingernails."
~ *Horror World*

"This is a beautifully written, gripping, and chillingly atmospheric book. You've done a great job with it, Pat."
~ *T.M. Wright, author of A Manhattan Ghost Story, Eyes of the Carp and Blue Canoe*

"I hope that Ms. Snodgrass plans on writing more in the future, because if this book is any indication, the woman has talent in spades."
~ *Shannon C, The Good The Bad and the Unread*

"Warning: Reading Mercer's Bayou may increase the likelihood of developing insomnia and/or nightmares. Uncontrolled bouts of jitteriness may also occur. In addition, readers may feel the sudden urge to grab an axe and cut down every tree in their neighborhood."
~ *Smoky Trudeau, author of The Cabin*

Mercer's Bayou

Patricia Snodgrass

A Samhain Publishing, Ltd. publication.

Samhain Publishing, Ltd.
577 Mulberry Street, Suite 1520
Macon, GA 31201
www.samhainpublishing.com

Mercer's Bayou
Copyright © 2009 by Patricia Snodgrass
Print ISBN: 978-1-60504-169-8
Digital ISBN: 1-59998-935-2

Editing by Sarah Palmero
Cover by Natalie Winters

First Samhain Publishing, Ltd. electronic publication: June 2008
First Samhain Publishing, Ltd. print publication: April 2009

Dedication

To John and Jonathan
The loves of my life.

Author's Notes

Mercer's Bayou is a real place, which is in the same general area as the infamous Boggy Creek, about 15 miles or so from Texarkana, Arkansas. Although I can safely say I have never seen the Fouke Monster, (though I know of people who have) I have caught some decent-sized catfish off the banks near the boat ramp as a child, long before I discovered boys and decided that putting the worm on the hook was yucky.

The First Light Church of Prophecy, the town of Tatum, Walter Mc Knight House, along with the Cold Hanging Tree, the cemetery and all the characters are fictional, and any resemblance to any persons (or places) is purely coincidental.

The lore of this particular tree (there are actually two hanging trees) is as described in the book—to a point. A plantation owner, distraught that the South had lost, hanged all his slaves instead of setting them free. It is indeed said that the Hanging Tree will rip out your soul if you touch it.

I doubt the tree can actually yank out your soul, but I'm in no rush to find out. It does not, to my knowledge, glow green either, or entice wolves to howl, or force the dead to rise from their graves. At least, I haven't seen any dead people walking down my street lately. If I do, I'll let you know.

The gospel songs and lyrics mentioned in the novel are all public domain and are found at http://www.negrospirituals.com. Thanks guys for the help!

Cheers,

Patricia L. Snodgrass

New Boston, Texas

Part One
The Itinerant Preacher Heads East

Prologue

Excerpt from Lecho de Muerte, the Obscure Journals of Hernando De Soto, translated ed. 2004:

September 12, 1541

Our [Indian] guide betrayed us he led us into a swamp where a strange tree glowed, killing everything around it, including several of my men. I ordered a retreat, but we were ambushed by a crazed pack of wild animal men. They ripped apart twenty-five of mi soldados [soldiers]. We hanged the guide for his treachery ...

Article Abstract from the "Journal of Caddo Indian Archeology and Folklore," vol. 2, PG 27-29, January/February issue, Central Oklahoma Press. Anadarko, OK. 2005:

A Caddo burial mound recently unearthed at the Mercer's Bayou site excavated a mass grave containing twenty-six bodies near the First Light Church of Prophecy's legendary Cold Hanging Tree.

The mound is 1500 feet away from the tree on the northwestern edge of the cemetery. It contains bodies, but no burial items such as jewelry or pottery. Since the mound has remained untouched, it appears these individuals were cursed. Therefore no ceremonial items were placed with the bodies.

Myths and legends abound in the Southwest Arkansas area. The most famous is the legendary Fouke Monster, a

Sasquatch like creature that reportedly roamed the area during the late Twentieth Century.

A lesser-known story comes from the controversial *Lecho de Muerte*, the Obscure Journals of Hernando De Soto.

Desoto writes of encountering a race of wild men who lived with wolves. In conjunction with this myth is an enigmatic area that Desoto previously described while trekking through the Natches Trace as "witch dances," where large swaths of mysteriously scorched land and grasses spread for miles. The Indians considered these areas cursed and would not go near them.

Desoto reports a second witch dance site where a strange glowing tree sits upon the edge of a bayou. A similar burned area circled the tree. The Caddo Indians believed it was an evil place and the tree could possess the living by stealing their souls. Finding the mound so close to a cursed site suggests the individuals interred at the site were punished in the afterlife...

-3-

From the diary of Molly Stokes Mercer, Mercer's Plantation, June 19, 1864:

When Orville found out the Yankees won, he completely lost his mind. He had all the buck niggers hauled out to the church and hanged them on that scary old tree. What he did with the mammies and young'uns I don't know, but I'm sure it was gruesome and a waste.

-4-

Excerpt from the *Miller County Register*, August 30, 1890 vol. 2, PG-A.

A record number of hangings occurred this month when forty white men, one Negro tenant farmer and two Comanche squaws were executed for the robbery and murder of the occupants of the Butterfield Stage Coach. The ambush occurred five miles southwest of Tatum Arkansas. The executions took place at the gallows behind the First Light Church of Prophecy...

-5-

Headline from_*Miller County Register*, dated October 9, 1923 vol. 4, PG 2-b, 3-c.

WHITE MEN LYNCHED FOR WITCHCRAFT

Fourteen hunters swore under oath Sunday morning that they witnessed, and then lynched two Gypsy men who were holding a weird ritual involving wolves. The hanging took place at the First Light Church. "It's the most brutal lynching I've seen in the past twenty years," Wochowsky stated. The hunters are being held without bail pending hearings...

-6-

Obituary clipping from the *Miller County Register*, dated October 30, 1923 vol. 4, PG 3-b.

His partner, Ronald Simmons, found Deputy Sheriff Peter J. Wochowsky, from Tatum, Arkansas dead in his apartment Tuesday morning when he failed to report for duty. Services will be held at the White Chapel Memorial Church, on White Chapel Road Tatum, Arkansas at 2:30 p.m. Graveside services begin at 4:00 p.m. Wake at 6:30 p.m.

Chapter One

-1-

"He's here."

"It won't be long now, will it?"

"Not long at all. Praise God…"

-2-

A promise, carried along by a hot Santa Ana wind and a fatigued Greyhound bus, brought Pastor James Kilpatrick Thomas to the heat-exhausted border town of Tatum, Arkansas. The bus groaned to a halt as it rested itself onto the sand-swept terminal, easing down on its air shocks the way a dog settles on its haunches. Heavy, gray-hinged doors squealed open, and sweaty, travel worn passengers disgorged onto the reddish dirt-strewn pavement. Thomas gasped as diesel fumes slammed down his throat and burned his eyes as he stepped onto the tarmac. Tiny red dirt devils swirled around his feet as he shuffled around, looking for some sign of the man who was supposed to meet him here.

No one spoke as they wandered across the terminal toward the IHOP, and he wondered if he should join them. "It would be pointless though," he muttered to himself, knowing that all he had in his pockets were the remains of his ticket stub, the letter that brought him and the cottony grit of dryer lint.

He looked wistfully at the sign proclaiming "SENIORS EAT AT HALF PRICE." *Someone might be charitable enough to buy me a cup of coffee if I asked,* he thought, arguing with the rebellious rumbling of his stomach. *But I'd better not. I might miss Mr. Jim, and I literally can't afford that.*

Thomas turned his back to the restaurant. He stepped aside and watched the remaining passengers mill around the side of the Greyhound, waiting for their luggage.

"Got any baggage?" the driver inquired, indicating the half empty berth, which held a hefty number of bags and parcels.

"Uh, no, I don't."

"Well," the driver said, "you need to move aside."

Thomas complied. It was ten in the morning, according to the large round clock protruding from the corrugated metal hull of the bus station, but it was already breathtakingly hot. He took a few steps toward the road, hoping to see the white Chevy pickup the letter described pulling into the parking lot.

"When will Mr. Jim get here?" he muttered to himself. He hated waiting, but more than that, he feared the uncertainty. The letter in his pocket allotted him a cool place to stay, food—his empty stomach reminded him—and a job, thanks to the Taos Homeless Shelter for Men's director, Horace Shipley, who had connections with several shelters through out the Southwest.

Thomas was grateful for the ticket, the pat on the back and the opportunity to start over. Yet, he was nervous. *What if the deal has fallen through?* he thought as he wandered back to the bus. *What if he doesn't come? What if I'm stuck here? At least Taos was familiar, but now I'm broke and I have no way of getting back.*

"Excuse me," Thomas said as the driver heaved a flowery suitcase out of the baggage compartment for an elderly passenger.

"Unhh?"

"Excuse me," Thomas repeated, "Can you tell me where the Walter Mc Knight House is?"

"On Broad Street." The driver grunted around his thick Maine accent as he hefted an overstuffed suitcase out of the berth. "Follow the interstate west, and when you come to the nearest overpass, turn left and keep walking till you hit downtown."

"How far is that?" Thomas asked.

"Oh, about ten miles or so."

"Thanks." Thomas muttered.

Ten miles. A ten-mile hike in this heat might as well be ten thousand. I'd never make it. I'd have to either hitch a ride or start walking at sunset, he thought. *I might get there around midnight or so.*

"Mister, ya got someone waiting for you?" the driver asked. "I was kidding about the hike. You know you can go inside the terminal and wait, or call a cab."

"Thanks," he said, realizing with a stab of relief that, yes, he could indeed sit inside the air-conditioned lobby, perhaps even sleep there if he had to. *But that's if Jim doesn't show up, and Horace promised he would.*

"Good. You go and do that," the driver said.

"Thank you." Thomas returned the curtness. "I will."

Lukewarm air welcomed Thomas as he opened the glass door. Several people sat on long benches, using their itineraries and tickets for fans, while others stood in line at the ticket desk. Thomas stepped inside. Many of the passengers moved aside without paying attention to him, while others stared in frank disbelief at the deep scar on his throat.

Self-conscious, he tried to pull his t-shirt over the wound, but finding it constrictive, he yanked the ragged hem of his shirt down. He nodded at passersby, forcing a smile as he sat next to an elderly black woman who had managed to squeeze into a pink dress that was a good two sizes too small.

Apparently shocked at his boldness, she harrumphed loudly and shuffled further down the long bench, settling next to a tall, gaunt white woman with a black patent leather purse in her lap. The two conversed in urgent whispers. Although he did not hear all of the conversation, he knew it was about him. For the first time since he left Taos, he craved a drink. *Don't think about it,* he told himself. But it was too late; his brain slid the mental DVD into his mind and began to play, in Dolby Stereo, the last two wretched years of his life.

Two years and countless bottles of Johnnie Walker Red ago, James Thomas was living the American dream. He had a wife, a daughter in high school and he ministered a small but faithful flock of Zunis who gathered every Sunday morning for their weekly spiritual manna. It didn't make much money, but it paid the bills and gave him satisfaction that he was indeed doing the Lord's work, or at least to the best of his ability.

That all changed in the blink of an eye when a homeless man drifted into church one afternoon, shoddy and pale, asking for a place to stay for the night.

I should have sent him to a shelter or let him sleep inside the church, he thought bitterly as he overheard the black lady mention the police and vagrants. His gaze focused on the plate glass window that overlooked the interstate. It was only for one night, he recalled telling Rachael, his wife. In the morning, the drifter would be on his way.

I was naked and you clothed me. I was a stranger and you took me in.

He pushed the Bible verse that had haunted him since the attack out of his mind. His hand touched the deep scar on his throat. *I did what you commanded, Lord. I did, and now look at what I am.*

Thomas stopped, squeezing his eyes shut against the mental pain. *I lay next to my wife with my throat gaping open and my life flowing out, listening against my will to his steady grunting and my Rachael screaming in my ear while he—*

The intense need for a drink shot through him, clear and sharp.

No, he told himself firmly. *Stop it. You don't need a drink. You don't. It's the devil talking. They caught the bastard who did this. They caught him that very afternoon and now he's on death row for double first-degree murder.*

...Was a stranger and you took me in...

Someone bumped into him and his mental DVD jolted to a stop. He steadied himself and then opened his eyes. Six teenagers were speeding past him on inline skates. A boy, roughly fourteen or so with a crop of thick reddish blond hair, wearing a Slipknot t-shirt, bumped against his arm.

Thomas slid back into the seat while the kid did an impressive circle in front of him. "Sorry, Pop." The boy grinned. Seconds later, he took off after his friends.

"No problem," Thomas muttered, more to himself than to the kid. "Don't pay me no mind, I'm just another drifter."

"Get the hell outta here," shouted the short, heavyset station manager as he rampaged past the ticket counter, shaking a handful of bus schedules at them as they sped away. By the time he stepped into the lobby, the boys had gone, laughing as they shoved open the glass door and shot down the tarmac.

"Damned heathens," the station manager grumbled.

"Come on, Rudy, where's your sense of humor?" his assistant asked.

"Down the toilet with my social security."

Thomas found himself smiling despite his morose trip down memory lane. Movement beyond the glass pane caught his attention. He felt his heart jump when he saw a large white pickup with Walter Mc Knight House embossed on the side gliding into the parking lot. The vehicle stopped in front of the window. Thomas sighed. As promised, his ride arrived. Thomas felt infinite relief. *Thank you, Lord,* he prayed. *Thank you.*

-3-

"You can't carry me, Brody, I'm too heavy." Megan Wallace cried out in a mixture of delight and terror as her husband of twenty-five years lifted her off her feet, then took a tentative step onto the porch.

"You're not heavy," he laughed. "Besides, it's tradition."

"I haven't been a bride in a very long time."

Despite her trim shape, Brody still had trouble carrying her over the threshold. She giggled while he partially dumped her onto the brown pit group sofa. It was large, taking up nearly one-third of the living room, which was more than adequate for an afternoon session of heavy breathing.

"You could use a few hours in my aerobics class," she teased as he threw his arms around her and pushed her down into the soft cushions.

"I'll give you a workout," he muttered happily as he nibbled on her neck.

"Brody, you left the door open, someone can come in."

"Then that'll teach 'em a lesson," he mumbled as he slipped his hands under her shirt. He kissed her while he explored her hard, lean body.

She sighed with pleasure. "Let's go to bed," she whispered.

"It's not set up," he moaned in her ear. He unzipped her jeans, slipping a hand inside. The sensation of passionate sparks shot up her belly. "Then shut the door," she said as she pulled his hand out of her jeans. "At least do that."

"Prude," he exclaimed as he stood and walked to the door. "Remember that time when we got caught behind those bushes in the park?" he asked as he closed the door.

"I was eighteen years old and mortified," she said as she slipped out of her clothes. "And you were twenty three, you cradle robber—"

"I never heard you complain," he said as he crawled in beside her. His eyes were shining with laughter and love.

She snuggled against him. "I'll never complain," she whispered.

"Then get over here, you Latin hottie, you."

She shrieked in delight then, laughing as he held her close. "It feels so weird, making love in Gramma's house."

"It's our house now," Brody said, distracted by his fly that refused to unzip. "And we can make love in every room of it if you want."

"Promise?" she whispered.

"I promise," he said, laughing as he finally won the battle with the zipper. "I promise, I promise, I promise..."

Chapter Two

"Afraid I'd forgotten about you?" Mr. Jim Balfour, a tall thin man with neatly trimmed blond hair and striking green eyes whom Thomas recognized as the Mc Knight House assistant director, boomed cheerfully out of the opened driver's side window.

Thomas opened the passenger side door and climbed inside. "No," he lied, "not at all. I just figured you were hung up with work or something."

"Well, you'd be right about that," Mr. Jim said as he backed the truck out of the terminal and headed for the access road that ran along the side of the freeway. Balfour frowned. "Old Pa Neidi is after me about getting you over to Mercer's Bayou as of yesterday. Can't imagine why he's in such a rush; services don't start till Sunday and that's two days away. In fact, he cornered me about you before I left. He even threatened to come along. I told him I could get you there quicker if he'd just let me be. Nice old man, but pushy." He stared at Thomas. "Still interested?"

"Absolutely," Thomas said.

"Well, it's not much," said Balfour as he shifted gears. He edged the truck onto the on-ramp and waited for the light to change. "It's just a little whitewashed church building and a cemetery with a historical marker. It was established in 1822 and was the chapel at the old Mercer Plantation. It's on the historical registry if you're interested in that sort of thing. The church comes with a small travel trailer parked near the building that's used as a rectory. It's pretty isolated out there, gets real quiet, especially during the week. Of course, the fishing's good, if you've got a mind to drown a few worms."

The thought of dozing on the bayou while fishing in the afternoons appealed to Thomas. Even more appealing was the idea of being left alone for a week. He wasn't much up on company after Rachael and Becky died and he found he cherished his moments alone with the Lord and a good fishing rod. "I'd like that."

"Now, if you're not comfortable out there, you're welcome to stay out at the Mc Knight House until you find a place of your own. Mind, the pay ain't very good though, so you might want to think about either staying with us or out at the bayou for a while anyway. Or you may be interested in taking up a second church to supplement your income. It's up to you. And if you do that, you'll need to find transportation."

"I'm sure the trailer will be fine," Thomas said.

"Well, I'm sure it's better that what you've had out in New Mexico. Horace runs a clean place, but who wants to spend the rest of their life in a homeless shelter?"

Thomas thought about the featureless building that had been his home since Rachael and Becky died. "I'm looking forward to staying at the church," he said. "I do prefer the privacy. And it's good to get back to work again, saving the lost and all."

"Good." Balfour said, "Now, there's some kids who like to go mudding around there on Friday and Saturday nights. You know, kids and those dang old four wheelers. And a few of the local boys like to use the church parking lot to skateboard on, but Lonnie keeps them from getting too out of hand. But if they get to being too much trouble, you can call Lonnie and he'll send a deputy out to run them off." Balfour frowned. "And there's a Gypsy camp about two miles from there but they pretty much keep to themselves."

"Do they attend the church? The Gypsies, I mean."

"Oh, Lord no," Balfour said, laughing. He stopped at a busy intersection and a group of teenage girls dashed across the street, giggling and waving to the pickup as they went. Balfour tapped the horn and waved back. "Oh, no. No. They're afraid to go there. They think the church is haunted."

"Haunted?" Thomas laughed aloud.

"Yeah, dumb, enit? But you know how those folks are. You probably don't want them coming no how."

19

"No, I'd welcome anyone who wishes to serve the Lord."

"Well, you might change your mind about that. They're strange ones down there, yep."

"So, what is the attendance like?" Thomas asked.

"There are about twenty-five souls who still worship there. Most all of them are about three days older than God—beg pardon. Old Ma and Pa Neidi are the oldest family. Their folks have been on the bayou since Old Man Mercer set out the boundary markers for his plantation. In fact, Neidi's great grand pap was the overseer there."

"Is that right?" Thomas asked.

"Oh yeah, and Pa'll tell you all about it if you give him a breath to take and your ear to chew off. He and Ma take care of the place now. They have a little band; they and the kids play every Sunday. Don't take it anywhere else, thank God. They're probably the worst singers you've ever heard. But their hearts are in the right place, I suppose."

The light changed and they were moving again. "You'll find out real quick that old Pa thinks he owns the place. He's a cantankerous old fart, so don't let him run over you. It's your congregation, not his, and you make sure he knows that. Once you do, he'll back off," Balfour said.

"I'll remember that. What denomination?" Thomas inquired as his stomach growled over the engine's droning.

"Holiness," said Balfour. The light changed and he turned left. He gave Thomas a sideways glance. "Will that be a problem?"

"Not at all," Thomas said. "I started out Presbyterian, but my last church was interdenominational."

"Good. Glad to hear it." Balfour said with excessive enthusiasm. "I know Pa Neidi will be thrilled. They lost their preacher two weeks ago. Found dead, slumped over his office desk. The coroner's office said he had a stroke. Not surprising though. After all, he was eighty two when he died."

"That's quite a legacy," Thomas said. "Still preaching at that age."

"Yep, don't make them like that anymore," Balfour replied.

The conversation ground to a halt. Thomas gazed out the window, watching the buildings as they passed by. The newer portions of the city gave way to the old downtown section. They turned onto Broad Street, then continued past antebellum facade buildings, antiquated abandoned factories, and finally, on the edge of town, a two-story yellow Victorian sprawled spaciously across a red and white rose-infested lot. A sign tacked across the gingerbread siding proclaimed, "WELCOME TO THE WALTER MC KNIGHT HOUSE. 2 Chronicles 28:14-16"

"Here we are," Balfour said cheerfully as he pulled into the designated lot. "It was once a bed and breakfast, but it went out of business about five years back. It went to seed, so we picked it up for back taxes, fixed it up, and here we are, serving the Ark La Tex region's homeless men. We're a 501-C charity, you know. We do our best to get them back on their feet, so to speak. We help out with employment and housing, and we work with our veterans to get them any help they need. We have a liaison with us who keeps us in touch with the VA Hospital down in Shreveport. She gets them their medications and sets up appointments and such." He frowned again which made Thomas wonder why. "We tend to men who genuinely want to start their lives over. If a man's a bum and wants to stay that way, then we give 'em a bus ticket and send them on their way. It sounds kinda mean, but it's our way of separating the wheat from the chaff, as the old saying goes."

"It's lovely," Thomas said as his mind returned to the concrete and corrugated steel building that housed the hundred and fifty drifters and day-working drunks out in Taos. "The house, I mean."

"Come on in," Balfour said as they left the truck and walked toward the huge veranda that skirted the building. "I know you're hot and tired, probably hungry too. Knowing Horace, he loaded you up with some of those slimy bologna sandwiches he likes. He never gives out cash because he's scared it's too much of a temptation to buy booze with it or just plain run off, so he sends bologna sandwiches on white bread with about a six-inch layer of mustard. Hell, that'd make a goat puke. So I'm thinking you're ready for a real meal right about now."

Thomas's stomach growled, answering the question.

"Well, let's get you fixed up then," Balfour said, clapping a friendly hand on his shoulder. "Then, tomorrow morning, we'll go out and see that church of yours."

Feeling happy and safe for the first time in two years, Thomas replied, "That sounds like a plan."

-2-

Megan woke, feeling disoriented and vaguely frightened. Long, late afternoon shadows haunted the once brightly lit living room. Now, the air was stale and humid, smelling vaguely of lavender talcum powder and musky, crumbling wallpaper. Sweat prickled on her body as she lay on the pit group. Although it was soft and comfortable earlier, the cushions were now itchy, hot and smelled of stale fabric softener. Her head ached with a dull thudding sensation that made her feel slightly queasy.

Brody lay beside her with his arm across her chest. He was snoring in her ear, unaware of the formless unease that woke her.

This was Gramma Elly's house, she remembered, *but it's ours now. The weird feeling is from waking up too hot and in a strange house, nothing more.*

She sighed. Brody muttered in his sleep and rolled over.

When Megan and Brody married, she tried to do the traditional housewife and mommy thing. But she was a terrible housekeeper, and motherhood became impossible after a number of failed pregnancies and a hysterectomy at the tender age of twenty-four. They tried adoption, but their counselor told them it could literally take years. Megan plunged into depression. Brody, unsure how to cope, discussed their problem with their priest, who suggested that she should start a daycare center.

Brody asked her how she felt about it, and she told him that she wanted to put her Phys. Ed degree to good use. That afternoon, he came home with a present: an exercise studio. She was reluctant at first, but within a few months, Megan discovered she loved running her own business, and had become quite successful, adding two studios in Austin and one in San Antonio. Now, Megan was planning on starting a new project, something, in her opinion, the oversized women of Tatum desperately needed.

As she passed through Tatum earlier that morning, Megan recalled seeing a space available in the small strip mall next to the Kroger's grocery store. It had a plate glass front and was easy to see inside. The store was quite deep and seemed to have a storage area in the back. She copied down the real estate agent's phone number from the sign propped up in the window, then rushed home to tell Brody what she'd found.

The gloomy heat of the house made her drowsy but Megan was determined not to return to sleep. She rose and walked across the hardwood floor to the air conditioning unit shoved into the window. She turned down the temperature, her body suffering from goose bumps as the cold air scoured her skin. *Well, at least the window unit works,* she thought wryly as she stepped away from the air conditioner.

The vague feeling of unease touched her again and she shivered. "I should put something on," she muttered as she padded from the living room and into the front bedroom. It, too, was gloomy with late afternoon shadows. The bed, a huge four-poster job that was a wedding gift from Brody's parents, rested against the far wall, while the dressers and chest of drawers were shoved into the middle of the room. Boxes and boxes of items were piled onto it. She groaned. There was so much unpacking to do, and she hadn't started.

"I won't be as bored as I thought," she said to herself as she opened her third carton, then finally finding her favorite blue bathrobe, put it on. She sat on the floor next to the cartons. She started pulling on her slippers, when she noticed a shadow race across the window. Startled, she wrapped her bathrobe closer and went to the casement.

A wisteria bush had gone wild and was climbing up the side of the house. She looked through the thick grape-like petals that were plastered against the thick, leaded panes. The wind, she noticed, had picked up. It swept red-brown dust out of the driveway and across the parched yard. The nearby grove of pecan trees picked up the breeze and chatted among themselves. Megan's skin prickled. *A storm is coming,* she thought. *I need to roll up the van windows before it hits.*

Megan left the bedroom, hurried up the short hallway that emptied into the spacious living room and went to the door. Brody began to snore, unaware of anything other than what was going on behind his eyelids. An enormous boom made her jump. Brody muttered in his sleep and rolled over on his stomach. Megan considered waking him, but changed her mind. She stepped outside.

The wind was whipping madly now, and she could see the tops of the thunderheads above the tree line. They were pearly white, glistening in the last glow of the afternoon sun. Another huge kettledrum of a boom sent her running across the yard to the AeroStar that waited like a faithful dog in its spot in the driveway. Raindrops the size of silver dollars pounded the dust, causing little sanguine puffs of dirt to explode into the air.

Megan yanked open the driver's side door and rolled up the window. Sheet lightning scorched the western horizon. *Hurry, hurry,* she thought as rain spilled down hard and fast as she rolled up the passenger's side window.

Drenched and cold, Megan finished her task and started across the front yard when she caught a glimpse of something out of the corner of her eye. Startled, she stopped and peered into the silvery veil of rain that obscured the forest just beyond the house. A crooked streak of lightning slammed into the pasture behind the house. Seconds later, a long rolling report of thunder echoed across the woods. Megan wiped the wet hair from her face.

A young woman, about fifteen or sixteen years old, stood at the edge of the woods. Her long, dark hair streamed down her shoulders and her flowery printed dress was plastered to her body. A huge red wolf sat next to her, grinning as his tongue lolled out of the side of his mouth. The oddest thing about the pair, Megan noted, were the eyes. Both had eyes of glowing yellow-gold. There was a stark familiarity about them, but nothing she could pinpoint. It was the same sensation she felt about the house.

"Hey," Megan shouted at the girl. Both the girl and the wolf melted into the deep wet greenness of the forest.

"Wait," Megan called again. "You're not in trouble; I just want to talk to you."

Rain fell harder. Small crystalline hailstones pelted down upon her. Megan was forced to retreat to the porch. She turned around again, hoping to catch a glimpse of the girl and the wolf.

But they had gone.

Chapter Three

The early summer storm that sent Megan retreating into the safety of her house lasted throughout the night. James Thomas lay in bed and listened to the wind and rain as it pelted down upon the metal roof and forced tree limbs from the ancient magnolia tree next to his window to lash against the glass, creating eerie patterns as the water rushing down the panes distorted the street lights.

This had been the first night in two years that Thomas had slept in a real bed that was made with crisp clean sheets and a Navajo-patterned comforter and smelled faintly of lilac, instead of the urine-stained cot and woolen army blanket that the Taos shelter provided. Back then, he had no need of anything other than a place to sleep off the day's attempt at dulling the pain of living while the two most important people in his life had not.

Thomas listened to the thunder roll across the night sky. The spiritual glue that bound his soul together dissolved the night Becky and Rachael were murdered. After those dark and awful days where he lay in a hospital bed, breathing from a tube inserted into his mutilated trachea, he questioned, for the first time in fifty-six years, the God he served.

"God has a plan for you," Bishop Freeman told him, but Thomas didn't believe that. *What kind of God makes plans like this?* he wondered. *What kind of God allows the murders of a woman and a child in order for me to follow some vague plan?*

Those questions were seared upon his soul as his body slowly healed and he was able to go home. But it wasn't a home anymore. It was only a house, a sad, deserted place that no longer carried the laughter of his daughter as she combated aliens on her PlayStation, or the scent of enchiladas baking in the oven, or the voice of his dear Rachael welcoming him home.

Thomas closed his eyes against the hard lump of grief forming along the scar, causing it to ache. He spent his nights, so silent then with just him in the house, reading the book of Job and drinking Johnny Walker Red until the soft teal light of dawn etched across the horizon, seen from the big bay windows that Rachael loved. *You shouldn't be doing this to yourself.* Thomas scolded himself... *You should leave it be. Let the dead bury the dead.*

Thomas couldn't. His mind was fully focused on the past and all he could do was wait and watch until the memories played themselves out.

Thomas recalled not preaching for those first weeks, calling his isolation a retreat. Instead he allowed the assistant pastor to take over. He claimed his throat hurt too much to speak, and that was partially true, but the truth was he no longer believed in what he preached. After his thirtieth rereading of the book of Job, he concluded that God and Satan played Job for a fool. That the entire book was about a cosmic bet, that the devil could sway Job after his wife and children were killed and he lost everything he had. And, to up the ante, God allowed Lucifer to give Job a roaring case of leprosy. True, Job was rewarded for his faithfulness, but for the first time in his life, Thomas questioned the wisdom of these actions.

Why would God, who was all-knowing and all-loving, put Job through that in the first place? *If God knows the hearts of all men, he knew in advance that Job would remain faithful, so why kill the ones he loved to prove it? And even though he was rewarded with renewed health, another wife, more children and all his goods returned, didn't Job ache inside for the first family he had? How can you replace human beings, especially the ones that you love the most?* he wondered. *How could Job be content with substitutes for what he was already happy with?*

Thomas rolled over and pulled the comforter over his shoulders. *I passed the test, Lord,* he prayed. *It was the hardest thing I've ever done, but I've got myself back together and I am ready to serve you again.*

It took a long time to forgive God, and he still hadn't gotten around to completely forgiving himself. And although he had not received the riches of Job after his two years of personal tribulation and salvation, he had been given a second chance. He smiled, but it was the grim, harsh smile of a man determined to make the best of things while his life on earth continued, when he rather wished it had not.

Thomas pushed the anguish aside and focused on the future. He could see himself sitting upon the bayou's shaded bank with a canopy of green above him and sunlight glistening as he cast his lure. The desire for peace and serenity calmed him, stilled the deep ache in his heart and eased the lump in his throat. He could almost hear the calls of blue jays and the raucous squawking of mockingbirds fighting over territory. The water would be lustrous, rich and deep, filled with a bounty of catfish and bass.

He was much calmer now, enjoying the soft scenes he played in his mind. He saw himself sitting in the office of his little church, preparing his sermons and ministering to the flock during the week, preaching on Sundays and having old-fashioned Southern potluck suppers under the stars at night. *Life is good*, he told himself. *God really has rewarded you. Look at all the gifts He's provided.*

He reveled in the simple pleasure of a soft bed and clean sheets. Balfour—or Mr. Jim as he preferred to be called—took Thomas to the thrift shop earlier that day and invited him to pick from the better clothes on the racks. He had experienced the true Southern flavor of pan-fried catfish, hush puppies, coleslaw and pickled green tomatoes. His clothes were neatly pressed and waiting for him in the morning. He had a shower and a nap, spent time in the living room talking to the residents who, thanks to the Mc Knight House, had been given second chances. In just a few hours, he would start his life over again, thanks to a kind man and a bus ticket.

I have been redeemed, he thought, feeling warm and secure under the covers, knowing that tomorrow things would start turning out for the better. *I doubted, but I was saved again. God has given me a second chance, and this time I won't blow it.*

-2-

The darkness and pouring rain did not deter the ritual in progress. Six people—a husband and wife and their four children—stood around the ancient tree. Sheet lightning illuminated the cemetery, casting garish purple shadows upon the withered ground. Wind whipped around the women's skirts and tugged upon the overalls of the men and children who participated.

Despite its dead appearance, the tree rustled as though it were very much alive. The creases in the black bark pulsed with a soft greenish-golden light. The family's faces were bathed in its light, their features gaunt, like withered skulls.

Overhead, purple lightning streaked across the sky. Thunder grumbled. The tinkling sound of hailstones striking the tombstones went ignored.

The old woman spoke as she cast chicken bones onto the ground. "He's strong willed this one. Not like the last. Old Preacher McCain couldn't be touched."

"Or gotten rid of."

"Patience, boy. The right 'un's here and that's all that counts."

"He's toting burdens that will make him easy handling."

"What will we do if he puts up a fight? The bones say he will."

"He won't for long. I got faith."

-3-

Lightning struck the transformer and reduced it to a smoldering husk, leaving Megan and Brody stranded in darkness. Brody, still feeling romantic after the afternoon's interlude, fumbled around in the darkened house until he found a flashlight. Then he wandered from room to room, the small pool of light dimly illuminating one after another, until he returned, humming happily to himself, bearing candles, a bottle of blackberry merlot, a cork and a lighter.

Megan laughed as she took his burden. She set candles around the room and began lighting them as he stumbled back into the kitchen for glasses.

The house was stuffy despite the storm. She opened the front door, allowing the cold air to burst in.

"That's what it was designed for," Megan explained as Brody returned to the living room with two glasses.

"Huh?" He set the glasses on the floor and began working

on the cork.

"The veranda," she explained. "As well as the big windows and high ceilings. This house was built for Gramma and Grandpa when they married in 1901. There wasn't electricity here then, so the house was built to withstand extreme heat in the summer and bitter coldness in the winter. The high ceilings were designed to allow the hot air to rise, and the big windows positioned around the house let in cool air in the summertime. The veranda was built so you could sleep outside in the summertime, and it kept the rain from coming into the house when you opened the door."

"How do you know so much about this old house?" Brody laughed as she sat across from him. The candlelight illuminated his face, bringing out sharp planes and angles around his cheeks and chin that in reality did not exist. For a moment, Megan thought about a séance she and her friends held when she was sixteen and invited to a sleepover at a friend's house.

"I did some research. Did you know that this was one of the first houses on the bayou that was wired for electricity?"

"Really?" Brody frowned slightly. "In that case, I need to get an electrician out here to have the wiring checked."

"I'm sure that it's been rewired several times since, but go ahead and have it checked. The house was vacant for over a year now, there's no telling what might be nibbling around up there," she said. Megan took a sip of her wine, contemplating. "Will that fit into our budget?"

"I've earmarked twenty thousand dollars for renovation," Brody said. "If we need more, then I'll have to budget that in. We'll know more about that when the electrician comes. I'll call first thing Monday morning."

Megan watched him as he sipped his wine. "Have I told you lately how much I love you?"

"Not recently, no," he said cheerfully.

"Well, I do, and I want to know one thing."

Brody sat his glass onto the floor. "What's that?"

"Are you happy? I mean here, in the country. I know how much you loved Austin."

"I'm very happy. Sure, there's things we both are going to miss, especially Bethie and Sherman, but hey, like I said, there's email and the telephone, and there's nothing stopping them from coming up here on vacation."

"I know that, but life is going to be so different here."

"Sure it is, but look at it this way. We have this grand old house, you are expanding your business to accommodate the expanding rears of the wealthier ladies of Tatum, who just love their Southern-fried food," he said with an exaggerated Southern accent, "and I have a job that's not going to perforate any more ulcers. I think living here is going to be wonderful, and Austin isn't going anywhere. We can go back on weekends, visit all the old hot spots, have a good time and then come home to an easy, ulcer free life."

"I just wanted to make sure you are really going to be happy here," Megan said.

"We wouldn't have done it if it would have been a problem for either of us," Brody replied. He stared hard at her. "Is this a problem for you, though? Do you want to go back to Austin?"

Megan thought about it. "In a way, but I think it's because I'm used to living in the city. We've been there over twenty years, and that life is hard to let go of."

"Yeah, I understand. You're homesick. In time you'll find this is home too.

"I know."

"Let's give it six months. If neither of us can adjust to life here, we'll sell out. How's that?"

Megan smiled. "I love you, Brody."

Brody's eyes sparkled in the candlelight. "I know you do."

"Well?" she asked.

"Well what?" he teased.

"Well, do you love me back?"

"Gee, let me think about it." Grinning wickedly, he slid the candle aside and grabbed her, pulling her to the floor. Megan cried out in delight. "I have a wife I just can't stop kissing," he said between smooches.

"Brody, stop."

"Only if you answer one question," he said as he lay against her.

"What?"

"Who were you talking to today?"

"That's not what I thought you wanted to talk about."

"Just curious," Brody said, propping his head up with his elbow to the floor. For an instant he looked like a teenager. "I woke up when the storm started. I went to look for you but you weren't in the house. I was about to step out on the veranda when I heard you calling to somebody."

"Oh that," Megan said, pushing herself up on her elbows so that she and her husband were eye-to-eye. "I almost forgot about that. And it was so strange, too. I'm surprised I didn't tell you."

"What happened?" Brody said, suddenly serious.

"It wasn't anything dangerous, just odd. I went out to roll up the windows on the van when the storm hit. I saw this girl standing under that grove of pecan trees. You know, the ones next to the propane tank?"

"Go on."

"She wasn't very tall, about five-two or three, scrawny like she hadn't had a decent meal in a while. She had long, stringy hair and was wearing a hideous blue-and-pink flowery dress, like the girls used to wear back in the fifties."

"Did she speak to you?"

"No, she didn't. She just stood there and stared at me."

"I see."

"Oh, and that's not the weird part. Get this. A wolf was sitting next to her."

"A wolf?" Brody said, surprised.

"Yes, a big old red wolf. It was sitting next to her like it was her best friend or something."

Brody bit his lower lip, considering. "Well, I wouldn't worry too much about it. She's probably a neighbor girl curious about us."

"But why would she run away when I called her?"

"Her folks probably told her not to pester us," he said.

"Okay, Detective Colombo. If that's all it is, then explain the wolf."

"This is the bottoms," he explained. "Maybe wolves here are kept as pets."

"Oh really."

"Yeah, really." Brody laughed. "Don't you remember Jack Roberts, that guy who was breeding that Mexican Gray wolf with his Malamute and selling the pups?"

"Yeah, but he was just weird," Megan said.

"You'd be surprised how many people bought them. It's exciting owning something feral. Hell, folks still hunt out here, darling. It's quite possible that her father found the pup when he was out hunting, brought it home and the girl raised it."

"I suppose," Megan, said, doubtful.

"Hey, stranger things have been known to happen. My step-brother, Kenny, owned a cougar once."

Megan stared at him, incredulous. "I'm assuming we're not talking about the car."

"No, the animal. He kept it in his apartment, although to this day I have no idea how he got away with that."

"Okay, now my curiosity is up. What happened to it?"

"Okay, this is amazing," Brody said as he sat up. "He had this girlfriend who lived with him. She worked days while he tended bar down in this pub at night. This was when he and I lived in New Orleans, just before I went off to college. The cat slept on the foot of the bed with his girlfriend. One night when Kenny was at work and she was asleep, somebody broke in on her."

"Oh, good God!"

"Good God is right," Brody said. "The creep got into bed with her, and put a knife to her throat. He told her to be a good girl and cooperate, but he apparently didn't notice her two-hundred-pound bed partner sprawled on the foot of the bed."

"How did he miss it?"

"I have no idea," Brody said, finishing off the last sip of wine in his glass. "All I know is that I got a call at about three that morning, Kenny hysterical, telling me that the cat ate the rapist."

"He ate him?" Megan mouthed the words, her eyes wide.

"She did, yes. Howler was a female. I went up there and, Megan, I had never seen so much blood in my entire life. It was splattered in places where you'd expect, like the bed, on the floor, but it was also on the ceiling and the walls."

"Did she kill Kenny's girlfriend too?"

"No, but she was cowering in a corner, white as a proverbial sheet, which is something because she was Creole. She couldn't talk for weeks afterwards."

"What did they do with Howler?"

"Well," Brody said, "Kenny got scared of Howler after that. He donated her to the zoo. I understand she's very happy there. Still just as docile as ever."

"I don't think anything like that can be tamed," Megan said. "It's insane to own an animal like that."

"Yeah, I know, but some people like the rush it gives them, owning something dangerous. I suspect your little friend in the pecan orchard is the same way."

"Maybe so," Megan said.

"Well," Brody said, rising and stretching. "I think that's enough about Kenny and his big pet pussy. How about we turn in for the night?"

"Okay. I'll go and put the glasses away."

"All right. I found where the linens were hiding," Brody said. "I'll get some sheets. That way the pit group won't be quite so itchy."

"That's a good idea," Megan replied as she picked up the glasses, the bottle and the wine cork. "Go ahead and make the bed, I'll be right back."

"Don't stay away too long."

Megan blew him a kiss as he ambled down the hallway with the flashlight. She put the wine bottle under her arm and juggled the glasses and wine cork in one hand while managing one of the short fat candles with the other.

She pushed open the kitchen door with her elbow. Darkness fled from her as the candle illuminated the room. She set the candle down upon the cabinet and nudged the wine bottle out from under her arm and onto the counter. Yawning and thinking about over-sized house cats, Megan went to the sink and was about to set the glasses into the antique enameled sink when something caught her attention.

A small window perched over the double sink and looked out on a large empty pasture beyond. Megan made a passing glance at the window then did a double take. She felt the glasses slip out of her hand and was vaguely aware that they had smashed when they hit the bottom of the sink. Unreasoning terror gripped her throat and strangled her. She stood, rooted to the spot, staring outside while an icy cold waterfall of adrenaline poured through her.

Finding her voice, she screamed, "Brody!"

"What?"

"Brody, Brody, get in here."

"What is it, baby, see a rat?" he joked as he shoved the kitchen door open and strode toward her.

Megan was breathless. She shook her head, the candlelight flickering golden against her dark hair. Brody stood looking over her shoulder and out of the window.

The storm wandered away from the bayou and was currently threatening Shreveport. He could see dull lightning exposing huge anvil-headed clouds off in the distance. But here on the bayou it was quiet. There was something odd happening in the distance. The soft, sloping rise that carried the pasture up the hill and toward the bayou levees was bathed in a dull greenish-gold glow.

"What is that?" she whispered. Brody's face was white and his Adam's apple performed a wild jig up and down his throat.

"Brody, what is that?" she repeated.

"Heat lightning," he said finally.

"But Brody, lightning flashes. That's one long steady glow."

"Then it's street lights."

"But there aren't any—"

"Street lights." His voice rose. "It has to be. There's electricity out here, right? Then it's got to be sodium streetlights."

"But it's not the right color."

"Let's just go to bed. Get on the pit group and I'll put out the candles and lock the door. Come on, let's just go. And watch for glass. Some of it might have hit the floor."

Megan turned away from the window and followed her husband into the living room. The pit group was not properly made, but that didn't matter. She left her clothes on, but took off her shoes and climbed in while Brody, white faced and obviously shaken, put out the candles, then shut the door and locked it. She noticed he did not undress either, but slid beside her and held her close.

It was hours before they went to sleep. Although Brody pretended to, she could tell he was awake because of the tension she felt in his arms as he held her.

"Brody?" she whispered. "You're still awake."

"Hush," he whispered. "Listen."

She strained to hear, but all that she heard was the wind whining through the eaves and the occasional rumble of distant thunder. She tried to relax as she cuddled next to him, but his body was rigid, as if he were trembling and trying not to.

She dozed off sometime shortly before dawn, but her sleep was restless. She found herself wandering lost through a great forest while yellow-eyed animals peered at her through the foliage and wolves howled as the horizon turned an eerie ghostly green.

Chapter Four

James Thomas woke to the sounds of sparrows chirping and flitting through the magnolia's branches while the warm summer sun poured down through the window, creating a mosaic of leaf-strewn golden blocks of light against the foot of his bed. He lay on his side, enjoying the beginnings of this most precious morning, while reciting the twenty-third Psalm.

The smell of sausage frying in the kitchen below enticed him to close his morning devotional and leave the warm security of the bed. Putting on a threadbare bathrobe, he wandered down to the end of the hallway to the bathroom, where he showered and washed his hair.

He found himself whistling a merry tune as he shaved with one of the disposable razors he found in the medicine cabinet. He looked at himself in the mirror, clean, prepared to receive the day and the Lord's blessings. He smiled and his reflection returned it. *I really am happy to see you back*, he told his reflection.

The bathroom door rattled and he realized that the other men must be rising also, and needing to get their day started as well.

"Getting out now," he said cheerfully as he replaced the bathrobe over his faded striped pajamas. He opened the door and smiled out at the weary, whiskered men who were waiting their turns.

Thomas nodded. "Morning," he said to them.

The men grunted. One went into the bathroom, while three other men walked up the landing.

"Morning, Preacher," one of them muttered as Thomas passed him by.

Thomas acknowledged the man with a smile. He returned to his room feeling happy for the first time in ages. He continued whistling his merry tune as he dressed. *This is going to be one of the best days of my life*, he told himself. *Everything is going to turn out just fine.*

A bell rang downstairs. *Must be a visitor,* Thomas thought as he tucked his shirt into his slacks and cinched up his belt. He heard the front door open, the muffled sound of male voices entering the living area, and the sharp slam of the front door as it shut. *I wonder who it is,* he thought. *Could it be the man Mr. Jim told me about? What was his name, other than Pa?*

Feeling nervous, he slipped into his loafers, and then went downstairs and into the kitchen where a handsome, middle-aged black lady was scraping scrambled eggs into a large green ceramic bowl.

"Morning, Preacher," she said cheerfully as he appeared in the doorway. "Did you sleep well?"

"Yes, ma'am, I did," he responded with equal cheer as he stepped up to the table. "My, this sure looks good."

"My name is Eula Blanchard," she said, extending a warm hand. He took it, and for a second was unsure whether to kiss it or shake it. "I'm the accounting and job placement officer for the Mc Knight House."

Thomas gave her hand a little shake. She smiled. "Is that right?" he asked.

"Sit yourself down anywhere you like. The other residents will be here shortly."

"Thank you, Mrs. Blanchard," he said gratefully as he sat at the table.

"This ain't my usual job as you've already guessed," she explained as she peeled a large yellow cantaloupe, cut it in half, then scooped out the seedy entrails with a large spoon. "Cindy Matthews runs the kitchen, but she and her helper both caught the flu and that left us short handed."

"Oh," Thomas said, "then you must let me help."

"No, no, no," Mrs. Blanchard said emphatically. "You'll get yourself all dirty and you have to go out to the church today. I'm sure you'll be meeting—" She cut herself off, frowned and then said, "the congregation this afternoon."

"I don't want to be a bother."

Mrs. Blanchard glanced at the doorway. She sliced her melon, put it into a clear glass dish, and placed it on the table next to the eggs. She looked at the door again, her eyes wide. The corners of her mouth twitched and her hands began fumbling for something to do.

"Is something wrong?" he asked her.

Mrs. Blanchard took another apprehensive glance at the doorway and then sat at the table beside him. She moved close and put her hand on his wrist. Thomas felt his insides twist. *Does she want to confess something to me, or does she want prayers or what? It's too early in the morning; I'm not prepared...*

"Listen," she whispered with a harsh urgency that sent prickles of alarm shooting up his spine. "That church they want to send you to—don't go there, whatever you do. They's other, better places you can go than to that...place. I'm telling you..." Her voice dropped until he could barely hear her. "That old man, Pa Neidi, he ain't right. He's got the devil in him. And that church is possessed by that same devil. If you're smart, you'd get back on that bus and get as far away from here as you can."

"Now, Miss Eula," said an easy Southern drawl at the doorway, "surely you're not making the preacher work for his breakfast this morning."

Both of them jumped. Mrs. Blanchard cast a worried glance at the doorway. Mr. Jim Balfour stood smiling down at them. A gaunt, elderly white man wearing overalls and carrying an oversized Bible under his arm was standing next to him. Mrs. Blanchard crossed herself.

"Morning, Mr. Jim," Thomas said.

Mrs. Blanchard squeezed Thomas's arm. "I-I was just telling the preacher about my brother, Shakenian. You know Shakenian, Mr. Jim. He's the one with that bad case of gout."

"Oh yes," Mr. Jim said, his eyes hard despite the smile. "How's he doin' these days?"

"Oh, Lord, not good, not good at all," Mrs. Blanchard said. "That's what I was talking to Preacher Thomas about. You see, Shakenian's foot is swollen so bad he can hardly walk at all. I just wanted to know if Mr. Thomas would be so kind as to say a little prayer, that's all I wanted to say."

"I'll remember your brother in my prayers," Thomas said, patting the woman's hand.

"Well, I sure understand that," Mr. Jim said, his face turning to stone. Mrs. Blanchard stared at him, wide eyed. "But what I don't understand is why a good Catholic girl like you would ask a Protestant preacher for prayers."

"Any prayer to the Lord is a good prayer," Mrs. Blanchard said, her own face an ebony mask.

"So it is, so it is," Mr. Jim said. "You can go on back up to the office, Mrs. Blanchard. We can handle it from here, and I know you have that budget report to finish."

"Yes, of course. I'll go and do that," she said, wiping her hands on her apron and straightening her skirt as she rose from the table.

"I'll make sure the men clean up after we're done," Mr. Jim said.

"Thank you, Mr. Jim. I'd like that."

"Anything to lighten your burden, my dear lady," Mr. Jim said.

Mrs. Blanchard cast a quick glance at Thomas, and then left the kitchen, giving the old man a wide berth as she walked past him. For a second, Thomas thought she made the sign of the evil eye at the old man's back before she climbed the stairs.

"Miss Eula-Mae is something else," Mr. Jim said with his customary cheer as he slid into the chair Mrs. Blanchard vacated. The old man took the chair on the other side. He placed his Bible on the table and rested his right hand upon the worn leather cover as if he were about to swear an oath.

"She's the sweetest lady you'd ever hope to meet," Mr. Jim was saying. "And we can't run this place without her, no, sir. But she's a little off, if you know what I mean."

"No, sir, I'm afraid I don't," Thomas said.

"Well, she's half Cajun. She's from out around Dixie Inn, Louisiana. Her pa was from Lake Charles. He was full-blooded coon-ass—sorry bout that—Cajun. What I mean to say is that she has some peculiar ideas about some things."

"I see," Thomas said, feeling like he was on display.

"Mr. Thomas—"

"Uh, James, please—"

"Right, James, I'd like to introduce you to Pa Neidi. He oversees the First Light Church of Prophecy down at Mercer's Bayou."

"How do you do?" Thomas said, extending his hand.

Pa Neidi stared at it, and then looked up to Mr. Jim. "You sure he's the one?"

"Yes, Pa, this is Preacher Thomas. He's the one from New Mexico we brought in to preach."

"Looks rather puny," Pa Neidi observed, looking Thomas over as if he were contemplating buying a mule. "How long you been preaching, boy?"

"Twenty two years," Thomas replied, feeling self-conscious.

"College boy?"

"Well, yes..."

"I ain't got no use for no college boy," Neidi said. He pushed his face close to Thomas so they were looking each other in the eye. Thomas got a point blank view of the <u>old</u> man's broken teeth, the crooked, hooked nose, smelled the rancid stench of spoiled snuff. Thomas wanted to pull away, to look away from those queerly green eyes, but he dared not. He was afraid to show any sign of weakness.

"I don't give a Confederate Damn about no college learnin'," Neidi was saying. "What I want to know is how many times have you read the Good Book?"

"All the way through?"

"Hell yes, all the way through."

"I don't know off hand, five, maybe six times."

"That's it? How do you preach then? Using them useless, Satanic commentaries, are yuh?"

"Yes—well no, not at all."

"Where's your own Bible? Why ain't it on the table before yuh?"

"Well—I—"

"Now, Pa," Mr. Jim said smoothly, "Preacher Thomas lost everything he had. We've got plenty of Bibles here he can have."

"Now what kinda preacher is this what ain't got his own Bible?" Neidi demanded.

"I know the Bible," Thomas blurted. "Ask me anything, I'll

answer it."

Pa Neidi glared at him. "All right, college boy, I'll put you up to the test, then."

Thomas smiled. "Bring it on."

"Which is the true Bible, the only one inspired by God Almighty?"

"Well," Thomas said, "I suppose that would be the Old Testament written in the original—"

"Wrong, wrong, wrong," Neidi shouted, slapping his hand down hard on his Bible. "That's college boy talk, and it's just plain wrong." He picked up his Bible and shook it at him. "Here's the only one true Word of God, the King James Bible, praise Jesus. I don't want to see you preaching out of nothing else, neither."

Thomas looked at Mr. Jim, hoping for assistance. But Mr. Jim was shoveling eggs and sausage onto his plate. He plucked out plump slices of cantaloupe and fresh red tomatoes and dumped them beside his sausage.

"Excuse my boarding house reach," he muttered as he leaned across the bowls of eggs and fruit to snag a large biscuit from a wicker basket.

Thomas's belly grumbled and his heart sank. Not only was the food getting cold, he was convinced that Pa Neidi was completely mad. King James Version? Didn't he know when it was written?

"Ready to give up, or are you up for more, Mr. College Boy?"

"Like I said before, bring it on."

"Give me the verse for 2 Timothy 2:16."

"But shun profane and vain babblings; for they will increase unto more ungodliness."

"Mimicking ape," Neidi taunted. "You can recite it, but do you know what it means?"

"I—"

"1 Corinthians 14:34!"

Thomas's mind froze.

"Let your women keep silence in churches: for it is not permitted unto them to speak but commanded under obedience as also saith the law," Neidi said before Thomas could respond.

41

"Speak up, man, you're supposed to be the preacher. Do you believe women should speak in church or not?"

"Well, I—"

"Good Lord Almighty," Neidi said to Mr. Jim, who was fishing in the basket for another biscuit. "What kind of idiot did you send us, who can't quote or interpret the Lord's Word?"

Thomas looked at Mr. Jim, hoping that perhaps he would say something in his favor. Mr. Jim shrugged, then filled his biscuit with butter and bit off a large chunk. "That Eula-Mae can sure cook," Mr. Jim muttered.

"Here's your last chance, Mr. College Boy Preacher Man," Neidi spat. "It's judgment day so don't screw up. What's Job 1:19?"

Thomas's heart felt as if it had suddenly turned into a block of ice. He knew this scripture; in fact, he knew the entire book of Job by heart. This was the verse where God destroyed the house Job's children were in. Once again, he glanced at Mr. Jim for guidance, but the man was too busy shoving food in his mouth to notice.

What should I do? Thomas wondered. *Should I just bid this man a good day and try and find some other kind of work elsewhere? Maybe I'm not as good a minister as I ought to be.* Mrs. Blanchard's warning sent tentacles of ice skewering his intestines. *Maybe I should just leave now,* he thought. *Maybe that'd be the best thing to do.*

"Well? Come on, man, spit it out," Neidi shouted.

He's just the groundskeeper, so why am I even listening to him? Thomas thought. "Look, Mr. Neidi," Thomas said. "I know my Bible, and I know the Lord. I'm not playing your silly game any longer. You're not my employer; the Mc Knight House is. You're just the caretaker and the band director and I want you to stay out of my business." He almost added, *you nasty old wretch,* but cut himself short.

Neidi rocked back in the chair and gaped at the man.

"And another thing: I'm proud I went to seminary, and I am not ashamed of my college education. If you don't like it, I trust you'll get over it soon enough."

Pa Neidi's jaw worked as if he were about to speak but was unable to. Instead, he slapped his hand down on his Bible and cackled, causing goose bumps to stand up on Thomas's arms and salute.

Neidi guffawed. "By gum, don't he have a set of brass balls on him? You're right, Mr. Jim. Mr. College Boy will do, he'll do real fine."

"Congratulations," Mr. Jim said, putting a biscuit on Thomas's plate.

"You mean I've got the job?" Thomas said uncertainly while Mr. Jim added eggs and sausages to his plate.

"Sure do," Mr. Jim said merrily. He stabbed a cantaloupe slice and offered it to him. "Melon?"

"Thank you," Thomas said, feeling confused.

Neidi stood, scooping up his Bible and placing it under his arm. "Have him out to the church by this afternoon. Gotta get ready for services Sunday, and we all can do with some rehearsing,"

"Stay for breakfast?" Mr. Jim asked.

"Naw, I've gotta get moving. Ma's gonna worry."

"Have a good 'un," Mr. Jim said, distracted by another piece of melon.

Pa Neidi let himself out, and as he vacated the kitchen, sounds of daily life swooped down upon them. Men came downstairs, washed and dressed, and made their way to the table, helping themselves to breakfast, laughing and gossiping among themselves as they filled the kitchen.

As Thomas ate, it occurred to him how quiet everything had become while Neidi was there. It was almost as if the old man sucked the very life out of the place, and now that he had gone, everything returned to normal. It was an eerie sensation, as if the house was waiting for the old man to leave so it could exhale.

But that's just silly, Thomas scolded himself. Neidi was just an old man. He was a creepy old man, that's for sure, but harmless nonetheless

"He sure has some odd ideas," Thomas said to Mr. Jim. "Old Pa Neidi, that is."

The room became silent once more, as if the old man's name had the power to evacuate even the air inside the room. Thomas noticed several men flinched; one man genuflected.

"Did I say something wrong?"

"Nope," Mr. Jim said around a mouthful of scrambled egg. "He's an odd bird all right, but he don't mean no harm. Like I said, stand your ground with him and you'll be okay."

Thomas wasn't sure he liked the sound of that. *Maybe I shouldn't take this job,* he thought. But at the moment, Thomas didn't have a choice, and he knew that. If he didn't take the job, there was literally nowhere to go.

I can stay for a short while, Thomas reasoned as he moved food around his plate. *I can stay for a couple of months, and then move on. I can keep putting my resume out, and surely some larger congregation will take me in.*

"Still taking the job, ain't ya?" Mr. Jim asked, and Thomas had the spooky sensation that the man had read his mind.

"Yes," Thomas replied. "In fact, I'll be ready to go as soon as breakfast is over."

"Good deal," Mr. Jim said. "I'll drive you down there myself."

"That would be nice, thank you," Thomas said. But his insides had grown cold again. The lukewarm food settled hard on his stomach and he began regretting a number of things, breakfast being far down on the list.

It's just first day jitters, he assured himself. *Things will be fine once I get to know everyone.*

Chapter Five

It was nearly lunch time when the Southwest Arkansas Power Company's utility truck lumbered up the long muddy driveway. Megan and Brody watched from the porch swing as the truck sputtered to a stop. The electrician got out and approached the veranda. In the distance, Megan heard the grinding roar of chainsaws.

"Morning," Brody called, rising from the swing to meet the tall, thin blond man who was mounting the steps. "We're sure glad to see you."

The electrician smiled, and said as he shook Brody's hand, "You folks got quite a storm last night. There's trees down all over Deer Creek Road."

"I'm glad you were able to make it," Megan said. "We just moved in two days ago, so I haven't had a chance to buy groceries, so we were lucky and hadn't lost anything."

"Well, ma'am, I'll get that taken care of here in a bit," the electrician said. "Which transformer was it, Mr. Wallace, the one on the road or the one on the pole behind the house?"

"Behind the house," Brody replied. "Come on, I'll show you."

Megan remained on the porch swing while Brody escorted the electrician around the back of the house. The blown transformer still smoldered on its stump on its pole, curling thin blackish smoke into the sky.

Despite the humidity, she felt chilled. The girl and the wolf had made her curious yesterday, but the glowing green—something—hovering along the horizon last night had unnerved her. She had gotten up twice during the night and checked the kitchen window. The light remained low against the earth and continued to glow, diminishing only when the sun rose. She returned to bed, frightened and uncertain about remaining on the bayou.

Was it a UFO? she wondered. Surely not. Megan never believed in such things, although her sister, Consuela, did. Her sister swore she saw one hovering over an open market in Mexico City two summers ago. Megan teased her about it, saying it must have been a weather balloon or something, maybe even the planet Venus.

"There has to be a logical explanation for that light," she muttered to herself. "There has to be."

Brody hadn't brought up the subject. He had left at five in the morning to go to Tatum and brought back orange juice and a bag of Southern Maid donuts. Megan had scolded him about the purchase, donuts being all sugar, fat and empty calories, not to mention what they did to her svelte figure. He laughed when she ate four anyway, swigging down two large bottles of orange juice in the process.

Despite her lectures on health and fitness, Megan did secretly crave those forbidden things, and when she encountered them, she found her resistance melting along with the clear sugar glaze.

She wiped the beads of sweat forming on her forehead with a paper towel. It wasn't quite noon yet and the temperature was soaring into the lower nineties. She found herself staring at the spot where the girl and the wolf stood underneath the trees. An eerie sensation flowed through her. *I swear I've seen her before,* she thought. *But when?*

Megan's train of thought was interrupted by a loud clattering sound coming off the highway. Her eyes strayed away from the pecan grove to the driveway, where a battered orange trash truck swished and bounced along the gravel path until it screeched to a halt next to the utility truck.

A grungy white man of undetermined age got out. He was dressed in greasy coveralls and wore a red Arkansas Razorbacks ball cap. The cab of the vehicle groaned and swayed as he shut the door and approached her.

"Hello," Megan called, curious. They had already arranged

service with Kingston Rural Trash pickup, and she was somewhat confused by the presence of the raggedy gentleman and his broken down wreck, especially on a Saturday.

"Howdy," he drawled, mounting the steps and crossing the veranda. "I'm Charlie Estille," he said, extending a greasy hand. Megan swallowed hard against the old man's strong aroma of bourbon running neck to neck with the stench of garbage, and took his hand. As she pulled away, she made a mental note to wash her hands after he left.

"Megan Wallace," she said, trying her best to be polite, which was difficult because the truck had brought along its own stench, as well as flies, which swarmed the sagging rear of the vehicle. Estille, she noted, wasn't much better, as flies were perpetually buzzing around his head.

He swatted absently as he said, "I'm here to tell you about my trash pickup service. I'll be by every Monday and Wednesday and I pick up everything, including heavy appliances."

"I'm sorry, Mr. Estille, but we've already signed on with the Kingston group."

"Well, that won't take much to get out of their contract. They may have fancier trucks, and their boys have pretty uniforms, but I am cheaper and will do a much better job for yuh."

"I think we'll stick with the Kingston Group," Megan said, adding firmness to her voice. The old man was obviously drunk, and she was not even sure he was aware of where he was. He seemed to contemplate what she said. She could almost hear the gears of his mind working: *she won't sign on, she's just a woman so what does she know? I need to talk to the man of the house, the real muscle behind this—*

"Your husband be about the house, ma'am?"

How predictable, she thought. "He's around back," she pointed, indicating the rear of the house. "He's with the electrician."

Charlie Estille tipped his cap. "Well, this really is men's talk," he said with predictable condescension. "I'll go and have a word with your husband. Afternoon, ma'am," he said, easing off the veranda and down the steps.

"You're wasting your time," she said to his retreating back.

47

"He won't change our contract, either." She stood and called, "And it's not even noon yet."

She sighed and returned to her swing seat and picked up a paperback novel that was lying beside her and thumbed through until she found her place. The flies buzzing around the truck began to wander farther afield, invading the coolness of the veranda. Megan tried to read, to concentrate on the lovers who were doing unusual things in oddly described positions, but the strong aroma of the truck coupled by the flies trying to use her forehead as a landing strip made concentration impossible. She set the book down, finding her mind wandering to a song she heard when she was a child.

There's a skeeter on my Peter can't you see?

There's another on my brother don't ya know?

There's a dozen on my cousin,

Can't you hear those bastards buzzin'

There's a skeeter on my Peter, can't you see?

Megan giggled. *I hadn't thought about that in years.*

She shooed the flies away with her novel. Megan sighed, wiped the sweat off her neck and shifted in the swing. Her gaze unconsciously wandered back to the pecan grove and her heart jumped.

The girl was back. She was standing in the shadows, blending in so well that if it hadn't been for the breeze billowing her skirt, Megan wouldn't have seen her.

Megan stood and walked to the railing on the far end of the porch. "Hello," she called.

The girl jumped.

"Come on over," Megan invited. "I've got orange juice if you're thirsty. I have a couple of donuts left, too, if you're interested."

The girl swayed slightly as if she were unsure. "Come on," Megan prompted, "it's okay. I don't bite."

The girl stepped forward, as if ready to accept her invitation, but the sound of male laughter stopped her in mid-stride. She turned and ran into the forest without making a sound.

"Wait a minute," Megan called after her, waving. "You don't have to go."

"I'm sorry, Mr. Estille," Brody was saying loudly as he and the garbage man appeared from around the side of the house. Brody escorted Estille to his truck. "We're happy with the trash service we've contracted. The Kingston Group is environmentally friendly and we like that in a sanitation service. But we'll keep you in mind if things don't work out with them."

"Them's Kingston boys be as queer as three dollar bills," Estille slurred as Brody assisted him to his truck. Estille pulled himself into the vehicle. "But if you want dem faggots hauling your trash for you, it ain't no skin off my ass."

Brody shut the door for him.

"Are you sure you won't stay for some coffee? I think we have some left over from this morning—"Brody said.

"I'm fine, just fine. Just wish you hadn't signed up with them damned queers, though. They won't do you half the job I woulda."

"Well, be that as it may—"

"It's your choice," Mr. Estille said, a little too loudly, as he glanced in Megan's direction. "If you let your women do your thinking for yuh, ain't anything to me."

"I think you need to go now," Brody said, his voice as well as his face hardening.

Charlie Estille nodded, fumbled for the key, found the ignition and started his wreck. He backed out, the rear of the truck skewing weirdly as the shocks on the right side of the truck gave way, spilling out trash as it went. Megan cursed under her breath as the truck turned around. It bounced down the driveway, and onto the highway, and disappeared around a curve.

"My God, what was that about?" Megan asked, waving her hand in front of her face.

"Just an old drunk trying to make a little money."

"Make money my eye, look at the mess he left."

Brody laughed. "I'll clean it up, just as soon as the electrician leaves."

"Well, that's a comfort, having the power back on," Megan said as the living room lights flashed on. Relieved, she slumped back into the porch swing. Brody joined her.

"So who were you talking to?" Brody asked.

"That girl," Megan said. "She was over there." She pointed toward the pecan grove. "She's as skittish as a wild animal."

"She's probably one of the Gypsies," Brody said. "Mick, the electrician, told me that there's a community of them about half a mile from here."

"Really?" Megan asked, intrigued. "My mother was Gypsy. Gramma and Grandpa left the tribe, or group or whatever you call it, years ago. They bought this property and settled here. I didn't know there were any of them left."

"Mick tells me that they have a thriving little community down in Mercer's Bayou, about fifty or so brave souls. Oh, and I found out what that weird light was last night," he said, changing the subject.

"Really?" Megan asked, scooting closer to her husband. "What was it, a flying saucer? Consuela will be thrilled."

"I'm afraid it was a little more earth-bound than that," Brody said.

"Oh? Then what was it?"

Brody laughed. "You won't believe this. It's a tree."

"No way."

"Yes, it's a tree. Mick told me about it. You see, out on Mercer's Bayou, there's this little church and cemetery that's been around since before the Civil War. It started out being a family cemetery and for the plantation but expanded to include the local town folk. I understand that the descendents of the original settlers around here still attend."

"How very interesting," Megan said, although her voice said that she didn't think it was interesting at all. "So what does that have to do with the glow on the horizon?"

"I'm getting to that. There's this old tree; nobody seems to know what kind of tree it is, it looks like an oak tree with cypress knees. But it's all black and charred. People think it was struck by lightning and it caught fire or something. Dunno. Anyway, it glows in the dark. But what causes it to glow is that the grounds have a high phosphorous content. It's leeching phosphorous and that's what causes it to radiate that weird light. I understand it can be seen for miles around. Yeah, it's eerie, but harmless."

"I've never heard of such a thing," Megan said. "Didn't the phosphorous kill the tree?"

"It did," Brody said. "But it's so full of the chemical that it still shines."

"Then why doesn't someone cut it down?"

"Because of the historic value. Back during the Civil War, or so the legend goes, the plantation owner hanged his slaves from that tree instead of setting them free. Afterwards, the tree was used for local executions. I understand they stopped using it after hanging was replaced with the electric chair sometime back in the thirties or forties."

"What a strange story." She pursed her lips. "But do we have to look at that weird thing for the rest of our lives?"

Brody smiled, stood, fumbled in his pocket and removed his wallet. "We won't have to if you go out and buy some mini-blinds for the windows," he said as he handed her the credit card.

Megan took the card and said, "I'll go take measurements."

Chapter Six

Charlie Estille's faded garbage truck went into an odd sideways skid as it slid up the muddy dirt road leading to the First Light Church of Prophecy's gravel-strewn parking lot. It took a bit of handling to coax the aged vehicle up the road even in good times, but after the night's storm, the road was heavily rutted and slick despite the gravel top the state put down back in February. The rear shocks had long since broken loose and the hopper performed a bizarre jig as it bounced and boomed and banged against the truck body.

Charlie slid the truck into the parking lot and then took the vehicle out of gear. The truck idled in a grumpy old mannish way as he pulled the plug on a half-empty bottle of Old Charter and took a long, satisfying drink.

It hadn't been the best of days. Charlie was counting on the contract with the Wallace family, which would have added two folks who took his services more out of pity than of efficiency. But five families and trash pickup for the First Light Church of Prophecy didn't pay the bills, and Charlie was about to lose his electricity if he didn't make some money quick.

Trash pickup was ordinarily done on Tuesdays and Fridays, which were the opposite days the Kingston Group did their pickup per court order and this chafed Charlie to no end. But Charlie ignored the order and worked whenever he felt like it. And if he felt like hauling on the days the Kingstons were hauling, then it was their own tough luck. Most of the time, he arrived on Wednesdays and Saturdays. The rest of the week was fair game as far as he was concerned. Often he'd collect particularly large items such as appliances and furniture, things the Kingstons wouldn't carry.

Today was not such a day. He had only one other stop after his contact with the Wallaces, and that was the First Light job.

He took another drag from the bottle. Estille particularly hated doing First Light's pickup, even though they rarely had much to get rid of. His loathing for the church came along with the innate fear of what resided within the cemetery. He hadn't seen *it* glow in many years, but last night, the tree had come to life. At first, he had no desire to come out here, but after receiving the cutoff notice from the electric company, he decided he had to go to work, hence, visiting the church.

He drained the last of the soft golden-colored liquid and discarded the bottle by tossing it into the floorboard with the rest of his empties. Charlie looked at the church. *Hopefully, there won't be much today,* he reasoned. But he was wrong. Judging by the plastic containers stacked alongside the building, their garbage cup had runneth over. Groaning, he forced open the door and staggered slightly as his unsteady feet touched the ground.

Old Man Neidi better pay me like he promised. Otherwise I'm gonna snap his neck, Charlie thought as he walked around the rust-infested side of the truck where the gearbox mechanism for operating the hopper squatted like an infected wart on the rail. *If that old bastard will pay me what he owes me without arguing, I can settle my bill Monday and still have enough left over for a bottle or two of Wild Turkey.*

The thought comforted him somewhat. Charlie leaned against the side of his truck, waiting for his alcohol-induced vertigo to subside a bit before making his way across the parking lot toward the trashcans stacked against the wall. He picked up the closest one and half dragged, half carried it to the truck. He hauled it on top of the hopper and emptied it. He extracted the can and dumped it alongside the truck.

It would have been better if I had gotten the Wallaces signed up, he thought. He scowled when Brody's face came to mind. *You can tell by the look of that well-kept heifer of his that they don't have no money troubles. But no, they had to go with the Kingstons, and wouldn't change their minds. Silly wetback bitch and her pussy-whipped old man. Damn.* He swore as he dragged the second can to the truck and unloaded it into the hopper as well. *What's the world coming to when women wear the pants in the family? Don't men have balls anymore?* He swore under his breath. *There hasn't been a real man since John Wayne,* Charlie lamented. *God rest his cowboy soul.*

The late afternoon sun and dense humidity made him drowsy. Sweat beaded across his forehead and poured down his nose in great galloping drops as he lurched toward the third can. Once there, he leaned next to the building, enjoying a moment of thin shade.

His rheumy eyes rested upon the cemetery, its stones jutting up like rotten teeth along crooked rows. Occasionally a Woodmen of the World's cement tree stump or a shabby concrete angel covered with Spanish moss and kudzu would adorn a grave, but most of the others were hand hewn concrete or granite slabs, the writing having worn away a century ago or more.

The tree glowered on the edge of the cemetery. A small fenced-in area strewn with tiny stones without names stood in front of the tree. Estille found himself standing in the midst of the stones, feeling scared and somewhat confused because he could not remember leaving the shade of the church building, nor could he recall why it suddenly seemed so late in the day. Hadn't it been near lunchtime when he went to the Wallaces? He squinted up at the sun which was sinking toward the bayou. Where had the time gone?

Befuddled, he looked down at the sad little stones. Dead children, no doubt, died during the flu of 1910, or maybe earlier, when that crazy fucker Mercer slaughtered all his slaves... *No decent man woulda done that. No sir.*

The heat—or was it the booze?—distorted the markers. Charlie looked around, confused and deeply disturbed, as if he had taken the wrong turn off the highway while daydreaming.

"God grant me the serenity," he whispered, backing away. "You should be cut down and your roots yanked up from hell," he slurred.

The tree seemed to regard him. Estille shuddered. Something in the back of his mind was beginning to take form. It was disconcerting because it was clearing away the comforting alcoholic fog and replacing it with something sinister. Something whispered and chanted and wrapped around his mind like a heavy blanket. He gazed at the blackened trunk and the leafless branches, naked as a tree in November. But at night, the damned thing glowed and glowed. It had seemed much brighter last night than it had in a long while, but now it appeared to be drained of everything, including life itself.

"Well," Estille said, fear tapping like a woodpecker in the back of his mind, "is it true what they says about you? Can you really yank out a man's soul?"

A soft breeze caught the upper branches and it clattered as if in reply.

"Let's see how bad your ass really is," Estille said as he stumbled toward it. Despite the alarms going off in his head, he reached for the tree. Or maybe it lurched toward him. It was hard to tell in his inebriated state. Either way, he grasped the trunk.

The odd tingling sensation began immediately. He snatched his hands away, but the tingling worsened, becoming a full-fledged burn. Estille staggered backwards, looking at the palms of his hands. They looked as if he had rested them on top of a charcoal broiler.

"Jesus Christ," he howled as he stumbled away from the tree. "You evil demon possessed thing," he shouted as he staggered toward the truck. "Goddamn you."

Charlie half lurched, half ran back to the truck, alarmed not only by the burning, stinging sensation, but also because he could feel the ground vibrating against his feet as he staggered to the vehicle. He rested against the driver's side door, and then yanked it open. He slid inside and put the truck into gear.

The side panel on the dash board lit up. The yellow 'hopper full' light flashed.

"Oh hell," he said aloud. "I'll have to empty the hopper before I go. It won't run if I don't."

Suddenly very sober, he turned over his hands. The palms had turned a brilliant shade of red. *Now what evil possessed me to touch that damned thing?* he asked himself.

There was no good answer, other than being too shit-faced to think straight. He looked across the cemetery toward the tree, which was standing, gnarled and black against the brilliant green canopy of living foliage, then down to the light on the truck panel. The tree whispered to him, tugging him back toward it. Charlie shook his head, then stopped himself when he realized that he was actually about to get out of the truck and go back.

All his instincts screamed at him to get as far away from Mercer's as he possibly could. *Run and keep on running, all the way to Shreveport, down to New Orleans if you have to,* he told himself. *Get hold of a boat and cross the ocean, hide in the mountains; just go far enough away so you'll never see that tree or hear those awful voices ever again...*

But the hopper was full and it had to be emptied. Swearing at fate, as well as his newfound sobriety, Estille exited the truck and walked to the gearbox. He pushed the gear to the automatic cycle mode and the load packer rose from the bottom of the hopper and hung.

"Damn, damn, damn," Charlie swore. The load packer had to rise and then push the trash into the body of the truck, cleaning out (more or less) the debris left over by the hopper. But the packer was hung on something, meaning he would have to get inside the mechanism and pull it loose.

It was dangerous. The newfangled trucks, like the Kingstons' shiny green rigs, had safety mechanisms installed that kept the workers from getting ingested by the hopper. But Estille's Heil truck was ancient and missing a number of key safety components, such as the tailgate and various safety panels.

Estille wasn't worried about that. He was far more concerned with getting away from the damned tree, which was now actively talking to him, making his hands shake as he worked. He climbed into the hopper and then pushed against the load packer. For a brief eerie moment before the packer gave way, he thought he could actually feel the tree watching him, measuring him up. He heard a grinding sound as the packer released, lifting itself off the floor of the hopper, and tipping him off balance and dumping him into a heap of trash. He landed with a jolt. Estille heard a mechanical squeal as the automatic cycling feature took over, freeing the mechanism and shoving the packer toward him. He tried to scramble out of its way, but there was literally nowhere to go but down and that wouldn't happen until the packer thrust, crushing garbage, as well as his own body, against the back of the hopper.

The last thing he saw was the blackened wall of garbage coming at him. He heard the screaming screech of steel-on-steel as the packer pushed forward. There was a moment of pain, horrible, hot and red. Then, like the crushed beer cans he had tossed into the hopper earlier that day, his compressed body tumbled into the body of the truck.

-2-

Mrs. Blanchard quit during Thomas's breakfast. She left a hastily scrawled note on her desk, begging an emergency and took off immediately for Slidell, Louisiana. Or so she claimed. Thomas felt uncomfortable. It was obvious to him that maybe there was more going on with Mrs. Blanchard that Mr. Jim wanted to say.

Instead of dwelling on Mrs. Blanchard, Thomas decided it would be best to make himself useful. He organized the men into teams and they cleaned the house while Mr. Jim finished the budget report. Afterwards, Mr. Jim came down to the kitchen where Thomas was finishing up the lunch dishes and presented him with two mismatched, shabby but workable suitcases and a Bible. Thomas thanked him, dried his hands and went upstairs to pack his meager belongings.

Moments later, he was downstairs again. His heart throbbed in a strange mixture of dread and anticipation as Mr. Jim led him to the truck where he placed his luggage in the back seat of the king cab. Thomas got into the truck and shut the door.

"Pa's called four times since we talked this morning, wondering when I'm bringing you down," Mr. Jim was saying as he started the truck and pulled it out of the drive and onto the street beyond. "I tell you, that old man will run you ragged if you let him."

"He does seem strange," Thomas said.

"Oh you two'll get along," Mr. Jim said. "He doesn't like being without a preacher or someone out there minding the place. He's always scared one of the kids is going to come down and vandalize the church if there ain't someone down there keeping an eye out."

"Is that really a problem?" Thomas asked, not liking the idea of being caretaker as well as the minister. After all, wasn't caretaking Neidi's job?

"Naw, that's just Pa," Mr. Jim said as the street widened and merged into a highway. "And I suppose he's right in a way. Even though he's the groundskeeper he can't be out there twenty-four hours a day. He's got Ma and all those kids to think about."

Thomas grunted, half afraid Neidi would indeed be out there twenty-four hours a day.

They traveled five miles further, going deeper into the heavily forested countryside. Mr. Jim slowed the truck and turned right onto clay packed, gravel-strewn road. Thomas could smell the brackish scent of bayou water. He looked out of the window and realized they were driving on a red clay wall. Bright flashes of water glinted around cypress knees and large tree branches. Occasionally, Thomas got a good view of the area, which reminded him of a Louisiana calendar his father purchased at a bait shop when he was ten years old.

"This is the bayou levee," Mr. Jim explained. "It doubles as a road."

"How practical," Thomas said, his eyes widening as a bobcat ambled along the side of the road with an enormous catfish in her mouth.

"It's just around this bend," Mr. Jim said. As they turned, Thomas could see the small, whitewashed building and the adjoining cemetery sitting upon a small rise. An antiquated travel trailer, perhaps seeing its best years around 1967, crouched nearby. The parking lot was the most modern portion of the place, having had a fresh coat of dark gray gravel laid down. Mr. Jim shifted gears and the truck ambled up the muddy driveway. As they approached, Thomas noticed a broken down garbage truck idling in the parking lot near the side of the church.

"I think you'll like it here all right," Mr. Jim was saying as he pointed towards a low spot near the levee. "There's a good place for going after channel cats," he said, "They often come down from the overflow."

Mr. Jim parked the pickup on the opposite side of the parking lot, giving the garbage truck, still idling away, a wide berth. "Looks like Charlie is making a pickup," Mr. Jim observed. "He's a good old boy, has trouble with drinking, but other than that he's not so bad." He stopped the truck and killed the ignition. Both men could see inside the broken down end of the hopper. The packer was rising, shifting, then falling back into the bottom of the hopper, and then rising again.

"Something's wrong," Mr. Jim muttered as he got out of the truck. Alarmed by the urgency in Mr. Jim's voice, Thomas got out as well and followed the lanky man to the vehicle, which was steadily cycling.

As Thomas jogged toward the idling garbage truck, he saw Mr. Jim looking inside the hopper. He ran to the side of the truck and killed a switch. The packer groaned and returned to its resting spot on the floor of the truck. Thomas felt his heart pounding. *Oh God,* he thought as he looked at the packer floor, *that's blood.*

"Oh Lord have mercy," Mr. Jim said. "Brother Thomas, don't look inside that thing, just get back into the truck and get my cell phone. Dial 911 and that'll get you Tatum police."

"Why?" Thomas said, feeling suddenly very frightened. "What's happened?"

Mr. Jim couldn't answer. He was leaning against the truck, vomiting profusely.

Thomas returned to the pickup, picked up the cell phone clipped upon the visor and walked toward the garbage truck with it. Mr. Jim, still leaning against the truck, waved him back.

"You don't need to see this," he said, gasping, as another wave of vomiting assailed him. "Just call the police and tell them to get out here. Poor old Charlie has been ground up by his own trash truck."

"Oh Lord." Thomas shuddered as he switched on the phone. His hands trembled as the cell phone's screen woke and greeted him with a green smile. He punched in the numbers and hit "talk".

Mr. Jim killed the ignition. Thomas felt foolish and frightened as he stood in the parking lot of his church waiting for the dispatcher to answer. For an instant, Thomas thought he heard something whispering behind him. He turned a round quickly, but there was nothing there. Goose flesh raced up his arms.

I don't want to be here, his mind whimpered as the

dispatcher answered the phone. *If I leave now, maybe I can get back on that bus going to Taos. The shelter wasn't the best thing in the world, but if I leave now, at least I'd be...*

Alive...

Chapter Seven

Twenty minutes after Thomas made the phone call to the Tatum emergency dispatch, rescue workers arrived. Shortly afterwards five patrol cars from the Miller County Sheriff's Department, along with an ambulance and the county coroner's black station wagon, filled the church parking lot.

Thomas stood beside Mr. Jim's vehicle while the rescue team worked to remove Charlie Estille's remains from the belly of the aged Heil. A young black woman, trim and petite in a sheriff deputy's uniform, looked inside the truck's cab and took some notes on a small pad. After completing her task, she stood next to the gearbox while another officer stood talking quietly to Mr. Jim. Mr. Jim was quite pale, Thomas noted. Jim's eyes were wide and haunted as he spoke to the sheriff who was jotting notes in his own pad. Mr. Jim gestured toward the truck. The sheriff nodded as he continued to write.

"Got him," the paramedic inside the Heil said. "Someone get me one of those corpse sacks."

The men standing around the vehicle removed their hats and looked at Thomas. *They're expecting a prayer*, he thought, feeling caught off guard. Thomas cleared his throat and said, "A moment of silence I think would be best."

Everyone bowed their heads and prayed. A few crossed themselves. The only sound came from the trees as they gossiped to each other in the breeze. "Amen," Thomas said. Everyone returned to work. In the respectful silence reserved for the dead, the rescue team moved to extract the body.

Thomas approached the sheriff and his deputy. Mr. Jim,

seeing Thomas as he meandered around the aged Heil, motioned to him.

"This is Lonnie Cox, the Miller County sheriff," Mr. Jim said, introducing the tall, gangly man in a blue-gray uniform and customary Smokey Bear hat. Thomas extended his hand and Cox shook it.

"James Thomas," he said. "I'm the new minister for this church."

"So Mr. Jim's been telling me," Cox replied. He watched as the body bag containing Charlie's body was hoisted out of the hopper. Two more rescue workers retrieved the bag and placed it on a stretcher. "Don't even bother taking it to the hospital," the gray-haired coroner was saying as the crew swung the gurney into the ambulance. "Just take him on down to the funeral home. Lord knows..."

Cox shook his head. "What a waste," he said. "Charlie was a pretty good old boy before he took to drinking."

"Do you know how it happened?" Thomas asked, indicating the truck.

"Well, it looks like a freak accident," Cox replied. "For some unfathomable reason, old Charlie climbed into the hopper, then got caught up in the machinery and was crushed by the works."

"Unbelievable," Thomas said, incredulous. "I thought those things were pretty much idiot proof."

"Sanitation trucks have safety mechanisms that prevent someone from falling inside," Cox replied. "That is, ordinary ones that do your curb side service twice a week. But this one," he jerked his thumb toward the decrepit vehicle behind him, "this one has had the safety equipment removed from the tailgate, exposing the machinery inside. Goddamn stupid if you ask me, but knowing Charlie, the equipment must have quit working and he just pulled it off."

"Isn't that illegal?" Mr. Jim asked.

"No real county ordinance against it," Cox said. "Sanitation department takes care of all that, because they have OSHA riding their asses if they don't keep their safety specs up. But Charlie freelanced and didn't have any helpers. I've wanted to see a county ordinance passed against sanitation freelancers for this very reason. They just plain ain't safe. Just look at that thing, it's a rolling dumpster. Why DOT didn't pull him over and condemn it instead of ticketing him for littering, I'll never know."

"Did he have any family?" Thomas asked "Someone should be notified."

"I heard him mention a granddaughter living in Little Rock somewhere but I don't know her name," Mr. Jim said. "He pretty much kept his personal life to himself."

"Well, I guess it's all over now but the crying," Cox said as the coroner's station wagon ambled down the driveway, followed by the rescue vehicle and the ambulance. Up on the levee, Thomas could see a large wrecker idling, waiting for the driveway to clear so they could pick up the garbage truck.

"They should just take that damned thing straight to the dump," Cox said. "I don't see any reason to impound it, seeing as there was no sign of foul play." Cox clamped his hand down on Thomas's shoulder. "Well, Preacher, seems like this is your first duty here on the bayou. Sorry about that."

"Couldn't be helped," Thomas replied. "I wonder if his granddaughter will claim him."

"I'll go to his place this evening and see if I can find some phone numbers," Mr. Jim said.

"You do that," Cox stated.

"In the meantime," Thomas said, "I should get to the church and settle in. Services are Sunday."

"You sure you want to stay out here?" Mr. Jim asked. "You can come on back to the Mc Knight House if you want."

Thomas thought about it, but the idea of being alone was enticing. "No," he said. "I'm fine. There's a phone at the trailer and in the church office, I take it."

"Yes," Mr. Jim said. "And you'll find that the trailer has a television and a satellite dish, so you can check out the Razorback game after you get done fishing."

Cox laughed. "I think that's what he's really after, enit? Fishing, that is."

"You found me out," Thomas said, blushing.

"Well," Mr. Jim said, "if you change your mind, I'm just a phone call away."

Thomas extended his hand, and Mr. Jim shook it. "I'm grateful for everything you've done for me, but I think it's time I get to work."

Mr. Jim said, "I understand that. I'll help you with your luggage, then I've gotta go to the station and witness for poor old Charlie. There's worse ways to die, but off hand I can't think of any."

"I know that's right," muttered Cox.

"Then I'll go on down to his place and see what I can find for contacts," Mr. Jim said. "I'll call y'all when I find out something."

"Thanks for your cooperation. Gentlemen," Cox said, tipping his hat slightly to Thomas. "Preacher," he said respectfully.

Cox walked away from the men, got into his cruiser and followed the coroner down the muddy slope to the highway. Within seconds, he disappeared behind dense foliage of sumac, wild jasmine and kudzu.

"Sure is a tragedy, but the Lord has plans," Thomas said vaguely as he followed Mr. Jim to the white king cab. Mr. Jim opened the passenger side door and extracted Thomas's suitcases.

"Oh, I almost forgot," Mr. Jim said, setting a case down. He dug in his pants pocket and pulled out a set of keys.

"You're going to need these," Jim chuckled. "Now, this one," he said, indicating a large brass key, "opens the church." He flipped over another key, a slender silver one, "This one is for the church office, and this one," he added as he showed him a similar brass key, "this one is for the trailer. I'm sure you'll need that," he said, the laughter in his eyes returning. "And this little spindly one here," he added, showing Thomas a small blue aluminum key, "this one here unlocks that shed behind the church. It's supposed to be for extra storage, but Old Preacher McCain kept his fishing tackle in it. All of it's still there, too, if you have a mind to drown a worm or two this afternoon."

Thomas smiled and took the keys and said, "Thanks."

The men shook hands once more. "Sure you don't want to come on back to the Mc Knight house with me? I'm sure we can rustle up something decent for supper tonight."

"Nah," Thomas said, his mind returning to sitting on a creek bank with a fishing pole, the red-and-white cork bobbing along with the current. "Save the bed for someone who needs it.

I'm sure I'll be fine."

"Well, if you're all set then," Mr. Jim said, getting into the truck. "You've got my number, and Pa Neidi will check in on you from time to time."

Thomas watched as Mr. Jim started the pickup, then followed the sheriff's car out of the parking lot and traveled down the driveway and out of sight.

The wind picked up again, rustling the forest canopy. Thomas looked up and waved at the vehicle that had now mounted the levee and was driving away.

The wrecker crew finished latching onto the garbage truck, and they pulled their cargo out of the parking lot and heaved it down the driveway, making Thomas feel sympathetic toward Charlie, but impatient for everyone to leave.

Moments later, he got his wish. Thomas sighed, feeling content now that everyone had left. He'd wanted privacy for some time now, and now that he was here, he needed it the way a starving man craved a steak.

His mind returned to the breakfast conversation with Mrs. Blanchard and her sudden need to leave for Slidell. *Emergencies do happen,* Thomas told himself. *Try to relax and not be so paranoid.*

I guess I should look the place over, Thomas thought. The cemetery and the church building suddenly looked sinister and he immediately regretted not accepting Mr. Jim's invitation. He shook off a chill. *It was just an accident,* he thought. *The sheriff said the man was drunk. It was his own fault he died, the poor old soul. And Mrs. Blanchard's sudden departure was just a coincidence. And Mr. Jim seems to be a decent sort. A little odd, but maybe that's just his way.*

Despite this, Thomas felt exposed standing in the open. He turned and walked toward the trailer. It was quite old, but clean, with blue siding and small roll up windows. He noticed that an air conditioning unit squatted in the rear window of the trailer, as if someone had to make room for the unit by slicing open the trailer's thin metal skin, so insertion would be much easier. Thomas mounted the porch steps, set down his suitcase and fumbled with the keys. He found it on the third try and unlocked the door.

"Home sweet home," Thomas said as he stepped inside.

It was much better than he expected. There was a recliner and a television set, a kitchenette with a built-in table and a miniature stove and refrigerator. Thomas moved into the kitchenette and opened cabinets, delighted to see that it was already stocked with dry food and canned meat. He found Dr. Peppers in the side panel of the refrigerator and opened one, drinking it as he wandered throughout the little trailer. He found the bathroom, which consisted of a shower stall, a very small sink and a toilet.

The bedroom was equally compact, with a tiny closet, a twin sized, neatly made bed with a couple of pillows and a shabby orange-brown bedspread smeared on top. A nightstand squatted like a brown mushroom next to it. A New Testament—King James Version, of course—lay upon the table. *Ma Neidi must have come in here and tidied up, bought the groceries and all,* he thought. *I have to remember to thank her.*

Just above the bed, the air conditioning unit blew refrigerated air. Thomas groaned, thinking about the earache he'd receive in the morning if he slept under that thing.

Thomas returned to the living room and retrieved his suitcases. He placed them both at the foot of the bed. He went back into his living area and sat in the recliner. It was black, old and patched vinyl, but it felt comfortable. In fact, almost as comfortable as his old lazy boy back in Taos. He reclined all the way back. Finding the remote in the side pocket, he switched on the television. He sipped his soda and watched as the Chicago Cubs pitched the first inning against the Astros.

The comfortable recliner, the blessed solitude after living in a men's dorm at the Taos homeless shelter, the pleasure of watching, or at least listening to the game, made him feel at home. The day's unpleasantness drifted away. He found himself dozing, the television becoming little more than white noise as he sank deeper into slumber.

A portion of his mind remained active and felt guilty that he should feel so content after the tragedy that occurred not more than a hundred yards away. But that too receded as he fell deeply asleep.

Outside, the daylight retreated from the bayou, and the canopy became alive with sounds of insects and animals. The tree, brooding in its confines on the cemetery, whispered as it glowed. Somewhere in the distance, a wolf howled.

Chapter Eight

-1-

James Thomas's first sermon since his fall from grace was mundane, beginning with him preaching for about forty-five minutes on the evils of gambling not only with money but with your immortal soul—one of Rachael's favorites—and ending with the invitation and communion for the twenty-two souls who attended.

Thomas got the full blast of the Neidi family band. At that point, he silently prayed for sudden but temporary deafness.

Pa played guitar—badly—but like the rest of the Neidi clan, he played with gusto. Ma Neidi, the pianist and Pa's wife of forty-three years come April, he was informed, was a reed-thin woman with a mulish face and buckteeth. She slammed her hands down on the untuned keys with enthusiasm but no talent, while the twin teenage girls in bright gingham dresses, and barefoot, stood holding hands and croaking out the words to "The Way of the Cross Leads Home."

Thomas shuddered, despite his prayerful demeanor. The sight of the Neidi family made his skin crawl. Dougie, their oldest son, was a young man who was thin like his mother, played drums for the band on Sundays and worked out at the paper mill during the week. The youngest of the Neidis, a slack-jawed towheaded boy of about ten years of age, was rummaging in his pants as his family sang.

The rest of the congregation was of retirement age or older. Other than the Neidi family, there was not one youthful face among them. The final song was sung, the closing prayers made by a man in a once-white Colonel Sanders looking suit with a Bible firmly tucked in his armpit, and the services were dismissed.

"Now remember, Preacher," Mrs. Neidi wheezed as she stepped aside for Thomas to walk around the pulpit, "you're coming over for dinner, and you know you don't open the church for evening service. Nobody comes down here after dark."

"Now, hush," Pa admonished. "What Ma means is that most folks don't drive after dark, and there's only one or two people who come down for worship, so there's no need to bother, but you come on down to our house after you change out of your fancy preaching duds, and Ma'll fix you a Sunday dinner that can't be beat."

"I wish I could, Mr. Neidi," Thomas said. "I really do. But I can't. I've got to perform a graveside service at one o'clock this afternoon so I won't have much time to socialize."

"Graveside service?" Pa asked. "What graveside service? For old Charlie Estille?" He sneered, and the man's blatant hatefulness rocked Thomas on his heels. "I'm right, ain't I? Where do you intend to plant that old sinner? Here in our cemetery, Preacher?"

"Yes I do indeed," Thomas replied.

"The hell you are," Neidi roared. The congregation, who was milling around the sanctuary waiting to meet the new parson, stopped and stared. Several of the elderly women blanched, then slipped around the two men and escaped out the front doors.

"Who gave you authorization to use my cemetery to bury that old drunken blasphemer?"

"I don't need your permission," Thomas replied, making a point to stand toe-to-toe with the old man without flinching from the eerie eyes and rotting breath. "And it's not your cemetery. It belongs to the church, and the church belongs to the Lord. I'm the minister and someone needed our help. Mr. Estille left nobody to attend his affairs, and the state has paid for a coffin and the use of a backhoe. Mr. Jim and I marked off the plot ourselves this morning. Mr. Estille will be laid to rest at the edge of the cemetery nearest to the parking lot and far enough from that old hanging tree as to not be a bother."

"I wish you'd said something aforehand," Pa said, obstinately. "I'm the caretaker of the property and I shoulda known."

"We tried to contact you but your wife said you were out," Thomas replied. Mrs. Neidi blanched. "I'm sorry if this inconveniences you," Thomas said as amicably as possible, "but a poor unfortunate soul has died, and it's our duty as Christians to help out where we can."

"No truer words were ever spoken," stated the Colonel Sanders clad gentleman who stepped up to stand beside Pa Neidi. He extended his hand. "Smalley's the name, Reverend Ike Smalley, founder and chair of the Victory in Jesus Mission for Lost Souls, located at 410 Ivy Street, Tatum, Arkansas, praise Jesus." Thomas shook the man's hand, which felt like a limp fish. "We ain't as fancy as the Mc Knight House but we take care of their overflow."

"Nice to meet you," Thomas said.

"Yep, we don't get the faith-based grants the Mc Knight House does but we do the best we can with what the Lord provides," Ike Smalley said in a booming voice. "Come to hear the new preacher preach. I tell you what, you got the touch, I guarantee."

"I'm trying to conduct business," Pa said, clearly exasperated with Ike. "Now if you'll just move on."

"Move along nothing," Smalley said, pushing Neidi aside. "Just came on out here to see the new preacher. Reverend Thomas," he said, "Mr. Jim has told me all about you, yes, sir. And one piece of advice I can give you freely is to not let this old demon boss you around. This here is your church now, praise God, and you do what you think's right."

"Old demon, my eye," Pa exclaimed "Look at you...you good for nothing old drunk." He glared at Mr. Smalley. "Still got that flask with yuh? Eh? The one filled with Donald Montello's shine?"

Smalley patted the right side of his chest. "Just a touch of God's healing virtue," he said, smiling. "For my rheumatism."

"The hell it is. You come down here to spy on the new preacher, ain'tcha?"

Thomas smiled and slipped out the door, leaving the two men to their quarrel. It was apparent that his coming was merely an extension of an old argument, one these two men had kept alive through sheer will.

Thomas was disappointed the rest of the congregation had left before he had a chance to meet them. He felt a pang of anger at the two men who held him up. He glanced over his shoulder. They were still quarreling, gesturing vehemently at one another. *Well,* he thought, *I'll visit with the congregation individually this week, which would probably be better anyway. I'll have Jim come get me.*

He walked toward his trailer, secretly glad none of the other Neidis was pouncing on him. *I don't know how the last preacher took it,* he thought. *That has to be the queerest family I've ever met.* He glanced over his shoulder. *They're like cartoon cutouts. For some reason they don't seem quite real. And those kids...* Thomas shuddered.

Thomas stood on the top step leading to the trailer's front door. *I'll focus more on my ministry,* he told himself. *That'll keep me away from that obstinate old man and his weird family.* He frowned, considering. *What I really need is a vehicle of some sort, so I can drive around and minister to the local folk, try and get more people into church. Shoot, we don't even have a youth ministry, and I'd really like to hear the sound of children and young people again.*

The thought brightened him somewhat. He slid the key into the lock. Just behind the door was air-conditioned bliss, but it had to wait. Charlie Estille needed burying. A bright patch of blue flicked past his field of vision. *What was that?* he wondered. He lifted his head and stared into the forest where the movement caught his eye.

A man with long, stringy black hair pulled into a topknot, and a girl of about fifteen years old, wearing a tattered poodle skirt and gingham blouse, stood at the edge of the forest.

"Hello," Thomas greeted. The man motioned for the girl to remain behind, and she disappeared into the forest as the man Thomas assumed was her father approached.

"Good afternoon," Thomas said, extending his hand, "I'm Reverend James Thomas, the new minister for the First Light Church of Prophecy." The man stared at him, and Thomas, feeling self-conscious, withdrew his offered hand.

"You should go now," the man said solemnly. He glanced at the church. Neidi and Smalley had taken their argument to the parking lot. He could hear the fracas but couldn't understand the words, which was just as well.

"You shouldn't be here," the man was saying, "this is a dangerous place."

"What do you mean?" Thomas said, alarmed. "How can this be a dangerous place when it's the house of the Lord?"

The man shook his head. "This isn't a house of God, it's a house of the devil, and that old man over there, the one who calls himself Pa, he ain't human, not as men go. He's a—"

"Get on outta here," Ma Neidi shouted as she rocketed across the parking lot towards them. Thomas was surprised a woman her age could move so fast.

"You dang old booger man, get on out. We don't want your kind around here." She lunged at the man and Thomas grabbed her by the arm.

"What do you think you're doing?"

"Turn me loose, Preacher, this is for your own good," Ma shouted as she yanked her arm out of his grasp.

The black-haired man winced as if he were struck. "I thought you should know," he muttered, nodding to Thomas as he turned and went back into the woods.

"What was that all about?" Thomas demanded.

"We don't want his kind here," Ma Neidi ranted. "He's one of the Mercer boys, a filthy, stinking Gypsy who lives with that rattle trap bunch down in the bottoms."

"He's still a man who needs the Lord," Thomas said, growing angrier by the minute by the old woman's prejudice.

"He ain't a man," she shouted. "Ain't you been listening to me? He's a Gypsy. They ain't even human beings. They're vermin. They live like rats in those filthy old trailers and cávort with wolves. They're devil worshipers and witches. We don't want them in our church, and the Lord sure doesn't."

"No, they're not, and how dare you presume to know what the Lord wants and what he doesn't?" Thomas asked. He was trying to hold down his temper, but wasn't doing a good job of it. Her attitude reminded him of certain members of the white community in Taos who held similar opinions in regards to his Zuni flock. He swallowed hard, knowing that getting angry at this point would not help the cause.

Ma Neidi straightened her dress, obviously agitated. "I don't care if you disagree or not, if you bring one of those nasty Gypsies into our church, Pa and I'll see to it that you're fired on the spot." She shook a long, trembling index finger at him. "And don't think we can't do it, either."

"Good afternoon to you, Mrs. Neidi," Thomas replied, opening the door to his trailer and stepping inside before she could protest. He shut the door and locked it, catching an afterimage of the angry woman standing on the steps, shaking her scrawny fist at him.

"We ain't having those damned Gypsies in our church. And don't think you can bring in any of those uppity niggers from Tatum down here either. I won't have it! God made this church white and that how it's gonna stay."

Thomas leaned against the door, feeling her fists pounding against his back through the thin aluminum casing. He wished fervently that he were back on the bus on its way back to Taos. Mrs. Neidi's voice diminished to an angry squabbling as someone led her away. Thomas realized he was holding his breath and released it in a grateful gasp. *Thank God, that's over*, he thought.

Thomas retreated to his recliner, closed his eyes and tried to clear his mind. In half an hour, Mr. Jim would be here with the man from the funeral home and the state's backhoe. He would have to perform the funeral in front of the Neidis, who were showing no signs of leaving judging from the loud voices in the parking lot. It's the Lord's Day, but it wasn't going to be a kind day, he thought. *If Old Man Neidi keeps this up, I may not last out the week. Heck, I'd be happy if Ma carried out her threat and had me fired.*

Thomas put the thought aside and focused instead on the cool bayou water glistening on the other side of the levee. The thought calmed him. He dozed, and in the twilight world between dreams and awareness, he saw strong men erecting a tent on the church proper. Coleman lanterns strung along on large poles while the women served a potluck supper.

Now, that's what this old place needs, a good old-fashioned tent revival, he thought as the dream paraded across the theater in his mind. *That'll bring in more members. It'll give us a fresh infusion of young people and new ideas and if it harelips Old Man Neidi and his clan, tough. He can get glad in the same pants he got mad in.*

...God willing...

That's not much of a Christian attitude, he chided himself. But his mind returned to what the Gypsy said and Ma's high-pitched railing cut through his brain. Those people ain't Christian, she said. They did not follow the teachings of Christ and weren't about to. So there's no point in having them around.

The question is would Jesus welcome the Gypsies? Thomas wondered. *Yes, he decided, yes, he would.*

The loud roar of the backhoe's arrival jolted him into full awareness. *They're here. It's time to go.*

Gathering up his courage along with his suit jacket, he stepped out into the rich, muggy air. He watched Pa Neidi directing the backhoe away from the spot Thomas and Mr. Jim had already selected to grounds out of the cemetery perimeter. *Lord give me the strength,* he prayed as he walked across the lot, *to deal with that awful old man.*

Chapter Nine

Brody swung Megan around in a happy arc as they celebrated the opening of Tatum's first aerobics studio. He gave her a congratulatory smooch and she smiled up at him, her expression vibrant. "It's going to be a great summer," she said, leaving the comfort of his embrace. She returned to her favorite spot on the porch swing, tucking her legs under her as she opened the black leather briefcase. Happy, he sat beside her and watched as she extracted a fistful of contracts.

"Look at this, Brody. We're in the black already and we haven't had a session yet."

"Word gets around, you know. That's the best advertising in the world."

"Because it's free," they said together.

Megan bounced slightly, which made Brody think about other things besides business. "I can't wait. This is going to be the best studio we've got," she said, settling back down in the seat. Grabbing a pen, she bowed her head and went to work.

"You feel that way about every studio you open," Brody replied. She smiled up at him and then returned to work.

Brody gazed at her hair glistening in the slight breeze and his heart skipped a beat. *God, I love her*, he thought. *I love her more than anything. I'd do anything in the world for her.*

"What?" Megan looked up, suddenly aware of his intense stare.

"I'm just glad you're happy, that's all. And wondering when I can retire now that you're the big time executive type, and if I can, can I sleep with the boss?"

Megan laughed and pushed him playfully away. "You're making it hard to concentrate. Why not take a walk or something?"

"Well, if you put it that way," he replied, "I think I'll walk inside and watch television. Six Days of Bond is on TNN."

"Oh Lord, not six days of bondage," she groaned. "What you really need to do is get some exercise. Go take a walk."

"I'm about to. I'm going to walk to the fridge, get a beer and sit down and watch *Die Another Day.*"

"Well, that's just what you're going to do if you don't take better care of your body. But if you're so dead set on being a couch potato, go ahead. You can have one beer, but stay out of the bundt cake. That's for the potluck supper tonight after mass."

Brody stuck out his lower lip, looking like an overgrown petulant child. "Well, if that's the way you're going to be..."

"Be grateful I don't sign you up for one of my classes. I still have a few more openings."

"Shame on you," he muttered as he shuffled back into the living room. "You're awful, serving bundt cake to overweight ladies at church. And me, your husband, doesn't get any at all."

"You get plenty," she said to the screen door, indicating more than just the cake. "Don't forget we leave at five."

"I won't forget."

Megan chuckled to herself and returned to work. *God, I love him,* she thought. *He's the funniest guy I know. He's the most loving, and most supportive...* Megan shuffled through the contracts, adding names and phone numbers and occasionally an email address to her Rolodex.

Fifty-eight girls and women of various shapes and sizes signed on, and Megan, feeling somewhat overwhelmed that so many people were wanting to get into shape, decided she had to hire at least two more girls to help out with the studio. She added them to the Rolodex and placed little red stars next to their names. *Work schedules and w-4 forms, I've got to get them to sign those Monday. Thank God Brody's around to help me with the business aspect. There's so much to keep track of.*

"Well, I'm back to managing again," she said to Brody's dark outline as he sat on the pit group's recliner feature. Megan shifted her weight, making the swing move slightly. "I knew this would be a good thing for the community, but I had no idea how positive the response would be. And guess what? I had five more women call today wanting to sign up. Where on earth am I going to put all these people?"

Brody's voice filtered through the opening music. "Are we going to have to find a bigger place already?"

"Not yet." Her brow furrowed. "But I'm seriously thinking about it. The studio is packed in the mornings. I have enough clients wanting to come for the evening sessions. That'll keep Sally and Lisa busy, but the studio really isn't very big." Megan frowned. "You know, you may be right after all. The studio won't be able to handle any more people. And I'm sure we'll have clients coming in from Genoa and Fouke as soon as the word spreads." Her frown deepened. "It's so crowded now we'll have clients bumping into each other."

"Let's shop around and see what we can find," Brody said through the porch screen. "There's that derelict A&P up on Magnolia Boulevard that's got plenty of floor space, and office space too."

"Sounds good," she replied. "Do you know who owns it?"

"Sorta. The owner's son works at the plant. I can get him to let us in and have a gawk."

"Excellent," Megan said, putting the contracts into a neat stack. She composed a work schedule for Lisa, Sally and herself. She bit her lower lip as she concentrated. The schedule was somewhat awkward because Lisa went to college and Sally was taking cosmetology classes, which meant that Megan would have to fill in between shifts.

"I'll have to hire two more instructors," she said. She dropped the form down dramatically. "The free weights and the exercise machines," she exclaimed. "Oh good God, I forgot all about those. There's no place to put them."

"Worry not," Brody's voice carried through the screen door. "We'll find a place."

-2-

"Well, here we are," Mr. Jim said as they pulled into the circle of run-down mobile homes nestled in a small clearing surrounded by dense forest. "You can go and talk to them if you want, but I'll tell you now, they won't be interested."

"It's my prerogative to try," Thomas replied, feeling put out. He got out of the truck and made his way toward the trailers. Several people were sitting on porches or in rusted lawn furniture, and one man was hovering between the legs of a large horse, trimming its hooves with what looked like an over-sized pair of salad tongs.

Mr. Jim sat in the truck and waited. Thomas could virtually feel the man's eyes boring into his back as he walked into the camp. *This is unbelievably frustrating,* he continued. *I can't properly do my ministry if I have people standing over my shoulder while I'm working. And that's exactly the point. I constantly have someone looking over my shoulder. If it's not old Pa Neidi*—who he gave the bum's rush after the funeral when he stepped out of the shower and found the old man standing in front of his refrigerator helping himself to his last Dr. Pepper—*it's Mr. Jim dropping by unannounced.*

Mr. Jim wasn't much better, although he didn't force himself on him every day like Pa did. But Mr. Jim did have peculiar ways of just turning up unexpectedly. Like after the funeral when he finally had time to go down to the bayou and fish. After he was sure Pa was gone, he left the trailer and went to the shed behind the church and found fishing tackle, rod and reel—all still in excellent shape.

He extracted the goods, feeling somewhat awkward that he was using someone else's tackle, despite knowing the elderly preacher would not be back to get them. A man's rod and reel were personal things, and he felt as peculiar about taking them as a woman would have felt about another woman using her cosmetics.

Something odd happened as well and Thomas wasn't sure how to articulate it. It was more than just the peculiar feeling he had when he removed the tackle from the shed. For a moment, he heard voices, and not just the distant mumbling he heard at night and attributed to the sound of water splashing along the levee, but clear, distinct voices—ancient voices—chanting in the summer air.

He turned sharply toward the sound. With the exception of the cemetery's inhabitants, he was alone. *But the song is still there,* he told himself. It was a strained, sing-song chant that he caught just off the edge of his hearing. Since his arrival last Saturday, the old hymn had followed him into his dreams and left him waking in the wee morning hours thinking about Rachael and Becky. He raised his head and listened. There it was again, coming down the bayou levee, clear and as brilliant as sunlight reflecting off the dark greenish-brown water.

Swing lo, sweet chariot

Coming fo to taking me home

The chorus retreated into dim muttering and then vanished altogether. Thomas shuddered and considered abandoning his post then and there. But without a vehicle, how could he get away? And if he called Mr. Jim and told him he was hearing voices, well...

Maybe it's just my imagination, he thought. *There ain't anybody down here, nobody down here at all but the dead and they're not talking.*

At least his conscious mind told him so.

He shrugged off the mantle of superstitious fear and left the shed and went down to the bayou, where the cool water, green from algae, and the colored canopy sparkled in the sunshine, driving away the shadows and faint voices of an old Negro hymn.

He made his cast, sat and propped up against an elderly cypress trunk, feeling all the world was at peace at last, so much so that he could see himself as a picture in one of those old Louisiana Bayou State's calendars his daddy was so fond of. The water, warmed by the dense jungle-like heat, mesmerized him. He dozed as his cork bobbed up and down on the current. Thomas heard the song again, sharp and intense, accompanied this time by childish laughter. He jerked up, realizing he must have drifted off. He looked up and saw Mr. Jim standing beside him, his hands on his hips, grinning.

Although the conversation turned to business—having an old fashioned tent revival was a fine idea, a fine idea indeed, Mr. Jim had said—Mr. Jim's presence unnerved him. For a moment, Thomas was convinced that the lanky man who looked like a cowboy from an old Audie Murphy film had appeared out of nowhere, almost as if he descended from the sky or rose from the ground. Or perhaps the chorus summoned him. For days afterward, Thomas wouldn't be able to get the idea out of his mind.

Thomas returned to the present. He frowned as he gazed at

the Gypsy camp. Mr. Jim told him on the way out that he couldn't loan him a vehicle. He gave some vague excuse about insurance and loss of faith-based monies the Mc Knight House relied upon had been cut back this quarter. But Mr. Jim was more than happy to drive him around. In fact, he insisted on it.

Spy on me, you mean, Thomas thought. *That's what you're really doing.*

Thomas set his mind on two things that afternoon: as soon as he got paid, he was leaving, and the second thing was he wouldn't leave a forwarding address.

Mr. Jim's attitude toward the local Gypsy population was more polite than Ma and Pa Neidi's, but no less hostile. He clamped his face into a Halloween mask grin when Thomas asked if he'd mind taking him down to the encampment. And as he turned to look back at the truck, Thomas saw he still held the same expression.

The Gypsies noticed him. Thomas adjusted his jacket, feeling hot, sweaty and nervous. The men ushered the women and young girls into their trailers. Mothers dragged children of both sexes inside. What appeared to be large dogs slid into the forest after a man in fatigues gestured them away. The two elderly women paused on their porches and did something very peculiar. They spread their index and middle fingers to their lips and spit between them. They scuttled into their homes, but Thomas was certain they weren't far from the screen door.

The men approached him. Even the blacksmith stopped trimming the gray mare's hooves and stepped toward the preacher with a hammer in his hand.

"Good afternoon, gentlemen," Thomas said, astonished at how calm his voice was when he wasn't feeling all that well-composed. A large nest of snakes had traveled up his gut and was now squirming around in his stomach. For a moment, he thought he was going to become sick.

"Afternoon," a man replied. The voice sounded friendly, although the expression on the man's face implied otherwise. "What can we do for you today?"

"I'm Reverend James Thomas, the new minister of First Light Church of Prophecy," he said, extending a hand that trembled at the fingertips. The man stared at it as if it were laden with Ebola.

"We know who you are," a man with greasy brown hair said. He jerked his head toward the truck. Mr. Jim was opening the driver's side door. "You're with the devil."

"You misunderstand, sir," Thomas tried to explain. "I am the minister of the church, and I'm here to invite you to attend our services—"

"Don't bother," said a younger man who was standing near Thomas's shoulder. He realized he was entirely surrounded by the men. They smelled musky, odd, like a combination of dried rosemary and old fashioned Barbasol. The heat within the small circle, as well as the hostility, was palpable.

"It was just an invitation," Thomas mumbled. "I didn't mean any offense."

"None taken," the old man replied. He motioned with his right hand and the men dispersed. "I think you're an innocent." His eyes shifted to Mr. Jim bounding across the compound toward Thomas. "My name is Mark Buckland, and I—" his voice dropped to a whisper—"have something to tell you, but not now, not with the devil's man with you. You come on out here later tonight, we'll talk then."

"I don't have transportation, I—"

Mark frowned, considering. "You can walk a mile, can't you?"

Thomas nodded.

"You walk along the levee about a mile south. You'll come to an access road and a boat ramp. My son, Stevo, will wait for you."

Buckland nodded in the blacksmith's direction. "My son," he said, loud enough for Mr. Jim, who was fast approaching, to hear. "My son and his wife would like for you to remember them in your prayers. They're expecting their first child." Buckland glared at Mr. Jim who stopped behind Thomas and put his hand on the minister's shoulder. Thomas tried hard not to squirm away.

"I'll pray for your family," Thomas said. "And I would like to invite you all out to the church. We're going to have an old-fashioned tent revival. It'll be great fun."

Buckland shrugged and walked away. Mr. Jim nodded in satisfaction.

"Told you," he said as he led Thomas back to the truck.

"They're Gypsies, heathens and devil worshippers. They ain't welcome at that church and they know it. Besides, they're thieves and we don't put up with that. Pa had a mower stolen by them last summer. Heck, they'll steal your eyeballs out of your head while you're not looking."

"It was my duty to God to at least try," Thomas said as he got into the truck. "Church after all, is for sinners."

Jim muttered an agreement. However, some deep instinctive call, the same call that warned Thomas about the homeless man who murdered his family, was now shrieking an alarm. *Take it easy,* Thomas told himself. *It's just anxiety. It'll pass.*

"You did your duty to those folks, James," Jim was saying, the tone of his voice sounding faintly sinister. "You tried. That's the best any man can do."

Chapter Ten

-1-

The sun slid behind the thick canopy of trees and foliage, promising an early dusk. Peepers sang and bullfrogs grumbled a mud-thickened tune as Thomas left his trailer with a fishing pole and a small amount of bait, as well as a flashlight, seeing as he would have to find his way back to the church in the dark. He didn't trust the light from the tree to guide him back. The rod and bait were his excuse for being out late, in case Old Man Neidi should happen to show up demanding what he was doing outside after dusk.

Thomas walked down to the base of the levee and wandered down a narrow, beaten path where deer and other animals went down to the bayou to drink. He turned on his flashlight and walked carefully, mindful of the musky scent and the occasional lapping sounds of water against the levee wall.

Every now and then, vehicle headlights from the bridge above shattered the darkness. Thomas slipped quietly into the foliage and waited until the traffic passed.

Satisfied no one was following him, Thomas continued his trek along the waterline, listening to the careful lap-lap-lap of water as it sloshed against his side of the bank. It was hypnotic and he soon found himself daydreaming. So he wasn't paying attention when he stepped into a fire ant mound. The ants filled his shoes, stinging with such ferocity that he scrambled up the hill, yanking off his shoes in the process.

"It hurts all the way down to the bone," he grumbled as he swiped the last of the ants out from between his toes. He shook out his shoes, surprised that the ants that spilled out did not scurry into the underbrush but instead came right at him.

Cursing under his breath, he scrambled out of the way, pulling his shoes on as he went.

Shining the flashlight onto the forest floor, Thomas found his tackle and pole. The tackle box, he noted was swarming with fire ants. Carefully stepping around the colony, he retrieved his pole and continued down the path.

He hadn't gone far when Thomas gasped with astonished anguish. He stumbled into a cloud bank of buffalo gnats. Gagging and sneezing, he dropped his pole as he threw his hands to his face, his flashlight skewing its beam violently into the canopy, startling a flock of starlings. He scrambled for his rod, and half ran, half stumbled along the bank. He rested against a pine tree, gagging on half-swallowed bugs and wiping tiny black insect bodies out of his eyes.

My God, what was that? Thomas wondered, startled when he heard a weird sliding splash into the water. *Was that an alligator?*

He realized how truly wild the bayou was. Thomas recalled the bobcat walking along the side of the road with a fish in her mouth. *I stepped outside the safety of my trailer and out into this,* he reprimanded himself. *What possessed me to do this? Why do I keep getting into these predicaments?*

Something caught his attention. Thomas swung his flashlight beam into the trees. Perhaps startled by, or attracted to the light, thousands of whitish-green moths the size of his hand slipped from the trees, and like soft petals, spiraled down toward him. Fascinated, Thomas watched them as they floated away and out over the bayou. The water glistened beneath them as they skimmed just above the surface.

It's beautiful, peaceful and just plain spiritual, Thomas thought, forgetting the gnats and fire ants and alligators. *And I'm an unwelcome guest in these woods. Forget it, I'm heading back. If the Gypsies want me, they know where to find me.*

Thomas started back toward the church. *I'll have to go through the gnats and ants again,* he realized. He stopped, considering. *I don't dare take off through the woods. I might get eaten by God's bounty.* He shined his flashlight along the earthen wall. *I'll have to go through it,* he told himself, *and I'll just have to endure it.*

He steadied himself, preparing to return home. He caught a

glimpse of headlights reflecting along the water and the high levee wall. *It's Stevo*, he realized. *He is down by the boat ramp.* He laughed aloud. *He came after all.*

Still laughing with relief, he headed toward the direction of the headlights. *Stevo can give me a lift back to the church,* he told himself. *Yes, Stevo can let me off down the driveway and I can walk back.*

Saplings and undergrowth rustled and cracked. Thomas, startled, back peddled and stumbled. The ground crumbled beneath his feet and his arms pin wheeled as he plunged ass-first into the blood-warm bayou water. Heart pounding, he scrambled back up the bank.

A long, narrow gun barrel protruded from the foliage, along with the heavy-set Gypsy man he had seen earlier that day.

"Stevo," Thomas exclaimed as he stood, "I'm so glad you're here, I—"

"Quiet," Stevo scolded, his tone cryptic. "They're watching." He motioned toward the church. The tree glowed ghostlike in the darkness. In the distance, a wolf howled.

"Here." Stevo shoved an envelope into Thomas's pants pocket. "Now get out before *he* catches you."

"But wait," Thomas said to the retreating back. Stevo vanished into the undergrowth and he was alone again.

"I was hoping for a ride home," he whimpered to himself as the lights from Stevo's pickup went dark.

Abandoned, Thomas turned and walked toward home. He held his breath and ran through the buffalo gnats and stumbled up the bank away from the fire ant colony, which was still furiously defending its territory as he scrambled up the levee.

He hadn't gone far when he heard the rumble of a four-wheeler. Startled, Thomas saw its headlights skewing bright white beams as it went up and down the bank. He was about to slip into the woods and wait for the vehicle to pass by, but whoever was driving the ATV must have seen him. Praying that it was a friendly face, Thomas waited. The ATV came to a halt next to him, the engine grumbled. A small flashlight ray touched his face.

"Well, it's the preacher," the young man, whom he recognized as Pa Neidi's eldest son, Dougie, said. "What are you doing so far out, Preacher Thomas?" he asked.

"I went fishing down by the boat ramp," he said, feeling strange that the lie would slide out of his mouth so easily. "I fished too long and it got dark—"

"Catch anything?" Dougie asked.

Chagrined, Thomas raised his pants leg. "Fire ants and they got my catch along with my tackle box," he replied.

"Well, you shouldn't be wandering around out here at night," Dougie said. "There's varmints out here, and some of them are worse than fire ants." Dougie scooted higher up on the machine. "Climb on. Ma sent me after yuh, said you needed a hot meal."

"Okay," Thomas said, feeling very helpless, but knowing that he couldn't refuse. "I'd like that."

"Well, hop on, the skeeters are getting righteous."

Thomas slid onto the back of the ATV. He made sure the envelope Stevo had given him was shoved deep into his pocket. He held his rod with his right hand and held onto Dougie with his left. The young man opened the throttle and they moved back up the bank.

He felt Dougie's muscles ripple beneath his shirt. Holding him felt odd, like he was holding onto a rotting log, and the smell the man exuded wasn't much different. The muscles rippled and flexed under the shirt, and for a moment, Thomas wasn't sure if what he felt really were muscles or writhing tree roots.

Truly afraid, he considered jumping off the back of the vehicle and running for his life. *But there's no chance of that,* he thought. *I have no idea where I am.*

Dougie veered into the woods where a logging skidder had cleared off a rough-hewn path through the undergrowth. The ATV rocked and bumped along, nailing Thomas in the groin a number of times. Something, perhaps a root, scraped across his ankle as they drove past.

The forest gave way to a pasture. Thomas looked over his driver's narrow shoulder and saw the warm glow of a house up ahead. Such a scene would make anyone feel glad for warmth and food and perhaps comfort within the household walls. *There is no comfort here,* he thought. *I'll have to spend the evening listening to Pa's nosy inquiries into my past and Ma's*

unabashed racism. But I suppose there's no getting out of it.
They were bound to catch up with me sooner or later.

Might as well get it over with, he thought. *Maybe it won't be
as bad as I think, and if I'm very lucky they won't ask me over
again.*

-2-

After finishing the evening dishes left over from the potluck
supper and Bingo at the church—Megan added a black bean
casserole to balance out the caloric horror of the bundt cake—
she pulled the kitchen curtains closed against the horrid glow
of that old tree.

"That damned tree" she called it, especially when she
discovered the mini-blinds did very little to keep the harsh light
out of the kitchen. She purchased heavy drapery material and
made curtains that still didn't fully keep the light out.
Exasperated, she painted the window itself black, replaced the
mini-blinds and then draped it. Even with all the extra work,
the garish glow physically pressed against the panes,
demanding entry. Megan shuddered. *Forget the historical value,
why doesn't someone cut it down?*

Forcing herself to dispel her disquiet, Megan joined her
husband on the sofa.

The living room was dark with the exception of the
flickering glow of the television screen. Brody was chuckling to
the remains of *Married with Children.* Megan couldn't care less.

She curled up next to Brody, and his arm, so accustomed
to its privileged place around her shoulders, slid around and
held her. She laid her head on his shoulder and, feeling
comfortable and loved, drifted in and out of sleep.

The canned laughter filtered through her weary mind as an
actor made some smart-assed comment. Moments later,
someone apparently arrived on stage because the audience was
applauding and shouting as if in the throws of hysterics.

*You can always tell when a sitcom is about to go under. The
laughter sounds like it came out of a tuna fish can and the actors
get standing ovations just for showing up.*

Megan felt an odd tugging sensation, as if something had
snagged her in the back of her head and pulled her out of her
body. *I feel like a big old bass,* she thought as the tugging

continued and she felt like something was reeling her in. *They really should use stronger tess-line*, she thought through the haze. Whirls and eddies drew her along the strange current. She was floating now, feeling the gentle lapping of waves around her spiritual body as the invisible force dragged her forward.

The spiritual undercurrent slid away and Megan's soul took flight, soaring above the brilliant canopy of greens, golds and reds as a Georgia Red evening sun set, drowning itself in a murky ribbon of bayou water.

A Dodge Ram that someone must have taken literally because of all the dents was parked just beyond a boat ramp. A stocky man with a long black pony tail and a gun got out and headed toward the woods. A few yards away, another man was faltering along the banks of a reddish-green ribbon of water.

Megan focused her attention. Another man was driving an ATV, coming toward ...*no, for*...the man with the fishing rod. The scene reminded her of the time when she was twelve and saw the film *Rosemary's Baby* for the first time. She wanted to shout at the movie screen, straining in her seat, mentally trying to warn Rosemary, but it wasn't possible. After all, it was just a movie, right?

Megan felt the same way now, concerned for the man staggering along the riverbank, suddenly faltering and then thrashing with all his might to free himself from something— mosquitoes? When the real threat was driving the ATV. But she couldn't warn him. She couldn't tell him not to talk to the man on the four-wheeler.

Megan abandoned flight and now stood in the cemetery at Mercer's Bayou, the Cold Hanging Tree throwing great flames into the violet sky.

I have to destroy it, she thought. It was a reasonable thought, something that she could do as easily as her early morning jogging sessions. *Let's pencil that in, shall we? Let's see, there's the morning workout at ten, go to the studio at noon, my manicure at three...and yes, kill an evil tree at five.*

She looked down and a wolf, yellow-eyed and black as the night, was holding something in its mouth. *Take it,* the she-wolf urged. *Take it. Take it.*

The wolf wasn't talking, she realized. *Something is talking through her. Oh how strange,* Megan thought. *The voice is familiar yet unfamiliar as well.* She looked at the tree, feeling truly frightened.

You have to kill it, the most reasonable voice said, *because if you don't everyone you love will die.*

Megan hesitated, not sure exactly how to do it.

Do it now, the voice commanded. Megan jolted. From another world, she vaguely felt Brody's arm tighten around her.

Take it, the she-wolf urged. *Do it.*

Megan took the object from the wolf and examined it. It was a pendant designed like an eight-spoke wheel, carved with strange markings. It spun, small and silver-blue, in her palm. The tree was making noises now, uttering a strange high-pitched wail that made the ground beneath her feet vibrate.

"I don't know how," she said to the wolf. "I don't know what this is. How am I supposed to use it to destroy a tree? And how is a tree dangerous? What could it possibly do to kill everyone I love?"

You ask too many questions, the reasonable wolf voice said. *Follow your instinct.*

Megan stared at the wheel in her hand and then looked at the wolf. She lowered her gaze to her feet, feeling frightened and confused.

"I don't understand," Megan said.

You don't have to, the she-wolf replied. *Just do as you're told.*

The ground lurched. Megan fell. As she rose, she saw the graves open. Dark gray and blackened hands pushed open coffin lids. The earth covering them spilled away as the corpses rose, blank faced and vacant eyed. Megan gasped as they left their crypts and started toward her.

It's opened. It's opened and you failed, the voice wailed.

"What's happening?" Megan cried as she felt the line pulling her back toward her body.

You failed. The wolf's voice faded as Megan flew away. *You failed and now there's going to be revival.*

A wolf howled. Another one nearby replied, and deep in the forest, another answered. Megan lurched awake as her spirit plunged back into her body.

Brody, startled out of his television-induced hypnosis, clutched her close. "What happened?" he asked.

"I had a falling dream," she said, feeling unsteady. The dream was receding and was now faded and wispy like early morning mist. She snuggled deeper into her husband's arms, but was unable to return to sleep. The sitcom had ended and the ten o'clock news from out of Shreveport, Louisiana began.

Megan barely listened to the story about a riot in Ledbetter Heights. The perky blond news anchor discussed the breakup and arrest of a dog-fighting ring, followed by a story about timber rustlers east of Texarkana, Texas who had stolen a large quantity of high quality pines from the Warehouser Tree Farm.

Brody chuckled. "Timber rustlers." His chest rumbled as he spoke. "I wonder if they'll hang?"

Megan didn't answer. Her mind was swirling. *What just happened?* she wondered. *Did I really leave my body, or was it a dream?*

Brody eased his arm from around her shoulders as she sat up. She rubbed her temple with the heel of her left hand, then realized she was clutching something round and somewhat heavy in her left palm. She wrapped her fingers around it, her heart pounding, afraid to see what it was.

"Going to bed?" Brody asked as she rose and crossed the room.

"Uh, yeah. Headache. Too much excitement, I guess."

"Save me some room. I'll be in bed in about half an hour. I want to catch the sports. I want to see if the Astros won."

I would rather see you play baseball instead of watch it, she started to say, but clamped down hard on the impulse to nag. Besides, she needed to find out what was in her hand and didn't want to explain what happened. Not until she had it sorted out in her mind anyway. "Good night," she said.

"Night."

Megan virtually ran down the darkened hallway until she came to the bedroom. She switched on the light and flopped onto the bed. Holding her breath, she opened her left hand.

The eight-spoked wheel gleamed silver in the light. The center of the hub spun without moving the spokes. As she looked deep into it she could see a long blue spire within the center. It occurred to her that whatever was inside the wheel was alive, pulsing with an alien energy. It frightened her. She gazed at the long, almost abnormally straight letters carved around the wheel's rim. Megan gasped and then resisted the impulse to fling the object away.

How in the world did it get here? Megan wondered as fear, thick and biting as bile, rose to the back of her throat. *And did that wolf really talk to me or am I losing my mind?* She clamped her hand against her mouth, partly to keep from vomiting, partly to keep from screaming.

Megan waited until Brody was thoroughly asleep before she crept out of the house. Standing at the edge of the forest, she took the pendant and hurled it as far as she could out into the woods. Satisfied it was lost forever underneath the forest floor, Megan returned to bed.

Chapter Eleven

Otis Miller's failure at the calf barn torqued him to no end. It was bad enough that last April's tornado laid his wheat crop to waste, but the heifers he took to market at the Texarkana stockyards didn't amount to squat when everything was said and done.

He ended up selling his Brangus crossbreeds for significantly less than he did last year, roughly forty cents a pound instead of the sixty five cents per pound he received the year before. It didn't sound like much of a difference until the check was cut and he found his profits had dwindled down to next to nothing. Miller cursed under his breath. *I barely made my feed money back. Rita's gonna be pissed.*

Otis grunted as the truck and trailer rig hit a pothole the size of a small crater. "Damn," he muttered as he nearly bounced out of the seat. "When are those county boys gonna drag their asses out here and fix that?"

He bemoaned the recently adjusted suspension system, which would need another alignment no doubt, and said a brief prayer of thanks that the gooseneck hadn't taken on a life of its own and decided to swing in the other direction. He negotiated another tight turn, kicking up red dust as he went.

It wasn't just the seed he needed now. He also had to pay for some much needed repairs to his tractor. The bush hog needed some work too, but it could wait till winter when it was too wet to work and he could use it as an excuse to keep busy.

I'll do the north forty in soy, he decided as he drove his aging flatbed and attached gooseneck cattle trailer up the gravel driveway that made an impressive arch around the front yard. *It'll be ready for harvest by fall, and it'll enrich the soil. Next year, I think I'll just let it go fallow, and put corn in the south pasture this coming spring.*

Otis swung his rig around the circle drive and parked underneath an old ironwood tree. *I'll have to get another loan to do it,* he grumbled. *After begging at the bank, I'll have to plow the pasture under. The carburetor works half assed, but I can get that old rattle trap started long enough to get the plowing done.*

He approached the house. Rita, his wife, was sitting on the porch. *Waiting on the news, no doubt,* Otis thought. *Ah, hell, this ain't gonna be good.*

He muttered to himself as he mounted the porch, almost gagging from the overwhelming aroma of magnolia blossoms from the tree beside the house. He threatened to cut it down because it aggravated his sinuses, but Rita-Mae, the wife, the lady of the house, the she-who-must-be-obeyed, as Rumpold of the Bailey, from his favorite British comedy put it, threw a wall-eyed screaming fit about it.

The tree stayed and he contented himself with handfuls of Allegra to keep his allergies at bay.

The house, which was the original Mercer plantation house, welcomed him with a soft yellow glow from the porch lights. It wasn't grandiose like the plantation houses he'd seen in Nachedoches, Texas, or the spectacular high-columned mansions in New Orleans, no. The Mercer place was a heavy-planked, tall, thin ship of a house that looked as if it'd be more comfortable moored off a pier in Galveston Bay instead of sitting dry dock on weary antebellum land.

Rita-Mae was sitting next to the front door on the wicker chair she bought in Canton, Texas three years back. She was fanning herself, more to shoo away mosquitoes than to stir the still air, which had grown rancid from heat, magnolias and rotting plant life.

"How'd yuh do?" she asked, her face partly concealed by the evening shadows.

Otis shook his head and handed her the check. Even though he couldn't quite see her face, he could imagine the indignant pursed lips that indicated she wasn't pleased.

"That bad," she commented, slipping the check into an

apron pocket. "Well, it'll be enough to buy seed, I suppose. Maybe get the carburetor fixed on the tractor, but nothing else."

"I'll fix the rattle trap myself. Borrow Big Paul's old Ford to plow with tomorrow."

"I figured. I already called Big Paul. He'll have it out to you first thing in the morning."

"I'm glad you thought of it."

"And tomorrow after plowing, you'll get Ed down at the dealership to fix ours. You know as well as I do they'll probably need to order parts."

"It would help if I bought a new one instead of patching up the old one. The damned thing's three days older than God—"

"If you'd gotten a better price off them heifers, you might be able to afford a new one," she said without malice.

Otis sighed. *And there's "mights" on a chicken's ass,* he thought. "I'll see the loan officer Monday," he said instead.

"The cows down in the barn pasture are ready to calve," Rita-Mae added, her voice softer, as if she realized she was being far too harsh. "Maybe this spring you can retire old Rattle Trap."

"Yeah." Otis propped his right leg on the porch steps and lit a cigarette. "But that's months away. If we get lucky and the soy harvest comes in good, and we turn the south pasture for winter wheat, we'll have enough." He looked up at her, blowing blue smoke from his nose. "Maybe even have enough left over for that newfangled dishwasher you want, though God knows why."

"We'll just have to do the best we can with what we got, and if I get a dishwasher, I will, if I don't, then I won't," Rita-Mae said, her voice fatalistic as her mother's who endured the Depression but never quite recovered.

Otis knew that was a huge part of Rita-Mae's cynicism. Even though she was born on the tail end of the Dust Bowl days, she inherited the innate fear of government and destitution from unseen forces from her parents. In her mind, poverty and Republicans meant the same thing.

Otis's folks never worried much about the Depression. His people were Choctaw, so his pa considered the white man's troubles a minor inconvenience. His father was a fervent believer in cash and carry, and so the farm was paid for, therefore, nobody took them on. He kept up his taxes, and the family survived as they had before Columbus stumbled on the Bahamas.

Otis was only a little fella when the Depression receded to the marching cadence of goose steps. To him, the government was a vague and intimidating organization that wanted to poke around in his business, which pissed him off to no end. He never asked them for money, although they had no problem taking his. He refused their loan and subsidy programs, which were tantamount to welfare in his mind. He'd rather starve to death than take a handout from Uncle Sam.

Otis was the first member of his family to attend college. He went to Texarkana College back in the fifties, majored in agriculture and received an Associate Degree. After his brief but memorable stint in Korea, he returned, married Rita-Mae and used his GI bill to buy the old Mercer place. He did as his father did, paid off the property as quickly as he could and then kept up on the taxes.

There was something romantic about owning a piece of history, no matter how run down it had become, and he and Rita-Mae, still young and expecting their first child, restored the plantation house, tilled the soil and brought at least a small portion of Mercer's Plantation back to respectability.

Things had gone pretty well over the years—the kids had grown and blew away like the chaff on winter wheat—and financially he was always able to break even. But this summer tore a hole in his pants and his money was seeping out of his proverbial pockets faster than he could mend the hole.

It wasn't a pleasant thought. He might even have to sell the forty acres of land running along the north pasture, but he really didn't want to do that. Selling the land was like carving a chunk out of his soul, and he wasn't prepared to do that, at least not yet.

"Preacher came by today," Rita-Mae said, jarring him out of his ruminations on the past and worries about the present.

"Preacher? You mean the new one down at the Southern Baptist? Lackey's his name, I think."

"No, no. The new preacher from the First Light Church. You know. *That* one."

"Oh," Otis said. His skin squirmed at the thought. "What

did he want, money?"

"No, he wanted us to come on out there. He's planning a revival."

"No revival's gonna save that church. An exorcism, maybe, but no revival."

"Well," Rita-Mae said, "I told him we'd think it over."

"Shoulda told him we go to Tatum Southern Baptist and been done with it."

"I guess." Her brow furrowed. Even in the shadows, he knew her lips were puckering again. "But he seemed like a decent sort. Friendly enough. Had old Jim Balfour with him." She paused as if gathering her thoughts, like eggs in a basket. "The preacher has this awful gash on his throat. I wonder if he's been in some sort of accident."

"Ain't no telling." Otis dismissed the conversation by sniffing the air. "Supper ready?"

"Chicken pot pie. It's in the oven. Should be done by now."

"Well, if you've got me some time, I've gotta see to Alice."

"Alice ain't dropped that foal yet. I checked on her about an hour ago. You'll have time for supper."

Otis dropped the dead end of his cigarette onto the ground and snuffed it out with a boot heel. "I'll be on up directly."

Rita-Mae stood and opened the screen door. "Suit yourself. But don't blame me if it gets cold."

-2-

There was no need for a flashlight. Otis had walked up the path to the old barn for the past thirty years and knew the way by heart. It helped that Jeb, his eldest son, became a master electrician and wired the barn for power as one of his projects before graduating from school. The loft was devoid of hay for many years and was now used as storage.

The barn glowed like a jack-o'-lantern. He smiled, thinking about his son and daughter-in-law who moved down to Texarkana, close enough to still see them, but rarely did. *We need to go and see them this week,* he told himself. *The farm can make do for one afternoon.*

As he approached the barn, he noticed a thick fog developing along the ground on the pasture beyond. *Odd,* he

thought, *it's not cool enough for that.*

The tree line fringing the larger meadow looked sinister, the ancient hardwoods appearing almost ready to uproot themselves and wander the earth. The air was hushed, still, without so much as a breath stirring. Otis realized he was holding his breath. He let it out slowly.

Stupid shit, he scolded himself as he let his breath out. *It's only fog. It ain't anything.* But the feeling of *wrongness* was settling deep inside his bones. Alarmed, his testicles sought safe refuge inside his body.

He was next to the barn now and he could hear Alice grunting and snorting in nervous labor as she banged around in her stall. The feeling of dread grew deeper, and Alice neighed at that moment, making him jump as the dead silence was broken.

Otis stood beside the barn, watching the fog as it grew deeper and thicker, swirling, writhing, then morphing into thick lumps that made him think of people huddled under blankets. Otis was truly anxious now, but was too fascinated by what was going on to leave the barn's side. A faint wailing noise was coming out of the fog.

What is that? he thought as he watched the hunched forms coalesce. They mingled, becoming more defined and distinct. More solid and *real.*

Otis bit his lower lip until a thin trickle of blood ran down his chin. His heart pounded in his ears as he watched the fog form into distinct body parts. Heads rose from the rising lumps of mist and he could see men with hats and women with cloth head covers. They seemed to be picking something off the ground. The forms rose and fell in the fog, vanishing, reforming, then becoming human again. And the noise, which at first sounded like an autumn wind whistling around the barn eaves, was now a chant, heavy with the sound of Negro voices.

Otis's hair stood up under his cowboy hat. He shuddered and realized that the air had turned ice cold. He noticed that his breath was coming out in quick puffs; an ethereal frost was now covering the side of the barn as well as the grass under his feet.

The field hands reaped a long dead harvest. The fog swirled around the hunched forms, thin and gauzy as a shroud. They were singing in earnest. It was melancholy, a deep, rich Negro spiritual that Otis hadn't heard since he was a kid sitting in the Rexall store back when they still had soda jerks. He was six years old and he remembered his feet swinging from the green vinyl stool as he sucked on a root beer float. He was listening to an old black man singing softly under his breath as he shined a white man's cowboy boots...the same song he was hearing now...

Slavery chain done broke at last,

broke at last, broke at last,

Slavery chain done broke at last,

Going to praise God till I die.

My God, Otis realized, *they're slaves. They're slaves and they are still picking cotton. That's why they're bowing and weaving...*

The scene hypnotized him. More slaves emerged from the fog now, picking and chopping at the dirt they hovered over, singing as they went.

The bodies are becoming more real now, Otis thought. *There are details that weren't there before.* He could see the men wearing ragged pants and shirts, the women bound up in heavy cloth, over-sized bags gliding just above the ground...

Way down in-a dat valley

praying on my knees

Told God about my troubles,

And to help me ef-a He please

The song drew him in, the chant holding him firm as he watched the field hands picking their ghostly crop. One of the slave women had moved away from the rest and glided toward him.

Otis could see her face, eerie white against the black night. The eye sockets were empty. Her mouth was a round, blank hole. She was wrapped in the fog that made her. At this moment, Otis realized he was literally too scared to move.

"Come with us, red niggah," she drawled, her voice thin and far away as if she were talking into a tin can. "Come on down with us, come on down with us to da river and know Glory—"

Her hands were reaching out to him, unnaturally white, the

fingers long and tapered. Otis stood, fascinated as she approached. The woman was beautiful, deadly and coming closer. Her body shimmered and swept inches above the ground. With eerie grace she swept towards him.

From inside the house, Rita-Mae screamed.

Otis jolted to full awareness; the desire to leave the world with the lady vanished as quickly as the specter that hovered before him. *Oh Lord, Rita-Mae's in trouble,* he thought. Otis felt as if he'd been punched in the gut when he realized the big house had once been occupied by servants as well, servants who were now long dead, but with white arms and vacant faces and a desire to send a humble man such as himself to Glory.

The scene vanished as quickly as it came, leaving a blank silence where the field hands worked and sang their heart-chilling song. But Rita-Mae was still in the house, screaming for all she was worth.

Otis backed away from the barn, then turned and ran for the house, his seventy-year-old body complaining as he went. "I'm coming!" he yelled, even though he knew that Rita-Mae wouldn't hear. *I'm coming, just hope I don't break a hip along the way...*

Chapter Twelve

Dougie Neidi led Thomas into the linoleum-crinkled foyer of his parents' run-down house. He bowed slightly as he opened the door that led into the kitchen. He waved Thomas inside. The good minister reluctantly entered, not knowing exactly what to expect. He found the family sitting around a large table that dominated the kitchen. Ma Neidi shut off the flame to the stove that squatted like a fiery-eyed troll next to a door that must have entered into a living area. Pa was sitting at the head of the table, a stack of plates at his right hand, while Ma took her place down the far end of the table.

"Have a seat, Preacher," Pa said, motioning him to sit next to him. Thomas nodded and eased himself into the seat, feeling strange and unwelcome despite the insistence from Ma to come fetch him.

Dougie sat next to him and the other children sat across the table. The twins were staring hard at him, while the youngest boy, whom he had only heard referred to as Brother, was trying to filch a piece of chicken off a platter.

Ma swatted the child's hand. "Stay out of that," she snapped, perhaps sharper than Thomas thought was necessary. The little boy curled his hand into a fist and then slid it under the table. Judging from his expression, he was hitting his leg.

Two baked chickens rested on Dutch blue china platters. Ma's best, no doubt. Vegetables and bread also filled the table, and on the counter top, a huge pitcher of iced tea gleamed in the yellow light. *The table arrangement is odd*, he thought, and especially so since everything, he observed, was within Pa's reach.

The children stared at the food like starving dogs, but said nothing. Again, his eyes fell on the plates resting next to the old man's elbow.

What a control freak, Thomas thought.

"Since you're the guest of honor, you can say the blessing," Ma was saying.

The family bowed their heads and Thomas, suddenly at a loss for words, stared at their crowns and wondered once again how he had gotten into such a predicament. Just how long a blessing did they want? Saying a small prayer to himself, he bowed his own head and said, "Lord bless this food for our perishing bodies, we ask in Jesus name. Amen."

"In Jesus name," Ma repeated.

"An oldie but a goodie, Preacher," Pa said in approval as he reached aside and picked up a plate and began filling it with food.

The kids watched as the old man packed the plate almost past capacity and handed it to Thomas. Ma, in the meantime, filled his glass with ice water. Thomas was disappointed and somewhat confused. He gazed at the pitcher of iced tea, with its gleaming condensation crawling slowly down the sides, and wished for a glass.

"Mrs. Neidi," Thomas said as she finished filling his glass and was about to proceed to Dougie, whose plate had been handed to Thomas and he was shifting it over to the young man beside him. "Mrs. Neidi, could I trouble you for a glass of that iced tea?"

The room became devoid of air. The children stopped shifting plates—with substantially less food on them than his—and stared at him with large frightened eyes.

"Did I say something wrong?" he asked.

"Now, Preacher," Ma gently scolded, "you know that tea goes with our cobbler after supper."

"I didn't mean to offend," Thomas stammered.

"Ma, you know the boy's not from around here," Pa said as he finished filling plates and was now heaping mashed potatoes onto his own. "His ways are different from ours."

Ma nodded as she took the unclaimed baked chicken from

the table, wrapped it in cheesecloth and placed it in the refrigerator. The children looked rabidly disappointed. They returned to picking at their food with the expectation hungry children get when they want their meals to extend far beyond what they actually have. It stumped Thomas. All of the kids looked healthy, well-boned and muscled, and weren't showing any signs at all of starvation. Although each of them had plenty of vegetables and bread, the chicken was spread sparsely among them.

There's so many of them, Thomas thought. *And the Neidis are not young and certainly not rich. They must conserve what they have.* He felt a pang of guilt as he gazed down at his own plate, heaped with more food than he could eat, but knowing it would be an offense if he didn't.

"Go ahead, Preacher, eat up," Pa grumbled around a plateful of gizzards, livers and a couple of pieces Thomas couldn't identify and tried not to think about.

Ma sat at her place and waited with her hands folded with southern primness upon her lap. Thomas smiled at her and raised his fork.

"I know it must have been a terribly long time since you've had a hot meal and all," Ma was saying. He knew she was staring at him while he ate. The kids stared too. Only Dougie and Pa kept to their tasks.

"You shouldn't have gone to so much trouble, Mrs. Neidi."

"It was no bother at all, and call me Ma."

"Thank you again, Ma," Thomas said.

"Well, you do need to be taken care of," Ma said, her face expressionless as she sat, the food on her plate neglected. "You not having a wife of your own to cook and do the washing or anything else. Do you plan to remarry, Preacher?"

"Ma," Pa scolded, "stay out of the man's affairs. That ain't none of your business."

"Just a question."

"Well, I hadn't thought about it. After Rachael died, I spent all my time trying to start my life over again. In service to the Lord, that is."

"Well, that's a mighty fine way to start," Ma said. "I'm sure he'll find you someone pretty when the time comes."

"I expect so," Thomas said, feeling enormously embarrassed.

"Where didja get that scar?" Brother blurted. Brother, he noticed from the past Sunday's encounter with the Neidi clan, was a hopeless stutterer. But his singing was stutter free, although it was just as awful as the rest of his siblings. He was astonished that Brother spoke out so clearly.

The air vacated the room once again. The common clatter and low-grade conversations of supper time chatter came to an abrupt halt. Thomas could hear his heart pounding.

"Get on outta here, boy," Pa roared.

"Pa!"

"Go on. Get up to bed. The girls can have the rest of your plate."

"Pa," Thomas whispered, seeing the child's face flush white, his lip trembling as he gazed down at his half-finished plate. "The boy didn't mean any harm."

"Go do as I say," Pa said to the child, ignoring Thomas.

Brother hung his head low, shifted his chair away from the table and ran between Pa and the stove, disappearing through the door behind the old man.

"Boy's getting more uppity every day," Pa commented as he picked up his fork.

"I'll tend to it," Ma said.

"Maybe I should head on home," Thomas said, feeling more anxious and uncomfortable by the minute. His food was now sitting hard on his stomach and he wasn't sure he could continue.

"Not till you finished with supper," Pa said, "and we've had a little talk aforehand. Then I'll take you on back."

"Thanks, but I think I'd like to get on back now."

"Now, hold your horses, Preacher. Ma's done gone all out today and cooked just for you. Now you can't go off and hurt her feelings, can you?"

"No, I wouldn't want that," Thomas said, feeling desperate as he realized the twins had finished their meal and were now staring at him with bright green eyes. "How can I refuse such good company?"

"Now that's a good deal," Pa commented. He pushed his

plate aside and Ma rose and took the plates away. She then divided the food from Brother's plate and split it between the twins. Thomas struggled to finish his own meal, which was difficult. Brother's punishment was far too harsh in his mind. The boy was curious, that was all.

"Mr. Jim told me y'all went out to Boggy Creek Landing and visited those Gypsies," Pa said. Ma grunted in disapproval as she returned with a large peach cobbler she extracted from the oven. "How did your talk with them go?"

"Not good. They don't want to come to church with us."

"Well, that's good. They don't need to come down here and worship with us," Ma said as she took Thomas's plate and placed it in the sink with the others. She opened a cabinet, extracted bowls and handed them to Pa, who dipped the dessert up and passed them around. Ma returned with the iced tea and refilled everyone's glasses.

"They got their own churches, just like the Meskins and niggers, ain't that right, Pa?"

Thomas cringed at such vulgarity coming out of what seemed like such a dainty woman's mouth. He stared down at his serving of cobbler, wondering where he was going to put such a huge slice. *I'm eating a bigot's food*, he thought. *God help me I don't think I can keep it down.*

"He tells me that you want to start up a tent revival," Pa was saying, nudging Thomas out of his reverie with a bony elbow. "Brother Jim, that is."

"I am," Thomas, said, happy at last to change the subject. "I was thinking about having one of those good old-fashioned tent revivals, with lanterns strung outside and a place for a potluck supper afterwards. Maybe even baptize a few folks down on the bayou."

"Now that's a wonderful idea," Ma approved. "Why, we haven't had a good old-fashioned prayer meeting down here since I was a little girl."

"I thought you'd approve," Thomas said, eager to bring his plans into focus. "I wish I had a computer though. A computer would make it easier for folks to find us. I could build a website and start a newsletter."

Pa waved his comment aside. "We've got everything you need. You don't need that old devil's machine to do what we need to do."

"Really," Thomas said, trying to keep the sarcasm out of his voice.

"We have a mimeograph machine and a typewriter. Got lots of paper and masters for the mimeograph too. You can run off some flyers and post them in Tatum or even stand on a street corner and hand them out. Folks'll get to know the new preacher that way."

"There's nothing on those dad burned computers anyway but necked pictures and devil worshippers," Ma stated. "It's a tunnel straight into hell."

"Well, be that as it may," Pa said, pushing his bowl aside, "we've already settled on what the preacher's gonna do."

"We have?" Thomas asked.

"I'll go on down to the funeral home and ask to borrow one of those big tents of theirs, you know the one I'm talking about, Ma? The one they used to bury the mayor about two years back."

"It's a lovely size," Ma agreed.

"Besides, they owe you a favor, Preacher Thomas. After all, you did agree to bury old Charlie without so much as make a fuss, and I understand the state paid them off so I figure a favor's a favor."

"That's great," Thomas said, feeling excited. "I'll set up the times and dates and let you know what to tell them."

"A mighty fine idea all around," Pa said as he rose from the chair. "I'll do that for yuh. All you gotta do is set up your sermons."

"And I'll get the ladies organized," Ma said. "There'll have to be food and we can't have everyone bring a chicken casserole."

"And singing," Pa slapped his hand on the table. "By God, we'll need to rehearse every day now."

"How exciting," Ma replied.

"I'm glad for you all's help," Thomas said, believing every word of it. He rose also and Pa escorted him into the living room, which was indeed behind the door where the old man sat.

"Just make sure you don't have no darkies coming to church," Ma called through the opened door as she began to eat. "I won't hold to having no riff raff in the church."

"No ma'am," Thomas agreed, but it was a shallow agreement. He intended to allow anyone who wanted to come to do so. After all, wasn't church really for sinners regardless of color? Besides, it'd harelip that bigoted old bitch to no end. That thought pleased him, even better than the prospect of a tent revival.

Thomas was shocked at his own vehemence, which made him feel strange, disconnected, almost as if the thought belonged to someone else. For an instant, he could hear the moaning of the trees and the eerie singsong chant that rose, velvet soft, like mist rising from the cemetery.

"You okay, Preacher?" Pa asked. His face expressed genuine concern.

"Oh," Thomas said, finding himself lying again for the second time today, "I'm not feeling too well. I'm sorry, I'm not used to all that good Southern cooking. I guess I got a little greedy tonight."

"I'll take you on home then." Pa's voice colored with disappointment. "You need to get some rest, I suppose."

"I do retire early," Thomas agreed, feeling utterly relieved. He stood in the threshold between the living room and kitchen and bowed slightly to Ma. The children, he noticed, were still sitting in utter quiet, eating their cobbler. "Ma'am," Thomas said, "thank you for an excellent meal."

"You're quite welcome, Preacher," she said. "Now I expect to see you at the supper table more often."

"That'll be a pleasure and a privilege," Thomas said, lying again. *That makes three in one day's time. My,* an ironic voice in the back of his mind commented, *the devil's words do become a habit, don't they?*

Chapter Thirteen

-1-

Abendego Jones hated his name. Why his father forced it on him was a mystery. After all, there were much better Biblical names to be had than that one. Abendego reduced easily to A Bad Negro; even his friends called him that. Because of this, his childhood and adult years were fraught with fistfights, sometimes resulting in overnighters in the Miller County Jail Complex. It was also the last thing his father had given him.

A.J. was seven years old when his father was killed. He was a brakeman for Santa Fe Railroad and was cut in half when a freight car backed over him during a linkup. What the railroad insurance paid did not make his mother wealthy, but it left her well off enough to be able to raise three kids without relying on what amounted to slave labor for black folks during the fifties. And Mama, being the strong-willed, self-reliant woman she was, "weren't going to niggah for no uppity white bitch. Period, end of story."

"They ought to come on down here and scrub my floors," she once said. A.J. smiled at the memory.

But she also kept her illness a secret, and no one knew, or wanted to know, that she was sick until she passed out on the kitchen floor one bright sunny Sunday morning just before church. His sister, Flo, found her and called the ambulance.

A.J. was sixteen years old and was convinced that God was systematically killing off everyone he loved. He didn't know why God had a vendetta against him, nor did he especially care. Everyone in the neighborhood stood and watched as his mother was loaded, protesting all the way, into the ambulance. She was rushed to The Old Cottonbelt Hospital in Texarkana. The diagnosis was dismal. She died six weeks afterwards.

A.J. never forgot the look on the nurse's face, pale, drawn and flushed from vomiting. "It fell off," she whispered to another staff member. A.J. overheard. "Doctor Moran was examining her left breast. Her nipple just fell off. And the smell! Jesus, I wretched for fifteen minutes—"

And I got you fired for that little comment too, so I did, A.J. thought. He may have hated the name his daddy had given him, and resented his mother for forcing him to keep it, but he wouldn't let anyone disrespect her, especially no snotty, white, bleached blond slut of a nurse standing next to the nurse's station gabbing with her equally slutty friends.

A.J. waited for his mother's end to come, and when it did, he did the one thing he'd dreamed of doing since he was a little boy. Change his name. So, forty years after the change, which did him good in his opinion, the new and improved A.J. Jones swung his tractor around the dimly lit pasture and mowed down the last of this season's Coastal Bermuda hay. The headlights beamed with an unsteady light as the machine jolted and bounced around the field, while the bailer at the business end of the tractor shat out its last huge round bail for the day.

It was getting dark, sure, and Emma would have supper ready by now, and he was hungry and tired. Besides, Emma would worry if he stayed out much later and would come looking for him. He sighed. *There ain't no peace in the world, no sir.*

This day, like most days now it seemed, was pressing in hard on him. He was thinking seriously about giving up the farm and retiring to somewhere comfortable and less humid. Like Arizona, for instance. Emma wouldn't go for it, though, he knew. She'd been to Arizona twice, thank you, when she was driving for Bagwell Truck Lines, and that was plenty.

A.J. sighed, readjusted his rump into the tractor seat, then, as the bailer finished taking its last dump of the evening, he put his shiny green—or would be in the daylight—John Deere into gear and drove it to the fence.

The sagging barbed wire divided his property from old Otis Miller's. He thought about walking over before going home to Emma and chewing the fat with the old Injun about what went on at the auction. Calf prices were most important in A.J.'s mind. He hadn't taken his steers to auction yet, but he heard about the dumped price on heifers so it wasn't looking good.

He was debating whether or not to put the calves in the freezer this year instead of trying to sell them, when he noticed something odd going on in Otis's pasture. At the same time, the tractor grumbled to a sudden and uncomfortable halt.

"What the hell—"A.J. swore as he tried restarting the motor. The engine flatly refused to engage, refused to make a sound. "Damned battery cables," he grumbled and swung his leg over the gear box, getting ready to dismount. Shocked, he remained in that pose as his eyes riveted to what was happening in Otis's field.

Miller's barn was in sight, glowing from the electrical lights Otis's boy installed years ago. It reminded him of that old Amityville House that his sons insisted on seeing back when they were just kids. But that wasn't what troubled him.

A.J. swung his leg around and sat sidesaddle on the tractor seat and watched as thick dew condensed into dense mist across the pasture. *It's just fog,* he told himself. *Happens this time of year, especially in the lowlands.* But the thought didn't comfort him. Something was decidedly wrong with this particular mist, and he shivered from the sudden drop in temperature.

Just as Otis had witnessed moments before, the mist swirled, grew into lumps, into forms, into people—no, not just any people—A.J. noted, *but my own people, black folks.* Black folks chopping cotton and chanting an old spiritual he hadn't heard since he sang in the choir before his voice broke. *It's a beautiful thing to watch,* A.J. thought. *It's beautiful, eerie, but scarier than shit.* What were those folks doing out there, digging and chopping when they should be in Heaven getting their final reward?

He heard Rita-Mae's screams coming from the house, followed quickly by Otis shouting reply. Dear Lord he was out here too? A.J. startled from the trance, woke with cold sweat streaming down in his eyes. *I wanted to follow them. God help me, I want to go along with them. Oh lord,* he realized. *What if I had? What if I had and walked straight into oblivion with them?*

A loud noise, like a door slamming shut, preceded a sudden inrush of reality. The spectral field hands vanished. A.J.

felt disoriented as if he were sitting underwater. The tractor restarted abruptly, nearly knocking him off his perch. He grabbed for the steering wheel and shut the tractor off before it lurched into gear and wandered off without him.

A thin green line spread across the horizon on the west. *It's that tree,* A.J. realized. *It's that old devil's tree, and it's come alive again and it's gonna do the devil's mischief.*

A.J. Jones, formerly known as Abendego Jones, wiped the sweat from his brow with a checkered handkerchief. After spending a brief but spectacular six months in the Hanoi Hilton during his stint in Vietnam, he was damned sure not going to be scared of some haunted tree. "I'll finish this," he said. "I'll put a stop to this once and for all."

-2-

Gasping for breath and fighting off an enormous stitch in his side, Otis Miller rushed up the porch steps, taking two at a time. Panting hard, he yanked the screen door hard enough to dislodge it from its hinges. "Rita, Rita-Mae," he shouted as he ran into the living room and stopped, stunned as if he'd been slapped across the face with a wet towel.

Rita-Mae stood in the middle of the living room. Her face was pale beneath large splatters of blood. Her dress and apron were soaked. Thin tendrils of gore dripped like rotten mop strings on her hem. Rita's eyes were wide as she clutched her left shoulder. Otis gaped, trying to decipher what he saw, to make sense of it somehow.

"Otis," she whimpered.

Otis, shocked beyond words, took a shaky step towards her.

"It's coming out of the toilet," she explained, her voice rough as sandpaper. "I heard a noise in the bathroom. I checked the toilet because it was rattling and moaning like something fell in it. I thought, maybe an animal..." Her lips trembled. "I opened the lid and it...it just came up." Tears slid down her face, mingling with coagulated blood.

He looked down then and realized blood was pouring over his steel-toed boots. "For the love of Christ," he exclaimed. "What's going on in here?"

"And that's not all." Rita-Mae slipped her hand into her

apron pocket and extracted a gold-rimmed locket. She offered it to him, palm up, the thin chain hanging limply between her fingers. "See what I found in tonight's supper?" she asked. "It was in the casserole. I don't own one of these, don't know how it got in there. I cleaned it off and set it on the table when I heard this awful sound coming from the bathroom. When I went inside—"

Her voice broke and she began to cry again, which wasn't her nature. Rita-Mae's hysteria unhinged him worse than the spectral field hands or the blood on the floor.

Otis took her by the elbow and guided her toward the door. Blood hadn't oozed this close to the threshold. He stopped and turned around, fascinated as he watched the blood slide like thick, muddy water out of the bathroom door and into the living room. *It can't be blood,* he reasoned. *It's something else. The septic tank must have backed up.* But there was no scent of sewage. *It smells warm,* Otis reasoned. *It's coppery and feral, like blood gushing from a freshly butchered deer carcass...*

Rita-Mae shook her head and handed him the piece of jewelry.

Otis turned the object in his hand. It was a cameo, made from real ivory, no doubt, he thought, and old too. The cameo bore the creamy white silhouette of a woman's head and the background was blue. The locket was backed with gold, the rim around it gleaming dully in the light. Frowning, Otis turned it over. Reflected in the golden glow were words etched in fine rolling script. *Molly Mercer, September 5, 1835. With all my love, Ted.*

"What does it mean?" Rita-Mae asked, her voice high and trembling. She cradled her arm in a way that made him feel uncomfortable.

"Are you okay?" he asked.

"I'll do," Rita-Mae, replied, her expression tense.

"I don't know what's going on," Otis confessed, thinking back to his own experience in the pasture. "But I know I don't want to stick around to find out what it is. Let's get out of here." He moved to push the door open, but Rita-Mae's face froze, whitened, her eyes wide and her lips tinted blue. "Let's go now," he emphasized.

Rita-Mae opened her mouth to answer, then lurched

forward and screamed. And screamed and screamed. Clutching her left arm, she gagged and sagged toward the floor.

"Rita-Mae," Otis shouted, grabbing the wiry old woman and holding her tight as her knees gave way.

Her mouth opened and closed like a bass out of water. She pointed over his shoulder. Otis looked over his shoulder. "Jesus Christ," he swore.

Hands blossomed from the pink and white flower wallpaper. More appeared, bulging under the wood, the fingers pushing outward until the hand was exposed. The hands were calloused, some cracked and seeping blood, all of them were black. They reached out of the wall, grasping and groping blindly. Otis laughed at the idea. *Of course they are,* he thought, *hands don't have eyes.*

More hands emerged, peeling paper off the wall. The chant he heard in the field moments before returned, loud and metallic, grating on the nerves.

Rita-Mae groaned and slid against her husband. "Make it stop, Otis, please."

His entire body trembling, his nuts drawn up so tight he thought he'd choke on them. Otis watched as more hands pushed themselves out of the walls, blood oozing from around the hard-worked wrists and wrecked knuckles. The hands multiplied, filling all the living room walls, scraping off wallpaper, slapping pictures off the wall as they emerged.

"Can you make it to the truck?" he asked.

She whimpered and then nodded. "Don't have much choice, do we?"

The lights flickered and dimmed, brightened and dimmed again. The walls gushed with blood. Hands along with arms burst through the ceiling. A long, loud howl uttered from somewhere outside sent them both screaming. Rita-Mae slumped again and Otis half dragged, half pulled his wife toward the threshold.

The phone uttered a bizarre chilling cry as it was ripped out of the wall by a hand and flung at them. Otis opened the door, only to have it slammed in his face.

Hands came up out of the floor, reaching, grasping at them. One tore the hem of Rita-Mae's dress, dirty yellow nails shredding the paper-thin flesh on her leg as Otis struggled to open the door. Another rogue hand yanked off one of her shoes. A hand exploded out of the muck, snatching at Otis's feet. Swearing, he kicked and stomped on the hands, which retreated back into the floor, with wails like grief stricken children. The song was deafening, the old spiritual that once comforted was now a torment; the voices moaned and were answered by the baying of wolves just beyond the door.

Otis didn't question their presence, nor was he particularly frightened by the knowledge that they were outside. He was living in the moment in ways most humans never experience. All that mattered was to get out and quickly. Everything else was detail.

He held his wife around the waist while one of the hands extended up to the elbow from the wall and slugged him in the ear. He stopped, stunned for a moment. Enraged, he slammed his own fist into the wall. The spectral hand jerked back. Otis, growling under his breath, kicked open the door and dragged his wife through.

The exterior walls vibrated, filled with an eerie golden-green light. Otis kicked aside the wrecked door as the hands tried to swing it shut. Once fully away from the front porch, Otis dragged Rita-Mae to the truck and heaved open the door. He shoved her inside the cab, ignoring the wolves as they scattered across the lawn.

"Oh hurry, hurry please," Rita-Mae moaned, her body shaking, clutching her arm tighter. "I'm in a bad way."

Otis climbed into the driver's side, slamming the door shut and swearing profusely while the engine groaned and growled and refused to turn over.

"For God's sake, Otis," Rita-Mae screamed.

The house shuddered and groaned as the roof caved in. The walls slid inward in an insane comic dance as the house imploded. There was a dull explosion toward the back, and Otis realized the propane stove must have blown up. Rita-Mae sagged against him, and for a terrifying moment he thought she was dead until he heard her deep heaving sobs.

They're pulling it down, he realized. *They're tearing down my life's work.* He could almost see the hands ripping the walls and yanking up floor planks, pulling wiring like plastic spaghetti along walls and down the ceilings.

The house caught fire. It burned mightily, brightening the side of the old barn, becoming a torch that blazed a good forty feet high. *They must be seeing it all the way to Tatum,* he thought.

The truck cranked with a startled lurch. Refusing to release this moment of good fortune, Otis turned the truck away from the remains of the house and sped away. A pack of red wolves huddled in the light moved aside as the truck sped down the driveway.

His heart hammered in his chest as he took the Mercer's Levee Road and headed toward Tatum. Rita-Mae moaned beside him.

"It'll be all right," he reassured her. His face was grim as he caught a glimpse of himself in the side view mirror. "Just hang on, old gal, it's going to be all right."

Chapter Fourteen

-1-

A.J. had never forgotten the story of the Cold Hanging Tree, and he remembered his grandmother's voice as she told it. He remembered the pause as she took another dip of snuff, her rocking chair creaking as they sat next to the old Franklin stove that kept her little cabin warm. A.J. thought about all of this as he drove grimly down the Mercer's levee, heading toward that unnatural glow in the forest. Despite his grandmother's warnings, he knew exactly what he needed to do. He was going to lay hands on that old tree, all right, and when he did, that tree would fall.

But he wasn't a foolish man, no. He brought along a heavy pair of welder's gloves because he knew that the tree glowed not because of Satan—although deep down in his soul he believed it did—but because it was leaching phosphorus from the ground and that would scald the flesh right off the bones.

Well, I have a solution for that bullshit, yes I do. He grinned. A.J. brought along some friends: a heavy duty chainsaw, along with two double-bitted axes in case the chainsaw failed to start the same way the tractor had died in the pasture about twenty-five minutes ago. He had fuel for the saw, and for his personal comfort, a tattered copy of the Bible and a twelve gauge shotgun.

A.J. moved his pickup aside and allowed the Tatum fire engine and entourage of trucks and rescue vehicles to pass. They roared by, causing his little truck to sway from the wind they kicked up. In his rear view mirror, he could see a tower of flames grasping for the evening stars.

"Lord have mercy," A.J. prayed. "Lord, let my job be swift

and sure."

Otis Miller passed by, the truck horn blaring, his flatbed and gooseneck swaying dangerously all over the road. "That crazy Injun's gonna get himself killed," A.J. said aloud. He was worried, though. Old Otis Miller didn't drive crazy, but was careful, especially when he had his prize gooseneck trailer hitched to the back.

He glanced back at his rear view. The flames were tossing themselves high into the air, well above the tree line. The horizon glowed in an unnatural dull sunset, and A.J. realized then, with his faith waning, that Otis's farmhouse was on fire.

"That's why he was driving so fast. Rita-Mae must have gotten herself hurt; otherwise he would have stayed and waited for the fire department."

A.J. shoved the accelerator to the floor, his pickup bumping and bounding along the levee, toward the green glow. As the levee turned, he could see the old white church house bathed in the supernatural light. It looked like a haunted house he and a few friends of his from the Jaycees put together for Halloween one year. It was fun and raised a nice profit too, until some of the more fundamentalist members of the community raised a ruckus and had it shut down because they felt it was Satanic.

"No baby, dat wasn't Satanic but dat church down there sure is."

A.J. passed the tree and the cemetery, the water in the bayou rising and falling as if it were breathing. He felt chilled again and afraid. He turned off at the intersection and drove down the dirt road toward the church, singing, "His Eye is On the Sparrow."

Feeling better, A.J. pulled up into the parking lot. He didn't pay any attention to the preacher's trailer house, which was the same unearthly color. "Preacher ain't in there," A.J. muttered as he opened his toolbox and extracted a chainsaw. "If he was, the lights would be on or he woulda come on out, because there's no way he couldn't have heard me driving up."

Gathering his courage, A.J. prayed, much as he did when he was a POW and squatting in a filthy tiger cage back in Nam. "I ain't scared of no old tree," he told it as he walked through the cemetery. "I ain't scared of you, no, I'm not. I've seen worse in this world than your sorry ass. My eye is on the sparrow."

The ground around the tree vibrated in a deep humming thrum as he sat the chainsaw on the ground and put on the heavy gloves. The intense thrumming reminded him of standing too near a ground hornet's nest. He swallowed, choking down the dread that rose along with bile to the back of his throat.

"Let not your heart be troubled," he sang as he adjusted the choke on the chainsaw. "His tender word I hear and resting on his goodness."

The chainsaw erupted into a loud wrup, wrup, wrup. It came to life in his hands, the noise drowning out his song. *Lord, steady my hand,* he prayed, *I'm ready to do this.*

A.J. stepped forward, but hesitated. A green shape formed in front of the tree. The thrumming sound was louder now, drowning out the crazed wrupping of the chainsaw. The ground shook as if lightning touched it.

The shape twisted and coalesced, much like the spectral field hands he saw earlier. A body emerged and A.J. recognized her at once. The chainsaw died and he began to cry.

"Mama?"

"Yes baby," the woman said, holding out her arms. "I'm right here. I hadn't died, just slept for a while."

"But Mama, why are you here? How did you get here?"

"A miracle," she replied. Her arms spread wide, inviting him in. "Come to me, baby." She smiled, her hair gray tinged, her eyes warm and loving. "Come and get close to your Mama. Lord, I've missed you so much."

He wept, tears streaming down his face and smearing the day's grime on his throat. "You ain't my Mama," he said. "You ain't, you can't be. My Mama died a long time ago."

"I said it was a miracle." Her brow furrowed. "Why do you question what the Lord has done? Hasn't he kept his eye on the sparrow?"

"Oh, Mama," he wailed, feeling lost, like a little boy who wandered into the woods one day and couldn't find his way back. This is a dirty trick, he knew. An evil trick played on him by the devil's tree. But he wanted to believe it, oh so much. He took a tiny step forward, ready to embrace the image before him. Yet the annoying, logical side of his mind shrieked, *Look at her, boss. She ain't changed in forty years! How can that be?*

And why's she here instead of standing at the right hand side of God?

"...Mama, yes," she was saying, though he had lost most of the conversation. "Now come here, chile, let me have a look at you."

"No, A. J. moaned. "No, you ain't my Mama. You might look like her, but you're not. This is wrong. You are wrong. You can't look the same after all these years, it ain't right."

The apparition howled. The eyes and mouth melted away. The sockets shot out beams of light. "You will come," a voice demanded, as the face warped and distorted, melting like a plastic doll's head. The ground rumbled, unsteadying him.

"No," A.J. shouted as he yanked hard on the chainsaw cord. It refused to start. Not one single wrup came from the motor. Sobbing, he grabbed one of the double-bitted axes and, shrieking in anguish and fury, lunged for the trunk.

The ground softened around the roots, and he stumbled, falling at the foot of the tree. The axe tumbled away. He looked up, too horrified to scream. The bark was peeling away, slowly at first, but then quicker, exposing a brilliant emerald green interior that seemed to burn with a nuclear heat.

His mind was distant, hypnotized. *There's something inside, something alive and squirming around in there like glowworms.* A.J.'s mind snapped back into reality. He scrambled backwards, trying to avoid the glowworms that weren't glowworms at all but thick, woody cords that launched themselves toward him. He screamed as his wrists and legs were bound so quickly he didn't have time to react. The cords yanked him forward. He screamed as he was dragged on his hands and knees towards that awful sight.

"Oh Mama, Mama," he bawled, as he was dragged head first into the tree.

Within seconds, A.J. Jones, formerly Abendego Jones of Mercer's Bayou, Arkansas, was absorbed along with his screams. The tree sealed itself, the lights dimmed, the vibration lowered until it dropped completely.

Around the base, the dead patch of earth expanded another ten feet. The fallen chainsaw and the axe lay abandoned. Moments later, wolves slid into the cemetery, wandered among the graves, singing their death song.

Chapter Fifteen

-1-

"What in the world is that?" Thomas asked as he stopped just short of pulling the truck door open. He pointed toward the east, where a dull orange glow towered above the treetops.

"Something's ablaze up on that ridge," Pa Neidi observed. "Might be a brush fire, happens around here sometimes." He stared at Thomas, who felt his skin prickle. Neidi's eyes glistened. "Let's go check it out."

No, Thomas thought. *I don't want to spend any more time with you than I have to.* "I don't think so, Pa," Thomas said instead, making his voice sound appropriately weary. "I'm pretty tired right now. Besides, we'd probably just get in the way."

"What kinda preacher are yuh?" Pa demanded. "There might be souls up there looking for guidance and consolation. And here you want to go to bed."

Consolation my ass, Thomas thought. *You just want to go up there to stick your nose into other people's business.* Thomas was momentarily shocked at his personal venom. *But it applies, doesn't it?* They were almost parodies of poor white trash. He would have laughed, but his mouth was too dry. "Or it might just be a brushfire, like you said. Then we'd only be in the way."

"Get in," Pa demanded. "We're going on up anyway just to make sure."

Thomas sighed, dropped his pole and tackle box back into the truck bed, then slid into the cab and closed the door while Pa started the engine. The raggedy old GMC rolled down toward the thin ribbon of highway, and mercifully not the rugged clear cut trail that Dougie brought him on in the ATV.

I'm tired of being held hostage to old Neidi's whims. Why can't I just say so? He sat and watched as the glow in the distance grew brighter until he could see flames and black smoke, blacker than the night, rising from what looked like a field up ahead. *It's just a brushfire*, he thought. *Pa dragged me out here for a brushfire. And I don't have the balls to tell him no.*

Most of all he was curious about the note pressing against his hip and he wanted nothing more than at that moment to open it. *That's not going to happen right away*, he told himself. *Go see what the fire's about. That'll satisfy old Neidi's curiosity, and then I can go home. Providing he doesn't find anything else to get curious about. And if he does, I'll tell him where he can shove it.*

Thomas was developing an intense dislike for the Neidi family, and even though their enthusiasm for the revival was a positive note, he was almost afraid they'd throw a fit about it. They were unpredictable, so it was hard to tell how they'd react to anything new. He glanced at Neidi's profile as he continued his journey down the road, his face contorting into a mixture of triumph and alarm as he headed toward the fire.

"Lord Almighty, this is Otis Miller's place," Pa said.

Thomas's insides squirmed. The fire was under control. At least, it hadn't spread across the lawn and into the adjoining pasture. Two more rescue vehicles howled behind them, and Neidi took the truck off the road as the fire trucks, one with Fouke" embossed on the side and the other "Texarkana," passed them by at a fast clip.

A man stepped in front of Neidi's truck, signaling him to stop. He did so and rolled down the window. "Did everyone get out?" Pa asked.

The man approached the vehicle, and Thomas saw it was Lonnie Cox, the sheriff he met a few days ago.

"Yeah," Lonnie said, pushing his standard issue Smokey Bear hat away from his forehead. The bright red flames illuminated one side of his face, etching dark shadows around his eyes and mouth. "Evening, Parson." He nodded to Thomas. "It seems like you're always in the right place but at the wrong time."

"Was anyone hurt?" Thomas asked.

Cox leaned against the side panel of the driver side door. "Rita-Mae had a heart attack. Billy Wong and Sullivan Sylmar caught up with them when they made the Deer Creek Road turnoff. Otis was driving like his ass was on fire. Suppose in a way it was."

"Will she be all right?"

"Far as I can tell," Cox drawled. "Last thing I heard she was in the emergency room at Tatum Memorial and was stable."

"Thank God," Thomas said, and meant it.

"What caused the fire?" Neidi asked.

"Best we can tell, the fire started in the kitchen. She must have been cooking dinner when she had the heart attack."

"I see."

"Well, the dangdest part of it was Otis. That crazy-assed old Injun. He was rambling about slaves in the fields and hands pulling the house down."

"Drunk?" Thomas asked.

"Hardly. Otis was a big time teetotaler. Never touched booze, had this thing about Injun stereotypes. Harley Stoker called him Chief one time out at the stockyards and Otis busted him up good."

"Then what would make him say those things?" Thomas asked.

"Scared crazy, is all I can figure," Cox said. "But don't worry about that. The boys have the fire under control and you're not needed here, thank God."

"Thank God indeed," Thomas agreed. "I'll remember Mrs. Miller in my prayers tonight."

"I'm sure she'd appreciate it." Cox dismissed them. "Go on home. We need the road cleared for the fire trucks."

"Will do," Thomas said, enjoying Pa's scowl.

Neidi grumbled and put the truck in gear. "Need to head on back anyway, Ma'll wonder where I went."

We went to do no good, Thomas thought, and again experienced angry shards, sharp as a sliver of wood shoved under a thumbnail and every bit as annoying, go through him. Pa turned the truck around and drove in the opposite direction. Soon, soon, Thomas would be home and opening the little paper that Stevo had given him.

As they made a right hand turn onto the highway, something odd captured the corner of his eye. Thomas's skin prickled into gooseflesh. He opened mouth to speak, but shut it again. *He'll think I'm crazy*, he thought. *And the thing is, I'm not sure he wouldn't be right.*

Thomas looked at the side view mirror again, but all he could see was the flame-brightened pasture on the left hand side. *There's nothing there*, he thought with relief. He glanced at Neidi, his sharp profile silhouetted against the bright light.

I saw people out in that field. I'm sure of it. People picking something; people who didn't cast shadows.

Chapter Sixteen

The headlights bounced halogen gold beams against the whitewashed church as they drove up the narrow driveway and into the parking lot. Pa Neidi stopped the truck and, for a frightening moment, Thomas thought he was going to invite himself in.

"Pa," Thomas started to say, hoping he could thank the man for dinner and then hurry off to his trailer and lock the door, but the old man motioned him to be still.

"See that truck over there?" Pa motioned toward the pickup parked on the edge of the cemetery. "I think that's A.J.'s ."

"A.J.? Is he a member of the congregation?"

"No, he's Otis Miller's neighbor. Wonder what he's doing out here while his neighbor's land is in trouble?"

"Maybe he went fishing and doesn't know."

"Well, I'll go on down and take a look. It's probably what you say. If I catch up with him, I'll let him know what's going on."

"You're a great help," Thomas said, feeling desperately weary. "And thank Ma again for that delicious meal. I'm glad I got to come."

Pa nodded and then exited the truck. Thomas took the opportunity to make his escape. He virtually fled from the vehicle, taking time only to snatch up his tackle, and walked quickly toward to the trailer.

Once inside, he didn't turn on the lights, but he did lock the door. He laid his rod and tackle box—retrieved earlier that evening by Dougie—beside the door, and then moved into the bedroom, where he peered through the narrow window. The eerie light glistened off the window panes. He could see Neidi standing at the tree, his lean body etched by the bright beams of his pickup. For a second, Thomas thought the old man was talking to it. The hair on his arms rose. *That's crazy,* he told himself. *He's just looking at it, but why? Why is he paying so much attention to that creepy old thing?*

Thomas pressed his face against the cool glass. He watched as Pa wandered out of sight down the bayou path, then moments later, he reappeared. Automatically, Thomas twitched the curtains closed, but made sure he had enough of a crease to look through.

It didn't seem to matter. Pa was obviously preoccupied by something lying on the ground. He bent down and picked up several large awkward-looking objects, but from this distance, Thomas couldn't tell what they were. He placed them into the bed of the truck; Thomas heard the rattle of the objects as they landed on the truck bed. *What is he doing?* Thomas wondered. *Should I call the sheriff? But why? He's not really doing anything illegal, but it does look very strange.*

Neidi walked back to the foreign pickup and got in. He started the engine, then drove it to the church parking lot and parked it beside his. *This is so bizarre,* Thomas thought as he watched Neidi play musical pickups. Neidi left the truck and got into his. Moments later, Thomas could see the brake lights glowing as they went down the driveway, and then finally, blessedly, out of sight.

"Thank God," Thomas said, feeling true praise and utter relief.

Yet, there was something disconcerting knowing he was left alone with the Ford squatting in the parking lot like a faithful dog waiting for his master's return. *Somehow, I don't think A.J. or whatever his name is will be back any time soon. If ever. If nobody claims it by morning, I'll call the sheriff's department. Then it'll be their business.*

Satisfied, Thomas watched until he was certain that Pa Neidi was gone for good. After about ten minutes or so, according to the red glowing lights from the alarm on the nightstand, he felt relatively safe, so he switched on the light.

Bright red fireflies shot across his vision as his eyes

adjusted to the light. He pulled the paper out of his pants pocket, sat on the bed and opened the note.

"YOU WALK WITH SATAN" was all it said.

"What is this supposed to mean?" he said aloud. "I thought there'd be some sort of explanation, not some cryptic message telling me who I walk with." *It doesn't matter what they think. I've made my decision. After the revival, I'm leaving. Then I can get out of here and start fresh somewhere else.*

Somewhere else. That had a pleasing ring to it. *I'll let Jim know in the morning so he can start looking for a replacement.*

Overwhelmed by homesickness, he placed his hands on his head, leaned forward and cried. "Oh Lord," he prayed aloud, "I'm in the wilderness, in a far and strange land. Please deliver me from this dark and dreadful place."

He lay down on the bed and curled into a fetal position, pulling a pillow over his head to keep the eerie green afterglow from invading the bedroom and—somehow he knew deep inside—his soul. He wept, feeling ashamed and relieved at the same time. *It's not unmanly to weep,* he thought. *It's not, it's not. Jesus had wept, hadn't he?*

Sometime after midnight, he drifted into a strange and disturbing sleep where he was riding a bus bound for nowhere, Rachael and Becky waving to him as he drove by. He wanted to get off the bus, but he could not. There was neither a driver nor a door. And the bus was heading toward a bright green-golden glow that burned and writhed as if it were alive.

-2-

A loud rumbling, followed by the sound of air brakes and men's voices, drove Rachael and Becky from his dreams. Thomas woke feeling disoriented, lost and forlorn. He sat up and realized that sunlight was invading the bedroom in thin slices through the blinds. He ran his hands through his hair. *Why is it daylight already? It doesn't feel as if I've been asleep.*

He heard another heavy bang, metallic clanging followed by a spectacular string of curses. Thomas went to the window and peeked through the curtains. A red wrecker, much smaller than the one that took away Charlie Estille's old trash truck, but judging by the paint job, must be from the same wrecker service, was hoisting up the older model blue Ford onto a secure position on the wench.

Several men were in attendance, including, he noticed as his stomach fell, Pa Neidi, who was speaking to Lonnie Cox from the sheriff's department judging from the blue and gray uniforms and Mr. Jim from the Mc Knight House. Pa was pointing toward the trailer, gesturing as he spoke to Cox who was nodding in a way that suggested he was only half-listening.

Fearing what Neidi might be rambling about, Thomas vacated his refuge and stepped into the muggy air. He hadn't taken ten steps from the front door when Cox, Pa and Mr. Jim met him.

"What's going on?" Thomas asked. Pa lowered his head as if he were about to pray. Thomas caught a strange expression on his face. It made him feel as if he'd swallowed a banana split whole.

"Another damned strange accident," Cox said. "Poor old A.J. Jones was found washed up on the boat landing this morning. It looks like he went fishing and fell in and drowned."

"Bless Jesus," Mr. Jim whispered, and Thomas stifled a flinch. *Bless Jesus for what?* Thomas wondered.

"I'm so sorry to hear that," Thomas said. "Is there anything I can do to help?"

"Well, I sincerely hope so," Cox said, all business. "I understand you took a walk down to the boat landing yourself last night, ain't that right?"

"Now, surely you're not going to accuse the preacher of any wrong doing, Lonnie?" Mr. Jim said his face pale with surprise.

"Now hold on, Jim. I'm not accusing anybody of anything. But it looks to me like there have been a number of accidents since Preacher Thomas showed up and I'm just asking a few questions. Strictly off the record."

"Maybe it'd be better if it were on the record," Mr. Jim said, his voice turning to granite.

"Now there's no call for that. Mr. Thomas, since you're down here, have you seen anyone out here? Anyone doing anything that might look suspicious?"

"No, not at all," Thomas said, although he suddenly found it odd that Jim had told him weeks before that kids mudded and skateboarded around the church grounds. In fact, it occurred to him, other than the regular congregates who turned up on Sunday and Pa, he hadn't seen a soul on the bayou at all. He didn't count Stevo; that was prearranged, he corrected himself.

"Other than Pa I haven't seen a soul down here," Thomas said earnestly. "In fact, I went fishing myself last night. I walked down to the boat ramp, just like you said. And I was heading home when Dougie Neidi came by on his ATV. His mother had sent him to get me."

"Really?" Cox said, jotting down notes as he spoke. "How did Dougie know where to fetch you?"

"I don't know," Thomas said. "I figured he came to the church and found me gone, then went down the bayou looking for me." He laughed slightly, which made him feel nervous, and of all things, suspicious. "I just assumed that's what he did. Ma, I mean, Mrs. Neidi, she's been wanting me to come out and have supper with them, and I was hungry and just went along..." His voice trailed off.

"So you didn't see anyone on the bayou while you were fishing?" Cox asked.

"No, sir. I didn't."

"A.J. might have gone further upstream," Mr. Jim suggested. "You know this was once an old river channel. And the currents do get treacherous, especially when Lake Wright Patman's floodgates open."

"Yeah, that's true enough," Cox muttered. "If he went upstream, or even if he were sitting on the banks right here," he pointed to the levee behind them, "and if he fell in, the current would have taken him downstream toward the boat ramp."

"Well, if he didn't get tangled up in someone's trot lines, he's on his way to Shreveport," Mr. Jim said. He shrugged. "It's just another tragic accident."

"There's been way too many of those lately," Cox said, scowling. "And there's weirdness going on that nobody can explain." He wiped the sweat off his brow, contemplating. "Earnest Wilcox called this morning saying he could hear screaming from his well. Thought a panther had fallen in. It was dredged but nothing came up." Lonnie Cox looked down at his feet, shuffled some red dirt and swore.

"Screaming," he continued. "And it's the damnedest sound I've ever heard. The University of Arkansas is coming down to investigate. It's got to have a logical explanation. Wells don't do that unless something's fallen into them."

"Maybe it's just air blowing through the pump, sometimes that makes an odd sound," Mr. Jim offered.

Cox looked relieved. "It very well could be. I'm sure those boys from UA will know what it's all about."

"It has been a hard summer," Pa complained. "First poor old Charlie, then this."

"And don't forget the Miller's house. And A.J. lives right next door." Cox scowled, considering. "I wonder what he was even doing down here so late. And he didn't even tell Emma where he was going. Just up and took off. Doesn't sound like him at all." Cox stared hard at Thomas. "Where'd you get that scar?"

Thomas hand automatically went up to his neck. "I was attacked. My wife and daughter were killed. I was the only one to survive."

"Now who in the world would do that to a preacher man?" Pa asked.

Thomas felt foolish and ashamed. He lowered his head and spoke to the ground. "A homeless man arrived at my church one Sunday morning. He stayed for the services, and when it was over, I spoke to him. He seemed to be so gentle, so kind, almost Christ-like. I felt sorry for him. He told me—he told me he was an Afghanistan veteran down on his luck. I invited him to have dinner with us. After dinner I let him stay the night in the living room. I told him that I'd drive him to the bus stop in the morning. Instead—" His voice broke as memories of the murder pierced his soul. "Instead, he repaid my kindness by raping and strangling my daughter. He cut my throat and killed my wife. I was left for dead. If it hadn't been for a member of my congregation coming by early that morning and finding the door open, I would have died too."

Should have died, he thought.

Mr. Jim's sympathetic hand gripped his shoulder. "You did the decent, Christian thing, James," he said softly. "You're not to blame for someone else's evil."

Cox nodded, his eyes softer. "You can't trust anyone these days. It doesn't matter how kindly they seem, there's always an underside." Cox rubbed the back of his neck. "Well," he said as he watched the wrecker carry the Ford away, "I have everything I need. Thanks for your help, Preacher." Cox tipped his hat to Thomas. "Try and have a good un."

"I'll try," Thomas said, smiling faintly.

"Imagine the gall," Pa exploded as Cox got into his patrol car and left the church. "Now that takes brass balls, to stand right there in front of God Almighty and accuse a preacher of murder."

"Pa."

"No, no, no." Pa stamped his foot, looking for all the world like the adult version of his youngest son. "I won't have it, I tell yuh. I won't. Of all the gall danged impertinence. He had no right to do that. None at all."

"Now Pa," Mr. Jim said, taking the old man by the shirt sleeve, "Lonnie was just doing his job that was all. There's no harm in asking questions."

"I'm fine," Thomas said. "He was just wondering if I saw anything suspicious, that's all."

"Well."

"Well nothing," Mr. Jim said. "We've got a revival to plan, remember?" He turned to Thomas and said, "Pa was telling me all about it. It's a grand idea, simply grand. Why, we haven't had a revival out here in a long time."

"Thanks," Thomas said.

"Hey, Pa, how about going on down to the funeral home and talk to the boys there about borrowing that big old tent of theirs. While you're out doing that, I'll show James how to use the mimeograph machine." Thomas caught a crafty gleam in Jim's eye. "You know you're gonna need flyers to hand out."

"I suppose so," Thomas said, feeling strangely nervous.

Muttering to himself, Pa wandered to his own truck, climbed in and drove away.

Thomas felt infinite relief. "I don't mean to be unpleasant but he does get annoying after a while, doesn't he?"

Mr. Jim laughed as he led Thomas toward the church. "He doesn't mean any harm. Besides, he's taken quite a liking to you. He wouldn't have stood up for just anyone you know."

"Well," Thomas relented. "I guess he's not such a bad guy."

"Naw, he's not. He's just old and obstinate, but good as

gold."

Thomas slid his hand in his pocket and pulled out the church key. "Mr. Jim, I was wondering something," he said as they arrived at the door.

"Well, ask away."

"It's not like I don't welcome everything you've done for me, I'm really grateful. But I'm missing New Mexico, and I think I'd like to go back home to Taos after the revival is over."

"Go back to Taos?" Mr. Jim asked as if that were the silliest thing he'd ever heard. "Why on earth for? You nearly starved to death there. I thought you wanted to start a new life here? And the congregation just loves you to death."

Thomas sighed. He really wasn't expecting an argument. "I just feel more comfortable ministering to the Zuni and they know me well, and I believe that after I get paid at the end of the month I can get a job preaching at the reservation there."

"Is this because of all the queer happenings?" Jim asked. "Because ole Lonnie, he was just doing his job—"

"—It's not that," Thomas lied. "I'm grateful for everything that's been done for me, I really am But I want to go back home."

Mr. Jim sighed. "I'm sorry to have to tell you this," the man said with a smoothness that convinced Thomas he wasn't sorry at all. "Very unfortunate, but I thought you read the contract."

"The contract?" Thomas stammered. "No, I—"

"We withhold the first month's pay," Mr. Jim stated. "It's for economic reasons. First Light is such as small congregation and they can only do so much. We at the Mc Knight House help out as much as we can, but they still need to pay utilities, and there's Pa's salary as caretaker. And we pay your utilities and buy your food..."

"Oh," Thomas said, crestfallen. "It's not that I'm being ungrateful."

"Oh, I know that," Mr. Jim replied. He leaned forward confidentially. "Now if it's a question of being out here by yourself," Mr. Jim said lowering his voice as if he were afraid anyone would hear, "hey, I'd be scared to stay out here all by myself, especially with that old ghost tree glowing like it does at night. I'm surprised you stood it this long." He shifted his feet as if he was about to say more but decided against it. Instead

he said, "You can always come on back to the Mc Knight House.
Stay with us and I'll bring you on down in the mornings and
evenings and of course during services."

back
IN the

"Thanks for the offer," Thomas said, trying to keep the
devastation out of his voice. "I'm fine down here. Really."

"Are you sure?"

"Yes, I feel like I'd just get underfoot up there. And I do like
the privacy," Thomas said.

"Well, if you change your mind, I'm just a phone call away."

"I'll keep that in mind," Thomas said. He unlocked the
church door and it eased open. "But I still plan on moving out
by the end of summer at the very latest, so don't get too used to
me being here."

Jim laughed. "Don't worry, I won't."

Part Two
Summoning the Faithful

Chapter Seventeen

-1-

Megan kept the dream and the pendant hidden from her husband. The nightmare was stunning and oh so real. She could pass that off as a vivid but disturbing dream that would leave her shaken for a few days and she'd get over it.

No, it was finding the little wheel in her hand after she woke that left her shaken to the core. Megan hated anything that dicked with her personal sense of reality. She was a practical woman by nature, pragmatic, stable and lacking the vivid imagination her sister inherited from their father. Megan considered that a blessing, because she really didn't want to know about anything other than solid, stable, reliable *realness*.

This is something Consuela would know about, understand and revel in, Megan thought absently as she watched her husband get into the van and with a flamboyant wave, drive away. Megan faked cheerfulness as she returned his wave. The last words in the dream resounded in her mind. *You failed. Now there'll be revival. Now everyone you love will die.*

For the second time since they moved in, Brody asked if she was happy living on the bayou. That surprised her and she wondered if he wasn't picking up on her unhappiness. Until yesterday, Megan believed she was and said so. She enjoyed the early mornings the most, the rich air, muggy, laying so close to the earth, creating soft mists that hovered around tree trunks like white petticoats. She loved the sounds of mourning doves calling their mates. The bright fluttering of hummingbirds around the feeder delighted her.

But when the sun went down...

Megan shivered despite the heat. At night, the bayou became a dreadful world of sound and lights and whispers that Brody never seemed to hear.

"I want to go home," Megan whispered. "I want to go back to Austin where everything is familiar, sane and steady and the only weird thing in the neighborhood is the local Moonies.

We should just go, Megan contemplated, drawing her knees up under her chin and circling her legs with her arms. *We should pack up and go back to Austin this very minute and spare ourselves a great deal of grief. I'll start packing now,* she decided. *And when Brody gets home—*

—Brody.

But how do I tell Brody? He's settling down so well here. I've never seen him so happy, and he hasn't had any trouble with his ulcers since he started this new job.

She rested her head on her knees. *And then there's the studio. I can't abandon it, especially now that it's already starting to take off. It would take a month or two at least to train a new manager before I can leave. Even if she was experienced—*

Movement, a sudden flutter of cloth and curls caught her eye. Megan unfolded her legs and stood. She walked to the railing. Her heart pounded, though she wasn't sure why.

A rustle, a glimpse of bright cloth flashed among the wild jasmine, sumac and red honeysuckle.

"Hello," Megan said tentatively, expecting the girl in the purple-and-orange flowery dress to bolt back into the woods. This time, she did not, but stepped into the clearing, then picked her way gently toward the porch.

"Can I help you?" Megan asked. "Are you hungry? Would you like some breakfast?"

The girl stared at her. She had strange amber colored eyes and shoulder-length black hair that hadn't seen a comb in a while. The girl motioned for her to follow and then glided back into the woods. Megan hesitated. The girl stopped, smiled tentatively, and then motioned again. Abandoning her apprehension, Megan followed her.

-2-

Mr. Jim followed Thomas into the church office. He grinned and opened a narrow door a few feet away from the desk. The desk, Thomas noted, had an antique Royal typewriter perched on a side table. *Why do these people have such an issue with technology?* he wondered. *They let me have a satellite TV after all.*

"Come look at this," Jim said. He pushed the door wider and exposed a small print shop squatting on a narrow cabinet lining the back wall.

"Here's where you'll find the stencils," Mr. Jim said, opening a cabinet. "And the duplicator ink is in this drawer."

Thomas laughed. "I haven't seen these since the Seventies," he said, giving the drum a short spin.

"The mimeograph works well, and we can still get supplies from the office supply store in Tatum," Mr. Jim explained. He stopped for a moment, his brow furrowed as if he was trying to remember something he had forgotten.

"Is something wrong?" Thomas asked.

Mr. Jim smiled and shrugged. "Just seeing all this old equipment takes me back to my college days."

"Yeah, it is kinda antiquated," Thomas agreed.

"But it gets the job done. They don't need much down here."

"Why hasn't the church gotten technology?" Thomas asked. "I know Mrs. Neidi thinks computers are evil, but it'd be so much more efficient if I had a computer and printer."

Mr. Jim waved off the comment. "Computers are expensive and don't do well down here with the humidity. Besides, why replace something that works?"

"But the satellite TV..."

"The phone system is antiquated and won't work with modern technology. And since there are so few folks down here, the phone company doesn't see the point in upgrading."

"Well," Thomas said, disappointed. "I'll make do then."

"Good man. Know how to run this?"

"Yes, I used to help my father when he put together the church newsletter."

"Well, I'll let you get on with it then." He turned to go, and then said, "Have you decided on a date?"

"Will this week be too soon?" Thomas asked. "I was thinking about the weekend of the nineteenth."

"Sounds like a plan," Mr. Jim said. He clapped Thomas on the shoulder. "Well, I'll leave it with you, then."

"I'll do the best I can," Thomas replied.

Thomas sighed when he heard the church door shut. He went to the office window, saw the lanky man ease into the truck and within moments he was gone. "Thank you, Jesus," he muttered. Grumbling to himself, he went back into the antiquated print shop and extracted a handful of stencils from the box. He returned to his desk with his supplies and placed them next to the typewriter. Next, he removed the ink cartridge. *Here comes the tricky part,* Thomas thought as he slid the first stencil into the machine and began to type up the flyer. *I haven't done this in years. If I am not careful, I'll be spending the next several days working on this one thing.*

A soft whine came from just beyond the door. He jerked his head up. *Oh Lord,* he prayed, *please don't let that be Pa.* Thomas sat and listened, but the noise he heard, or thought he heard, did not repeat. *It might be the building settling, or maybe just my imagination.* He chuckled to himself and returned to his task. *I need to get a radio or a CD player,* he thought. *I know I wanted quiet but this is too quiet. I need something to break up the monotony.*

Thomas grumbled to himself as he tore up a mangled stencil and tossed it into the trash. "I'd already be finished if I had my Mac," he muttered. "And it would look a dang site better than these purple horrors. No one is going to look at these things. They're terrible."

Thomas leaned back in his seat and contemplated. *I guess it doesn't matter does it? I'm leaving, and if nobody shows up at the revival then there'll be no reason for them to insist I stay.*

Realization gut-punched him. *If I don't get more people into this church, the collections will still be woefully inadequate. Mr. Jim will go on about the faith-based money shortage. They'll use that and low tithing as an excuse to keep me here another month. Then another and another until I'm still down here, growing as old and gray as the Spanish moss that covers the trees and working for slave labor, just like that last poor old preacher who was found slumped over this very desk. Was he thinking the same thing I am before he died?*

Thomas stared down at the completed stencil, surprised because he was sure it wasn't quite done. He made two more, just in case one of them wrinkled on the mimeograph drum, which was bound to happen, then relaxed.

The phone rang, jarring him out of his reverie. He looked down at the instrument, an old black rotary as antiquated and nondescript as the rest of his office furniture. He picked up the receiver. Thomas felt chilled, as if he'd toiled all day underneath the hot summer sun and developed a case of heat exhaustion.

"Hello?"

"Preacher?" Pa Neidi's voice crackled through the wires. "The boys say we can use their tent, but I need to put it on reserve. You never told me the date."

"Tell them it'll be on the weekend of the nineteenth."

He heard muttering on the other end of the line, Pa speaking to someone else, no doubt. He thought he heard Pa say something about "nigger freedom day," but wasn't sure. Thomas waited, half tempted to hang up. Just as he moved to place the receiver back into the cradle, Pa's voice blurted, "Hey, Preacher, are you there? They say that unless some big shot dies that weekend, the tent's ours."

"Thank you," Thomas said.

"They'll be down the morning of the revival and set it up. Said they'd bring the chairs too."

"Tell them I'm glad for their help."

"Will do."

The circuit closed. Thomas placed the receiver back into its cradle. He rose, took the stencils to the print shop and set them next to the mimeograph machine.

He filled the tray with paper then studied the duplicator. "Let's see if I can remember how to do this," Thomas said aloud as he coated the drum with duplicator ink. He slid the stencil very carefully into the designated slot on the drum. The one his father used had two slots. But this one had only one. In a way it made it easier to work with. This duplicator wasn't motorized, so he had to crank the copies out by hand, which was tedious but still efficient enough to do the job.

It was messy work. Within minutes, his hands, as well as

the front of his shirt, were covered in dark purple blotches. Thomas took a break, washed up in the small half bathroom in the sanctuary and returned. He grabbed the crank and turned. The machine complied, grabbing sheets of white paper out of the box as the drum turned, stamping the stencil image on the sheets, and shifting the flyers into the dump tray.

The drum rolled. The machine thumped out a rhythmic beat as it worked. The sound was hypnotic and his mind drifted along with the careful thump, thump-thump of the machinery. The tiny shop became stifling from the afternoon heat. The ink-filled air made him groggy and a little light-headed.

It was a while before he felt the cold, electric chill leech up from the crank handle and into his hands. Thomas's arms buzzed as the sensation shot up into his brain. His mind turned to putty as he continued to turn, the duplicator drum whirling, the machine thumping out the paper, shitting out blurred purple copies. *Graple,* he thought, recalling the childish name his father gave the color. *Graple.*

A song, faint at first, grew stronger as it wove through his mind like tattered silken threads. He began to dream, or perhaps hallucinate. It was difficult to determine. For all he knew he was stoned on printer fumes and at that point he didn't give a good goddamn.

Thomas dreamed of the future. Or was it the past? That, too, was hard to tell. He was feeling woozy yet continued turning the handle. The sound of the mimeograph thump thump thumping out pages and pages of purple flyers that took on a strange green tint. *Oh it's green all right,* Thomas thought as his mind sailed through the hallucinogenic fog bank. *But it's a green I've never seen before. It glimmers and shines...*

The thumping became drumbeats, rhythmic and primeval. Through the eerie cadence voices sang an old Negro spiritual.

I'm just a po wayfaring stranger
Travellin' through this land of woe.

A silent film played in the theatre of Thomas's mind. It was watermarked in sepia and white. It was grainy but clear. And the surprising thing was that he was in the film. Thomas watched himself standing in the church parking lot which was unpaved and graded down into an even, bare block of red clay. The cars parked in the lot were old, Desotos and Nash

Ramblers, and there was a cotton wagon too, with a pair of ginger mules hitched to a post where his trailer now stood.

Strong men erected the tent in the grass plot beside the cemetery. The canvas blew cloud-like in the breeze as the men set the tent poles. Children in overalls and gingham dresses played tag among the tombstones. Many of the stones looked fresh and recently set. Older men helped women set up chairs and strung kerosene lanterns from ropes strung from pole to pole. A long table was placed alongside the church building. Mrs. (call me Ma) Neidi and a group of other women he didn't know burdened the table with food. Why were they doing that? Thomas wondered, his mind feeling vague and insubstantial. Why not put the food inside the church where it was surely cooler?

There was no answer. He drifted back into the mind movie. A pulpit was placed upon a stage. People filed into the tent, laughing and gossiping as they went. Ladies in their dresses and hats fashionable in the 1930s and men in blue jeans, overalls and work shirts sat and waited for the service to begin.

These folks are salt of the earth, Thomas thought. *They've come to hear me, come all this way just for me...* It was beautiful, perfect, exactly the way he wished, no yearned for it to be. But there was something disturbing about it. The perfection of the dream was too right, too brilliant, too, too exact. An alarm went off in the back of his mind.

Thomas tried to remove his hand from the crank and found he could not. He struggled to open his hand. He demanded it to open up but it would not. The music, loud and very real, hammered in his ears.

I'm just a po wayfaring stranger,
Traveling through this land of woe.

Truly scared now, Thomas yanked his hand away. Suddenly free from the handle, he staggered back, his palm burning as if it had been shoved in dry ice.

The song vanished, taking the air in the room with it. Thomas stared at the machine as if it were a monster ready to rise and leap from its perch on the cabinet top.

This is ridiculous, he told himself. *I was working and my hand went to sleep, that's all.* Thomas's mind was convinced, but his body was still pumping adrenaline. *Stop being foolish,*

Thomas chastised himself. He took a tentative step toward the machine. He saw that the mimeograph's drum swung to a stop in mid stride. A half completed page peeked out from underneath the duplicator.

He shook the numbness from his fingers and pulled the paper out from under the drum. Stunned, he leaned against the door frame and stared at the words, words that weren't typed on any stencil.

You can have what you want.

Shaken, Thomas dropped the page as he staggered away from the machine and virtually bolted into the office. He slammed the office door closed. Thomas headed for the outside door, but stopped when something odd caught his eye.

Sitting on the desk, where the stencils previously lay, was one bottle of Jack Daniels whiskey and a shot glass.

In the distance, Thomas heard the plaintive strain of the old Negro spiritual, the voices rising and falling as they worked, "travellin' through this land of woe..."

-3-

Megan followed the girl deeper into the forest. She was surprised at how fit the teenager was and how quickly she was able to navigate around briars, thick ropes of honeysuckle and low-hanging kudzu as she made her way deeper into the lush green wood.

"Where are you going?" Megan asked. "Where are you taking me?"

Before the girl could answer, a clearing appeared abruptly from behind a stand of sweet gum trees. Megan stopped, surprised.

The glade was filled with cars and pickups, mostly rusted out hulks. Those that looked like they might have been able to work if they underwent serious repair were being loaded to capacity.

"We're going to De Queen," the girl whispered. "That is, until the troubles die down anyway. Don't know if we'll come back or not." She shrugged. "The way Granny Joyce talks, I doubt it."

A group of women were stuffing what looked like

mattresses into a rusted out hulk of a station wagon. Talking in low voices, they pointed toward Megan. They stopped what they were doing and approached her. The girl abandoned Megan and helped several others as they loaded boxes into the trunk of a black Plymouth Fury.

"Hello," Megan said tentatively as she watched the older women approach. Feeling suddenly shy and self-conscience, Megan wondered why she had made this trip into the woods with a girl she knew nothing about.

An ancient woman wearing layers of blue skirts over a leopard leotard stepped forward. She glared at Megan through watery brown eyes. "I knew your grandmother. She lived in the house you live in now."

"Yes," Megan said, feeling her palms prickle with sweat. But she was too nervous to wipe it off.

"I have advice for you. If you are smart, you'll take it."

"Will it cost?" Megan asked. *So this is the scam, huh?* she thought, feeling angry and foolish. *The girl was a ploy to get me into the encampment for a bogus fortune telling session,* she reasoned. The advice, of course, would result in discovering a family curse that only a substantial amount of cash would remove. *There's no mystery here, just a pathetic attempt at a little petty larceny.* Megan glanced over the old woman's shoulder. *This is probably the real reason why they're leaving, she thought. The cops must be on to them.*

"No money, and no fortune telling," the old woman said evenly. "I have advice, which you can keep or throw away." She frowned, her face puckering with thick wrinkles. "The choice is yours; it always has been."

"I see you're all moving," Megan observed, ignoring the woman's cryptic remark.

"Yes, and if you are wise, you will go too," Rowena said. Her eyes narrowed. "Or stand up to the evil and fight it, as you are destined to do."

"What destiny? Why is it important for us to leave?"

"Strange you should ask me such questions when you see the answer burning outside your window every night."

"You mean that spooky old tree?"

The women genuflected. "Yes, yes you foolish girl. That spooky old tree. It's calling the dead to it, and when they come,

141

they will revive the devil's church. You must leave and soon, because the demon within is craving fresh souls and this time it ain't particular about who it takes."

Megan laughed. "Why, that's the silliest thing I've ever heard. That old tree is just a dead husk, and the only reason why it's glowing funny is because it's leeching phosphorus from the soil."

"If you believed that you wouldn't have painted your window black."

"How did you know?"

"You are a fool, shallow and vain. And you failed to stop revival, even after God gave you the chance."

Megan jerked as if she'd been jabbed in the back with a cattle prod. "How did you know about that dream?"

Rowena ignored her question. She pulled the little silver wheel pendant out of a skirt pocket and handed it to her. Megan stared at the offering, her right palm itching for it, but she was afraid.

"Take it," Rowena commanded, and placed the object in Megan's palm and closed her fingers around it. "This is your last chance. Do not fail again."

"Where did you find it?"

"It is a gift from God, you foolish woman. Now go. We have lots to do."

"But—"

"No," Rowena said. "No charge. Now go and do as God bids, or ignore the signs and let the devil take its own."

The elderly woman and her entourage walked back to the station wagon and finished loading it. Megan watched as the small convoy geared up and drove down a small dirt road and out of sight.

A small knot of men who remained behind stood at the doorway of one of the trailers. One of the men was staring openly at her. He leered and tipped his hat. The others laughed.

Suddenly feeling very much alone, Megan pocketed the necklace and strode quickly back into the woods, listening intently in case they followed her. When she got to what she perceived to be a safe distance, she slowed down.

That was the most bizarre thing I've ever experienced in my life. She stopped and looked back. The clearing was obscured by brush and honeysuckle vines. Megan bit her lip. *But they knew about the necklace,* she thought. *They found it and the old woman...*

Stop it, she scolded herself. *Just stop it right now.*

Megan resumed her trek home. *That girl must have found it when I threw it away the other day,* she reasoned. *Yes,* Megan thought, comforted somewhat by the logical explanation forming in her mind. *Yes, the girl found it, and then gave it to Rowena who made up some shuck and jive story about it. And the dream? That must have been a coincidence.*

Megan laughed with relief when she saw the house peeking through the trees. She stopped at the edge of the property where the lawn joined with the forest. She studied the amulet. *There is no such thing as a demonic tree. That's stupid. And this is just a ridiculous necklace, and the basis of a sham.*

Megan laughed. She threw the necklace high into the air. It glistened briefly in the sunlight just before arching over the undergrowth and disappearing under the lush foliage.

"Now stay gone," she told it.

-4-

"Go ahead," Rachael's voice coaxed. Thomas stared at the bottle. "Go on. You know you want to."

"I can't." Thomas uttered a soft whimper as he stared at the bottle of Jack Daniels. He could almost feel the warm, tingling burn of the liquor going down his throat, curling into his belly and then spreading golden liquid warmth throughout his body.

It is a hot day, he reasoned. *And I worked hard. Don't I deserve one small drink?*

"Yes, you deserve it," Rachael agreed.

"No," he groaned, backing away from the desk, "I won't be tempted, not this time"

"But you know you want it."

"God grant me the serenity," he prayed.

Drawn to his desk, he sat in the seat and stared at the bottle.

"To accept the things I cannot change."

How did it get there? Thomas thought. *Who brought it and why is it on my desk, taunting me and why do I hear Rachael?*

"Go ahead; just one little drink won't hurt," Rachael whispered in his ear.

"God grant me."

"You know you do"

"The courage to change the things I can."

"Not even for me?" Rachael teased.

"You're not there," Thomas said. "Rachael's dead. You're just a figment of my imagination."

Giggles.

"And the wisdom to know the difference!" he shouted. Thomas's entire body shook with effort as he picked up the bottle and glass and placed them into the bottom of his desk drawer and slammed it shut.

He leaned back in his chair, tears etching down his face. His hands trembled, begging to take the bottle out and have one drink. After all, just one little drink couldn't hurt.

Maybe someone came in when I was in the print shop working, he told himself. *An old drunk, perhaps, or one of the Gypsies must have placed the bottle on the desk and walked away.*

But that didn't make any sense, he thought. *Every drunk I knew never left a bottle alone, much less an unsealed one with a complimentary shot glass.*

Thomas put his hands on his temples and leaned his head down until his forehead touched the desk. "God help me," he whispered, his lips brushing against the false wood finish of the desk. "Please help me. I'm losing my mind."

-5-

Jim pulled off the road and waited for Pa's battered old pickup to catch up. His heart pounded as he watched in his side view mirror as the vehicle slowed down and pulled alongside him.

I don't want to do this. Jim's mind turned round and round as the old man put his truck into park and leaned across the vacant passenger's side to talk to him. *Why can't that stupid preacher be sensible and come on back to Mc Knight? I can keep track of him that way, maybe even stop what's about to happen.*

God knows I feel bad enough—

"You ain't having a change of heart are yuh?" Pa asked, interrupting his thoughts.

"No, Pa," Jim said obediently.

"That's good to know," Pa said. "Very good to know." He grinned, showing snuff-stained rotting teeth. "Because I'd hate to see what happened to that poor old nigger man happen to you too."

"I'll do as I'm told," Mr. Jim said.

"Good and faithful servant," Pa approved. "You'll be rewarded when the end comes."

"Yes, Pa."

-6-

Late afternoon shadows crept across the face of the church office and the little room was quite dark when Thomas awoke. He jolted upright, feeling dazed, confused and wondering how he managed to fall asleep at his desk.

Sharp fear pierced him as he remembered the bottle of whiskey in his desk drawer. Thomas stared at the drawer, too afraid to look inside but too afraid not to. Holding his breath, he eased it open.

The bottle as well as the shot glass was still there. He closed the drawer and exhaled. "I didn't drink," he said. "No matter how tempted I was, I didn't drink."

A cold eeriness settled in the room. Anxious, he rose, vacated the office and locked the door.

The late afternoon had receded into twilight. *Where did the day go?* Thomas wondered as he stood on the step. *The sun was up just a little while ago. I'm sure of it.*

Or was it? He looked down at his hands. The hand that turned the crank was red and tender, as if he had touched a car's manifold while it was running. *It's on the verge of swelling. If I don't put some ice on it, it's going to blister.*

A soft autumnal breeze caressed his face and ruffled his hair. He looked at the darkening sky. *Maybe a storm's coming,* he thought. *That'd explain the drop in temperature, the night coming early.*

The wind picked up, cold, sharp and unnatural. It rustled

the treetops. Thomas shivered. He leaned forward, folding his arms across his chest as he made his way across the parking lot. Thomas was nearly to his trailer when he realized the music he heard earlier had returned. It was strained, eerie, chanting-like... He stopped and listened, really listened for the first time. *What is it?* he thought. *Is it just the wind, or a Satanic ritual in progress? It is dark and isolated here and I'm alone. The Klan meets in isolated places like this. So do devil worshippers who mutilate cattle and vandalize small out of the way churches and cemeteries.*

"No," Thomas whimpered as the song grew louder, almost palpable as it approached. *And what's that noise along with it? It sounds like something heavy, like a wagon creaking...*

O. Bye and bye, bye and bye
I'm goin' to lay down my heavy load.

The music, now accompanied by the jingling of harnesses and clattering hooves, filled the forest. Thomas gaped at what looked like a thick, writhing ball of mist forming in the cemetery. Seconds later, a wagon loaded with cotton and people emerged.

I know my robe's gon' to fit me well
I'm goin' to lay down my heavy load
I tried it on at the gates of hell
I'm goin' to lay down my heavy load

Two ginger colored mules shook their heads, making the harness jingle. Their hooves clopped as they hauled the wagon across the cemetery grounds. Thomas watched, amazed, as the wagon moved towards him. It was heavy with cotton and sacks. Young black men and women dressed in calico sat on top, singing their dirge-like hymn.

Stop po' sinner and don't go there
I'm goin' to lay down my heavy load

An elderly man in a ragged shirt and pants, his muscular dark brown arms bulging as he held the reins, urged the animals forward.

Fascinated, Thomas watched as the cotton wagon passed by, kicking up spectral dust as it went. The driver, his face half hidden by a straw hat, touched the brim with long hickory colored fingers and said, "Nice night for it, enit, Parson?"

"I-I suppose so," Thomas stammered in reply.

The driver flicked the reins, muttered, "Eheyuh." The mules shook their heads as they pulled. Their hooves clattered in rhythm to the wagon. The wagon receded into the forest and disappeared, leaving the haunting spiritual in its wake.

O, bye and bye and bye and bye

I'm goin' to lay down my heavy load...

The spell broken, Thomas sagged to the ground. *They went through the trees. Literally through the trees.*

Thomas remained kneeling in the parking lot, too stunned by what he saw to move. Finally the music as well as the heavy mist faded away. Shaken, Thomas stood and made his way to his trailer. Just as he approached the porch, a group of strange objects caught his eye. Resting against the trailer was a handful of heavy-handled wooden hoes used for chopping cotton. He touched the handle and flinched. The hoe was warm, as if its owner had just released it from his grasp. Puzzled, Thomas looked down and saw a pile of burlap toe sacks on the ground next to the aggies.

They were piled neatly, not haphazardly, and then it occurred to him, the ghostly workers would return for their equipment. For the first time since the hobo tried to murder him, Thomas screamed.

Chapter Eighteen

"Good run?" Brody called down from the veranda as Megan made her way up the driveway. She waved in reply. The sunlight glistened on her hair and her body bounced in ways she knew he greatly enjoyed. Her feet kicked up small puffs of reddish dirt as she slowed to a quick walk.

"Yes," Megan replied as she leaned against the railing and stretched. "It was a very good run. I saw a small family of deer grazing in the pasture a couple of miles from here. It was amazing."

"Very cool," Brody replied, handing her a towel. She accepted it and dabbed her forehead.

"Care for a rubdown?" he inquired.

"Not right now," Megan said. "Maybe later."

"Oh," he said, disappointed.

Megan laughed. "You need more exercise than bedroom calisthenics. Why don't you run with me in the morning? We can watch the sunrise together."

"I'm better at walking," Brody laughed. "I can barely keep up with you as it is."

"We can walk," Megan replied. "Walking is good too. We can go every morning before we go to work."

Although she never said it aloud, Megan was sincerely worried about his health. He never subscribed to her healthy diet and exercise lifestyle. Instead he spent the evenings hanging out in front of the television with a pack of chips or a beer in hand, or sitting on the swing with a carton of Cherry Garcia ice cream instead of sampling the fresh fruit she placed conspicuously on the counter top.

"Nah, I'd rather watch you run."

"Coward, I knew you'd bail on me." She laughed.

"Sorry, kid," he said.

"Well I guess I should be grateful you quit smoking." Megan sighed.

"I'll start walking. Tomorrow perhaps."

"Promise?"

"I'll do my best," he said. "Maybe we'll see those Gypsy friends of yours."

"They're not my friends and I wish you hadn't brought that up."

"They were just scamming you, you know."

Megan dabbed her neck. "Yes, I know. Now can we please not talk about them any more?"

"Sure," Brody replied. "I didn't mean to upset you."

"I'm not upset," Megan said. "Just annoyed I fell for their whole silly setup."

"Happens to everyone from time to time," Brody said. "I wouldn't worry about it. Chances are excellent you'll never see them again."

"I hope so," she said fervently. "They're supposed to have moved on anyway. Maybe they'll stay gone."

"Listen," Brody said, changing the subject. "If you want to check out the old A&P with me, you'd better hurry. I'm leaving in fifteen minutes with or without you."

"Ah you can't leave without me." Megan laughed. She gave him a quick kiss as she passed him by. "I've got to shower and get ready. Take twenty minutes at least."

"Well, get on with it." He gave her a playful smack on the butt. "Time waits for no man."

Megan blew him a kiss and went into the house.

Mary Kay pink tiles with a complementary pink sink accosted her vision as she entered the bathroom. Pink and black linoleum peeled around the baseboards. The toilet was a grimy yellow which seemed to glare at her after being assaulted with the pink and black color scheme. The bathtub was an antique claw footed job and was huge, white and filled almost one fourth of the room. It was the bathroom's only saving grace as far as Megan was concerned. It was excellent for long evening soaks, especially if Brody chose at times to rise from his television induced stupor and join her for an evening of good clean fun.

As she slid the sweatpants off her hips she noticed something bright protruding out of her pocket. Curious, she pulled the chain and gasped when the amulet came out.

How in the world did it get there? she wondered. *I threw it away. I know I did. Twice in fact. This time I'll put you in a spot where you can't find your way back,* she thought. She dropped the amulet into the toilet. Megan flushed and the pendant was swept away.

Feeling less disturbed, Megan got into the shower. She stood under the warm spray and allowed the tension ease out of her tired muscles. A quick gleam caught her eye. She looked up at the narrow window above her. *Sunlight,* Megan thought. *It's just sunlight.*

"Come on," Brody called. "The realtor is waiting."

"I'm coming now," she shouted as she stepped from the tub.

"Coming or just breathing hard?"

"I could do this faster if you weren't teasing me," she said as she toweled off.

"Okay I'll stop."

"Thank you."

Once finished, Megan dressed into her faded jeans and red tank top. She exited the bathroom. She skipped down the hallway as she slipped on her sandals. "Let's go," she laughed. "I can't wait to get started."

-2-

His mind happily anesthetized, James Thomas handed out flyers and words of encouragement to anyone who would listen. In the back of his mind, an old spiritual, interspersed with whispered words from Rachael, played on.

"Come witness the power of the Lord. Experience the gospel as your grandparents did beginning next Sunday at the First Light Church of Prophecy's tent revival," Thomas called. He was feeling strangely euphoric as he stood at the intersection in front of the Super Target and handed out his tracts to passersby. *And why shouldn't I?* he asked himself. *I'm in my element at last. I'm happy and healed and sharing the Lord with the lost.*

Apparently the giddiness was contagious because as soon as a person took a flyer their expression changed dramatically. Some walked away as if in a daze, while others enthusiastically agreed to attend the revival on the nineteenth.

Not everyone, however, took a tract, nor spoke to him as they walked by. Two elderly black women dodged his outthrust hand.

The oldest lady said, "Ain't no way I'm going into that devil's church." She turned to her companion and added, "And he's holding it on Juneteenth too. If that ain't a sin, then I don't know what is."

"Um, hum," her friend acknowledged.

Other folks simply stepped across the street and went around him. A Mexican woman gave him the evil eye as she crossed the street with her young son in tow.

Sinners and hypocrites, Thomas thought. *They think I'm belittling the Lord's word by preaching here.* He frowned. *And they'd be right. I'm prostituting the Word just as if I was hawking cheap women on the street corner.*

Thomas tried to fight the sensation of mind-dulling bliss, but found he really didn't want to. It felt good and there was nothing wrong with feeling good was there? No, he told himself, of course not.

Thomas relaxed and allowed the warm, pleasant sensation to flow through him. After the harrowing events the night before, it felt good to not worry about mysterious whiskey and cotton wagons and tumultuous nightmares. All the cares of the world ceased when he picked up the box of flyers for today's street preaching adventure. And he was glad.

Yes, he thought as he smiled at a woman wearing a bright yellow sundress who was coming toward him. *I'm mellow. Just as if I'd chugged down half a bottle of Thunderbird in one swallow.* He giggled and the woman reaching for a flyer snatched her hand away.

Thomas started humming. The woman, looking shocked,

hurried away, her pumps clicking sharply against the pavement.

A child approached and stuck out his hand but his mother slapped it aside and dragged the boy away. *That's two,* he thought. *Two going to hell. We'll call that a too-fer. Or a three-fer.*

"Whatcha got?" a young man standing next to a fashionably dressed woman asked as they approached.

"Flyers for the revival, son," Thomas replied. "Here, have one. See what the Lord can do for you."

"Hey, are these mimeographed?" the young man asked as he took one and handed the other to his companion. "I've never seen any befo—" The question forgotten, Thomas watched as their expressions changed. Their pupils flashed a brief but intense green, then faded to black.

Yes, they'll come, he thought as the giddiness cranked up a notch. *I'm sure of it. Bless you, Jesus. Praise Jesus.*

The couple walked away, their heads close together as they examined their handout. *Saved,* Thomas thought. *Hallelujah.*

-3-

"Take it easy now, Mama," Brandon Miller said to his mother as he guided her gently down the steps and into his Dodge Caravan. Otis was standing beside the van with the door open while Brandon and his wife Cindy, gravid with their second child, helped her mother-in-law into the vehicle.

Brandon got into the driver's side and Otis rode shotgun. Cindy held Rita-Mae's hand as they drove from Tatum Memorial and into town. Rita-Mae hadn't spoken since the incident that brought down her house. Otis didn't tell her what Lonnie Cox said about the accident. It would upset her, and being upset right now wasn't a good idea.

Rita-Mae spent one night in ICU before being shifted to a private room. After a battery of tests, including a complimentary angiogram, Dr. Parnowski determined that her heart was fine. There had been no damage, much to her family's relief.

The fact that she still refused to talk was most disturbing. Brandon was certain his mother would make at least one or two haughty comments, especially in regards to the food served. Not to mention—as she often did—Cindy's condition.

Instead, his mother sat still in the back seat of the car, her face turned toward the window.

"I'm glad you and Dad are going to be staying with us," Cindy said to her mother-in-law. "At least until—"

"Until we get the farm squared away," Otis finished. He frowned. "I put the place up for sale and have gotten two good offers on it. I figured we'd move on up to Mena. You like Mena, remember, Rita-Mae? I know how much you enjoyed going through those antique shops there." He shifted in his seat, feeling helpless. "Brandon and Cindy are transferring up there this coming October. So we'll be seeing a lot of them, and the new baby too. His job is going to take him up there, right, Brandon?"

"Yeah, right," Brandon said, glancing at his father. "I got that manager's job I told you about."

"See? Every thing's going to work out just fine. The fire may have been a blessing in disguise you know," Otis rambled. "It hit me the other day. Neither of us is able to take on a farm anymore. And it'd be good to sit back, relax and spend our time spoiling the grandbabies."

"But, Dad," Brandon said, lowering his voice, "that farm is your whole life. I'm stunned you'd be willing to sell it. Especially at such a reduced price."

"It's time to move on," Otis said, face turning stern. "I'm an old man, son. I'm not able to keep up like I used to."

"Dad, why don't you come clean and tell me what really happened out there that night."

"There was a fire and your mother had a heart attack. That's all you need to know."

"No, now, something squirrelly is going on here. Otherwise you'd just sell the acreage, rebuild the house and retire out there. So what's going on?" Brandon glanced at his father. "It's the Olesons, ain't it? Are they trying to force you to sell out again?"

"No."

"It's one of those big corporate outfits then." Brandon swore under his breath. "What did they do? Did they make you an offer that you couldn't refuse and when you did they burned you out?"

"You're thinking about the Godfather and no."

153

"Then what—"

"Nobody threatened us," Otis snapped. "Nobody is after our land. I'm old and tired and I want out. That's all there is to it."

"Come on, guys," Cindy said from the back seat. "Let's not quarrel. Mama's home. That's all we should be thinking about."

"You're right, Cindy, and I apologize," Otis muttered.

They traveled the next two miles in heavy silence. Rita-Mae continued to gaze out the window. Otis stared straight ahead, feeling as glum as the thunderheads that loomed on the horizon.

Brandon stopped at a traffic light. On the left hand side was the Super Target store, laden with shoppers. On the sidewalk next to the intersection stood a thin man in shabby clothes handing out flyers to a small knot of people gathered around him.

"What's going on over there?" Brandon asked. Otis turned and felt the hairs on his arms stand up.

"Lord, look at that," he said.

Rita-Mae saw him too. Her eyes looked wild, like a spooked cat. Her jaw worked as saliva dribbled from the corner of her mouth.

"Mama?" Cindy asked, alarmed. "Mama what is it?"

Rita-Mae's eyes rolled back into her head. She uttered a weird gurgling cry.

"Brandon," Cindy screamed.

"Mama, what is it?" Brandon shouted in return. He hadn't noticed the light had changed. Annoyed drivers honked, urging him forward. He ignored them. "Mama? Mama!"

"Oh God, she's having a stroke," Otis cried.

"No," Rita-Mae screamed. "Get us away! Take us away!"

Scared, Brandon floored the van and it lurched ahead, nearly careening into a green Plymouth before speeding away.

"Mama, you're scaring me," Cindy cried. Shocked at the reduced state of her once formidable mother-in-law, she burst into tears. Rita-Mae huddled close to her daughter-in-law.

"What happened?" Otis asked. "Do we need to go back to the hospital?"

"I don't know. I don't think so," Cindy said, composing herself. "She saw that shabby old man out there and got all upset." She shuddered. "He scared me too."

"Rita-Mae," Otis demanded.

"Revival," she whimpered into Cindy's sleeve. "Revival."

"What's that supposed to mean?" Brandon asked. His hands shook on the steering wheel as they left Tatum city limits and accessed the county road that would take them onto highway 71 and then to Texarkana.

"It means we're getting the hell out of here," Otis replied.

"But Mama—"

"If Mama ain't any better by the time we get to Texarkana, then we'll put her in the hospital. Otherwise we're leaving for Mena as soon as she's up to it," Otis said with finality.

"I'm up to it," Rita-Mae whispered.

"Are you sure?" Brandon asked. "Mama, you don't look so good."

"Never mind how I look," Rita-Mae said, regaining some of her spunk. "And the answer is yes, I can make it."

"It's settled then. We'll go to Mena tonight."

"But Dad."

"No don't Dad me, boy. My mind's made up."

"Dad, what the hell is going on?"

"It's time we all headed out. That goes for your brother in Texarkana too. I don't want to hear any fuss about it, either. Let's go to Jessie's play school and pick him up, go to Greg's and get the hell out right now."

"Dad, I can't just drop everything and neither can Greg and Jody. Besides, what happens if Mama should have another fit?"

Otis glared at his son. Brandon realized his father's hands were trembling. His face was pale and his eyes wide with fright.

"She seems calm enough now," Cindy said. She brushed stands of hair from Rita-Mae's face. The older woman rested her head on her daughter-in-law's shoulder. "And I agree with Dad. Let's just go."

"Tell your boss anything, tell them your mother has taken a bad turn, make up any excuse, hell I don't care. Let's get out of here. Now," Otis commanded.

"Sure Dad," Brandon said, defeated. "Sure. Anything you want."

-4-

"I like the building and the price is right too. It's going to make a great gym..." Megan's voice trailed off when she realized Brody wasn't listening. Instead, he was watching an unusual encounter taking place in front of them.

"I wonder what's going on over there?" Brody asked as they strolled down the sidewalk toward a group of people standing around what looked to be a hobo handing out sheets of paper. Megan spotted him too and the unease she'd felt since her encounter with the strange necklace jacked up notch.

"Brody, let's cross the street here," she said as they came to the intersection. Brody ignored her. Megan noticed people were either giving the bum a wide berth or were taking some sort of tract from him. Brody, obviously intrigued, approached the man in a shabby suit with threadbare elbows.

"No, Brody, I don't want to," Megan said, pulling his arm.

"Why not?" Brody asked. "Come on. Let's see what he's got."

Megan removed her arm from his. "I couldn't care less about what he's got. He's just an old bum handing out flyers."

Brody didn't seem to hear. He seemed riveted to the man. Not knowing what else to do, she tagged along. Now that Megan was closer, she could tell he was a preacher of some sort judging by the stacks of pamphlets at his feet and a worn out King James Bible resting on an unopened box, filled, Megan presumed, with even more flyers. He was smiling in a weird way as he talked to two young men in front of him.

"Brody, let's go. He gives me the creeps."

"Wait, baby," he said. Brody stepped up to the preacher, who turned and smiled at him. "Good afternoon," Brody said, "what's going on?"

The Preacher smiled wider—if that was possible—and Megan felt an intense desire to run as far as she could from the man with those eerie greenish-blue eyes.

"We're having a revival at the First Light Church of Prophecy," the preacher said. "You're welcome to join us." His gaze strayed from Brody's face to Megan's chest. She felt the sudden and distinct urge to cover up. "And your lovely wife as well," the preacher said amiably. "She *is* your wife."

"Yes, this is Megan. Megan, say hi to the nice preacher."

"Hi," she muttered.

"Come join us down on the bayou," the preacher said. "It'll be great. A real old timey affair. There'll be little gospel, a little bluegrass, and a potluck supper afterwards." His eyes gleamed. "Maybe even a baptism or two."

"That sounds like a lot of fun," Brody said, taking the flyer. "Something different to do on—"

Megan thought she saw a soft green glow pass from the flyer and up Brody's arm. Brody's face went slack. Shocked and unable to articulate what she saw, Megan said the first thing that came to mind. "Thanks but no thanks, we're Catholic." She grabbed her husband by the hand and pulled him away.

"Brody," she said once she got him moving across the intersection. "Brody, are you okay?"

He shook his head as if trying to clear it. "Yes, I'm fine."

"Are you sure? You look like you're going to be sick."

"No, no, I'm fine. Sure you don't want to go to the revival?"

"Hell no."

"Then I'll go by myself."

"Brody, we're Catholic remember? We're not going to any weird-assed holy rolling church revival." She glanced over her shoulder, half expecting to see the old man following them. "They may handle rattlesnakes and drink poison for all we know."

Brody stared at her. His eyes looked as if an unnatural light was filtering through them. "Come on, where's your sense of adventure?"

"I left it at the intersection," she said. "Come on, let's go home."

Chapter Nineteen

-1-

Evening mass was a dull rendition of kneeling, chants and prayers that Brody reduced to white noise. He was relieved when it was over, snubbing the priest as he walked past. He got into the van while Megan chatted up some guy in a blue suit.

"Come on," he muttered to himself. "Quit gabbing and let's go."

I wanted to go to Mercers for church this morning, but she wouldn't have that, he thought. He tried to assert himself but Megan put her foot down and that ended the argument. *Damned women,* he thought. *You can't live with them and you can't chain them out in the yard.*

Megan arrived, her face flushed. She got into the van and said, "You're still pissed off, I can tell." She snorted, exasperated as she started the van. "I don't know what's gotten into you. You've never been interested in charismatic churches before. And besides, that's the church where that spooky old tree is. There's not enough money in the world to make me want to go down there."

He dismissed Megan's angry diatribe and sank into a pleasant, mindless buzz. Megan finally became silent as she drove and he sat in the passenger's side and daydreamed. He glanced at his wife and saw that she had taken on a two-dimensional quality. It was as if she had suddenly turned into a cardboard cutout.

Brody despised her. *No,* he amended. *I don't hate her at all. I love her. She's the best thing that ever happened to me.* In response, he felt a sudden and sharp sensation. It was as if someone had taken an ice pick and shoved it between his eyes.

"Headache?" Megan guessed.

"Uh huh."

Brody rubbed his forehead. He gazed out the window as they passed the First Methodist Church. A big, red brick building regurgitated brightly clothed celebrants onto its perfectly manicured lawn. As they passed by, he noticed the sign in front of the building. The sign proclaimed in big black letters: Jesus Loves the Little Children. Even the Unborn.

Yes, of course that's true, he thought. *Jesus loves the little children, even the unborn.* He glanced at his wife, whose lovely— but paper doll-like—profile furrowed in frustration when some doofus in a gray Hyundai cut her off.

Yes, even the unborn. His mind clenched on the idea and ripped it the way a dog gnaws at a piece of meat. *How many of the unborn have you killed, Megan? I can think of at least six.* He was immediately ashamed and turned to stare at the landscape of dense forest. Megan turned off the main highway and onto the county road that lead to Deer Creek Road. A few moments later they were making their way up their long dirt driveway.

Of course Megan never killed the children she carried, he chastised himself. *I can't imagine why I thought such a thing. She wanted children desperately and was heartbroken when she—*

The comfortable fuzzy sensation in his head itched like wearing a wool jacket in the middle of the summer. He resisted. The itching turned into an angry, heated buzz. He shoved his fists against the sides of his head and whimpered. A voice accompanying the itch said, *Go ahead and say it. You know you want to. You need to know, especially now, after all these years. What did happen to all those poor little babies that Megan miscarried?*

"Are you okay?" Megan asked. "Brody, you don't look so good."

"Megan." He cleared his throat, astonished that he was actually going through with it. "Megan, I need to ask you something."

"Sure, what?" She parked the car in the driveway. Megan turned and looked at him. His heart ached. *My God, she's so beautiful, so sweet and loving. She has always been my greatest joy...*

Or has she? the voice prompted. *Or is she really Eve sent here by Satan to seduce you into believing that?"*

Brody?" She placed her hand on his arm. "Is something wrong? You've gone white. You haven't perforated an ulcer have you?"

"I'm fine," he lied. The voice inside his head was getting louder and more demanding. The strange itch behind his eyeballs was growing into an intense burning ache. "I just want to know if you ever regretted not having children."

Megan stared at him, her face unreadable. "What's brought this on?"

"I need to know, that's all. I've got to know if you ever felt like...oh God, I don't know. We tried so hard to have kids, and all those pregnancies ended in miscarriage." He swallowed.

The voice in his head prompted, *Go on, damn you. You want to. You know you do.*

"They did end in miscarriage," Brody said. It sounded more like an accusation than a statement.

"What the hell is that supposed to mean?"

"It means that Jesus loves the little children, and I want to know if our children ended up in Heaven although they were never born."

Megan's expression went flat. "You'll have to ask Monsignor."

"You did want them, right? I know a woman can get rid of a baby if she wants—"

"What are you saying?"

"Well, you went to the doctor. And he was an abortionist at another clinic. I mean, you did take all that anti-nausea medicine." He clamped his mouth shut, feeling shamefaced but strangely satisfied.

"I took that anti-nausea medicine because I couldn't keep anything down. And Dr. Gonzales was never an abortionist. He was Catholic, remember? We went to the same parish." She exhaled in exasperation. "I don't even know why we're discussing this—"

"But he did perform abortions. I'm sure of it," Brody persisted. The locomotive in his head was wound up now and wouldn't shut down although he desperately wanted it to. "He did, I remember. We saw him coming out of that clinic shortly after you miscarried for the third time. He was an abortionist and you killed our babies and it's a mortal sin to have an abortion—"

Megan's hand whipped out and slapped him hard. The mental locomotive shut down and the fuzziness in his mind cleared. Horrified, he stared at her. Her face was purple with rage. *I've hurt her*, he thought. *God forgive me, I hurt her and I don't know why.*

"Never ever accuse me of that again, Brody," Megan hissed. "Goddamn you."

Megan climbed out of the van and slammed the door so hard the window fell off the track. It smashed into the bottom of the door with a resounding crash. She stormed up the driveway and into the house.

"Megan!" Brody shouted as he tried to follow her into the house. But she was too quick and slammed the door in his face. He heard the lock click.

Brody put his face against the door and said, "Megan, I'm sorry. I don't know what made me say that. I swear to God."

"Screw you," came the muffled reply.

"Damn," he swore. He searched his suit pockets and swore again. *I left the keys on the kitchen table.* He sighed. Judging from the muffled crying just beyond the door it'd be a long time before he would get back inside.

Brody sat on the porch swing feeling perplexed and oddly satisfied.

I'd never suspected her of anything like that before. The thought never entered my mind, he said to himself. *I love Megan. I know she wanted to be a mom more than anything in the world. I'd never hurt her, especially not like that. But I just did. Why did I do it?*

Laughter. Brody flinched. For the first time he fully realized something awful had taken up residence inside his head. "Megan?" he whimpered. "Megan, please. Call Monsignor. Something terrible is happening to me." Warm fog flowed into his mind. *I've got to fight this. I've got to...*

His mind faded into a void. He heard the breeze rustling the trees and the slow churning of bayou water.

"Megan," he whispered, feeling himself slipping away, "something's got me."

He sat and watched the mental fog roll in. Soon his mind was numb and stupidly blissful.

"Jesus loves the little children," he sang under his breath. "All the children of the world. Even the unborn."

-2-

"Reverend Thomas," Cora-Lee Johnson said, shaking the preacher's hand "That was a fine sermon. A wonderful message from God."

Mrs. Cora-Lee Johnson was a fiery Southern Baptist and had been since her personal salvation at the age of fourteen. She was a formidable woman who had never missed a single service, thank you very much. She proudly raised her six children in the church, seeing that each one was properly baptized at the age of ten. Her two sons went to seminary and were currently pastors of their own congregations, which she was pleased to tell anyone who would listen. And the other kids? Well, they served the Lord in their own way.

Yesterday, Mrs. Cora-Lee had a life changing experience. And from her point of view, she was saved right this time. After shopping, she picked up one of Thomas's purple flyers. She was about to rebuke him for not being a proper Southern Baptist minister and leading people astray with a false religion but that didn't happen. Instead, her ordinarily fierce mind turned to a pleasant mush. She looked at Thomas and realized the upcoming revival seemed like a fine idea.

When she awoke Sunday morning, she had completely forgotten about the Tatum First Baptist Church that she attended these fifty odd years and went to First Light Church instead.

Praise and bless the man who tends the flock, she thought happily. *Here is a man in the wilderness, a regular John the Baptist among us. Praise God. We need a thousand more just like him.*

"You are a true warrior for Christ," she told him after services concluded. "I couldn't wait for your revival, no sir. I had to come today and hear you speak."

"I'm pleased you did," Thomas said in a friendly but half

listening sort of way. Which was of course right and good, she thought. Because there were so many standing around seeking the good man's attention and he had far more important things than to visit with little old ladies.

She smiled dreamily and wandered out to the parking lot and got into her Buick, navy blue of course. She chose it the day her grandson enlisted and went to Iraq to kill the evil Saddam and bring Christ to those starving, godless desert dwellers.

Yes, dear sweet Davy, she thought as she wended her way back to her little white house with bright yellow shutters and meticulously trimmed yard. Ouida, her eldest daughter and Davy's mother, sent her ten year-old daughter, Sammy, to mow the yard. *It was once Davy's job,* Cora-Lee thought. *But Sammy did a real nice job, even though she shouldn't wear shorts and do men's work.*

Davy was the one she missed most even though he was almost born out of wedlock. At least Tim and Ouida did the right thing by the family. God punished them, of course, by denying them any more children for the next ten years. Then Samantha Jean came along followed shortly by her twin brothers. Cora-Lee knew then that God was pleased with the marriage. *All my grandbabies are blessings,* Cora-Lee thought. *But Davy was the best and brightest of them all.*

Cora-Lee frowned as she pulled the car into the carport. Davy died on an aircraft carrier. How, she never really knew. But Cora-Lee was certain that her daughter did. Although she tried to approach her on the subject numerous times, it didn't matter. Ouida would not tell her anything other than he died in the line of duty.

A shadow has fallen across my heart, Cora-Lee thought. She was suddenly frightened but unable to determine why. She left the car and went inside. The house was warm, almost stuffy. Ordinarily she didn't mind. As she was approaching her mid-seventies, everything seemed cold these days. But today.

The hallway leading to the bedrooms was dark as was most of the house during the day. Cora-Lee held the antebellum belief that if the house was dark it would be cooler. It just made the air stale and heavy instead. She started to walk to the thermostat to lower the temperature when she saw movement in the hallway. "Ouida," she called out. "Is that you?"

163

"No Nana," said someone in the hallway.

Cora-Lee gasped. "Who are you?" she demanded. In her heart of hearts, she already knew the answer.

A young man stepped out of the shadows. Resplendent in his formal Navy uniform was Davy.

"No," she whispered as he approached her. He knelt before her, took her hands into his as if he were about to propose. He looked up at her. His face was earnest. His eyes glowed with an incredible green luster. *Wasn't his eyes brown?* Cora-Lee wondered. *No, I guess not. The mind plays tricks sometimes.*

"I'm back, Nana. The Lord sent me to you."

"No," Cora-Lee whispered, sobbing as his solemn young face gazed up at her. "That can't be. My Davy died five years ago."

"The Lord sent me to you," Davy repeated. "You've been such a good and faithful servant all these years. And he loves you so much. He sent me back to look after you."

"Did you come to fetch me, boy? Am I about to go to Glory?"

Davy smiled, his teeth perfect brilliant white. "In a manner of speaking."

She uttered a thin wail and threw her arms around him. He was no apparition. He was solid. He was real, warm and alive. She could feel the roughness of his uniform, smell the clean, sharp scent of his favorite aftershave. She felt the steady heartbeat under his jacket.

"Oh Davy," she whimpered. "I've missed you. Darling boy. My precious, precious boy."

-3-

Megan heard the door rattle. Moments later came a muffled swear. Megan threw a pillow at the door.

"Sleep outside for all I care, you bastard," she told the door. Megan sank back into the sofa and resumed her grief.

I thought he understood what I went through. I thought he knew how devastated I was. There would never be a baby for me. Ever. Couldn't he at least imagine what that felt like? She held her stomach while she wailed into the cushions.

Spent, she lay on her side and breathed in deep, ragged

sobs. She wiped long, clear tendrils of snot from her nose on her good blouse. Soon her breathing stilled, as did the anger and hurt. Numb, she stared into the early evening gloom as the sun moved from the windows.

Shadows lurked in the dim room. She could hear the faint squeak of the porch swing. She heard voices as if Brody was speaking to someone although she was certain nobody had pulled up. Moments later, she slid into a light doze. *Maybe some hunter or fisherman got lost and found their way to the house. Perhaps that's why I didn't hear a car. Brody is probably giving them directions. I may have to let him in after all, if someone needs to use the phone.*

The muffled conversation stopped. She heard the porch boards squeak as Brody walked off the steps. *If that's so, why didn't I hear anyone else's voice but his?* she wondered.

Megan rolled over on her side, facing the back of the couch. *I don't give a rat's ass who he's talking to. I don't care any more. Nothing matters.* Sleep crept up on little cat feet. Without warning, something red-hot scorched her breast. Crying out, she sat up abruptly, rummaging in her blouse for the unexpected object that burned her. She felt a delicate chain around her neck. She pulled it and the pendant came out.

Perplexed, she looked at the innocuous object hanging from its delicate silver chain. The center glowed bright red, then dulled to orange, then returned to its usual shifting purplish-blue color. The room was pregnant with sandalwood. "How in the world did you end up on my neck?" she asked aloud.

A thin white mist formed in front of her. Her heart skipped a beat. She gasped as fear as cold as artesian well water gushed through her. "Ohhhh," she whimpered as the mist coalesced into a person. Or at least part of a person. The head and shoulders appeared but there was nothing below the waist.

The man looked somewhat familiar and Megan might have recognized him if his head wasn't wobbling on its thick stump of a neck. The head was smashed flat on one side. The eye on the unaffected side was dangerously close to falling out. The horrible, lopsided mouth was moving as if he had a mouthful of tobacco and couldn't expel it. The destroyed nose dribbled bloody ropes of snot down the crushed chin. "For God's sake, help me," the apparition howled.

Megan opened her own mouth to scream but nothing came out. The rest of the mangled man appeared. He shuffled nearer. She smelled the corpulent aroma of garbage as he shambled closer. He worked his sideways jaw. She could hear bones creaking as he did so. "Help me. Please," the man groaned.

She recognized him. The knowledge plunged her into a terror she'd never experienced in her life. It was Charlie Estille, the trash man who showed up the day after the storm.

Megan screamed.

The apparition vanished. Light flooded the living room as if someone had just replaced a burned-out light bulb. The room was much colder than what the air conditioning vented. Her breath came out in short, white puffs. She rubbed her arms. Everything was unnaturally quiet. Not even the cicadas were making their nightly noise.

"Brody," she screamed. "Brody." Rooted to the sofa, Megan cried out her husband's name again.

He never came.

-4-

Their first evening service in fifty years concluded, Thomas left the church and headed back to his trailer. He was initially surprised when his congregation requested an evening service. Most folks were afraid to come to church after dark. But those who picked up his flyers arrived for morning service, then wholeheartedly requested attending that evening. Thomas was elated. *I have a church at last,* he thought. *I have a real church, complete with angels.*

Oh yes, he'd seen them flitting in and out of his peripheral vision since the day he went to street preach. They were softly clad, demure, beautiful faced cherubs that looked as if they had flown out of a Leonardo da Vinci painting. "Of course there are angels here," he heard Rachael say. "This is a church, isn't it?"

"But there were no angel sightings in Taos," Thomas said.

"Quit doubting, James," Rachael said quite clearly. "You've always been such a doubting Thomas. How can we ever be together again if you don't relax and have faith?"

"You're right, darling. You're always right." He smiled to himself as he unlocked his door. He turned and looked out at the scenery around him. It was a peaceful, gentle evening.

Everything was bathed in moonlight and heaped with the heady scent of cypress. Even the old cemetery and the tree that usually glowered at him seemed serene and content. *God is in Heaven. Rachael is with me. There's an angel on my shoulder and all is right with the world.*

He sighed, blessed by the beauty wrought by God's own hand. *Why did I want to leave?* he wondered. *I can't imagine living anywhere else. It's so beautiful here, so tranquil, so lovely. And I have a purpose. The Lord's hand is on me. I can feel it. His hand is on me and on the sparrow...*

-5-

Ouida Spruell was worried about her mother. Cora-Lee hadn't shown up at church, which was not only strange but completely unheard of. After evening services, Ouida had her husband drive her to her mother's house. "She may have fallen and broken a hip," she told him. "You never can tell."

"I doubt it's anything serious," Tim told her. "She probably overslept or something."

"Not my mother," Ouida replied, willing the car to go faster. "She's never missed a day of church in her life."

"Let's just think good thoughts till we get there, okay?"

Ouida offered him a wan smile and Tim encouraged it. He turned their Lexus off the main road and onto his mother-in-law's street. "There," he said, pointing to the car in the driveway. "She's home."

"She's probably lying in the shower with her leg broken." Ouida's expressive brown eyes widened "Or maybe... Oh God, you don't think someone broke in on her, do you?"

"Good thoughts, remember?" Tim said, trying to hide the anxiety from his own voice. "Like I said, maybe she stayed up late and overslept."

"She should have gone into the retirement community," Ouida said as Tim parked the car behind Cora-Lee's luxury liner of a Buick. "At least that way I know she'd be safe."

"Your mother's not an invalid," Tim replied. "She's in good health and still works part time. She doesn't want to go into no home and I don't blame her."

"She's not your mother and I'm not talking about a regular

167

nursing home. It's a retirement community with a sauna and tennis courts."

"And room for a pony," Tim said, quoting one of his favorite Brit-coms.

Ouida smacked his arm.

Tim placed his hand on her shoulder. "Ouida, stop thinking the worst. Now let's go in, okay?"

Ouida nodded. And together they went to the door. "It's unlocked," Tim said.

"Mama?" Ouida called as she gently opened the door. "Mama, it's Ouida, are you okay?"

"Ouida?" A tentative voice responded.

Ouida smiled at her husband. "You're right." She opened the door and they crossed the small foyer into the living room. Her mother was sitting on the sofa, looking small and pale but otherwise unhurt.

"We missed you in church today," Ouida said. She sat next to her mother. She took her hand while Tim sat on the other side of the older woman. "Are you all right?" she asked. "It's not like you to miss church."

Cora-Lee gazed at them through a fog of dreamy contentment. "Oh Ouida, I have the most wonderful news. It's the best news in the world." Her thin hands gripped her daughter's. Tears spilled down her cheeks. "Ouida," she whispered, her voice cracked with emotion. "Davy was here with me this afternoon. He was kneeling in this very spot."

Shocked, Ouida pulled her hands away. She heard Tim gasp. "Mama. Davy's been dead for five years now. He's not coming back."

"Oh I know it sounds crazy, but it's not. I'm telling you, I saw him right here. I talked to him too. I hugged his neck and he was real, warm and alive. It's a miracle; the Lord raised him from the dead."

"I don't know what you saw, but it wasn't Davy. He can't come back." Her voice broke.

"Mama," Tim said. "This man who talked to you, did he come to the door? Did he tell you he was Davy? Did he ask you for anything?" His face darkened. "Did he hurt you?"

"No," Cora-Lee said in a distant voice. "He appeared in the

hallway right over there." She pointed to the hallway.

Tim rose from his seat and strode down the hall. Seconds later, the women heard the sounds of doors opening and closing.

"Nobody wants my boy back more than I do. You know that." Ouida's voice fractured with the weight of emotion. "I think someone played a terrible trick on you."

"No," Cora-Lee said with conviction. "I know it was Davy. I know it was. He told me that God said I was such a faithful servant that he rewarded me by raising him from the dead."

"I know you're a good Christian," Ouida said. "But I don't think that God rewarded you in this way. It's just not possible."

"With God anything is possible," Cora-Lee snapped. Her voice rose an octave below shrill. "This is a God-fearing household. I raised you to be a Bible believing Christian."

Ouida opened her mouth to protest but Tim returned from his search, his brow furrowed in puzzlement. "No one was here and there's no sign of a break-in."

"Mama, I think you're confused," Ouida said.

"You're the only one confused, young lady," Cora-Lee snapped. "You don't believe in the Lord. That's why you don't believe me about Davy. If you repent and confess your sins right now, you can see and hear him too."

"How did he die?" Tim asked, his voice hard. "If he was here and spoke to you, then he must have told you how he passed."

"Well," Cora-Lee considered. "He said he died in the line of duty protecting America from those godless Arabs."

Ouida and Tim looked at each other.

"I'm getting the car," Tim said. "Ouida, get her purse and make sure you have a copy of her insurance card. Mama, we're taking you to the hospital. And no," he added when he saw she was about to protest, "this isn't up for debate."

-6-

Brody wasn't quite sure when he drifted off to sleep. Perhaps it was because of the heat and the steady rhythm of nature that lulled him into a light doze. Or perhaps it was because his subconscious mind yearned to free itself from the dense woolen coils that were trying to snuff out his thoughts.

Consciousness, like the remains of the day, ebbed away. Sleep came and Brody found himself standing inside a doctor's office.

This is Dr. Gonzales's clinic, Brody thought. *Oh how many times have we been in here?* he asked himself. *How many times have we entered these rooms in joy only to leave in heartache?*

Brody glided past the door to stand next to a gynecological examination table. Megan was lying on it, her heels resting inside a pair of stirrups. A thin paper sheet draped over her sprawled legs. A nurse, white faced and expressionless, stood next to the doctor who was sitting on a stool and working between his wife's legs.

Brody felt disconcerted about seeing another man groping around his wife's privates. As far as he was concerned that area was sacred and meant for him only. *But he's a doctor. He's just doing his job.* Nevertheless, Brody felt a mixture of outrage and embarrassment as he continued to watch.

Doctor Gonzales picked up a sharp surgical tool from the sterile tray next to the table. He held it up to the light. The serrated stainless steel edge glistened in the light. Brody held his breath. The doctor slipped the instrument between Megan's legs.

Megan moaned with pleasure. It was a sound Brody had heard a thousand times since they were married. But it was something he never expected to hear during an exam. Especially an exam that involved sharp objects.

But she was with the doctor now—who was supposed to be a professional although he was a man and was groping around where he shouldn't—and he seemed to be enjoying it almost as much as she was. Brody felt his face grow hot. It was grotesque the way she was going on. Brody cringed when a thin but distinct scraping sound came from under the sheet. Megan panted. Her hands explored her breasts and she moaned again.

Blood dribbled and stained the edge of the sheet. Megan gasped. She tossed her heavily maned head, her hands digging deeply into her breasts. The doctor smiled faintly as he continued to scrape. Megan uttered a deep orgasmic groan. She arched her back as the doctor removed the instrument. It looked even sharper now that he could see the bloody but still gleaming thing in his hand.

Dr. Gonzales inserted a clear rubber tube the size of a

garden hose underneath the sheet. Megan accepted it and enjoyed another orgasm while the doctor flipped a switch on a panel next to the examining table. The distinct sound of sucking air filled the room.

Bloody tissue gushed in thick clumps through the rubber hose. Brody watched fascinated, yet horrified, as the tissue, blood and what appeared to be thick clots of something that looked like hair and bone siphoned down and into a glass jug on the floor.

Megan cried out, gripped the edge of the examining table and arched her back for a second time. She screamed in tormented pleasure. Her body gave up orgasm after orgasm as bloody pulp thumped thickly through the tube and plopped into the jar.

Brody stared, transfixed as the thing inside the jar began to cry.

Brody's Adam's apple escalated up and down his neck. His mouth was too dry to scream, his belly hollow with angst. The procedure ended. The doctor removed the tube which was now stringy with clotted blood. He removed his gloves and bent down and picked up the jar.

Megan faced him. She was smiling, but it was a garish, gruesome smile. Brutal and vile. Her eyes had turned inward. Brody felt faint. The whites of her eyes turned a demonic red.

The doctor brought the container to him. He handed it to Brody and said, "Your son, Mr. Wallace."

The jar scalded his hands. The swirling blood and gore churned wildly inside the jar The bloody thing inside uttered a faint wail. Unwillingly, Brody held the jar up so he could see inside. He nearly dropped it when the destroyed face of an infant pushed against the glass and then swirled away.

Brody screamed.

Chapter Twenty

Brody awoke disoriented. The swing jerked, nearly tossing him onto the porch. He looked around, half expecting to find the horrible jar next to him. He leaned back in relief when he realized it was not. He closed his eyes and wiped the perspiration from his brow. It was just a dream.

The evening deepened. The twilight settled like a cloak on the bayou. Despite the nightmare, the gentle sway of the swing and the soft light of the evening made him drowsy again. He resisted sleep, opting instead to try and reach Megan and convince her to let him in.

A slow and steady mist filled in the dark gaps between the trees. Brody watched it approach. He was fascinated and a little apprehensive because the mist looked strange and not like the ordinary fog he'd seen in the past. It glistened although there was no outside light to give it much luster. "I'd really like to go inside now," he said to the door as he rose from the swing.

"Megan," he called, tapping on the door. There was no answer. *She must have cried* herself to sleep. *And it's no wonder. I was a real rat-bastard to her.*

The bitch, a voice deep inside his mind said, *the bitch killed her babies and no telling who else's...*

Shut up. I don't believe it. I won't believe that, Brody told the voice. The image of the mangled fetus in the jar, the look of triumph on his wife's face blazed in his mind.

She killed those babies, the voice insisted. *The bitch. The slut. The whore.*

"That's not true," Brody said aloud. He placed his face in

his hands. "God help me. I love Megan and I know she could never hurt a soul. Especially not one of our precious babies."

Precious babies, the voice mocked. *You know what kind of woman she really is. A filthy half Mexican piece of trash that's only good for lap dances and blowjobs in sleaze pits—*

"Shut up. Just shut up," he shouted. "She's a good woman. I love her and I trust her—"

You're a fool. Stop thinking with your dick and you'll know. The truth will set you free...

"Oh God, won't you just shut the fuck up?"

Something inside him laughed.

"Get out of my head."

You'll see I'm right. You'll see.

The temperature plummeted as the mist flowed up to the house. Brody, startled out of his internal battle, watched the vapor swing around the edge of the porch. The fog covered the veranda like quilt batting. Portions of the vapor broke away and began to spin, growing thicker and denser with each rotation. Brody watched as the objects coalesced. Within moments Brody could clearly see people stepping out of the fog.

No, he amended. Not just people. Children. Four girls and two boys of various sizes and ages stood before him. Their arms where ghostly white and their eyes were a brilliant emerald green. *Are these mine?* he wondered.

"Daddy," one of the girls confirmed. "Daddy, we've missed you."

"Oh God," Brody sobbed. The emotion heaved from deep within him. "Oh God, it's true, it's true. You're all my babies."

"Why did Mommy hurt us?" The smallest of the little boys asked. "Why did Mommy make us die?"

"I don't know, baby," Brody wept. He reached out for them and they ran toward him. Seconds later he was holding them, caressing their soft, fine hair, crying into their little arms.

"We've got a present for you, Daddy," the oldest girl said. "It's a special present and you'll like it."

He allowed his oldest daughter to take him by the hand. The spectral girl led Brody—willingly, oh, yes, so very willingly— down the steps, around the house and into the back yard. The other children followed as well, circling him as he made his way around heavy piles of brush he intended to burn this fall when the monsoons came.

His daughter smiled up at him. She pointed toward a building partially hidden in a grove entwined in wild roses and sumac. "See, Daddy? You like it, don't you? It's just for you."

Tentatively, Brody walked to what his mind dimly registered as an old tar paper shack he had planned on pulling down later in the year. But now it appeared as a perfect work shop. It was something to be cherished and envied. He smiled down at his children, whose little cherub faces beamed back up at him. "Go ahead, open it," his eldest said. Smiling shyly, Brody opened the door.

It was everything he ever dreamed of. Pegboards covered the walls, holding power tools of every sort and size. There were sawhorses and work benches. In the middle of the room stood miter, circular and table saws. And there was lumber stored up in the rafters, neatly stacked and labeled according to size. On the far end of the shop were several bins containing sized nails and screws.

"Would you build us something, Daddy?" one of his sons asked.

"Yes, of course I will," he said, his eyes still blurred by tears. "What do you want me to make?"

"Something to remember what happened to us," said his eldest. "Something Jesus would like."

Brody thought about the marquis he saw earlier that morning. *Jesus loves the little children. Even the unborn.* "I know what to do," Brody said. "Don't you worry. I know just what to do."

-2-

The once-strong scent of sandalwood evaporated along with the strained song that once echoed through the room. Megan curled up until her knees rested under her chin. She lay still, too scared too move. But even more, she was angry and hurt that Brody hadn't come to her rescue.

Brody, she thought. *Where are you? Who were you talking to? What's going on? First you make terrible accusations and then you leave when I need you. What's up with that? The Brody I know would have kicked down the door when I cried out. The*

Brody I know would have protected me. He certainly wouldn't have left me here alone to fend for myself.

The air was stale and heavy with the remains of incense and the edgy taint of garbage. The light seemed unnaturally bright, as if she were on the verge of a migraine. Even the walls seemed to breathe, relaxing and expanding, relaxing then expanding, making Megan think she was in the bottom of an enormous lung. *I can't take this. I've got to get out of here.*

Abandoning the house, she stepped out onto the porch. The late evening shadows engulfed her. It was cold outside, much colder than a late June evening in southwest Arkansas had any right to be. Megan shivered and rubbed her arms. Her breath came out in crisp white puffs.

The fog looks so weird, she thought as she watched it boil briskly along the sides of the house. The trees were completely obscured from about mid-trunk down. The underbrush stood out like prickly islands in a sea of spectral white.

Laughter, soft and as insubstantial as the vapor itself came from behind the house. Brody was talking, but she could not understand what he was saying. A faint chant or perhaps grumbled mumbling came from the fog. Brody laughed again and this time it was answered. *Those are children's voices,* she thought, stunned. *Who are those kids and what are they doing here?*

Maybe somebody dropped by to visit and their kids are playing out back. But there was no vehicle parked in the driveway, nor did she hear any adult voices. It was unlikely someone with children walked out of the woods, but it was possible. Maybe a family went fishing on the bayou and got lost. *Maybe Brody is helping them find their way back to their car.*

But then why would he be in the back yard? And what on earth was that weird grumbling sound?

"Brody?" Megan called. She took a hesitant step off the porch. The fog embraced her up to her hips. It was a strange, clammy feeling, as if thousands of tiny, cold hands were caressing her. She suppressed the urge to brush the sensation away. "Brody?" she repeated as she walked toward the edge of the house. The Cold Hanging Tree was glowing brilliantly tonight, she observed. The light spread an eerie green atop the mist. Disturbed, she turned away and concentrated on finding her husband.

Megan could hear Brody's voice as she approached the back yard. It was almost inaudible. It mixed in with the weird grumbling sounds she'd heard earlier. Then he picked up tempo and she could hear, for the first time, what he was singing.

"Jesus loves the little children, all the children of the world."

His voice was coming from behind the large clump of bushes which hid a rundown tar paper shack leaning precariously on rickety walls. The kudzu and honeysuckle that covered it was probably the only thing holding it up. Astonished, she noted that a brilliant golden light was coming from the hovel.

What in the world is he doing in there and how on earth did he get electricity to that shack?

Megan climbed through the dense brush and made her way to the old lean-to. The door tilted sideways on its hinges. The light coming from the door as well as the cracks in the walls was so dazzling it seemed to seep out of the wood's very pores. Megan could hear hammering, and singing. "...all the children of the world..."

The hammering stopped for a moment. The silence was punctuated by laughter. Tiny hairs on Megan's arms stood up. Gathering her courage, she shoved the door open further.

Brody was standing at what remained of a termite-decimated workbench. He was engulfed in the radiance. For a moment, she couldn't see what he was doing. Brody giggled as he worked. He stopped, wiped sweat from his brow and resumed his song. "Red and yellow black and white, they are precious in his sight." He raised a blinding white object up to his face for inspection.

Megan's fear jazzed up another notch. The light from the object faded and she could see clearly what Brody held in his hand. He was building crosses like the kind found on children's graves. He sighed, his face beaming as he gazed at his handiwork. Megan gasped. They weren't perfectly constructed religious objects at all. They were composed of termite-ridden wood and rusty six penny nails. Even the arms weren't straight.

"Jesus loves the little children of the world."

"Brody?" she asked. "Brody, what on earth are you doing

out here?"

Brody startled. He turned to look at her. The lights burst off, leaving them in the dark. Bright sparks danced across Megan's field of vision, but it didn't stop her from catching a glimpse of Brody's face outlined in the shadows. "What are you doing here?" he demanded. "What do you want?"

Oh my God, Megan realized. *He doesn't recognize me.*

Brody blinked as if he caught himself sleepwalking. "Oh I know you," he said. "I know you very well. You're the whore."

"What?"

"It was you. It's always been you." Brody stepped closer and she could see his face in the dim light. He looked maniacal. "You're the Whore of Babylon," he hissed.

"What are you talking about?" Megan asked as she slowly backed out of the shack.

"They're gone because of you," he roared. "You baby-killing bitch. You whore. Get out. Get out before I kill you."

"Brody," she whispered, shaking her head. "You don't mean that."

Brody rushed towards her, his arm raised, a corroded claw hammer clenched in his fist. She screamed and stumbled out of the shack. Her feet tangled in briars and she nearly fell on her face. She righted herself in time to see Brody lunging at her, swinging the hammer with all his might. Megan dodged the blow. She dashed through the brush and out toward the forest.

For the first time in her life, Megan was glad Brody was a couch potato. He staggered and cursed as he crashed through the shrubbery in a vain attempt to pursue her. Megan bolted into the fog and disappeared deeper into the woods. He tracked her for a few hundred yards. Gasping for breath, he stopped. Undaunted, Megan rushed through the undergrowth.

Just as she thought the undergrowth couldn't get any thicker, the forest seemed to lift its skirt and exposed the clearing that housed the abandoned Gypsy camp. Megan stopped, her heart pounding. *It's obvious that going home ain't an option. And I don't want to stay here either,* she thought. She looked around, uncertain if this was real or if she was still at home having troubling dreams while Brody languished on the porch. She wandered aimlessly around the site. *Are the men still here?* she wondered. *If they are will they help me or help themselves to me?*

Trying her best to be silent, Megan slipped deeper into the encampment. The trailers were vacant, she was sure of it. The windows appeared devoid of life as she approached. *I have to get help*, she told herself. *If one of these trailers has a phone at least, one that's still operational, I could call the sheriff's department. I could get help for myself and for Brody.*

She mounted the closest trailer's porch, a large red and white hulk listing on its supports. Heart pounding, she gathered the remnants of her courage and turned the knob. The door opened and she entered. *I feel like Goldilocks*, she thought. *I wonder when the bears are going to return.*

She stood in the cramped living room. Megan could vaguely see the lump of what appeared to be a sofa propped up against the wall. Thankfully nobody was sleeping on it. She stumbled around in the dark, using the edge of the sofa as a guide until she came to the table beside it. Sitting down, she reached over and touched the surface of the table. She explored the flat, rough surface, accidentally knocking off an ash tray. It landed with a dull thud. Megan held her breath, listening for anyone coming down the hallway. Satisfied that nobody could have heard, she ran her hands over the top of the end table once again. This time she felt the hard, distinctive plastic of a phone. She laughed with relief. She picked up the receiver and her hopes were quickly snuffed out when there was no dial tone. *I hoped the phone company hadn't had time to disconnect them yet. I guess not.*

Megan drew her knees up to her chest. *What am I going to do?* she wondered. *What's happened to Brody? Where's the man I love?* She stretched out on the sofa. It was hard, lumpy and smelled of beer and stale carpet deodorant. She lay alert, listening for anyone who might still be in the trailer. Or if Brody managed to track her down and was coming after her with his hammer.

The moon rose and she watched its silvery light spill through the large window onto the opposite wall. Then a dull green glow appeared, bracketing the moon on both sides. She whimpered. The amulet on her chain glowed a dull red. The room filled with sandalwood, taking away the musky scent of old mobile home and cheap carpet deodorizer. A soft breeze blew through the window, rustling the ragged curtains.

The light from the tree glowed brighter. The moon finally left its ghostly bracket and climbed high into the sky. *It's your fault,* she told the garish glow. *I know it is. And I'm going to kill you if I can.*

-3-

Tim and Ouida settled Cora-Lee into her hospital room. After the EEG recorded suspicious brain wave activity, her doctor ordered more tests, including a CAT scan first thing in the morning.

The couple left the family matriarch resting lightly with the television on and the preacher's wife quietly reading in the corner. Moments later, they arrived at Cora-Lee's house to pick up a few clothes for the elderly woman's stay.

Ouida sat on the sofa. Davy's picture was still lying face up on the sofa. She gazed at his affable face. *What brought all this on?* she wondered. Of course, Dr. Hearne was most likely right, Ouida considered. Mama's sudden confusion was probably due to a mild stroke and for the second time today she contemplated talking her mother into moving into a retirement community.

Oh not one of those filthy ones where everything smells of piss and the patients are drugged into stupidity. There are several really nice communities in Texarkana, she thought. One especially pleased her, with huge columns, lovely wallpaper and limousine service. There were tennis courts in the back. Tennis was something Cora-Lee had enjoyed doing while her husband was alive. They played at the country club every weekend until his heart attack in 2000. She could take the sport back up again. With the proper medication and exercise, she'd be fine.

She shouldn't be alone, Ouida thought. *And it's not safe these days. Who knows? Someone might really have come in, posing as her grandson.* Ouida had heard of veteran scams before. This was probably far fetched, but it certainly wasn't out of the realm of possibility, especially in this day and age of plastic surgery.

Ouida's eyes strayed back to her son's picture. *But if nobody posed as Davy then why did she fixate on him?* she wondered. *Unless it's because he's no longer with us—and I know she misses him so. I do too.* She felt the sting of tears and wiped them away with the palm of her hand.

Tim was sitting outside in the car, waiting for her to pack her mother's suitcase and come out. She'd already packed the small overnight currently resting gently against her calf. Ouida needed a moment to be alone to recharge and try to find her emotional bearings. It was one thing to fall apart in front of Tim, but not the kids.

The picture of Davy smiled up at her. His black hair sheared and the white sailor's cap perched jauntily on his head as if it would blow off any moment. Smiles were something that most military pictures she'd seen didn't have. *Everyone looks so stern. But Davy was such a happy child, even when he was a baby he—*

Stop it.

Tears spilled down her cheeks. She felt the sting of mascara and knew her makeup was spoiled. *I'll have raccoon eyes now*, she thought. She frowned as she fumbled in her purse for a tissue. Ouida never told her mother how Davy died. She was too afraid and deep down, too ashamed. Her mother was such a devoted Christian woman. She would have been appalled if she'd ever found out.

The officers who told us about Davy said that he was working down in the engine room during the midnight watch. He was oiling some bearings on the engine when he was grabbed by the machinery and crushed by the crank shaft's crosshead. That was why we had to have a closed coffin funeral. I know that devastated Mama but nothing would compare to the hurt of what we found out later. Joe Preston, his friend and shipmate came to see us while on shore leave. He told Tim, in confidence of course, that he caught Davy drinking while on duty. Joe saw Davy fall into the machinery. He tried his best to save his friend but he was too late. Poor Joe, Ouida thought. *The poor boy was devastated. He and Davy had been friends since junior high school. They even enlisted together. I thought they would have been best friends forever.*

Ouida jerked out of her reverie. *Tim*, she thought. *He's ready to go back to the hospital.* Ouida rose. As she did, a sheaf of paper resting on the end table caught her eye. Curious, she picked it up. The smeared purple print announced a revival at the First Light Church of Prophecy on June nineteenth.

Of all the nerve, she thought. *I'm amazed Mama even picked this up.* A strange sensation shot up her arm. Seconds later, Ouida's mind was drifting in an eerie, peaceful place. The horn blared again. She ignored it. *I'm in Heaven,* she thought happily. *We'll have to go to the revival. It'll be a sin not to.*

A rustle of fabric caught her attention. Startled, she half stood as her son strode down the hall and into the living room.

"Mama?" Davy called. "Mama, I'm home."

-4-

"I wish you'd come on to bed," Effie said to her husband George. She groaned as she peeked in on him. He was sitting at his standard place in the den in front of the computer with his face virtually attached to the monitor. It made her irritable, of course, because he seemed to—no, she knew beyond a shadow of a doubt—he spent more time with it than he did with her.

"In just a little bit," he said. "I found an excellent website on pro bass fishing."

"Wonderful," Effie said, not bothering to hide the sarcasm from her voice. "And does it come with a chat room too?"

"No" he said, missing the insinuation. "But it does have message boards. I'm registering for one now."

Effie sighed. "You're turning into a real web head, George. If you're not careful, that monitor is going to become grafted to the side of your neck."

"Would make things easier, wouldn't it?"

Effie grunted a spectacular obscenity. "I swear to God, if I find out you're screwing around with some slut in one of those chat rooms of yours—"

"Ah, you couldn't take a joke if it came with handles," George replied. "And don't look at me like that. I'll log off in a few minutes, okay? I want to send something to a friend first."

"Such as?" Effie asked, her arms folded. "Dirty pictures, no doubt."

"Just this flyer for that revival this coming Friday, that's all."

"Oh that." She shivered as if caught in a draft. "That hobo preacher. He was a queer one, wasn't he?"

"I liked him. I think we ought to go."

"The hell we will. I'm not going down there."

"Well I'll go by myself, then." He picked up the handout and gazed at it. He smiled in a weird, dreamy way that gave Effie the creeps.

She'd been married to George for twenty years and had known him for five before that. They were high school sweethearts. He was a halfback on the team and she was the president of the school's DECCA chapter. George currently hawked used cars at Fulton's Used Cars and Boats and Effie was a full charge bookkeeper and day auditor at the Twilight Time Inn, Tatum's only hotel.

"Here," George was saying, "just take a look at this flyer. It's been printed off a duplicator."

"Big deal," she said, moving his hand away.

"Well, just look at it."

"I don't want to."

"Just feel the quality of the paper. It's a virtual antique."

"George, I don't give a potter's damn about that piece of paper," Effie said, shoving his hand away.

"You should. It'll save your soul."

"I'll just bet it will."

"Just take the paper."

Effie backed away. "Why don't you wipe your ass on it?" She turned and strode back to the bedroom.

George heard the door lock. *You pushed too hard he scolded himself. You know how hard-headed she is.* George frowned. The warm, wooly blanket that had settled on his mind since he took the leaflet from the preacher yesterday twisted tighter. His doubts were smothered. He smiled. *Yes. It's so much better this way.*

George deleted the porn files he had accumulated, knowing that they were an abomination now that his eyes were open. He had been collecting pornography—adult porn only; never the kiddy stuff. He was hard up, not a pervert—for about a year now. It wasn't because he didn't love Effie any more, no. He still loved her very much. But he'd noticed over the past year or so, his, well his performance had begun to wane. He was still interested, obviously. But he just couldn't seem to get the old member to cooperate.

This was something no real man was going to tolerate, he told himself. And forget about those stupid "male enhancement" commercials. He snorted. *Nobody is going to buy that crap. "Honey, I walked the dog, called the baby sitter and told my doc I have a limp dick." Yeah. Sure. Now let me tell you the story about how Little Orphan Annie screwed the pooch.*

The fog drift in his mind thickened. *I shouldn't be looking at people having sex; it's a sin. It's an abomination, guaranteed to kill the spirit. I should just accept my celibacy and let Effie know*, he thought. *It would be honest and probably more scriptural too.* He picked up the flyer and caressed it. "You saved me," he said. "You saved me from a life of sin and denigration. And now I'm going to share you with the world."

Humming an old hymn he hadn't heard since he was a kid, George placed the flyer into the scanner and initiated the program. The scanner emitted its standard blue-white light. Just as the blue light passed halfway across the page, the machine made a bizarre noise.

Surprised, George saw the light change from blue-white to a deep, emerald green. The lid of the scanner jumped as the document underneath squealed. Yes, oh Lord it squealed like an animal impaled on a spike. The whole thing was really bouncing now. Frightened, George leapt from the chair and retreated to the back of the room. He watched in amazement as the monitor, keyboard, and the drives shot out green beams of light. The computer shrieked as the monitor exploded, shooting out black smoke and glass across the room. George ducked. The heavy blanket in his mind vanished. He shook his head, clearing the remains of the mental shroud. *My porn*, he thought. *Oh damn, I deleted my fuck files.* A tiny whimper escaped from his throat.

Effie came out of the bedroom, her aged, pale blue bathrobe dangling from her shoulders as she inspected the room. She stared at George and then at the remains of the smoldering computer. Astonished, she asked, "What in the world did you do?"

-5-

The "right" Reverend Ike Smalley had just finished his task and leaned back into his chair, enjoying a flask of God's healing virtue. It was also known as good Tennessee sippin' whiskey. He didn't go for the rot-gut that was still produced down in the bottoms, that was even if you knew where to find it. Occasionally some idiot would taint the mash by running it through a car radiator. Or they'd use runoff water coming straight out of one of the pulp wood plants instead of getting good distilled water from the store.

"That shit'll kill yuh," he told the flask. "But you. Why, you're a blessing straight from God's own blessed cornfields."

Now Ike had made some damned good corn mash when he was younger. He ran it, too, back in the forties and early fifties until he found Jesus and the joys of properly brewed hooch. No, the whiskey wasn't even drunk for pleasure any longer as far as he was concerned. It was strictly for his rheumatism among other ailments that the devil had afflicted him with. At least that's what he told himself. But the pain was real enough, and had been so since he was a youngster and fell from grace when a government agent shot him in the ass over bootlegging some shine.

But Ike Smalley learned the lessons of youth well. Now he ministered to the dregs left over from the Mc Knight House. He cared for men who were nothing more than day drunks who worked long enough for a bottle of cheap booze and a place to flop for the night. They weren't good enough for the Mc Knight who expected them to get decent jobs and become socially acceptable, oh no, sir. So they came to him because he preached to them, saw they were fed and didn't force them to attend AA meetings. The drunks liked it and Smalley was happy to tend a small flock that at least paid half assed attention to him whenever he had chapel for them in the evenings.

That was, if they wanted to eat, they'd sit down and shut the fuck up.

Smalley was changed, though. He looked up at the walls and smiled at his handiwork. Yes, he'd been thinking about it ever since he came across that new preacher from First Light Church of Prophecy. Smalley hadn't thought much of the preacher. What was his name, Thomas? *Yeah*, he chuckled. *Thomas. What a hell of a name for a preacher. He's a pussy, a lapdog for Mr. Jim and that cocksucker Pa Neidi.*

Smalley, however, had an abrupt change of heart about the man—among other things—when he took one of those shabby leaflets from Thomas that day. He was going to tell him to stuff it. Instead, he enthusiastically announced that he was called into service of the Lord and would be out at First Light to assist the good minister in his work. Yes, he knew instantly when he picked up another half dozen flyers and then motioned for one of his men to relieve Thomas of a boxful that he'd have to be a guest speaker at the revival.

And to his surprise, Thomas agreed.

Why, everything seemed so good that he poured himself another glass. He leaned back and put his feet on the desk.

Smalley spent that afternoon pasting the handouts on what was once a display window when the building was a dress shop in a former life. He hadn't stopped there. Smalley called upon several members of his flock to go to Thomas and get as many flyers as they could. Later, they stood outside the mission and handed them out to passersby. *But even that wasn't enough,* Ike Smalley thought as he pulled another drink from the flask. He smiled and gazed at the walls.

He had papered the walls in purple-smeared leaflets. He taped, glued and stapled them, some two or three pages thick until all the paneling was covered over.

Smalley giggled. He even managed to paper the ceiling with them as well although it was tricky and he had to stand on his rolling office chair and pray that he wouldn't fall and break a hip doing it. Sure, he could have gotten one of the younger guys to come in and do it but he felt that this required a personal touch. Just like the floor. He had started pasting them in the far back corner of the office and now had over half the floor done.

Smalley had the men go ahead and do the dining hall with them as well but they ran out about half way around the room. Frustrated, he called Thomas on the phone requesting more. But he was told that there weren't' any more and he'd have to make due with what he got.

That's no big deal, Smalley thought, finishing the flask. He picked up one of the tracts from a stack spilling onto his desk. "Rodney," he called. "Come on in here."

Rodney, a wormy little man with a two day growth of beard, peeked inside.

"Rodney," Smalley said, waving a flyer at him. "Go down to

Nexus Printing and get this copied off. You know where that is, right?"

Rodney took the handout and nodded. His eyes unfocused and Smalley smiled.

"We have an account there," Smalley added, "so you don't need any money." *Not that I'd give you any, you fucking retard,* he thought.

Rodney stood with the flyer in his hand, his jaw slacked.

"Yes, go have about ten thousand of these printed. And get some of those manila envelopes too. We've got a big day ahead of us." Smalley smiled. "We're going to send these to every church in the area."

Part Three
Angels, Tribulation and the Faithful Twelve

Chapter Twenty-One

-1-

When Thomas entered his trailer, he found an angel sitting at his kitchen table. Astonished because until this moment the creatures seemed to appear only out of the corner of his eye, Thomas stood at the threshold while the being, whose face glowed almost as white as his three piece suit, smiled and gestured for him to enter.

"Evening," the angel said with a distinct Louisiana accent. A tall green bottle of Jameson whiskey sat on the table. Two glasses appeared. He poured for both. "Come sit down," the angel said amiably. "We have some things to discuss."

"Discuss?" Thomas asked as he edged closer to the table. The angel motioned him to come. Thomas was scared enough to allow his socked-in mind to land a few independent thoughts. He shook his head, prepared to slowly back down the steps.

"Oh, there's nothing to be afraid of," the angel said. "We know you've been seeing us for a while now. God sent us down to help you out, that's all. Now, come on and sit down. I've got a message for you."

"For...for me?" Thomas stammered.

"No. For Elvis. Now sit yourself on down." The smile on the angel's face had taken on a hard set edge.

Thomas was obedient to the will of the being and sat across from him.

The angel laughed, filled a glass and handed it to him. "Neat?" he inquired.

"I, uh, I don't drink anymore."

"Ah, sure you do. Come on, drink up."

"What—why are you tempting me? That is if you're an angel—you are an angel—right?"

The angel glared at him. The eyes were blue, pupil-less and held a strange milky whiteness that made Thomas think of cataracts. "What gives you the right to question the will of God?"

"What do you want with me?"

"Me? Not a thing, dear boy. Not a thing in the world. But the Lord, now, he has big plans for you."

"I don't understand."

"He knows there will be a revival here come this Sunday and he's well pleased with that. Wonderful things, revivals. They're such blessed events. Have you ever wondered why they're called revivals?"

Thomas's hand shook as it rested next to the glass. Oh how he wanted to taste it, to feel it burn down his throat...

"You can have it if you want." Rachael's voice returned, quite loud this time. "Don't you want to be with me?"

"Not particularly," Thomas said to the angel as he continued to eye the glass. He ignored the voice in his head, the one with the itchy fur that made his thoughts hot and uncomfortable.

"What does the word revival mean?"

"It means to bring something to life or to bring it into awareness, I suppose."

"Very good. This church of yours has indeed been dead for a long time now. Look at what you've got for a congregation. A half dozen old folks and a couple of middle-aged women who bake on Sundays? Not one youth or one solitary babe-in-arms. Now what kind of church is there that doesn't have the laughter of children? Oh yes, old Ma and Pa have kids, but that ain't good enough. And look at you down here all alone and with the Neidis running everything including you."

"Nobody runs me."

"No, of course not," the angel said, waving his hand aside to dismiss the comment. A box of Lucky Strikes appeared on the table along with a small matchbook with a white cover and the word "Ziracuny" typed in red across the picture of an eyeless horse. He offered the pack to Thomas who shook his head. "Don't smoke, don't drink and don't screw around with wild women. My God, man, you're a regular paragon of virtue." The angel lit up, blew smoke out of his nose and then said, "No wonder God thinks so highly of you."

"I'm only his faithful servant."

"And you're so modest as well. You'll be pleased to know that he has a special project just for you."

"A project?" Thomas's heart thumped. "What kind of project?"

The angel sipped his whiskey. He smiled and then said, "Before I go into that, I have another question to ask."

"What?" Thomas asked.

"You know when the end comes those who are judged and found worthy will go to Heaven."

"Yes," Thomas said.

"You also preach that those who go to Heaven will be joint heirs with Christ."

"Absolutely."

"Well, has it ever occurred to you that if you're a joint heir then that makes you a joint ruler as well?"

"I'm not following you."

"It's not too hard, if you just think about it. If you inherit the Kingdom of Heaven and become joint heirs with Christ, then who are your subjects?"

"Well, that means," Thomas mused, "that when we inherit the Kingdom of Heaven we will be ruled by God and Christ."

"But if you're a joint heir with Christ, that makes you a ruler also. How can you rule and be a subject at the same time?"

Thomas's brow furrowed. "I never thought about it like that before."

"Well, I want you to think about it quickly. Because you don't have much time left." The angel blew smoke through his nose.

Thomas's heart fell somewhere into the vicinity of his nut sac. "Am I being called home?" he whispered.

The angel slammed his shot glass on the table and uttered a long deep-bellied howl. "Called home? Oh not today, dear boy. Not today. But it is sooner than you think. You see," the angel wiped tears from his blue-john colored eyes, "You see, after this Sunday, everyone will be called home."

Stunned, Thomas asked, "The Judgment? It's this coming Sunday?"

"Yes, indeed it is." The angel smiled. "And God has decided to reward you early. You see," his voice lowered, "not everyone is going to Heaven."

"Oh, I know that. The wheat from the chaff and all that."

"Indeed, indeed. But there are those who aren't villainous enough for hell, but not righteous enough for Heaven. Do you know what is going to become of them?"

"I-I don't know."

"Well, they get to stay here in the New Jerusalem. And the New Jerusalem will encompass the whole world. But there will be little sections off the main kingdom. Suburbs if you prefer. And you being a joint heir in Christ will have your own kingdom, right here on the bayou."

Thomas was silent, his eyes glowing with expectation.

"There are a few things for you to do first, of course," the angel said. His voice was brisk as if he'd just closed a deal on a new Cadillac. "You've already done the hard part, but now you will have eighteen—no," he said, cocking his head, listening to a voice only he could hear. "No, twelve righteous men and women who have heard the Word and will be saved at the revival. You will call to them and they will answer. They'll hear your voice in their dreams. They will not be frightened away like the weak that will flee upon seeing and hearing you, but you will be a source of strength and comfort to them. Because, you see, there will be tribulation."

"Tribulation..."

"Yes, yes. But they'll stay with you, these faithful twelve. And on the third day, you shall reward them with their own keys to your kingdom, the one you will share with Christ, here on earth."

"I have a request, if I may," Thomas whispered.

"Your wife and daughter. I understand. And yes, death will no longer have any meaning. The veil will be rent and they will join you."

"My wife? My...my Becky?"

"Anything you want," Rachael whispered.

"Yes, yes," said the angel impatiently. He took another shot, snuffed out his last Lucky Strike, stood and said, "You know what you have to do. I don't have to give you detailed instructions, do I?"

"No. I know what to do."

"Good. And one more thing. Watch out for a bitch of a Latina who's hell bent on kicking your ass. Kill her quickly and be done with it."

"As the Lord wills," Thomas whispered.

"Good and faithful servant." The angel glowed brighter. He turned white-hot and then vanished.

Thomas sat in the darkness that swept in after the angel left. He could still smell the whiskey, the pungent scent of the cigarette. He could hear the whispers from the graveyard beyond.

In the darkness Thomas prayed.

-2-

It was in those dark eerie hours of predawn when Megan was jolted awake by the rich scent of sandalwood permeating the room. Dull, thin moonlight created a gray block on the floor. As she cleared away the cobwebs of sleep, Megan realized fully that she wasn't home.

Memory of Brody's twisted, insane expression, the hammer in his hand, the macabre scene in the tar paper shack and the resulting chase through the woods swept through her. She sat up, rubbing her temple with the palm of her hand. *Oh my God, I've lost him*, she thought. She curled back into a fetal position on the musty old couch and cried.

She woke again with a start. She lay still, listening. She heard it again, louder this time. A strange sound came from the outside. Megan, sat up, cocked her head and listened.

"Swing lo, sweet chariot, coming fo to carry me home."

Curiosity pulled her off the couch. She crept to the window and looked outside.

The fog had returned, solid and ominous, caressing the ground around the encampment. Thick lumps formed from the mist and bodies emerged. A young black man, maybe eighteen or nineteen years old, was naked to the waist. His pants were ragged and gray. The young slave's back was raw and bloody with lacerations. He fell, groveling in the dirt. He convulsed, screaming, "No mo, massa. Oh please no mo."

A whip shot out of the fog, opening a gash across the youth's face. Another lump formed, then rose from the pool of mist, growing, towering over the slave. Whip in hand, the overseer beat his victim to death.

The scene spun itself out. The specters melded into the fog. Megan sat at the window, cold sweat prickling her forehead. *Incredible*, she thought. *Absolutely incredible.*

The scent of sandalwood was strong. She picked the pendant off her chest and looked at its innocuous engraving, which turned orange, then bright red. She could feel the heat pouring from the amulet. She feared it but couldn't find the strength to take it off either.

A noise like the soft rustle from thick curtains caught her attention. She turned and gasped as an elderly black man in overalls appeared at the far end of the room. "You've got to get rid of it," he said in a matter of fact tone.

"What?" Megan squeaked, not understanding the dead man's meaning. Early morning light filtered through his chest. His head and shoulders appeared solid, as did his legs and feet, but his midsection was eaten away by the light. *Oh my God.* Megan giggled, giddy from hysteria. *I can see dead people.*

"You know what I mean," the ghost said. He pointed to the window, his hand nearly transparent in the light.

"Who are you? Are you one of the slaves?"

"No, I was never a slave. But—" he turned to the window and lowered his hand. He tilted his head. "I only have a few seconds, 'cause dat angel is listening for me—he knows I'm up to something—but you've got to quit asking questions. Be still and pay attention to what I've got to say."

"I'm listening," she said, ignoring the sound of blood surging in her ears. "What do you want?"

"You've gotta get rid of that tree," he said emphatically. "It's gotta be yanked up by its roots and that necklace of yours thrown into the hole. That's the only way we can be free."

"I don't understand. What good will throwing a necklace down a hole do?"

"You'll know," the ghost said in the cryptic way ghosts explain things. He turned toward the window and vanished in the strong red-gold light of dawn.

"You'll know." The voice echoed in her mind long after the spirit vanished.

-3-

Cora-Lee awoke to the brilliant image of Davy standing at the foot of her hospital bed. His face was vibrant in the darkness, his eyes deep green emeralds that glowed with a rapturous fire. Cora-Lee's heart squeezed. *I love him. Oh God how I love him.*

"Rise and dress," he commanded, his voice deep and Biblical in its power. "Revival is at hand and you have been called."

Cora-Lee squealed with glee. "I'm one of God's own chosen."

She struggled to sit up but was too weak from the tranquilizers the doctors pumped into her. She cried out in despair. "Davy, I want to come with you. But I can't get up. Can't you see what they've done to me? You have to help me. I will leave right now if you can unplug me from all these tubes."

"Rise," Davy said again. "Rise and join us in the Lord's house."

She whimpered, reaching for Davy's outstretched arms. "Please help me. I can't do this by myself. I'll do anything to be with you again. Give my life to you."

"Rapture this Sunday," Davy said, vanishing in a thin green mist. "The little church on the bayou. Go to the blessed little church... Go today..."

"I can't get there," she shouted, frustrated. "How can I get there if I can't move? Davy, why won't you help me? I'm your own grandmother!"

"Mama will help," Davy whispered. "She will abide by thee."

-4-

Ouida had a plan. *Sure it's sneaky but it's for his own good, isn't it? After all, he needs salvation. I certainly can't let him and the kids remain behind when the Rapture comes.*

Tim wouldn't take the flyer she offered him that afternoon.

But the kids took it and were happy with the consecrated warmth that eased into their minds just as it did their mother's. And this disturbed Tim, she knew. Even though he didn't say so, she saw the disbelieving look on his face.

After dinner, Ouida lost her temper and insisted he take the handout. Instead, he stormed out of the house and drove out to the fields to check on the cattle. "You'll be condemned to hell for this," Ouida shouted after him as he slammed the door shut. "You're denying Christ and Davy."

Tim returned after midnight and she was certain he hadn't spent all that time alone with the cows. No, he'd gone somewhere else. She decided not to make an issue out of it. *It's better this way,* she thought. *I'll wait until he goes to sleep and I'll place the flyer in his hand. Then God can move in him the same way he moved in me, allowing me to see Davy and become one of the Twelve.*

Ouida lay on her side and feigned sleep as Tim slid into the bed beside her. She listened as his breathing slowed, signaling he had slipped into sleep. Slowly, she took the leaflet from the nightstand. She rolled over and slipped it into his hand.

Tim jerked awake. He lunged forward, seeing but not understanding the piece of paper clenched in his fist.

"Be saved, my sweet Tim. Be saved and see Davy," Ouida exclaimed, her expression rapturous.

He stared at her then down at the paper. Repulsed, he ripped it up and threw it against the wall. "What the hell are you doing?" he demanded.

"Why, saving you, of course," Ouida said. She paused for an instant, and then her face lit up. "Revival will be upon us this coming Sunday. Isn't that the most wonderful news? I've been anointed as one of the faithful Twelve, and you can be too. Just accept Christ and Thomas into your heart and come with us to the bayou and wait for the Rapture."

"What's gotten into you, woman?" Tim shouted as he stumbled out of bed. "You've gotten severely weird since you came from your mother's house and found that stupid flyer."

"It's not just some flyer," Ouida said, petulant. "It's a message from God."

"It's bullshit from a hobo preacher," Tim roared as he stuffed his legs into his jeans.

"No, Tim. Please, if you'll only hold it, cradle it to your breast and open your heart to the message you'll see. You'll know."

"And let in a message from hell? No thanks." Tim countered, shoving his feet into his cowboy boots.

"Where are you going?"

"I don't know. Some place where a man can find some peace and quiet until you get this out of your system." He tucked his shirt into his jeans. "My God, Ouida, where is your good common sense?"

"I know I can see Davy," Ouida screamed as she sat up on the bed. "I know he's here. The kids have seen him too. It's a sign from God. It's a glorious sign of his return."

"It's bullshit," Tim retorted. "It's a sign these things are laced with LSD or meth or something. I don't know. But I'm going to find out. You, Cora-Lee and the kids ain't been the same since y'all touched that stupid thing. I'm going to go down to the station right now and find out what's on it."

"The only thing on it is God's own words."

Tim grabbed his wife's shoulders and gave her a little shake. "Listen to yourself, Ouida. You're talking crazy."

"I'm just filled with the spirit, that's all," Ouida whimpered.

"You're filled with something but I don't know what. But I'm going to find out. This shit is going to stop now." He bent down and picked up the flyer, which to his astonishment had reassembled itself. His arm felt as if it was immersed in warm water. His mind fogged over and he felt somewhat dazed. He shook it off. "It's got some kind of drug on it, I'm sure," he said. He went into the kitchen. Ouida followed close behind him, wringing her hands and whimpering. He placed the paper inside a plastic bag. He washed his hands with hot soapy water while Ouida watched him with a puzzled expression on her face.

"You didn't feel it?" she asked.

"Feel what?"

"God's presence. You didn't feel God's love for you when you picked it up?"

Tim shoved the bag in his jeans pocket. He walked past her.

"Where are you going?" she demanded.

"I already told you." He shoved his Stetson on his head and left the house with Ouida practically running to keep up. Tim got into their Lexus and started the motor.

Ouida beat on the window glass. "I won't let you stop revival," she screamed. Her face distorted with rage. "Get out of that car. Blasphemer! Satan worshipper! You're going to hell, you no count son of a bitch."

Tim backed the car out of the driveway and turned onto the highway. In his rear view mirror he could see Ouida standing in the yard, her white nightgown billowing in the rise of soft mists that swirled around the house. For a second, Tim thought he saw images in the fog. He shook his head. *An after effect from touching the flyer,* he decided. *And having Ouida screaming like a wild woman at me.*

Feeling much safer now that he was on the road and heading toward the bright edges of town, he took the turn off that led to the sheriff's department.

-5-

"I tried," Ouida said to the apparition forming in front of her. "I tried to get him to see the light but he won't open his mind to the Lord."

Davy emerged from the fog. He gazed down at her with hollowed out eyes. His face was pale but glistening with a supernatural joy. *Oh,* Ouida thought, awed. *The Lord really is upon him.*

"If he's not for us, he's against us," Davy said.

"I understand," Ouida said. "Bless you, Jesus. Thank you Jesus," she muttered as she went back inside the house. She went to the hall closet and extracted Tim's 4-10 rifle. She pulled the box of shells from the shelf, glided to the sofa, sat and loaded the gun. She sat with the weapon resting across her lap, half covered by her nightgown.

Her mind struggled like a rabbit caught in a snare. *After all this is Tim,* she reasoned. The wet blanket smothering her mind squeezed tighter, and a feverish itching occurred behind her eyeballs. *This is the man I married. The man I love with all my heart and soul. The man I share my bed with and the man I had my children with. The man I swore to honor and cherish...forever and ever...until death do us part.*

The mental blanket compressed into straight jacket tightness. Ouida cried out, pushing her fists against her temples. The itching became catastrophic and for an instant she thought she'd have to claw her eyes out to get to it.

I can't do this, but I must do this. Oh someone please help me.

Chapter Twenty-Two

-1-

Tim Spruell didn't know what to think. He spent the predawn hours driving around town, feeling lost, confused and definitely unnerved. *Fuck that*, he amended. *I'm just plain scared.* Tim feared for his family and was angry because the source of his fear was a piece of paper, for God's sake. *But how did it become one piece again after I tore it up?* He scowled. Tim hated mysteries. *There has to be a logical reason. Maybe I just thought I tore it up. I was half asleep when she shoved that thing in my hand. I might have imagined it.*

But he doubted it.

At five o'clock he went into Tatum's Donut Hole and picked up a pair of cinnamon bear claws and a cup of coffee. He went back to the car and locked himself in. Ouida hated it that he ate in the car, fearing he or the kids would ruin the upholstery. He didn't give a rat's ass at the moment.

I've never known Ouida to go off the edge about anything before, he thought. *Sure, Cora-Lee is eaten up with religion, but Ouida? Nah. Sure she goes to church every Sunday, but that's just to please her mother. If she had her way, Ouida would sleep in on Sundays. And why the sudden interest in First Light? It's a holy roller church that the Neidis go to, enit? Now why on earth would she want to go there? Ouida hates holy rollers. And she loathes the Neidis. In fact I can't think of anyone off hand who even talks to those people. White trash if there ever was.*

He finished his second bear claw. He swallowed his coffee which resembled twenty-weight motor oil and started his car. Catching his grim expression in the rearview mirror, Tim pulled out of the Donut Hole parking lot and headed to the sheriff's department.

Tim drove deeper into town. The traffic lights hadn't awakened yet and were still blinking a steady yellow and red. He turned right and headed for the gray cinder block complex that housed the city police department, the highway patrol and the sheriff's departments. He sighed. *They can get to the bottom of this, I know. If anyone could figure it out, it's Lonnie.*

He and Lonnie had been friends since middle school, when Tim arrived from Dallas, feeling lost and disjointed after his mom and dad divorced and his mother moved him and his sister back to Arkansas where she was born. He and Lonnie became instant friends and went through high school together. They joined the National Guard the day after graduation, served together in Desert Storm. They returned home, married, settled down, had kids and worked on their American Dreams.

Tim trusted Lonnie more than he trusted anyone on earth, with the exception of Ouida, and she pulled the plug on that when he woke and found her shoving that stupid tract in his hand. *It's like the* Invasion of the Body Snatchers, *only this rendition is in Technicolor.*

Just as Tim approached what Lonnie affectionately referred to as the "cop shop," he noticed the billboard on the left hand side of the street. It contained a picture of a half-naked woman with a martini glass in one hand. Across her abdomen someone had spray painted in huge letters, "The End Times Am Come."

He noticed the graffiti wasn't limited to just the billboard. Along the sides of the buildings, similar statements were made. "Get right or get left," was sprayed across the window of a used bookstore. The curious phrase, "Revive us again," was written in purple paint across a parked sedan. Surprised by the audacity and vandalism so close to the cop shop, he nearly ran into a pedestrian while reading on the side of an aged strip mall wall, "Jesus Rocks." Some smart ass wrote underneath it, "But can he dance?"

Tim shuddered as he pulled into the police station and killed the engine. *Lonnie's the most reasonable man I know. He'll have the answer if nobody does.* The thought comforted him as he went into the station with the flyer in hand.

The lights stunned him for a moment, causing black spots to swim in front of his field of vision. He waited until his eyesight cleared. He walked to the reception desk where a lovely young black woman was manning the switchboard.

"AHP, Tatum City or Sheriff's Department?" she asked.

"I need to see Lonnie. I mean the sheriff."

"In county resident?" she asked as she typed something into her computer.

"Yes. Please, ma'am. I need to see Lonnie real bad."

"He's out on a call this morning," she said. "Is this an emergency? I can refer you to another deputy."

"I don't know," Tim said as he plunked the plastic-encased flyer on her desk. "Suppose you tell me."

She jerked as if he'd just dumped a rattler on her desk. "Billy Wong is the only duty officer at his desk at the moment." She tapped a switch and called for the deputy. "You can file your complaint with him."

"I'd rather see Lonnie."

"I know, but go ahead and file your complaint with Billy and we'll get you in to see him as soon as he comes in."

"Thank you ma'am," Tim said, automatically touching the brim of his Stetson.

A door opened and a large uniformed Chinese man appeared. "Morning, Tim, what's up?" he asked.

Tim showed him the tract. Billy smiled. *Ah shit, he's got it too,* Tim realized a second too late. The dispatcher lowered her gaze. *And she knew it too,* he thought. *Damn, she coulda warned a fella.*

"Come on inside," Billy Wong said, smiling in a way that made him feel profoundly uncomfortable. "Let's parley."

-2-

Sunlight crept through the workshop's half opened door, creating a narrow rectangle of golden light on what he perceived was a concrete floor. Brody sighed with contentment. His nocturnal labor complete, he stepped away and surveyed his work.

Two hundred and ninety six tiny crosses rested in six cardboard boxes. Two hundred and ninety six crosses for the unborn. *And it's only the beginning.* He smiled. *I'm one of the faithful Twelve. How do I know? Because an angel came by and told me so.*

He smiled at his children. His precious babies. They looked very pale, almost transparent, but that didn't matter. They were here with him and the bitch that killed them had fled for parts unknown. *The Whore,* he thought. *That's what the angel in the purple tux called her. She's the Whore of Babylon and she's fled into the wilderness. Well, she won't stay there for long. Those good anointed men Thomas sent will find her and she'll pay for what she's done, oh yes.*

"Daddy?" his eldest, whom he named Christina, asked.

"Yes, sweetheart?"

The child shifted on the wooden crate upon which she sat, her face pierced with shafts of sunlight. "What are you going to do with the crosses?"

"I'm going to plant them along the roadside," he replied.

"Why?"

He smiled at her, then at all of them. They smiled back. Tears stung his eyes. He wiped them away with the back of his hand and said, "I'm going to put them alongside the road so people will know that Jesus loves the little children, even the unborn."

"What if you put them at the First Light Church instead?" Christina asked.

"Yes," Brody agreed as if it were the most brilliant thought in the world. "Yes, of course. I'll put them there instead. What a wonderful idea."

"We love you Daddy," they said.

"I love you all too."

"What about Mommy? What are you going to do about her?"

"I loved her once, I know I did. I thought she was the most wonderful woman on earth. But now—"

"Are you going to kill Mommy?" Elijah, the littlest boy interrupted.

Brody cocked his head. He listened to the voice. Yes, it was vague and insubstantial at first. Now it was loud and imperious. Worse, it perched up front in his brain and constantly demanded his attention. It was, he determined after it buzzed in his head for hours while he worked, the voice of

God. "I'm not going to kill your mother. God's anointed will tend to it. The Lord has other plans for me." He giggled suddenly, unexpectedly. "Yep. Plans."

"Who are God's anointed, Daddy?" Christina asked.

"Men who heard the Word, men who are hunters and are able to take care of your mother and any other hedonist hell bent on stopping the Rapture." Brody hefted one of the boxes, placing it carefully into the back of the van. His lips pursed. "What am I going to do with you all though? I can't just leave you here. And the van isn't big enough, especially after I load it."

Christina stood. Her body became merely an outline as the streaming light flooded through her. "It's okay. We have to go anyway," she said. "And you need to rest before you labor in the vineyard today."

Brody sighed. "You're right. I think I'll take a little nap before heading out."

"There's no hurry," Christina said.

"Why do you all have to leave when there's plenty of room here?" Brody asked.

"The angels said we had to go back to Heaven during the day, but we can come back this evening."

"I'll be waiting," he said.

"We love you so much Daddy. You're the best daddy in the whole world."

-3-

"Well, what do you think?" Wong asked as he led Tim into the cramped office he shared with Lonnie.

"I don't know what to think," Tim said, cautiously treading through the minefield of conversation with the man. "Suppose you tell me."

"You know," Wong, said. "It's been wonderful, hasn't it? Revival is coming, and then we'll all go to Glory."

"What are you talking about?" Tim asked, feeling alarmed.

Billy Wong's eyes seemed to glaze over. "Why, don't you know?" he asked. "The world is coming to an end. It's the Rapture. Those who come to Revival will be saved. All others...well...we know what's going to happen to them. Eh?"

"Yeah," Tim drawled. "Do you know when Lonnie's coming back?"

"Should be any minute now. I saw you had our flyer. You liked them didn't you? The flyers?"

"They were fine," Tim said, wishing to be somewhere, anywhere other than in this room with Billy Wong. *The man's gone nuts*, he thought. *Just like Ouida and Cora-Lee. Stepford Christians. All.*

"Are you saved, Timmy?"

"Uh, yeah, I am," Tim stammered, not sure what the big man meant and not particularly wanting to. He started to rise. "I think I ought to wait outside for Lonnie."

"Why are you so all fired up to see Lonnie anyway?" Wong asked. "Sit down and stay a while. So you are going to Revival, ain't you? You've gotten the call. Right?"

"The call. Right. Yeah, sure," Tim agreed, watching the door. His mind moved at light speed. "It's just that Lonnie and I...We're best buds, you know? And I thought we could take some time off and go fishing this afternoon. We could, uh, even spread the good word while we're out."

"That's what I thought, fishing for men, right?"

Tim laughed. "Yeah, something like that."

Wong stared hard at him. "Have you been saved, Timmy? I mean really saved?"

"Why yes, as saved as well as I can be I suppose."

"And you are going to Revival this weekend?"

"I said I would."

"Well," Wong smiled. "I just want to make sure you're a believer, that's all."

"I believe," he said. "I do."

"That's fine, that's real fine, and I'm glad to hear that," Wong said. "Then you won't mind if I give you a little job to do."

"What kind of job?"

"Close the door."

Talk about Southern discomfort, he thought as he reached to close the door. *I don't want to be here with this crazy bastard, no sir.*

"What's going on?" Tim asked.

"Why nothing in the world," Billy Wong said with his usual cheer as he propped back in his seat. The front legs swung upwards as he balanced on the back two. "I have a little something for you to do from one brother in the Lord to another."

"What kind of job?"

"Oh, I'll get to that directly. Bend over for a minute and let me see your eyes."

Tim removed his glasses then leaned forward. Wong dropped the chair onto all fours, and leaned forward as well, almost touching his nose to Tim's. "Green, good," Wong said, relaxing back into his seat. "Not as green as I'd like to see, but good enough. That takes care of that, then."

"So, what do you want me to do?"

"I'd put out an APB on the bitch if I could, but she hasn't broken any laws. At least none of man's laws. Besides, there ain't enough of us on the force who are saved to go out and do it without it causing too much suspicion. I know you've been coon hunting most of your life, am I right?"

"I've got some coon hounds."

"Good. Can they hunt anything else other than coon?"

"I'm sure they can, given the right scent."

"Then I want you become one of the anointed. Since you're saved and all, you have a right to the anointing. And I'd like to give it to you rather than to some stranger."

"Anointing? That's the first I've heard of it."

Billy Wong cut him a sideways glance. "I want you to go out and find that Megan Wallace bitch. She's a threat to salvation. She's the Whore of Babylon and she wants to stop the Rapture."

"How can one woman stop the Rapture?" Tim laughed.

"How could one woman get all of humanity thrown out of Paradise? Besides, I told you, she's not just any woman. She's the Whore of Babylon. And she's going to stop Revival if she can."

"Why?" Tim asked. Wong was so ludicrous it was hard not to laugh in his face.

"Because she's evil that's why. She hates us because we're believers. She despises Jesus so much she's willing to destroy us to keep the Rapture from coming. And," he added for emphasis, "she's Catholic."

"I see," Tim said, noting the hypocrisy. Until last week Billy was also Catholic. "What do you want me to do?"

"Receive the anointing," he said, pulling a flyer out from his desk drawer. Tim shuddered.

"Problem?"

"Air conditioner vent is above me."

"Oh," Wong said, accepting the excuse. "Anyway, put your paw down on this and swear to God, Jesus and Thomas that you'll kill Megan Wallace, the Whore of Babylon."

Tim was too shocked to speak. *Kill a woman? I can't do that,* he thought. *I just can't. A man maybe if he's threatening my family. But some woman who's never meant me no harm? Besides,* his mind reeled. *Who the hell is Thomas and why should I swear any kind of oath toward him?*

"Well?" Billy Wong asked.

"Well what?"

"Put your hand on the paper and swear."

"I—uh—"

The office door swung open. Tim felt infinite relief as Lonnie strode in.

"Gentlemen," he said, not bothering to take off his Smokey Bear hat. "What's going on?"

"Nothing," Wong said as he casually slipped the tract into a desk drawer. "Tim just dropped by for a visit, that's all." He leaned forward and spoke into the antiquated intercom perched on his desk. "Sally, I need you to do some copying for me."

"Yes sir," replied the muffled voice.

"Yeah, I was wondering if you could take the rest of the day off, you know," Tim said, hoping his expression would fill in the gaps. "Go out to the lake with me, soak a few lures."

"Tim you know I—" Lonnie cast a wary glance at Wong, who was blatantly listening in. "I could use a break. Sure, why not?"

"Good," Tim said. "Meet me there?"

"I think I'll come along too," Wong said. "Hey, it's a slow day, enit? And the bass are running." He shot a glance at Tim. "Maybe even do another kind of fishing, eh?"

Tim and Lonnie stared at each other. "Someone's gotta stay

here and mind the store," Lonnie replied.

"Thank you Sally," Wong said as the secretary came into the cramped office. The officer handed her the tract. "Copy this for me and mail them off would you? I already emailed you the addresses."

Sally took the flyer. Her expression changed from near-death boredom to exultation. "I'll get on it right now," she exclaimed.

Lonnie and Tim watched as the girl sashayed out of the office. Then at each other. "Stepford Christian," Tim mouthed. Lonnie nodded.

"Well, you're not going to be gone all day, are you?" Wong was asking. "I mean, why not drive out and have lunch, then fish for a while then come back."

"Now, Billy that don't make sense at all. I'm not going fishing on my lunch hour. I go to fish, it's for the whole day," Lonnie stated.

A sudden, dazzling blast of light exploded from the room across the hall. The door burst open as smoke billowed out. Sally staggered out into the wide lobby, her hair singed and her pink sweater and skirt now a smoky brown. Behind her, the photocopier disintegrated into a melted black smoldering stump. As if to add insult to injury, the fire alarm went off with a resounding clatter.

"I went to make copies of your flyer, like you asked," she said. Her eyes were wide with fright and for a moment, she reminded Tim of a startled cat. "And it just—just—blew up."

Wong blinked. He looked around, confused as if he just stepped up to a podium and realized his pants were missing. "What just happened?" he asked.

-4-

Brody was surprised and pleased that he didn't have to break the front door down. Apparently, Megan left it open when she came out last evening. He frowned as he stepped inside. The house smelled odd, musky and somewhat dirty. It felt vacant, devoid of human occupation but also of human warmth as well. The lights, the sounds, the smells all seemed so artificial. Everything was so out of place. Overall, the house felt, well, haunted.

The phone rang, severing him from his reverie. Annoyed, he answered it.

"This is Bruce, are you coming in?" his supervisor asked.

"No, I'm not," Brody said, feeling drowsy now that his nocturnal labors had finished. "No, can't do it. I'm resigning my position."

"Are you one of the Twelve?" Bruce asked.

"Yes...Praise Jesus...I am."

"Then blessings upon you brother. So am I."

"Praise Jesus."

"How many have you convinced to come to Revival? I haven't had but a few takers," Bruce rambled. "Several on my staff flat out refused and I shit canned them on the spot. They said the church is Satanic or some such nonsense."

"There's so much sin in the world," Brody said.

"Yep, that's right enough." Bruce paused, considering. "You know, I ought to turn in my resignation too. There's no point in coming into work now that the world is coming to an end."

"Yeah," Brody laughed. "Ain't no point in it is there?"

"So are you going along with the anointed today? Do a little 'dear' hunting?"

"Dear hunting. That's funny."

"Heh, heh. I'm glad we can still share a chuckle between us," Bruce said.

"Nah, I'm going to let the big boys handle it," Brody said. A tiny fragment of himself screamed in the back of his mind. "But if she shows up here, I got a little surprise for her."

"Yeah, we don't need her messing things up."

"Yes," Brody concurred. "She's messed up way too much anyway."

"Women. God, you can't help but hate 'em."

"I hear you."

"Say," Bruce said, excitement filling his voice, "have you seen the angels lately?"

"Angels? Well, I—" Brody started.

"Oh my God yes," Bruce interrupted. "I saw two of them this morning on my way to work."

"You don't say," Brody said. He suppressed a laugh. *Seen*

them? he thought. *Hell, I've been talking to them, but you won't shut up long enough to tell you though will ya?*

"You live out by First Light, don't you?" Brody asked instead.

"Yeah, I'm just a couple of miles down the road from it," Bruce concurred. "Yep. The angels appeared about two days ago. Since then I've seen angels and haints and that old tree lit up like a beacon straight from Heaven."

"It must be wonderful, seeing angels and such," Brody said. "I've been spending lots of time with all my kids. The kids God returned to me, praise Jesus."

"Miracles are everywhere. Angels are walking the earth, the dead coming to life. It's like God's plan for the apocalypse is well under way. Won't the unbelievers be shit faced when Jesus appears in the heavens on Sunday?"

"Yeah," Brody said.

"Well, I ratchet jawed enough. You did say you'll be down for the revival, right?"

"I wouldn't miss it for the world," Brody replied.

"I'll see you then."

"May you have a wonderful day in the Lord," Brody replied. He hung up and sat on the pit group. *Christina's right,* Brody told himself. *I am tired. Just a little nap is all I need. And then I can go and labor in the Lord's vineyard for a while longer today.*

Half asleep, his lids drooping, he could see the angel wearing a purple tux through his eyelashes. The being appeared in front of the television set with his arms outstretched, his expression glorious. His orange running shoes, Brody noticed, were unlaced.

"Rest," the angel said. "And when you awake, come to the church. The Lord has a special task just for you."

"Yes," Brody replied joyously. "I'm up for any job you have for me."

-5-

The phone rang, jarring Brody awake. "Megan, would you get that?" he mumbled.

No, Megan isn't home to answer the phone, the voice inside his head stated. *She's gone.* A soft, insane giggle erupted from his lips. *She left you and your babies all alone. Now what kind of mother would do such a thing?*

The phone rang again. Brody picked up the receiver. "Yes?"

"Hi, Mr. Wallace," said the perky voice at the other end of the line. It was one of Megan's sluts. Mary, perhaps, he thought. Or maybe it was Karen. He didn't know and really didn't care. All the exercise girls were alike. Enthusiastic in a cheerleader sort of way, had great bodies and were dumber than a sack full of door knobs. Brody smiled as the girl chattered insipidly in his ear.

"Karen here," the voice continued, confirming his suspicions.

"Good morning, Karen, what's going on?"

"Well, I need to talk to Megan."

"She's out on an errand," he lied. His throat began to itch. "Can I leave a message?"

The girl laughed. "No, but you can take one if you want."

"Sorry, I just woke up," he said, wishing with all his heart he could choke the life out of her. "Yes, I'll be happy to take your message."

"Tell her that I waited for her to open this morning and she hasn't shown. I'm getting worried."

"Don't be, she's fine. Tell ya what, just take the day off, and don't bother opening at all today." He laughed. "In fact, you don't ever have to open it again."

"But, Mr. Wallace, please don't fire me. I'd open if I had the key."

"Not firing you, dear heart. I'm closing the studio down. It's actually mine. It's in my name and I have final say. So don't worry about it. Take the day off. Hell, go ahead and take eternity off if you want. It doesn't matter any more."

"Okay," she said, sounding doubtful and a little frightened. "If that's what you want."

"Go have some fun, and have a good day in the Lord."

"Well, yeah, okay," she said, sounding uncomfortable. "Same to you then."

Satisfied by the befuddled click, he hung up and laughed aloud. *Poor sweet Megan,* he thought. *People might worry for a bit about her absence, but the Lord has it all covered.* He imagined talking to the local hick sheriff about his sudden and shocking loss.

"My poor baby," he said aloud. "She was pretty but stupider than shit. She wandered out into the woods to hike or was out fucking one of the Gypsy boys and ran afoul of a few men out hunting razorbacks. Tragic yes, but God has plans. Yes, he has plans..."

Chapter Twenty-Three

-1-

"It's falling apart," Thomas cried. He paced his office like a caged cougar. "We're losing the faithful. How many have already fallen by the wayside? What are we going to do without them?"

"Just calm down," Pa Neidi said. He sat in a spare chair beside the desk while an angel, this time a young female wearing a powder blue Armani suit and smoking Cuban cigars, stood in the corner. She smiled and winked at him, then blew blue smoke in his direction.

"We'll pick up a few stragglers at the revival, that'll make up the slack. Besides, you haven't been in town lately. The flyers are causing up quite a stir. We'll have a good sized crowd by tomorrow, you wait."

"The Lord only promised twelve faithful. What about the rest who are coming?"

"Christ had twelve faithful. His apostles, remember? And he drew crowds wherever he went. And that's how it should be. You didn't think you could run a kingdom by yourself, did you? Nah, you need advisors and counsel. The Twelve will become your personal attendants when the Lord comes. Everyone else will become your subjects."

"And then we'll have our kingdom on Earth," Thomas said, feeling much calmer now. His brow furrowed. "What about the Whore? She's still running loose. She can undo everything we've worked for. And I won't let her take Rachael and Becky away from me again, I won't."

"You're getting all riled up again, Brother." Neidi said. "Your wife and daughter are only a small portion of the Glory that you will receive in the end. And the Whore, well, she's one woman alone in the wilderness. Even her husband has forsaken her. And keep in mind, he's the most faithful of your twelve. A regular Saint Peter, he is. And the anointed have their sites on that damned Mexican gal. Nah," he spat. "She ain't much of a threat at all."

The angel smiled, a wide-toothed Cheshire cat grin, and then pointed her cigar toward the window.

"And speaking of the devil," Pa said as the rumble of Brody Wallace's AeroStar clamored up the dirt road. "Here comes Saint Peter now."

"Him?" Thomas asked as he watched the balding middle age man unload a boxful of poorly made crosses composed of termite-ridden wood and place them onto the ground next to the van.

"Yep," Neidi concurred. The angel laughed and pulled deeply on her cigar, the cherry glowing cheerfully as she blew smoke through her nose and around her lips.

"You can't be serious," Thomas said. "He ain't nothing but a raggedy little man. What can he possibly do for us?"

"More than you will ever know," Neidi said with a wicked gleam in his eye. "Oh yes, you'd be surprised at what he's capable of doing."

"I don't like it. He's the Whore's husband. What's keeping him from getting all warm and fuzzy about their relationship and him betraying me? What's keeping him from becoming my own Judas?"

The angel sneered around her stogy and shrugged.

"He has issues," Neidi said. Pa pointed at the little broken-slat crosses Brody Wallace removed from the boxes. He was talking to someone. Thomas could tell by the way the man was gesturing between boxes.

"I don't trust him."

"You will once you come to know him. He's a good man, someone you will come to trust as closely as your own good right arm."

"Well..." Thomas said.

"And of course it's just the beginning," Neidi said. "More will come too. There'll be many more before sundown. Once people who were afeared to come down here are now rushing to the bayou in droves. Before you know it, you'll have a full house and the answer to your prayers."

-2-

Tim, Lonnie and Billy sat at a cement picnic table and fumbled with the remains of their lunch. The lake, a brilliant June blue, sparkled between the gaps of loblolly pines. A white speedboat blared by, slicing the water into white ribbons. Flocks of seagulls, blown ashore during the last hurricane and adapted to lakeside life, picked mussels from the gently lapping shoreline. Other gulls spiraled above a rusted out dumpster filled with trash and beer bottles.

Someone had written in large orange spray-painted scrawl, "Jesus Saves," across the front. *It's getting worse*, Tim thought, and judging by Billy Wong's downcast look, it wasn't over yet. Not by a long road.

"Damn, what I wouldn't give to be out there right now," Lonnie said, his tone wistful as he watched the speedboat gash the water.

"Maybe next time," Tim said. "Right now, I want to know what the hell is going on."

"Well," Lonnie said around a mouthful of taco, "your poster ain't the only one to turn up at the cop shop. I've got two more. Sent them up to the lab in Little Rock and the results came back this morning."

"What are they laced with?" Tim asked.

"Nothing."

"There's got to be something on them, Lonnie. They're driving people nuts." He shifted on the concrete bench, trying to get blood circulating to his butt. "Not to mention what they do to electronics."

"Tell me about it," Billy said. He hadn't touched his lunch. He looked pale and shaken, as if he had been on a bender and woke up in the wrong apartment...naked.

"Do you remember anything at all?" Lonnie asked.

"No, not really. I remember feeling like my head was stuffed with steel wool. I remember that distinctly enough."

"It does sound like some mind altering substance, doesn't

it?" Lonnie asked. "But the flyers are just stencils and ink. Nothing unusual to them. There's no residue of any kind. No toxic chemicals, drugs or off the wall hallucinogenic substances."

"What about the lab people who handled them?" Tim asked.

"All evidence is handled with latex gloves. They never actually touched them."

"Oh," Billy muttered.

"Just don't stick one in a copier," Tim said, as the vision of the once-blond but smoldering secretary staggering out of the office like a character in a Benny Hill skit crossed his mind. The three laughed.

"I wish I could remember more," Billy said, his expression glum. "We're all in trouble. I know that."

"You mentioned a woman to me while we were in the office this morning," Tim said. "A woman named Wallace? Her first name was Maggie? Mary? Hell, I can't remember."

Billy groaned and rested his head against the cement table. "I don't remember either."

"Wallace?" Lonnie asked. "Don't recognize the name."

"Me either. Newcomers?"

"Could be. I'll run a check. Shouldn't take too long. Small towns, everyone knows everybody else. Are you sure you can't remember that first name, Billy?"

"No, sorry."

Lonnie frowned. "Things started getting squirrelly as soon as that new preacher showed up. Since then, I've had some of the weirdest calls to go out on. Remember the Miller place? It burned down not too long ago."

"Yeah, that was a tragedy," Tim said.

"There was some serious shit going on down there. And it ain't stopped after the house burned either. Folks down on the bayou are seeing all sorts of crazy shit."

"Such as?" Tim asked.

"Ghosts, haints, walking dead. Angels."

"You can't be serious," Tim said. Billy groaned.

"Dead serious."

"What else?" Tim asked.

"Well, Charlie's death for starters. I know that old trash truck wasn't safe, but what are the odds of being crushed to death in one of those things, really?"

"He was drunk, though, Lon," Billy said. "Toxicology proved that."

"Okay," Lonnie acquiesced. "That one can be explained away, but what about A.J.?"

"He went fishing, fell in and drowned."

"Sounds reasonable," Tim said.

"A. J.'s death occurring not two miles from Charlie's accident."

"Could be a coincidence," Billy said.

"And buffalo could soar out of my ass," Lonnie said, annoyed. "This is all connected, I know it. Take the Miller place for instance. It's five miles from First Light Church and it burned down under very strange circumstances."

"I thought the propane tank went up," Tim said.

"That's the official story, yes, but there's more to it than that."

"Such as?" Tim asked, very interested.

"Such as the fact that Rita-Mae and Otis both reported some serious weirdness there after the house burned down. Both of them are in their seventies. They're stable, reliable, sensible people. They're not given into making up stories and especially not stories like the ones they told."

"What kind of stories?" Tim asked.

"Stories I didn't put down in my report, for one," Lonnie said. He leaned forward. "Like Rita telling me that she saw blood coming out of the bathroom. Said it flowed all the way into the living room. She showed me a locket she found inside her casserole and she claims that it doesn't belong to her. I had it taken to an antique dealer; the damned thing is one hundred and fifty years old."

"And don't forget the hands," Billy whispered. "That was the creepy part."

"Ah, yeah," Lonnie said. "She was screaming about hands coming out of the walls and floor. And you know the really scary part?" He leaned closer, whispering like a twelve year old about to tell a campfire horror story. "The really scary part is that when the ER staff examined her, she had deep scratch marks and bruises on her ankles. Like someone had grabbed her around the legs."

"Jesus Christ in a hoop skirt," Tim swore. "No shit?"

"No shit. I saw the pictures. Also Otis said he saw something in his field that night just before the house came down, but he didn't say what. You know how he is."

"Crazy tight-lipped Indian," Billy said. "I hear they moved up to Mena as soon as Rita-Mae was able to travel."

"They did," Lonnie said. "I heard they piled up what little belongings they had left and just moved. Both his boys quit their jobs and went up too."

"And they're not the only ones either," Tim said. He caught a glimpse of two men walking along the shoreline, both of them wearing suits and carrying something tucked under their arms. He jerked his head toward them. Lonnie nodded. Billy swore under his breath. "I know that five families in my neighborhood have left. No explanation for it either. Just folks who've lived in this area all their lives had an intense desire to be elsewhere," Billy said.

"This is scaring the living dog shit out of me," Lonnie replied. "Give me a still or a meth lab to bust up. Or someone knocking over a convenience store. Those things are solid and real. But this X-files stuff drives me up the wall."

"I know that's right," Billy agreed.

"How do you arrest the supernatural?" Lonnie asked. "And that preacher, things are going on around him but I don't have anything to run him in on."

"Even though Charlie was found dead in his trash truck, the Miller Place burns down, then A.J. disappears only to be found drowned in the bayou not far from the church," Tim said.

"All accidents," Billy Wong replied.

"That's how the DA will see it," Lonnie said.

The two men who were walking along the thin ribbon of beach left the lake. Now they climbed the tree-lined ridge and were heading toward them.

"Lonnie," Tim said.

"I see them," Lonnie replied.

"Freaking body snatchers," Billy muttered.

"Listen, y'all," Lonnie said. "I haven't told you the really weird shit yet."

"What kind of weird shit?"

"More weirdness that I don't dare put down on the daily reports, for starters. Not unless I want a stint in the Benton Mental Hospital. Like folks seeing slaves walking around. Out at the old Lavon's place there's a well that screams night and day and won't stop. It screams like a woman with her cunt hairs ablaze and nobody knows what's causing it. And that tree is glowing brighter each night. Have you noticed? You can almost see it from town now. Wolves are moving around in the daylight, even though they're considered extinct in this area. And the Gypsies have left. They've been camped down there since my granddad was a pup, and now they're all gone."

"Nothing's making sense," Tim said.

"It makes sense, a weird, X-file kind of sense. But that was just a television show. There ain't no such thing as ghosts, spooks, haints or goddamned Fouke Monster. There's got to be a logical explanation for what's going on."

"Company," Billy said, jerking his head toward the two approaching men. Lonnie nodded slightly.

"And folk's ain't acting normal, you know?" Billy said.

"Yeah, we know," Tim replied. "You scared the hell out of me this morning."

"Scared the hell out of myself," Billy muttered.

"Keep your yap shut, Timmy, while we deal with these two stooges," Lonnie muttered.

"You won't get any argument out of me," Tim replied as he watched the two men approach.

"Afternoon, officers," said a chubby blond-haired man with a copy of the Bible under his arm. His partner, wearing a similar outfit, smiled down at them.

"Can I help you?" Lonnie asked, sounding official and somewhat annoyed.

"We just wanted to drop by and tell you to have a wonderful day in the Lord," the youth said.

"And we wanted to give you this," his companion said, continuing to smile as he removed three of Thomas's tracts out of his Bible and offered them to the men.

Billy flinched. "Get that damned thing away from me."

"We just wanted to let you know about the revival at First Light Church of Prophecy. It starts tonight and runs to Sunday. Now's the time to be saved if you're not."

"Yeah," the other man said, casting a wicked glance toward his partner. "The Rapture is sooner than you think."

"I'll tell you what," Lonnie said, aggravated. "You take your trash and get on out of here before I ticket you for soliciting."

"Trash?" the white man said, offended. "Sir, the Lord's Word is hardly trash."

"Didn't you hear what I said to you, boy? Get on down the road before I run you in."

"You'll regret it," his partner replied. "You'll be on the wrong side of judgment when the end comes this weekend."

"What are you talking about?" Lonnie snapped.

The two young men looked at each other. "What I mean to say is that we're concerned for your well being and we want you to know Jesus as your personal savior."

"You never mind about my relationship with God," Lonnie said. "What do you mean that the world is coming to an end this weekend?"

"Well," the white man said, smiling, but obviously nervous. "What my brother in the Lord meant to say was that if the world were coming to an end tomorrow, would you be on the right side of judgment?"

Lonnie glared at him with a suspicious eye. "Yeah, right," he said. "Now I told you both to git. This is your last warning."

The two men nodded. "Y'all have a blessed day in the Lord, then," the leader said. They turned in unison and continued their journey around the rim of the lake.

"Shag ass," Billy said. "Was I like that?"

"Worse," Tim replied. "You nearly made me shit myself."

"Those boys are good enough reason for me to know something bad is going down at that church," Lonnie said.

"You don't suppose that preacher down there has turned into a kind of Jim Jones, do you?" Tim asked, alarmed.

"The world is coming to an end this weekend," Lonnie mused. "That makes me think that these folks are tired of waiting for the Rapture and are going to make it come themselves."

"How can they do that by being down in that isolated little church?"

"I sincerely doubt that they can cause any real damage to the outside world," Lonnie mused. "But they can do plenty of hurt to themselves. Just like that Heaven's Gate cult did a few years back."

"You don't suppose—" Tim said, horrified.

"I don't know what to think any more. They might just be well-intentioned kooks about to travel up to the Ozarks and stand on a mountaintop waiting for Jesus to come and get them. Or it can be more sinister than that. And we don't have any evidence these folks are a danger to us or to themselves."

"So what can we do?" Tim asked.

"Keep a watchful eye out," Billy replied. "Watch and report back to us, and just to us. If you see anything—more out of the ordinary than it is already—you know what I mean?"

"We all need to act as normal as possible for the most part. And don't discuss this with anyone on the force either, Billy. We don't know how many officers are under this church's influence, so let's keep this little party to ourselves."

"You don't have to worry about me. I ain't saying nothing to nobody."

"And what else?" Tim asked.

"I'm going to keep an eye on that church for one thing. And then, come Sunday, Billy and I will go to that revival and see what happens."

"I'll come too," Tim said.

"No, you don't either. This is police business."

"I'm already hip deep in this," Tim said, thinking back to Ouida and the kids' odd behavior. "Let me help."

"You can help best by keeping track of what's going on and reporting back to me," Lonnie said.

"I'll see if I can find out about that Wallace woman," Billy said. "See how she fits into all of this."

"Right," Lonnie said. "We all know what to do. I suggest we meet back here the same time tomorrow but keep everything we've talked about under your hats."

"Not a problem," Tim said. He touched the brim of his Stetson. "I wear a big hat."

-3-

Megan didn't leave the secluded confines of the abandoned camp despite the rising heat and humidity. Two men in hunter's orange walked past earlier in the day. Fearful, she retreated into the back room of the trailer and hid there until they left. After what happened with Brody, she wasn't taking any chances.

The sun passed the zenith mark and the air inside the aged mobile home became musty, stale and hot. The paneling began oozing its own particular brand of sweat. She was hungry too. She rummaged through the cabinets and managed to find a few abandoned canned goods left behind when the original occupants moved on. She found a small but old can opener. She opened a can of black-eyed peas and munched on them cold. They were lukewarm, slimy and slid in thick chunks down her throat. But as Brody used to say—before he lost his mind—it'd push a turd.

Her belly stopped crawling and complaining. And at the moment, that was all that mattered. She washed them down with water from the sink which she drank from a discarded jelly jar.

She lay on the couch and chanted her rosary. She was drowsy and headachy from the heat but too afraid to go outside. Not until dark anyway. She had almost drifted off to sleep when she heard a car door slam. Alarmed, she crept to the window.

The hunters were back. They arrived in a black truck. Both carried powerful-looking rifles with scopes. Her breath caught as she watched them move to opposite sides of the encampment, each of them taking a trailer to search.

They're looking for me, she realized. *Oh sweet Mary, what am I going to do?*

Frantically she searched the living room. *There's obviously no place to hide here,* she thought, *and I can't get out because they'll see me.* Her heart pounded as she heard footsteps approaching the trailer. Ducking so she wouldn't be seen from either window, she moved swiftly down the hallway until she came to the first door. It was a small bedroom with a closet, but too obvious to hide in. She looked out other window and saw the men both approaching the trailer now. One of them motioned for the other and he moved toward the back of the elderly mobile home. Megan slid down the hallway, listening, but startled anyway when she heard heavy boots stomp up the back steps.

Megan yanked open the bathroom door. She slid into the cabinet under the sink, pulling the door closed behind her. Her cheek rested against a rusted pipe and the cramped enclosure smelled faintly of Lifebuoy and rat shit. Her heart pounded in her ears. She bit her lip when she heard the back door crash open.

Despite the grinding discomfort of a leg cramp, Megan remained where she was as they ransacked the trailer. *They're going through the living room and the kitchen now,* she thought as she heard cabinet doors opening and closing. *What am I going to do when they get here?* She could hear their muffled voices, soft oaths coupled with deep Southern male voices. Her heart beat a cadence to their chant.

Something smashed to the floor. Something loud and made of glass.

The jelly jar and opened can of peas, she thought. Her mind raced. *I left them on the cabinet top. They'll see them. They'll know I'm here.*

"Looks like the jungle rats bailed," one of them said.

"Yeah and good riddance, praise God."

"Any sign of the Whore?"

"Not from any of the other trailers. Haven't checked the back yet."

"If she's here, bring her here. Don't hurt her. We're supposed to take her to the preacher so she can meet Jesus."

Pause.

"Well, go on down and check the rest of the rooms."

"Won't leave any stone unturned," his partner replied. His heavy boots made the floor underneath her vibrate. "Uh, since she's a whore, can we?"

"No," the other voice said. "Just find her so we can take her to the preacher."

"You ain't no fun at all, boss. No fun at all."

"Just cut the shit and go find her."

She could hear him moving down the hall now. Tiny beads of sweat broke out on her brow, stinging and blurring her eyes. It ran down to the tip of her nose and dripped onto the floor.

The heavy boots stopped moving. She heard the bathroom door open. *Hail Mary, Full of Grace, the Lord is with you,* she prayed silently. She scooted deeper into the cabinet.

As she moved aside, Megan saw a hole in the floor. It was the size of her fist, maybe a little larger. It was certainly not big enough for her to climb through. Her eyes widened when she saw movement in the hole. At the same time the hunter strode into the bathroom.

"Here kitty, kitty," he said as he moved around the room.

Megan bit down hard on her tongue. Her eyes were riveted to the hole. She sat, stunned as she watched a small, sharp muzzle investigate the edges of the hole. Megan caught her breath. A rat-sized skunk squeezed through the opening in the floor. It shook its greasy fur, clamored up her leg and began scratching at the cabinet door.

Too horrified to move, she remained squeezed against the back of the vanity. The rusted sink bowl shoved against her neck and side of her head while the skunk climbed off her knee. It explored the thin rubber sole of her shoe then began nibbling on the fabric. Megan remained still even though her heart pounded at the thought of contracting rabies if the animal's teeth should connect with the tender flesh just underneath the sole. She squeezed her eyes shut. *Oh God,* she prayed. *That man's right next to the cabinet door.*

She heard boots tromp up to what she guessed might be the toilet. She heard the sound of fabric scraping against the door. Sweat dripped off Megan's upper lip. Megan stifled a scream as its claws pricked her skin.

Outside, Megan heard the distinct sound of a zipper followed by a rustle of cloth. The skunk heard it too and scrambled around her leg. Megan struggled not to move as the creature squirmed around her thigh to position itself next to the door.

The hunter grunted and grumbled to himself. He sighed as he took a loud, obnoxious piss. The smell was unbearable. Megan heard his pants go back up. She heard as well as felt water pouring into the sink. The skunk shuffled against the cabinet door, making it clatter.

The door flung open as it was ripped from the hinges. The hunter jabbed the gun barrel into the opening. The skunk promptly lifted its tail and retaliated.

The thick, pungent stench exploded into the bathroom. The hunter screamed. Megan's eyes watered and she stifled a gag while the skunk shimmied down the drainpipe and back outside. The hunter swore profusely as he staggered out of the bathroom, coughing and retching as the stench permeated the room.

"Good Lord, what did you get into?" his companion roared as the reek followed the man out of the hallway and into the living room.

"Come on, let's get out of here."

"But we haven't—"

"Forget it," he said. "Ain't nobody going to stay in there after that skunk got flushed out."

"Oh Lord, *that smell.*"

"Come on," his companion said through various gagging noises, "let's git."

Stifling a gag, she covered her mouth and nose with the top of her shirt and stumbled out of the cabinet. She rushed into the back bedroom. She hid underneath the open window, desperate to catch even a small portion of fresh air while the truck cranked and the men drove away.

As soon as the truck was out of sight, Megan bent double and threw up.

-5-

Tim left his friends at the police station. He picked up Ouida's rumpled flyer from the cop shop and took it across the street to Insty Prints where he spread the paper on the copier's glass surface. Again he felt the strange warmth seeping into his palms. "Forget it," he grumbled as he spread it over the lens. "I ain't buying it." He closed the lid and for a moment he was certain the paper was trying to squirm away. He forced the lid down onto it with the palm of his right hand and fed the machine fifty cents with his left hand. As soon as the scan began, he walked away.

Tim grinned to himself as he left the print shop. The copier blew apart as he crossed the street.

"Hey, you," the manager shouted from the doorway. "You fucked up my machine. What the hell did you put in it?"

-6-

"Mama, why are you going hunting in your nightgown?" Sammy asked, perplexed.

Ouida blinked at her daughter as if startled out of a dream. "I'm not going hunting, dear. Why do you ask that?"

"Because of that," Sammy said, pointing to her mother's lap.

Ouida looked down and saw the shotgun resting across her lap. She stared down at it, confused. *I was at Mama's*, she recalled. *She had a bad spell.* Dazed, she looked up at her daughter. *How did I get here? I don't remember coming home at all. And where's Tim?*

"What's wrong?" Sammy asked.

"I-I thought I heard something last night and I sat up."

"What was it?"

"Just an armadillo."

"Oh," Sammy said. Her brow wrinkled. "But it's daylight now."

Startled, Ouida looked at the large gold faced clock on the wall. It was past noon. "What have the three of you been doing?"

"Watching Cartoon Network on the TV in the den," Sammy said. "I made us popcorn for breakfast."

"Oh I see," Ouida said, feeling befuddled.

"Where's Daddy?" Sammy asked. Her brow furrowed again. "We're hungry."

"He had to go to work early," Ouida said, frustrated that she had to lie but at the same time didn't want her child to know that she had no clue where he was nor what she was doing with the gun. "I'll go put this away," Ouida said. She hefted the rifle and put it back into the closet. "Sammy, are your brothers dressed?" Ouida asked as she closed the closet door.

"Yes."

"Good. Now how about we all go to Burger Bonanza for lunch and visit Nana afterwards."

The child's face lit up. "Yes." She ran up the hallway. She stopped about ten feet from the den and asked, "Is Nana going to be okay?"

Ouida tried on her very best smile. "I'm sure she'll be just fine. Now go get your brothers and let's get lunch, okay?"

Chapter Twenty-Four

-1-

"They're coming early," Thomas observed as six more cars pulled into the parking lot. He stood by the blinds and watched as his new parishioners milled around the churchyard, greeting each other like long lost relatives.

Thomas blinked. An unsettled feeling swept through him as if he had inadvertently stepped onto someone's grave. He looked at the angel still standing in the corner smoking. But she didn't look the same as she did a few moments ago. Her beautiful face distorted as if she was wearing a mask that slipped askew and he could glimpse for an instant what lay beyond the facade.

"Is something wrong?" Pa asked.

The entity in his head tightened, creating an intense woolen itch. "Nothing's wrong, Pa," he said.

"Getting cold feet?"

Thomas chuckled as the thing inside his head relaxed. "Maybe a little."

"Well, everyone's a little scared, I guess," Pa said. "After all, the world is coming to an end here pretty quick. Even though you know you've earned your rightful reward, the whole idea is gonna take some getting used to."

"I guess," Thomas said, still feeling uneasy even though his mind was blissfully socked in. He looked out the window. "Two more cars have arrived," he observed.

"I know," Pa said. "The town is nearly vacant. The Lord has already started winnowing the chaff."

"I don't understand," Thomas said.

"Those who have heard the call is coming down here.

Everyone else...is taking off...as if they can escape God's judgment. It's a hoot."

"I feel sorry for them," Thomas said, and meant it. "Those poor souls. I should have done more to reach them all. There just wasn't enough time."

"You can't reach the unwilling," Pa commented.

"I suppose," Thomas said. He leaned his head against the cool glass and watched as Brody Wallace knelt in the cemetery. He ignored the new arrivals. Instead he focused solely on planting rickety little crosses alongside the tombstones.

"He's following his own call from the Lord," Pa told Thomas. "It's best to leave him be for now."

The angel leaned against the wall and puffed away at her cigar. She leered and jerked her head toward the window.

"What am I going to say to them?" Thomas wondered aloud as four more cars pulled up.

"Welcome them," Pa replied. "They're here to see you, to be near you. They ain't interested in a bunch of fancy talk. Let them know how happy you are that they took time out of their lives to join us."

"Time." Thomas laughed. "There isn't any time left, is there?"

"Nope," Neidi said.

The angel laughed.

-2-

Tatum was abandoned within twenty-four hours. Those who hadn't received the call fled from those who had. Many left the area, traveling as far away as Shreveport or Longview. There was no panic, no frantic loading of vehicles. Nor were there any traffic jams on the way out of town. People seemed to seep out of the area, especially during the night. The tree, dazzling now, cast its malevolent glow across the swamps and lower places. It shined so brightly that it could be seen in downtown Tatum.

Lonnie wished with all his heart he could go with them. He sent his wife Amy and three boys to Shreveport to visit his sister. Lonnie promised he'd get there as soon as he could. Ironically, the same instinct that goaded him into leaving was also forcing him to stay.

I've still got my job, he told himself. He told that to Billy and to Tim as well. He did try to get Tim and Ouida to cut out and leave, but Tim wouldn't hear of it. Neither did Billy. As far as Billy was concerned, he had a score to settle.

Lonnie peered out the small thin office window and watched the substantially reduced flow of traffic coming and going from various cubicles in the larger area outside his office door. On the surface, everything seemed normal. But an uncomfortable undertow of interoffice weirdness put him on edge. *There is just too damned much sweetness and light,* he thought. *I don't mind seeing folks smile when they work, but damn.*

He continued to watch his co-workers pass by his office and felt himself actually shudder. *I feel like I just fell into that gaudy glitter dome of a studio on TBN. Any second now, that pink-haired chick with mascara streaming down her face is going to burst into my office demanding I have a "great day in the Lord".*

Billy Wong opened the door and stepped into the narrow office. He looked as if he'd just thrown up. Lonnie didn't ask whether he did or not, but suspected it was a close call either way.

"Lock the door, Billy," Lonnie said quietly. Billy complied.

"Have you been out in that yet?" Billy asked as he took his seat.

"No, but I've been getting some extremely creepy emails," Lonnie said. He leaned forward. "I sent Amy and the kids to Shreveport. They're staying at Mia Ellen's till this blows over."

Billy nodded. "Good idea. Do you know if they made it into Shreveport yet?"

"She called my cell phone an hour ago. I told her not to use any of the sheriff office numbers or any other land lines for now. Can't be too careful these days. But yeah, she made it down there okay. She ain't particularly happy about the bum's rush I gave her, but she'll get over it."

Billy nodded. "I finished up my patrol half an hour ago. I parked the car about two blocks away. No reason. Just felt like the thing to do. I'm half afraid our brothers in blue might decide to do something to it if I left it parked here."

"I wouldn't be surprised. Nobody seems to be making any

moves on the 'normals' that remained. At least," he added for emphasis, "not yet."

"Yeah, I thought for sure they'd set up road blocks to keep folks from getting out, but so far they're letting everyone pass."

"So what does it look like out there?"

"Abandoned. Most all of the stores are closed. The neighborhoods look like little ghost towns. All the farms are empty too. A few folks are staying. You and I, Tim and Ouida are the ones I know of. Ouida ain't leaving on account of her mom being in the hospital, and Tim won't leave Ouida so they're going to try and wait it out. He told me this morning he was going to put the kids on a bus to Dallas to stay with his folks, but last I heard he hadn't done that yet. Otherwise, it's been real quiet."

"It's too quiet," Lonnie concurred. He glanced out the window. "Look at them out there," he said, indicating the spacious lobby outside the office. "Doesn't that beat all? They're wandering around with fucked up expressions on their faces and not doing any real kind of work. I overheard the dispatcher taking calls this morning. Talk about freaking weird. The Triple A convenience store out on Deer Creek Road was robbed. You know what that silly skank of a dispatcher asked the clerk? Instead of sending out a car, she asked the clerk if she knew Jesus."

"What did you do?" Wong asked.

"I sent her ass to the house. Can't fire her; it's not her fault. She's under the influence of that church."

"I understand that but we can't do without a dispatch," Billy complained.

"Emily has taken over. She's not a happy camper, but she's doing it." Lonnie grunted. "She'll get over it. She's the only other one with dispatcher experience in the building that's not...influenced."

"I'm glad. We've got a number of officers abandoning their posts and going to that church. It's like the village of the freaking Damned or something." Billy replied.

"More like the *Invasion of the Body Snatchers* to me," Lonnie said. "And you were snatched too, remember?"

"I don't, and that's probably a blessing at this point."

"What exactly do you remember?" Lonnie asked. He leaned

forward, staring into the thin brown eyes of his partner and friend. "I know you, partner. You've spent some time mulling it over. You must have remembered something. No matter how small, any piece of information at this point will help."

"Well," Billy said as he contemplated the question. "It all started Saturday for sure. The wife brought home one of them creepy tracts and handed one to me. Then everything just kind of, I don't know, fogged out."

"Fogged?"

"Yeah. It was like trying to feel your way through a fog bank. My thinking got real slow and I felt—I don't know—funny. Like my mind was being smothered by something."

"How about Alison? Is she still under the influence?"

"No. Her mind cleared up like mine did after Sally stuck my tract into the copier. But Ally's scared shitless. She demanded I send her back to Hong Kong. I put her on a plane last night. Then I spent the night driving around. Didn't know what else to do."

"Have you heard anything about any of the surrounding communities? Fouke? Geneva? Texarkana? Overton?"

"No, the 'influence' seems to have a limited range."

"And the flyers don't like copiers." Lonnie grinned.

"Yeah, lucky for me, huh?"

"Any luck finding the Wallace woman?" Lonnie asked.

"Yeah. Her first name is Megan and her husband's name is Brody. They live out past Deer Creek Road. Went by there this morning but the house is empty. I figure they've been, uh, yeah."

"Think they're already down to the church?" Lonnie asked.

"I'm sure they are," Wong replied.

Lonnie considered. "From what I understand from those fools we met at the lake, the world is supposed to come to an end tomorrow. I have a feeling though, that before that happens, tonight is going to get plenty interesting down on the bottoms."

"Think they'll start that revival up early?"

"Wanna take a ride out there with me and find out?"

"Well, hell, yeah," Billy said. "Somebody's gotta pay for that brain fucking I got."

-3-

Brody ignored the newcomers' arrivals and focused upon the task at hand. The little crosses were a miracle. Each one he planted took root and began to grow. As soon as they reached a certain height, they emitted an intense glow. Nobody else seemed to notice, but it didn't matter. As far as he was concerned the miracle was a reward for him alone. He sang as he removed another bundle of crosses and began planting them between a set of dilapidated tombstones.

He was so busy at his task he lost track of time. The sun slid down behind the pines and the grounds cooled. He heard vehicles arriving, car doors opening and closing, happy voices, both human and ethereal swirling around him. In the distance, an old Negro choir sang a soulful tune.

He was untouched by all of it. He was so intent upon his work that he nearly bumped into the angel's legs. Brody knelt before the being who smiled benevolently down upon him. The creature was dressed smartly in an Armani suit, his white hair gelled, his eyes so blue they looked white.

"You haven't forgotten about what we talked about, have you?"

"No," Brody said, awed. "No, I haven't forgotten. I know exactly what to do."

"Good," the angel in the Armani said. He squinted up at the sky. "The sun'll set soon. You need to quit fooling with these silly crosses and get on with the business at hand."

"Oh, I will, I will. I promise." He bit his lower lip. "But I said I'd finish this for Jesus and the babies first."

"And Jesus has blessed what you're doing, but it doesn't matter any more. The apocalypse is in a few hours. Do you know what an apocalypse is?"

"Yes," Brody said.

"Good. So this foolishness," he spread his arms out indicating all the small crosses planted in lopsided rows between crumbling tombstones, "is a waste of time. You have a far greater task at hand, as the preacher's most favored apostle."

"I do?" Brody asked, his face slack, his eyes shining. Tears streamed down his face. "I'm to be the next Peter?"

"Not if you don't hurry," the angel replied. His voice was brisk and businesslike. "So get off your knees, dust off the graveyard dirt from your hands and get to the real work that needs tending."

"Okay," Brody whispered. "I'll go now."

The angel nodded. "See that you do."

-4-

"I can't stand him," Thomas said, referring to the man kneeling between a pair of broken moss eaten angels. Brody was carrying on an animated conversation with one of the crumbling statues. It was weird and it raised goose flesh across Thomas's forearms.

"He'll be your most loyal subject," Pa reiterated. "And after tonight, you'll never hate another human being again because you'll be filled with the spirit."

"But until then," Thomas said, "do I really have to talk to him?"

"Nah," Pa spat. "He's already got his instructions from the Almighty."

"That's a relief," Thomas stated.

Thomas walked out to the parking lot with Pa. The late afternoon sun sent shafts of white-gold light through the pines and cypress trees. He squinted. A large white truck labored up the drive. It maneuvered past cars and pickups and one maroon Harley Davidson Valkyrie. Other vehicles squatted alongside the drive and the grassy hillside near the cemetery.

The lot and grounds were filled with people. The church and grounds looked for all the world like the scene that had played out in Thomas's mind several days ago. Strong young men erected the tent while children played tag among the stones. Women wearing soft cotton dresses prepared a banquet table beside the church sanctuary, while older men set up chairs and strung Coleman lanterns.

I'm so blessed, Thomas thought. His discomfort over the strange man talking to the graveyard statues was forgotten. The sermon was already prepared, all he had to do was show up and start talking. All truly was well with the world.

-5-

Virtually blind, Megan stumbled around the park until she found another open trailer. She staggered into the first bedroom she encountered. For what seemed an eternity, she huddled under a urine-stained mattress and waited for sundown.

By dusk her vision cleared well enough to move about. She crawled out from under the mattress, washed her face in the kitchen sink, listening intently for any signs of humans returning to camp. Once Megan determined it was safe enough, she slipped out of the encampment and disappeared into the woods. She walked toward the fading glimmer of sunset until she came to a red clay road that she recognized as the one leading to Deer Creek Road. The Triple A store was just a few miles from the dirt road and it would be an easy hike for her. From there, she would call the sheriff's department and get help. At this point there was little else she could do. *Anyone could find me,* she thought. *All they have to do is follow their nose.*

Megan squinted at the forest, her vision still blurred from being sprayed at point blank range. She sighed, coughed on the fumes and tried to quicken her pace. She watched the final shafts of sunlight filter through the trees. She caught glimpses of deer nibbling on tender shoots of undergrowth. If things were different, she'd be enjoying the hike instead of flinching at every sound.

I have to get Brody back, she thought. *I've got to bring him back to his senses, even if I have to...*

...What?

She stopped, considering. Megan choked back a sob. *I'll do anything, even if I have to put him in a mental hospital. I'll do whatever it takes to get his mind right again.*

The rumble of oncoming traffic sent Megan diving for the ditch. She hid in the undergrowth surrounding a thick stand of pines and waited as the three cars rambled down the road.

Megan waited until the cloud of dust dissipated before she went back to the road. She walked briskly, breathing easy as she quickened her pace. *Forget the Triple A,* she thought. *There's no telling who's there waiting for me. I'll get to Tatum by midnight if I hurry,* she told herself. *I can go to the police station and get the law to help me.* Shoring up her resolve, Megan broke into a light jog.

Chapter Twenty-Five

It's almost time to go, Thomas thought. His heart pounded like a kettledrum as he dressed. Tears stung his eyes as he looked out of the living room window and at the sea of vehicles that sprawled across the parking lot, down both sides of the dirt road, and lined up along the levee. An elderly gentleman driving an antiquated Packard drove up the long incline toward the cemetery. He parked it, got out, and hugged Pa Neidi as if he knew the man all of his life. *And why not?* Thomas thought. *It doesn't matter if they know each other or not. After all, we are all brothers in the Lord. It's fitting we all should love—*

A fragment of a doubt lodged somewhere deep in his mind. Thomas's lips drew into a thin, hard line.

"It's just nerves, like Pa said," Thomas said aloud to a room he wasn't sure was entirely empty. Lately, the angels tended to come and go as they pleased, and he certainly didn't want to look doubtful—

—Doubt. Ah, there's the rub, Thomas realized. *We're all supposed to face the final Judgment together and nobody's said anything about that. Nobody mentioned separating the sheep from the goats which is what God will do in the end.* He gazed out of the window once more. A group of people were walking toward the tent.

God will dry every eye and wipe away every tear. And then we will forget. Besides, there's no marriage in Heaven, is there? Thomas shook his head, trying to clear it. *I should know this. I do know this. Why can't I remember?*

Thomas chewed on his lower lip, contemplating. His hands

were sweaty and he wiped them off with a paper towel. His Bible rested on the counter. He picked it up and thumbed through the gospels until he came to Mark chapter 12.

"Yes," he said aloud as he read the page. "It's right here, plain as day. 'They shall not marry or be given into marriage, but be like the angels in Heaven.'"

He closed the book. *Rachael will no longer be the woman I love after judgment.* He thought. *My Becky will just be another worshipper among the throngs walking along the streets of gold... She'll see me, smile, maybe nod, but will move on because her eye is not on her earthly father but her heavenly one.*

He gazed back down at the Bible. He ran his fingers over the rough black surface, and the faded gold lettering. *That's not how the angel said it would be,* Thomas thought. *But the Bible states differently. Angels are the messengers of God, but the Bible is God's word. How can the two be contradictory?*

He fell to his knees and agonized. *Why am I being so doubtful? Why can't I just accept things as they are and look forward to an eternity with Christ?*

Because, the fragment of doubt answered as it swirled in the pink and gray miasma that smothered his mind, *if I can't have my family with me family in Heaven, then Heaven would become—dare I think it?—hell.*

Thomas stood. "I trust the Lord," he told his reflection in the meager living room mirror. "I trust in him and in the angels he's sent. I know what I have to do."

Thomas buried his doubts and gave his tie one final twitch. He plastered a preacher's smile on his face and stepped outside into the heavy, humid air.

The fog rolled in over his mind. His doubts swept away as he put his trust and his faith in the angels that were now flitting amid the gravestones. Two of them appeared and wandered among the faithful, alternately touching someone as they passed by. Somehow, Thomas found this disturbing. Shouldn't the caress of an angel's hands and wings bring forth blessings? He tried to shake off the unpleasant sensation as one of them glided past him. The angel looked back as if he knew Thomas was watching. He had a vicious, almost....hungry...expression on his beautiful face.

Thomas shuddered.

You're being ridiculous, he chided himself. *They're blessing those people, not getting ready to eat them. What's wrong with you?*

The incident in the office came to mind. Again he saw the ravenous expression on the girl angel's face. Before she blurred her features, he swore he saw her sizing him up like a dog lusting after a beef steak.

Stop. Stop it now, he told himself. *God will punish you for being afraid just like he punished the children of Israel for worshipping that idol.*

Thomas pushed his misgivings into the back of his mind. He watched as the finishing touches were made on the meeting site. Ike Smalley appeared next to the dais, checking his watch and looking somewhat nervous. Thomas strode down the makeshift aisle toward the podium. Men and women touched his clothes and hands, offering him praises as he made his way to the dais. The congregation took their seats and the music struck up. The Neidis inflicted "The Way of the Cross Leads Home" on the gatherers. The congregants laughed and sang and praised God. The angels, Thomas saw, stood at the periphery of the tent, their hands folded, their heads bowed. As dusk fell, Thomas ended his struggle with the demon of doubt. He consciously snuffed out his last red ember of humanity and made his way up to the podium.

-2-

"Let me up, damn you!" Cora-Lee Johnson shrieked. She fought against the restraining vest that held her fast to the bed. Ouida frowned. Tim destroyed the tract that held her and her family's minds in bondage. *Why hasn't Cora-Lee's good common sense returned?* Ouida wondered.

"Let me up, Ouida Mae! Cut me loose right now, you stinking Judas. You filthy rotten little whore. You took us from Jesus and from Davy."

"Mama, please stop," Ouida pleaded. "You're going to hurt yourself."

"I'll kill you," Cora-Lee hissed, her once-hazel eyes blazing an eerie green. "I swear to God Almighty, I'll kill you for what you've done to that precious boy."

Cora-Lee dropped back to the bed. She gulped huge gasps

of air, the blue veins in her neck protruding against the paper-thin flesh as she heaved once again against the restraints. She moaned, swore, and then sobbed as she lay back against the pillows.

"Mama," Ouida whimpered.

"Shut up, you hateful, selfish little bitch. It was you and that blasphemer of a man you married that did it. You don't love me. You don't love Jesus despite how hard I raised you to, and you never loved Davy. Thanks to you I'll never see him again."

"Mama, please stop," Ouida whispered, cut to the bone by her mother's accusations. *She's never been like this before,* she thought. *Mama was always strict on us kids, sure, but she was a kind and loving mother. She never said a cross word to me my whole life.*

"How much?" Cora-Lee hissed. "Thirty pieces? It was thirty pieces of silver. Thirty pieces you paid and now you'll deep fry in hell."

It's got to be a stroke making her say these things, Ouida thought. *I've heard that strokes cause people's personalities to change. She probably doesn't even know I'm here. Not in a real sense, that is. For all I know, Mama might as well be talking to the shadows in the room.* "Poor Mama. You just lie there and get some rest," Ouida said as she squeezed her mother's arm. "I'll be back in a few minutes."

"You'll be judged," Cora-Lee raved as the tranquillizer took effect. "You'll be judged unworthy to enter into the Kingdom of Heaven. You should never have been born."

"Mama," Ouida chided.

"Lord," Cora-Lee prayed aloud. "If I knew Ouida Mae was going to betray us and deliver Davy to Lucifer, I would have strangled her at birth."

"You don't mean that. When you get well you'll forget everything you've said."

"Blasphemer. Satan worshipper. Child killer...Whore," Cora-Lee spat.

The door opened and Tim, white faced and anxious, walked in. Ouida sighed in infinite relief.

"Let's take a walk," he told her as he put a protective arm around her waist and led her out the door. Surprised that he didn't stop at the doorway, she followed him to the elevator, and then got in beside him. He pushed the first floor button. Just as the elevator descended, he pushed the red stop button, stopping them between floors.

"Tim, what are you doing?" Ouida asked as the elevator grumbled to a halt.

"We have to talk, and this is the only place I can think of where we won't get eavesdropped on."

"I don't understand," she said, frightened. "Tim, what on earth is going on? Mama's completely lost her mind. And the nurses are acting odd."

"I have a pretty good idea." Tim frowned. "How are you doing? Feel like going to a revival?"

"No, not especially," she said. She pushed aside the memory of Sammy standing in front of her when she woke with the shotgun in her lap. "Especially not to the one that's currently all the rage."

Tim scowled. "And Mama?"

"Mama is in a right state. And I can't understand why because you destroyed the flyer." She pursed her lips. "And the nursing staff is getting—I don't know—peculiar. And I haven't seen a doctor all day..."

"The whole town is screwed up," Tim replied. "Most of the sane ones left town and the rest, well...they're like Mama or worse."

"So much for the stroke theory then. I suppose she's still under that preacher's curse."

"Maybe she doesn't want to be out from under the preacher's curse, as you put it," Tim said.

"I don't understand."

"Think about it. Your mom has always been devout, almost to the point of fanaticism. She never misses a single moment when the church doors are open."

"I figure it's because she's just lonely. I know she likes going with the Evergreen Club and doing her weekly Bible studies," Ouida replied.

"I think it goes deeper than just her hen parties and Bible socials," Tim replied. "I think that preacher gave her what she wanted. She was always partial to Davy, even after the other kids came along. Mama was devastated when he was killed. For a while I didn't think she was going to get over it."

"I guess I should have told her the truth about what happened that day, but I couldn't bare her disappointment if I had," Ouida said. "Davy was her hero. I just couldn't bring myself to tell her he had clay feet."

"I know you wanted to spare her feelings, and that was a judgment call we both made, so don't you dare start feeling guilty about that."

Ouida offered her husband a wan smile. "I love her so. I'm scared I'm going to lose her."

"In some ways, we might already have." Tim leaned against the back of the elevator.

"The kids and I got off lucky. I don't remember any of it," Ouida confessed. "Other than my mind being filled with something. Something itchy."

"That's what Billy Wong said too," Tim replied. "I don't know why it affects some people and not others." He shrugged. "Maybe it's because the preacher didn't have what you wanted, or you already have what you want."

"I wanted to see Davy too," Ouida recalled. "But I have the other children, and you, of course. I have more to live for, so maybe I can move on because of that and others can't."

"That's right." Tim's expression softened. "And they didn't affect me because I already have everything I want and need."

Ouida's eyes widened. "Tim, what are we going to do?" she whispered, feeling very small and scared.

"You're going to grab the kids and get out of here. Tonight."

"I just can't leave Mama like that."

"She'll be fine. Trust me, she's safer here than you and I are. I'll see to her as soon as I get back."

"What? No, Tim what are you going to do?"

"I'm going down to that church and see what I can find out."

"Oh Tim, don't."

"I'll be careful. But Ouida, I want you to listen to me carefully now."

"Tim!"

"Now listen." He gave her a slight shake. "I want you to get out of town. Right now. Get the kids. Don't pack or change clothes or anything. Just get in the car and leave. I'll call you when it's safe."

"Tim, I can't drive off, not out in the dark like this. What if something happens?"

"Then go to Texarkana and get a hotel room and leave for Dallas in the morning. Don't tell anyone where you're going and keep to the interstate. And whatever you do, don't stop until you get there. And when you arrive, call me on my cell."

"Tim, I don't want to go without you."

Tim kissed her. "I'll be on my way to Dallas as soon as I take this little trip down to the bottoms. And as for Mom, I'll get her transferred over to Methodist hospital as soon as I can get it arranged."

"I'm still afraid."

"It'll be okay." He kissed her again. "I promise."

"No, you can't promise something like that. Oh, Tim, I can't do this without you. Please, come with me. Let's check Mama out and get away as fast as we can."

Tim shrugged, feeling helpless. "I don't think it'd be a good idea to take her out in her present state of mind. Besides, I can't leave right now. Lonnie and Billy need me to help out. The majority of the police department is affected and I'm one of the few people who they can count on right now."

"Then how do you know the police won't come looking for me? What if I get stopped? And what will happen to us if something happens to you?"

He leaned forward and kissed his wife on the forehead. "Folks have been leaving and nobody's tried to stop them. I doubt they'll try and stop you as long as you keep to the freeway and don't do anything to draw attention to yourself. Try to understand, and believe me when I say I'll be with you as soon as I can."

"I'll hold you to it," Ouida whispered.

Chapter Twenty-Six

For the third time in roughly ten minutes, Megan dove into the underbrush. Four cars and a pickup blew past. Just as Megan peeked out from underneath the heavy swatch of honeysuckle, two more cars flew by. After what seemed like an eternity, Megan crawled out from under the foliage and resumed her trek to Tatum.

The world became dark and somber. Humidity settled upon her, hot and dank, like a sweaty horse's saddle blanket that had been left out to dry after a long day's ride. Thin tendrils of fog rose from the overheated ground, spilling out of the heavy undergrowth and flowing across the road.

Megan shrieked when a startled flock of sparrows roosting in a nearby cedar tree took flight. Their tiny wings beat against her hands and face as they fled skyward into the deepening gloom. Megan's eyesight was still blurry and the steadily dimming light made it even more difficult to see. Megan pressed on, leaving the roadside and entering the forest. She lurched through the trees, pulling pine needles and cobwebs from her face and hair. The strong scent of pine and cedar resin bit her nose and burned down her throat.

Just when she thought it couldn't get any worse, Megan stumbled into a swarm of mosquitoes. She swore and slapped at the insects. Without warning, the ground slipped out from under her. She skidded face first down a small ravine and into a stagnant creek branch. "Ohhhh," she whimpered as she climbed onto her hands and knees. The amulet fell out of her blouse and swung pendulum-like between her breasts.

Megan righted herself. *Nothing seems broken,* she thought.

My knees are skinned but that's all. She straightened and tucked the amulet back into her shirt. She climbed out of the ravine and headed back toward the road. It didn't take long to find her way back. She walked along the road's edge, her feet kicking up little puffs of red dust as she went.

It's easier here, Megan thought, as she watched her environment as warily as a deer stalked by a panther. She pulled her wet hair away from her face. *It's easier, but not safer.* She frowned as she gazed up at the night sky. Mars had risen just above the treetops—was it really that late?—and glared down at her with its baleful reddish eye. *There's been a huge amount of traffic on this road, more than I've seen since we moved here. All those cars and trucks are headed toward Mercer's Bayou.*

Megan slid into a thicket as headlights slashed across the night sky. A white Bonneville rumbled past, throwing dust into the bushes. She coughed and gagged, spitting out muddy saliva. *Mercer babies,* she thought as another car made its way toward the bottoms. *But then again, I'm heading that way too, it seems.*

A lump of grief constricted her throat and she heaved down the pain. *I will not cry,* she told herself, feeling angry and frustrated. *Mary, Queen of Heaven,* she thought. *Please help me. Intercede for me. I need your strength.*

Megan ceased her personal ruminations when she realized that the air around her had become decidedly colder. It felt like a patch of winter that hadn't been swept away by the warmth of spring. She walked along, rubbing her arms for warmth. An owl complained about her presence. She flipped it off and moved on.

Thin tendrils of fog swirled around her as she walked. The mist, lovely and ethereal, parted. Areas of it thickened and stretched. Soon arms and shoulders emerged. Faces twisted with age and pain lifted skyward. *It's happening again.* Megan shuddered. *It doesn't matter how many times I see it, it still gives me the creeps.*

She could see them clearly now. Many of them walked alongside her. Others flitted in and out among the trees. "How many are you?" she asked.

"Legion," said an old man, thick and stringy as worn out

shoe leather, "for we are many."

"Why are you doing this?" she asked.

The old man began his woeful chant. His companions sang along with him. "Why are you here?" she persisted. "Why aren't you, I don't know, in Heaven or something?"

"I'm just a lone wayfaring stranger," they sang. "Traveling through this land of woe."

"No, wait," she said, jogging to catch up with the spectral field hands. "Please tell me what's going on."

The field hands ignored her as they went toward the east.

"Wait a minute. You're going to Mercer's Bayou, aren't you?"

"Lord knows our sorrow."

"Please, somebody talk to me. Tell me what's happening."

A bright beam of light shot through the darkness. Startled, she leapt out of the way. The ghostly field workers vanished as the car, Megan recognized with a laughing sob of relief, belonging to the Miller County Sheriff's Department, slowed to a crawl beside her. The patrol car turned on its lights and stopped. The red and blue lights virtually screamed as they overpowered her vision. She hesitated for a moment. *What if they're influenced the same way Brody is?* she wondered. *It's too late to think about that now. One of the officers is rolling down his window.*

"Can I help you?" asked the man in uniform.

"Yes, please," she said. Her voice trembled under stress as well as lack of food and sleep. "Please help me. Someone's trying to kill me."

A deputy stepped out of the passenger's side then went around and opened the back door. Grateful she climbed into the back seat.

"Lord, girl, what have you gotten into?" the Chinese officer exclaimed.

"Nothing tomato juice won't take off," the sheriff replied. He turned to Megan and asked, "May I see your ID?"

"My name is Megan Wallace, and I don't have my identification with me." She laughed, feeling the hysteria rise. "You don't think about such things when your husband is trying to take your head off with a claw hammer."

"No, I suppose not," the Chinese officer commented.

"I hid out at the Gypsy encampment. And this morning there were men looking for me. There were two of them in a big black truck carrying high-powered rifles."

"Hold on a minute," the sheriff said. He shined a penlight into her face. Red and black spots dotted her field of vision. "She's clean," the sheriff said.

They don't think I've gone crazy, like Brody, she thought. Exhaustion and fear taking its toll, Megan doubled over and wept.

-2-

"The Rapture is at hand," shouted Ike Smalley as he stood on the small dais, resplendent in his gravy stained Colonel Sander's suit. "Are you ready? Are you ready? I mean really ready?"

The congregation shouted and stomped its feet.

"Are you ready to receive the Lord in all his glory?"

"Yes!" roared the congregation.

"Are you ready to join him in the air?"

"Yes. Yes!"

"Are you ready to receive the keys to the Kingdom of Heaven?"

"Hallelujah."

"Then get ready brothers and sisters for the time is at hand."

Thomas wasn't sure exactly when the old preacher usurped the night's message, but it didn't matter any more. He was glad to stand beside the dais, his hands folded piously in front of him. After a while, the old hack stopped preaching and started screaming inane babble. It was the language of the Holy Ghost, or so Thomas was told. But deep down where the monster in his head couldn't quite reach—not yet anyway, but soon, he knew, oh yes very soon now—he knew it was all bullshit.

Thomas smiled down at his congregation, who celebrated the coming Rapture beneath the unnatural luster of Coleman lanterns. The Neidi band was banging along with its typical uneven cadence while the more reserved members of the audience sang, clapped and stomped to the beat. The more enthusiastic members actually took to dancing in the aisles. The elderly, their faces shining in joy, stood waving their hands as if they were paying homage to a newly christened luxury liner.

A man, his eyes gleaming with ecstatic madness, staggered to the front of the congregation. Shouting praises, he raised a water moccasin over his head and danced in front of the altar. As he spun, the agitated reptile struck his hands and wrists. The man fell to the ground and convulsed as the snake shot past the crowd and out into the night. Nobody noticed. And Thomas, who was gazing down at the dead man lying at his feet, didn't care in the least.

-3-

Just as Tim turned off the highway and onto the levee, a gunshot blasted out his back windshield. Swearing profusely, he swerved as another shot took out his back tire. The Lexus drifted, spun, then skidded along the guardrail. Tim's stomach twisted as he caught sudden glimpses of foliage and rich red bayou water far below the guardrail.

His heart pounded as the Lexus skidded to a stop. The airbag shot out of the steering column and smacked him in the face. Tim was thrown back against the seat. He gasped huge gulps of air. He could smell smoking rubber mingled with the dank scent of the forest. He heard a gunshot somewhere far below. As he looked out his window, he could see the church roof, the huge line of parked vehicles and the top of the tent billowing slightly in the breeze. To the left of the cemetery, he could see the tree squatting on top of the slight rise. It seemed to settle down into the hill and then blasted a huge column of brilliant green gold light high into the sky.

Holy shit, Tim thought as a second, much closer gunshot propelled him out of the car and down the long slanting gravel strewn embankment. Down and down again, sliding and skidding along on his backside until he came to rest at the water's edge. Tim slipped into the darkened undergrowth and held his breath as the third and final shot took out the car's gas tank.

The Lexus thudded with a deep gasoline-soaked echo as the tank exploded. *Damn*, he thought, *they're not playing anymore. It's no longer a matter of going down and spying on a bunch of wild-eyed fundamentalist fuck ups. These guys are in it for real.*

He looked up. In the fiery outline along the levee, two men with high-powered rifles stood at the guardrail. It was obvious that they were keeping unbelievers off the road and away from the bayou. *How would they know that?* Tim wondered. *I could have been on my way to attend the revival. Why shoot at me?*

Because, he thought. *They know the same way Cora-Lee knows.* The men on the bridge moved away from the car. Two more dull thuds caused the blackened carcass to dance along the breakdown lane.

A brilliant green-gold flash burned through Tim's mind like a psychic pulse. Tim turned, but he didn't need to. He already knew. The column of green light burst into flame, garish, obscene and towering at least two hundred feet into the air. It illuminated the levee in a bizarre, unearthly light. He could hear the men as they moved away, bellowing prayers, giving thanks. *That's it,* Tim thought. *It really is the tree that's doing it. And all this time I thought the legends were so much horse shit. It really does feed on your soul. Or maybe your faith. Or maybe your darkest fears. Hell, I don't know. Maybe it's all three. Or more.*

Tim heard the roar of a truck engine somewhere on the levee. His heart raced with fear and dreaded anticipation. *It's coming. And I don't think it's Jesus.*

-4-

"Let me up, you slut! Harlot! Damn you let me up!"

"Mama," Ouida said, alarmed and confused. "Calm down. Everything's going to be all right."

"No it's not," her mother cried. She flung herself against her pillows and uttered a long, anguished howl that jarred Ouida's nerves. She stood next to her mother feeling frightened and helpless. There were no nurses on the floor that Ouida could detect. *It's late,* she reasoned. *The staff might be at their shift change meeting. I should just go now,* she thought. *Mama will be fine. I need to get the kids and head out while we still can.*

"Mama, please," she said, trying to take her mother's hand.

But Cora-Lee yanked away. "Witch," she said. "Jezebel."

"Mama, you know good and well I'm none of those things."

"You were always disobedient, spiteful, blasphemous. Always questioning the ways of the Lord. And then you went and married that adulterer and now you have a passel of bastard babies!"

"That's not true. You know Tim being divorced has nothing to do with adultery."

"Adulteress...."

"Mama, now stop."

Cora-Lee's eyes burned an eerie gold green. "Let me up. Let me go to the revival. I need to go. Don't you understand? I'm one of the Twelve. I want to be with the Lord. I'm the preacher's apostle. He needs me."

"Mama..."

"I want to see Davy again."

"Mama, it's not time for you to see Jesus. And you're not that evil old preacher's apostle."

"If you were a good Christian woman, you'd know. But you don't. You abandoned the Word. Well, I won't."

"That preacher you talked to last week, Mama, he's a con artist or something. He put something on those papers he was handing out and it's done something to your mind."

"It's the Rapture," Cora-Lee cried, her face virtually blazing from the heat of misguided revelation. "The Lord has come. Like a thief in the night."

"That's what it is, isn't it?" Ouida whispered, backing away from the bedrail. "You're not being coerced. You want to go. Oh my God, Mama, Tim was right. Whatever it is that's got hold of you, you want to keep it. You're feeding it yourself and soon the thing that has possession of your soul and everyone else's isn't going to need flyers or preachers to dupe people into taking care of it." Ouida gasped. "That's why it's let the unbelievers go. That thing knows it's only a matter of time when it'll take hold of anyone whether they believe or not. And it won't stop with Tatum either, will it? It'll just keep getting stronger and stronger—"

"Unbeliever," someone behind her interrupted. Ouida jumped, horrified as three members of the hospital staff stood behind her. They all smiled, their eyes glowing green, their faces twisted in a garish righteousness that made her bile rise.

"What is this?" Ouida demanded. "What's wrong with you people? This is like some crazed horror movie."

"It's not a movie." The head nurse smiled. "It's the real deal, honey. Jesus is coming tonight and you didn't RSVP."

The nurse nodded. Two big, burly orderlies she'd seen smoking in the parking lot earlier in the day rushed at her. Ouida dodged them. She shoved the head nurse aside as she bolted down the corridor.

Ouida's heart pounded as she raced along the pastel wallpapered hallway. She slammed into the elevator doors, whimpering as she shoved down hard on the open button. The elevator slid open and she ran inside. The door slid closed. A hand reached out through the slit between the door and the heavy metal frame. Ouida screamed as the door automatically tried to open. The hand extended further inside along with the white arm and shoulder. Instinct and fear kicked in and she grabbed the man's hand and bit down hard. She tasted blood and flesh. The hand's owner shouted, swore and withdrew. She slammed the elevator doors closed and pushed the down button.

I can't let it go all the way down, she realized, panicked. *Someone will be there on the first floor waiting for me.* She glanced down at the control panel. Remembering what Tim did, she hit the stop button. The elevator skidded to a halt between two floors. She leaned against the safety of the sleek metal walls. She realized something was in her mouth.

She swirled the object around, feeling somewhat confused and disconcerted. *Maybe I broke off a piece of my bridge,* she thought. But she knew that was wrong. Whatever was in her mouth was thick, coppery and rough. She spit it out in her hand. Ouida screamed, throwing the object against the far wall. It bounced off the shiny silver wall and landed with a soft thump on the carpet. It finally rolled to a stop about a foot away.

Ouida screamed until the tiny vessels in her eyes ruptured.

Ouida had bitten the tip of the man's thumb off. The end of it was pointing upward as it rested on its bloody stump. Tiny black and blue dots swarmed her field of vision. Her stomach heaved. She stumbled into a corner and retched.

Chapter Twenty-Seven

-1-

"Hang tight," Lonnie said to Megan as he killed the lights. The cruiser crept along the foot of the embankment. Moments later, they came to a stop about a half a mile away from the church. *My sight is definitely getting better,* Megan thought. *I can see the lights from the tent revival gleaming along the waterline.*

"Stay put. We'll be back in a few minutes," Lonnie Cox said.

"Where are you going?" Megan asked, alarmed. "You can't leave me out here by myself."

"You'll be safer here than where we're going," Billy Wong replied. "Just keep your head down and be still and we'll be back in about half an hour."

"My husband is down there," Megan said. "He's caught up with all that nonsense."

"We'll be back in half an hour," Lonnie repeated, closing the driver side door. "Do as Officer Wong says and you'll be fine."

"Please don't hurt him," she said. "I know what he tried to do earlier, but that's not him. Brody has never laid a hand on me. He's really sweet and kind and I know he still loves me."

Billy Wong grimaced as he slammed the door.

Megan whimpered as she saw the two uniformed men fade into the darkness. She slid deep into the seat, looking through the grated diamond grid that divided the back seat from the front. This had been a K-9 unit at one time she noted, catching the scent of dog as she rested against the back seat.

From her position, Megan could see the levee between the wild undergrowth. *Something's going on up there,* she thought.

She leaned forward, straining to catch a glimpse of movement. A car cruised along the highway. A sudden report rang out, startling a murder of crows. At first Megan thought the car must have blown a tire. She heard two more shots. Megan sat stunned as the car careened into the guardrail, showering the edge of the levee with red-gold sparks as it came to rest in the breakdown lane.

A deep, sudden thump, followed by a reddish-orange flash lit up the levee. Megan jolted. She slumped deeper into the back seat when the column of gas-soaked flames boiled upwards, the reflection dancing on the hood of the car. She heard another deep, thudding explosion followed by a rally of sharp, unmistakable gunshot reports.

"It's the hunters," Megan said, horrified. "Oh, good Lord, they've gone and killed somebody."

Movement on the levee caught her attention. She saw the silhouette of a pickup reflected against the burning remains of the car they just destroyed. Someone was looking down the guardrail into the undergrowth and bayou water. *They're looking for someone*, she thought. *Whoever was in the car was thrown clear of the wreckage. They're making sure their victim is dead, I suppose.*

The man next to the railing stood and made a curious gesture. The red beam from the hunter's laser scope danced along the brushes and trees then glanced along the hood of the patrol car.

Oh God, Megan thought. *He's seen the car, and they're no longer particular about what they shoot. And there's no way to get out*, she discovered as she slid her hand along the door. *There's no handle on my side of the door. The cage was designed to keep prisoners in and the only way out is if someone lets you out.* She pushed against the grid, but it was welded into the frame. She rolled onto her back and tried to kick the cage loose but it wouldn't budge.

She laughed between sobs. *And of course it won't open*, she told herself. *What good is a grate between the seats if you can bust it down with one good-sized Jackie Chan kick?*

The bright red beam shot across the hood again, glancing along the windshield. Megan slid to the floorboard. The unmistakable sound of a shotgun bolt drawing back brought her upright into the seat. She turned and looked out the driver's side window.

A rifle barrel was pointed directly at her head. One of the hunters on the levee had radioed their buddy on the ground. Now she was staring at a barrel, long and gleaming in the orange and green lights. Behind the scope she could see a pair of green eyes blazing in the darkness. "Whore," the baritone voice from behind the gun barrel crackled. "Whore of Babylon."

Megan screamed. The man grinned, his face contorted. "I was supposed to bring you to him, but now I think I won't. I'll send you to Jesus myself. Praise God."

Megan watched helpless as he pulled the trigger.

-2-

The elevator rumbled, jerked and receded down the shaft. Ouida scuttled into a corner and huddled there, knowing that there was no escape this time. Whoever was going to be at the lobby when the doors opened would surely kill her. Or worse. She waited as the elevator grumbled below the first floor and continued to sink deeper and deeper until at last it jolted to a stop. The doors slid open.

Ouida was astounded when the only thing that entered the elevator was a thick, glistening fog. The temperature dropped as the mist poured into the car. She shivered, waist deep in icy dampness. She approached the opened doors and peeked outside. A pale green tiled corridor greeted her. Soft mist ebbed and flowed along the white and black tiled floor.

She was alone.

Ouida's mind buzzed. *They wanted me to come down here. That's why they didn't follow me. But why?* She retreated back into the elevator. *I'm in the morgue*, she realized as her heart slammed down into her belly. Desperation fueled her and she slapped her palm down on the Close Elevator Door button. The doors remained open. She sobbed, pressed harder on the buttons, trying to force the elevator up and onto the first floor. She wanted out of the hospital and on the road to somewhere. *Anywhere. Dallas, yes. That's where Tim told me to go. And I will too as soon as I get out. Mama. What am I going to do about Mama?*

She crawled back into her corner, crouched down and

grabbed her hair. She cried. She rocked back and forth, her back rubbing the sleek steel corner of her inadequate refuge. After a seeming eternity of self-abuse, the fit of hysteria passed. She rested, gasping in huge deep gulps of alcohol-tainted fog. She lifted her head.

The mist was now shoulder-deep as she sat on the floor. *I can get out,* she told herself. *There has to be a way to get dead bodies into the morgue without taking them through the main hospital where everyone can see them. They must come in through a door somewhere down in here. I just have to find it.*

-3-

The tent revival reached a fevered pitch. People yelled, whooped, danced in the narrow aisles or on the outside grounds of the tent, hugging and shouting in joy. The celebrants looked more like hedonists in an orgy than a congregation of charismatic Christians.

"Come unto me, you weary and heavy laden, and I will give you rest," Thomas shouted above the chaos below. His arms were outstretched, eyes blazing as the Neidi band played. "Come, my beloved disciples, the time is at hand," he called down to the congregation. "Come. Let the spirit of the Lord fill you."

Jim Balfour, to Thomas's delight, stumbled toward the altar along with Ike Smalley who abandoned the right side of the dais to join his brothers and sisters. They looked up at the pulpit, their faces glowing with a profound, blazing passion. They, like the rest of the celebrants, were drunken in spirit. They reached for him, trying to touch him. Thomas, his face radiant, his eyes beacons of green light, joined them as they approached. The congregation shouted praises as he laid hands on each of them. The faithful screeched as if they'd been shot. They fell to the ground convulsing, writhing. Slain in the spirit. Murdered in the spirit.

He acquiesced to an immense power. He felt energy shooting from his fingertips as he grabbed one of his disciples by the head. The man's eyes bulged in shock when Thomas shared the spirit that he contained. The man screamed as if his soul was being torn out. He collapsed to the ground. He twitched then was still.

The congregation shouted praises. Celebrants staggered forward, demanding, begging and pleading for the touch.

Thomas stepped in the midst of his parishioners, his face contorted with the fires that consumed his soul. The locomotive force drove any doubt from his mind as he waded through his congregation. He reached out, touching outstretched hands, grasping seeking fingers, grasping seeking fingers, sharing the spirit with his mentally sick and soul weary parishioners.

Without warning, a loud, anguished howl cut through the night, interrupting the service. The energy severed, the band shut down. The flock became silent. The lights were unnaturally bright as the wolves howled again. It was a sharp, piercing shriek that sent primordial nerves on edge. The wolves blasted again and somewhere within the cemetery another pack picked up the cry. Someone in the back row screamed, "It's turned to blood!"

It's happening, Thomas thought with a mixture of elation and terror as he watched the moon rise through the gap in the tent. The moon hung like a drop of blood between the upper branches of the Cold Hanging Tree. The ground beneath their feet shook. The tree blazed into life, the limbs writhing, the trunk groaning and trembling as a tower of green flames shot high into the night sky.

The angels walked freely in the midst of the congregation and began to feed. People ran screaming as the creatures fell upon the flock. Thomas saw them as they truly were. The pretty female angel who smoked stogies in his office swept amid the throng. The cigar and derby were gone. Her cherubic face exposed reddish eyes and an oversized jaw containing rows of shark-like teeth. She caught his eye and grinned at him. Thomas's mouth went dry.

Realization kicked in as did adrenaline-drenched terror. But the mental fog rolled back in and hid the jagged rocks and sheer cliffs from the lighthouse of his mind. Thomas relaxed. He stood in detached amusement as the angels fed upon the celebrants. He laughed outright as he watched several worshippers' heads shrink like rotting apples while the angels gorged upon them.

The wolves howled. People screamed. Jim Balfour, suddenly not as faithful as he first believed, bolted through the throng, pushing people out of his way as he fled through the crowd. The parishioners followed, screaming as they fled toward their vehicles. Thomas laughed. *They're running like their asses are on fire.*

"Don't go!" Thomas laughed as he heard the panicked shriek of tires, the thudding bumps as unbelievers crashed into each other trying to flee into the night. "Don't you know, Colonel?" he shouted as Ike Smalley, the man who had the audacity to take over his service, was now running for his life down to the parking lot, his white jacket flapping like moth's wings behind him. "Don't you know you can't get your God's healing virtue here?"

Only nine—his faithful nine—remained. *No, ten,* he amended, *because Cora-Lee is held captive in the hospital.* But it wouldn't be long. He knew that the nurses would free her shortly now that her slut of a daughter had run for her life. Yes, dear Cora-Lee would join them in the jubilee. Ten instead of twelve. He looked down and saw that the other two were trampled in the stampede.

The Nine looked up at him, their faces radiant like newborn children. *More will join them. Oh yes. Soon, soon. Praise Jesus. Praise the tree.*

He raised his arms and howled. The angels drifted out of the cemetery and entered the tent. "Hallelujah," he shouted as they surrounded him. He did not care that they were touching him now, caressing him with cold hands, their faces luminous and lustful. Neither did he care when the Neidis and the faithful Nine who, equally enraptured, sang and shouted praises as they lifted him down from the makeshift dais—when had he mounted it? He could not remember—and led him out toward the cemetery. The angels, even more beautiful now than when he first saw them, followed in procession like monks behind their priest.

"I'm coming home, Rachael," he shouted. "Bless you Jesus, I'm coming home," he shouted, his heart bursting with joy.

The tree was much closer now, glowing like the Glory of God himself. *Yes, it's burning without smoke, without scent and it looks just like the great hand of God. My own burning bush,* Thomas thought. *That's what it is and I'm going to stand before Him and receive my reward. Just like Moses. Yes, just like that.*

Something small but persistent disturbed him. Thomas

didn't want to dwell on it. He wanted it to go away, but it would not. It was something akin to doubt, sharp and uncomfortable like a burr in a boot.

The beauty of God's glory vanished. All the pretty angels who led him here were now twisted and their faces grotesque, gruesome as they stood leering at him, laughing at him. He felt suddenly very foolish, very gullible. And very, very frightened.

The tree, oh God, his mind shrieked as he saw, really saw for the first time, the limbs squirming black—charred—but glowing with an unearthly sheen as the branches reached out for him. He stepped backward but felt a sudden pull as his arms were yanked back. One of the apostles was holding him. "No," he moaned. "There's nothing about Jesus in this."

The angels departed in thin greenish vapor. He comprehended with sudden sick horror that Pa and Dougie Neidi were actually holding him by the forearms and pulling him toward the tree. The rest of the family along with the nine had circled the tree, their arms raised in invocation. "Come before the altar, brother," Pa cackled. "Come before the altar and be saved."

The tree shuddered. It snatched him with sharp, black tentacle-like branches. Thomas shrieked and staggered backwards. *Oh Lord, oh Lord,* he prayed, more fervently than he had ever done in his life. *The only thing that's getting revived is that thing inside the tree. That's what's been talking to me,* he realized. *All this time, it hasn't been Rachael's voice but that demon whispering poison into my ear.*

Thomas shoved his disciples' grasping hands away. He stumbled and slammed into Pa Neidi's chest. He screamed when his hands sank deep into the old man. *He's hollow,* Thomas thought, *hollow as if someone had taken an enormous ice cream scoop and scraped him out.* Pa leered and got a better grip on his arms.

"Oh God, help me," Thomas cried. "I'm surrounded by demons and hollow men." Neidi's hands twisted hard on his wrists. Thomas bore down on his heels, leaning against the men's weight.

Someone pushed him from behind. Thomas slipped in the scorched, lifeless grass. His screams reduced into hoarse sobs as he was dragged to the tree. The limbs lashed out, impaling him.

"Save me, Jesus. Oh, please," he cried as the limbs clamped down into his body, sharp points skewered through his chest, arms and legs. Hot barbs latched deep into his body. Thomas was helpless as the branches pulled him toward it. The tree opened up, exposing the blinding green-gold furnace inside.

Thomas uttered a hopeless sob. He felt the hot wet sopping between his legs as he pissed himself. The trunk finished peeling away, exposing a pulsating aperture large enough to hold a man in. Weeping, Thomas was shoved head first into the tree. Tiny fibrous shoots blazed up his spinal cord and entangled his brain. His mind ripped open as a great, terrible voice boomed like a kettle drum in his ears.

The tree fed on his soul until he was as hollow and as wooden as the creature that held him. It was blissful, erotic...orgasmic... He was dimly aware of ejaculating into his clothes.

"Oh yes," he sighed, letting the blessed coldness engulf his entire being. This is the peace that passes understanding, he thought, just as his brain died and the tree took his soul away.

-4-

Oh God, oh God, oh God, Mr. Jim Balfour's mind raced as he, along with a long line of panic-stricken congregants, bolted across the parking lot to their vehicles. Mr. Jim backed into at least two cars in his desperate attempt to get away. He left the long, thin ribbon of driveway and bounced across the fields. He came to an abrupt, jolting stop as his truck tires came in contact with the highway and skidded on the pavement.

Mr. Jim floored the truck and it blew past several cars. His hands shook like he'd been on a bender and his face wore a broken man's grimace. In the rearview mirror, he could still see the green flames leaping skyward. The red moon hung above it like a drop of blood brought forth by a vampire's fang. Mr. Jim tittered at the analogy. *I've gone bat shit crazy,* he reasoned. *After what I saw coming at me, anyone would have their sanity ripped loose from their moorings.*

The night enfolded him as soon as his truck reached the heavy canopy of trees. Bayou water glistened with a sickening green glow below the levee. Lights from the traffic behind him dwindled as many former supplicants found refuge in dirt-infested back roads. Jim's heart pounded against his back. His adrenals were still juiced and he felt as if he could run forever. *Even if I did,* he thought, *I'll never get rid of that image.*

Hysterical giggling rushed up out of his gullet. His hands shook. The truck careened down the road so quickly that he was barely able to keep it upright. Mr. Jim slowed down and caught his breath. He did his best to ease the slamming of his heart against his chest cavity.

It's not right, he thought. *I was one of the first led astray by Pa and his damned tree. I got that poor preacher to come down here, knowing he was going to become a sacrifice. Yes, I did, and I didn't care, no sir, I didn't.* Jim started to cry.

Why didn't he pay attention? I gave out enough hints didn't I? Even Mrs. Blanchard told him flat out and he was too stupid to leave.

He glanced back at the flames tossing themselves high above the foliage. *The fire is getting larger. I bet you can see it from Shreveport now. And it wouldn't be this way if I had bigger balls. I could have fought it... I could have made it stop...*

All of the wouldas, shouldas and couldas can't stop what's happening now, Jim berated himself. *You know what you have to do. You just have to grow the balls to do it*

Jim pulled over and parked the truck. Several cars blasted past him, honking their horns as they went by. He ignored them. He shuddered and squeezed his eyes closed. The afterimage of the monstrosity floating toward him with red eyes and long, stringy white hair, with a face like a deformed fetus, came into focus. Needle-sharp teeth glistened as it opened its jaws wide, ready to latch itself leech-like upon Jim's face.

Gathering up his courage, Big Jim Balfour put the truck into gear and went back to the Mc Knight House to gather what he needed.

Chapter Twenty-Eight

-1-

Thomas regained consciousness by degrees. As he rose higher and higher into awareness, the tree wrapped his mind in a cool green shroud. *Nothing can hurt me now,* he thought, his psyche dim and distant beneath the heavy verdant pall. *Through you,* he said to the demon, *I can do anything.*

A troubling thought swam through his mind. He ignored it. A cool substance was pressed to his forehead. Liquid dripped down his parched cheeks and flowed into his ears. *Rachael?* he wondered. *No, not Rachael,* he decided. *The hand belongs to a man. He's one of my disciples.*

Thomas opened his eyes and saw Brody Wallace staring down at him. *Brody Wallace, yes, I remember,* he thought. *This is the man who planted those dirty little crosses in the churchyard. And it's no wonder he's so sad, so distraught,* Thomas mused, *what with all those dead children following him everywhere.*

"We're in my office," Thomas said uncertainly.

"Yes," Brody replied. His eyes were bright and maniacal. "We brought you here after the service." The man cocked his head to one side and for a moment looked like a goofy cartoon buzzard. "Are you all right now, Lord?"

"Yes," Thomas replied as he eased himself up. He stood, finding his legs shaky. Brody Wallace steadied him. He eased him into a chair. "Do you know who I am?" Thomas asked Brody.

Brody Wallace's face literally lit up as he knelt beside him, "Oh yes," he whispered, his face glowing with exaltation. "You're our savior. You'll lead us up into the sky when he comes at dawn!"

"And do you believe that?"

"Oh yes my Lord, with all my heart."

Thomas looked around, confused. "Where are the rest of my disciples?"

"In the church, my Lord," Brody said. "I led them into the sanctuary after—after you appeared."

"You are a good and faithful servant," Thomas whispered absently, his hand caressing the man's cheek. "Do you know what we have to do now?"

"Yes, the angel explained everything to me," Brody said. "And I'll have everything ready very shortly."

"Will you be ready before sunrise?" he asked.

"Oh, yes. Absolutely."

"That's good," Thomas said, feeling weary. "That's very good. Then you need to get started." Brody Wallace, his face radiant as tears streamed down his cheeks, nodded. He looked ludicrous, even to Thomas.

"What about the Whore?" Brody asked.

Thomas looked inward and saw the Whore trapped inside a car facing the business end of a shotgun. He smiled. "She's no longer a threat."

"Is she dead?"

"No, but they'll bring her to the church. To face," he grinned, "the final Judgment."

"Oh Praise God."

"Now you have to get busy," Thomas admonished. "We don't have much time."

"Yes, my Lord," Brody whispered as he rose, then backed out of the room bowing. "It's almost time," he said with the excitement of a child expecting Santa. "It's almost here."

-2-

Megan screamed, lurching onto the floorboard as the gun barrel tilted crazily upward. The barrel belched a huge orange and yellow flame above the roof of the car. The driver's side window shattered from the concussion as the bullet soared into the night sky.

She lay on her side, panting, sweat mingling with shards of broken glass. Her gaze focused on the shattered window where a large white arm extended from the darkness. It grabbed the gun and was now wrestling with the hunter with the unearthly eyes. The newcomer jerked the gun toward the ground, the butt of the rifle striking the hunter underneath the chin. The hunter's heavy weight thudded against the side of the patrol car, and then slid onto the ground.

The man shoved the hunter aside, jerked open the car door, grabbed Megan by the arm and yanked her onto her feet. She screamed and twisted, trying to get away, but the man pushed her against the car's trunk and clapped his hand over her mouth.

"Shut up or you'll get us both killed," he said harshly as he jerked his head toward the levee. "There's at least two more of them up there."

Megan relaxed, nodded, her eyes still large and frightened. He removed his hand then said, "Come on. Let's get out of here."

Megan, who until today would never have followed a strange man into the woods alone, ran behind him into the forest.

-3-

Brody whistled a merry tune as he carried out the final instructions presented to him by an angel in a powder blue suit. He walked like a man of distinction between the church office and the tent that floated ghost like in the breeze. His form cast long and eerie shadows against the tombstones. His children trooped along behind him. Next to the AeroStar, an old black man sat on the ruined stump of a Woodmen of the World tombstone. He tipped his ethereal hat in their direction.

Brody got into his SUV and settled into the familiar warmth of the checkered cotton bucket seat. He waved at the kids as they watched from the cemetery. He cranked the engine and backed the van through the thin green patch of lawn that separated the parking lot from the church proper. The taillights splashed sanguine light against the white-sided wall as he braked.

Satisfied he had reached the appropriate distance from the building, he killed the engine. He enjoyed the familiar slam of the door as he closed his vehicle, probably for the next to the last time, because he had to get back inside and start it before going inside the church to await the Second Coming, didn't he?

He whistled as he rounded the back of the building where he found the little shed that contained, among other things, Thomas's fishing tackle. He sorted through the various odd and ends of broken tools, fishing rods and empty paint buckets until he found the remains of a garden hose that was coiled snake-like upon a bracket in the far corner of the shed.

"Jesus loves me, this I know," he hummed as he rummaged around dilapidated, worm-eaten shelving until he found old grease rags, partially melted rolls of duct tape and a cracked mixture of epoxy and wood glue dried in the bottom of a can. "Cause the Bible tells me so."

He took the rags along with the hose and duct tape, then returned to the van. Depositing the goods, he went to the building and looked for an opening around the church window. The old ghost watched him. He whittled, smiled and offered advice.

"They's a spot right over there, boss," the old black man said. His drawl was as slow and hypnotic as bayou water. The specter chuckled as he cut out a sizeable chunk of ghostly wood and continued whittling while he appraised Brody's work.

"Yes, Jesus loves me, yes Jesus loves me..." Brody sang. His fingers slid across a gap in the office window. The exact place the ghost told him. His searching fingers found a crack in the pane. It produced a small puncture, as if a child's pellet gun had made the hole. He pushed his finger into the dimple. "It doesn't go all the way through," Brody muttered.

"Oh you can fix dat right quick," the old man replied as if he were discussing the carburetor on a cranky lawn mower. "The thing you need to do is pop dat hole, make it big enough to shove the hose through. Den you can seal it off with dat duct tape you've got over there."

Brody looked at the ghost sitting on the tombstone. "You know, that's a good idea."

The former slave smiled, his teeth flashing in the garish light. The spaces where his eyes should have been blazed green.

"Oh yes sir, boss. I'm just full of good ideas."

-4-

Lonnie Cox and Billy Wong knelt in the bushes and watched as the middle aged man with his arms loaded with odd items shuffled from the back of the church to his van. The man unloaded his burden and squatted behind the SUV. At first glance, he looked like a mechanic inspecting the undercarriage of the vehicle. Lonnie heard his partner suck in his breath. "What the hell is he doing?" Lonnie asked.

"Looks like he's shoving something into the exhaust pipe," Billy Wong whispered.

"He's definitely up to something," Lonnie concurred, "but I can't tell what. There's a tombstone blocking my view."

"Let's get closer," Billy said.

"I'm on it," Lonnie replied.

-5-

"Ah yeah," the ghost on the tombstone approved. "Now dat's coming along real fine."

"Thank you," Brody grunted as he finished stuffing the rags around the nozzle of the garden hose he had stuck into the tailpipe. He knew the intense heat coming from the exhaust pipe would melt the hose and probably set the rags on fire toward the end. Though inefficient as insulation, the exhaust would still go through the hose and into the church. It would hold just long enough for the van to do its work.

Brody stopped momentarily as a thought, deep and troubling, surfaced. He looked at his work, trying to mentally peer through the fogbank like a sailor watching a ship gliding into a mist-enshrouded harbor. Scowling, he sat back on his heels and tried to focus.

The mental itching began at once, scorching his brains as if a colony of fire ants took up residence inside his cranium and were burrowing out through his optic nerves. He groaned and pressed his hands on his head. His eyes clamped shut as he doubled over. Red, gold and black splotches danced across his field of vision. In his mind, he could see Megan searching frantically for him. He could almost make out her desperate and frightened pleas for him to come home. "Megan," he whispered. "Megan is in trouble."

He struggled harder. The fire ants brought the pain up another notch. The agony compressed his mind, searing his brain. Brody screamed. A heavy thrumming pushed against his eardrums, and he writhed in agony beside the van.

"Daddy?" his eldest daughter inquired. She caressed his forehead with a wispy hand as he knotted into a ball and dry heaved behind the AeroStar. "Daddy? Why are you forgetting us? Daddy? Don't you love us any more?"

The anguish receded. The fire ants went dormant and the wooly fogbank once again descended into his mind. "I can't touch you. I could before but I can't now and I don't know why." Brody whimpered. "Oh Lord, I want to let you know how much I love you."

"It's okay, Daddy," she said. She smiled. Her eyes were so green, so dazzling, so utterly beautiful, like emeralds, like the Son of God who was now preaching in the church behind him. His face widened into a ghoulish grin that even the old man on the stump avoided.

But Megan...

The itching behind his eyeballs flared up. Brody heaved again.

"It's okay, Daddy," Christina said. Her small hand patted his back but did little good. "It's okay because we will be with Jesus and Mommy will be in hell where she belongs. And we'll be with you...together forever and forever."

Brody rose and then looked at his children. They smiled at him. His heart skipped a beat.

"We love you so much," Christina said.

He smiled and nodded, his throat too tight to speak.

-6-

It took a few minutes to decide on exactly what to do. After all, Mr. Jim Balfour wasn't used to going into a deep panic. But once he calmed down, the answer to his dilemma arose like a ship's prow cutting through dense fog.

Even though the old yellow Victorian looked empty, Jim took no chances. He left the truck running as he rushed to the small tool shed behind the house. There he picked up a come along, a chain and on second thought, hefted the heavy red Husqvarna chainsaw and a couple of double bit axes and tossed them into the back.

The plan was simple. He'd use the come along and the chain to wench the tree out of the ground, and then take deep satisfaction in turning it into cordwood. It was a shame that he didn't have any dynamite. He'd blown up stumps while clearing off about thirty acres for pastureland for an old boy who bought the Henderson place six years ago. *Yeah,* Jim thought. *Some dynamite would be extra spectacular. Launching that fucker to the moon would make my day.*

Jim climbed into the cab, slamming the door behind him. Just as he put the truck into gear, he heard the unmistakable sound of a bullet chambering into its cylinder.

-7-

Brody, returning to a state of mindless bliss, left "Jesus Loves Me" behind and replaced it with, "When the Roll is Called Up Yonder." Between choruses, he laughed, a thrill racing up his spine as he made his final—"and I do mean final," he stated—preparations.

Finished with the van, Brody uncoiled the garden hose and stuffed the other end through the office window and taped it down. It also helped seal off the building from the fresh air outside. Satisfied, Brody walked to the far end of the building and cut off the air conditioning from the breaker box mounted on the outside of the building. For a moment, he considered cutting the lights as well, but changed his mind.

Now, he wondered, *why would anyone in their right mind place a breaker box on the back side of a building like that? Someone could do a bit of mischief.* Brody smiled at his own wit. Not everyone would have thought to turn off the air conditioner, he told himself.

His children agreed. They had the smartest daddy in the whole world. Even the former slave who sat and worked his ghostly magic on a nonexistent piece of wood nodded his approval.

"You're right smart, ain'tcha, boss?" his spectral companion replied. "Just do what you gotta do, that's all I'm sayin'."

Brody felt especially good about himself. He stepped back and viewed his handiwork. Satisfied, he got into the AeroStar and turned the ignition. The SUV responded, the muffler rumbling thick blue smoke around the exhaust pipe. Despite this, Brody believed enough carbon monoxide was flowing through the garden hose to get the job done. He got out of the van, slammed the door closed and nodded to the ghost who offered him a jaunty salute.

"See you in a while," the old man said cheerfully as Brody walked into the church.

Bright lights, hideously loud gospel music and high praise assaulted him, making him feel a little queasy. Or was it the car exhaust seeping into the sanctuary? It didn't matter, he thought as he plunked himself down in the front pew. His children clustered around him. In a few short minutes, nothing would matter any more.

He gazed upon his children's lovely faces. Brody's heart ached for them. Christina placed her little hand on top of his. He was amazed at the paleness contrasting against his own skin.

Brody frowned. Christina looked at him, her eyes an incredible green-gold. They glistened in the light as if they were made of highly polished metal.

"Daddy? What is it? What's wrong?" she asked.

"Why nothing, baby, nothing at all."

Christina snuggled against his shoulder. "We love you Daddy," she said.

"I know," Brody replied. He snuffed out his doubts, relaxed and waited for dawn.

-8-

"Ah shit!" Billy Wong swore as he and Lonnie moved through the untended azalea bushes surrounding the church. "See what that crazy bastard just did?"

"I saw it," Lonnie said, grim. "I'll tend to it." He crouched low, crashing like a buck in rut through the undergrowth. Once he cleared the brush, he sprinted across the cemetery. He made maybe one hundred yards when he saw a red beam of light streak across his path. He stopped short, pivoted, and for a second his mind returned to a play he remembered when he was a high school running back.

The red light danced across Lonnie's chest. He scrambled out of the way. A blast, more felt than heard, shattered his right shoulder. Lonnie fell, grunting as the ravaged flesh protested as he rolled over on it. Half crawling, half staggering, he took refuge behind a crumbling concrete angel statue.

Lonnie heard the second shot. He cringed behind the deteriorating antebellum angel as a large chunk blew off next to his ear. "Who is that, Little Pete?" he called to his partner.

"Sure looks like it," Billy concurred.

Little Pete was a sniper during Nam and was quite good at it. Rumor had it he still did "jobs" but Lonnie never found any proof of that. At least nothing he could run him in on. Which, Lonnie thought ruefully, was a damn shame. *Now I'll just have to kill him, and the paperwork is going to be hell.*

He peeked around the corner of the statue. The laser beam glanced along the base. Damn. "Pete," he called. No answer. But then again, he didn't expect one. "Pete, this is the law. You don't want to get into any more trouble boy. You've had enough trouble in your life. Don't make a bad situation even worse by killing an officer."

The responding gunshot reported throughout the cemetery. Lonnie ducked as a corner of the statue flew in various directions. *Yep, it's Little Pete all right,* he thought.

He heard the angry cry of his partner's .45 as it sent its payload into the darkness. Lonnie held his breath. *I'm pinned,* he thought. *Pinned and bleeding like a stuck hog to boot.* He looked around, keeping the panic shoved down deep inside as he scanned the cemetery. *I sure hope there's nobody on my side of this statue,* he thought as he glanced over his shoulder. *If there is, I'm fucked.*

Wong squeezed off a few more rounds. Little Pete answered his challenge while Lonnie pulled his own revolver from the holster. *It's like the damned OK Corral out here,* he thought. *Just like the OK Corral, and everyone knows how that sucker ended up.*

Chapter Twenty-Nine

-1-

Trembling, Ouida slid along the slick tile walls of the morgue, occasionally encountering clusters of steel doors as she passed by. They reminded her of mini cold storage freezers she saw when she was nineteen and working at the local Sizzler Steakhouse. *But those ain't slabs of beef behind those gleaming silver doors,* she thought. *Oh no.* Mist spilled down the corridor, filling it until it was chest high. It clotted instantly, carrying with it thick globs of something that had the same consistency as whipped topping.

Ouida stifled a profound urge to scream. What looked like lumps of whipped topping coalesced until they formed bodies. Men, women and children of indeterminate age rose from the vapor and began their sojourn down the morgue proper. *I'm not really seeing this, am I?* she wondered as she followed the dead. Curious, she lagged behind them as they marched down the hallway filled with little rooms and what appeared to be laboratories, judging from the equipment she spied as she moved past the heavily paneled glass doors.

Sudden, imperative thumps coming from another cluster of doors just ahead of her caused her to shriek. Ouida turned to run, but saw that the cold storage unit doors behind her were also being kicked open on both sides of the hallway.

The freshly dead dragged their bodies out of storage and limped along with the ghosts for a few feet. Then like snakes shedding their skin, the lusterless light of the human soul peeled itself away, leaving the body to slump onto the floor.

Ouida ran, her heels clicking a desperate beat against the tile floor as she stumbled against the shambling corpses. The offices and labs receded as she followed the ghosts to a darker, grayer, cement-encased hallway that echoed the desperate tick, tick, tick from her heels as she ran. The ghosts did not seem to notice, however. And she followed the softly chanting beings as they made their way up a long un-tiled ramp toward a set of thick metal doors.

She uttered a high-pitched hysterical shriek between her fingers as the ghosts walked through the closed door and exited the building. *Of course, of course,* she thought, her mind bogged down with too much information. *That's what ghosts are supposed to do, after all. Would you honestly expect them to open the door?* Ouida yelped again, and the shriek contrasted against the low, agonized chant resonating from the exiting dead.

-2-

"Get your head down," Tim Spruell barked as he shoved Megan's head into the underbrush. "They're shooting and busting up everything over here."

"What's going on?" Megan asked, struggling to peer between the bushes. "What are you looking at?"

"Someone's getting shot at but I can't tell much else," Tim replied as he peeked over the hedge, his mind taking a comical turn as he did so. He was suddenly reminded of an ancient Artie Johnson skit on that old TV show, *Laugh In. Verry interresting,* good old Artie used to say as he peeked through the set shrubbery. As a ten year old in the sixties, that scene made him howl. And he repeated it over and over in class until his teacher became exasperated and sent him to detention. Now the memory resurfaced and he didn't feel like laughing.

A shotgun blast shouted in the darkness. A pistol, apparently belonging to one of the sheriff's deputies, answered. Another large chunk blew off the concrete angel. The Cold Hanging Tree blazed, gouging out deep shadows where the green light spilled onto the cemetery. More of the ground had died too, Tim noted. The scorched earth was already up to the parking lot.

Tim looked up. The sky turned a hazy greenish black, obscuring the stars, changing the moon a bizarre purple color.

The deputy on the edge of the forest fired his weapon. A

loud grunt and one of the rednecks fell out of his perch in a nearby cypress tree and landed like a dark pile of rags onto the ground.

"Lonnie, you okay?" a voice in the darkness asked, confirming Tim's suspicions. *Oh shit, it's Lonnie and Bill,* Tim realized.

"Hey Lonnie."

"Keep down," Lonnie roared, waving at their general direction.

Lonnie bailed from his cover behind the angel. He made a mad dash, holding one shoulder as he galloped Quasimodo-like across the cemetery and back into the woods.

"You need to lie low," Tim said as he pushed Megan's head down again.

"I can't," she said. "See that van over there? It's mine. My husband is here. He's—"

"—Well it's too late to get it now," Tim said, impatience rising along with his fear and anxiety.

"No," she said, "you don't understand. The engine's running. Can't you hear it? Why would it be left running so close to the church, unless—"

Tim and Megan stared at each other, the same thought occurring to them at the same time. Before Tim could move, she bolted out from under the bushes and headed for the AeroStar.

"Goddammit, come back here, you crazy bitch," Tim shouted.

-3-

Oh thank you Lord Jesus, it's unlocked, Ouida prayed with profound sincerity as she forced open one of the doors and let herself out. She shivered despite the hot, sticky air that clung to her, dampening and chilling her arms and face as she broke out in a cold sweat. She looked around and found herself in the maintenance portion of the hospital. This was where the basement opened into the bottom of an enormous concrete pit. Hearses as well as ambulances were parked around the periphery. A utility truck and two odd looking emergency vehicles squatted on the bottom of the enormous concrete bowl.

She scanned the rim. On the far right side, she saw a small

ramp where trucks drove down into the basin. Gathering up the tattered remains of her resolve, she ascended the steep driveway. *How do those trucks manage to get down here?* Ouida wondered as she scrambled up the steep incline. Desperate not to slide back down again, she crawled on her hands and knees onto the lip of the pit.

Once free of the hospital proper, Ouida rested against the side of an ambulance. The ghosts, now chanting a deep, woeful spiritual, moved down the street *en masse*. She could see the sparse traffic stopping abruptly then turning and speeding away in the opposite direction. More spirits rose from the thick lumps of fog and followed their companions. Seconds later, the ghostly troops moved away from downtown, out toward the luminous green haze on the horizon.

Without warning, the ground shook. Ouida grabbed at a nearby ambulance door handle and held on tight as the ground snapped and flicked as if God was beating a rug hanging from a clothesline. Just as suddenly as it started, it stopped.

Mama, Ouida thought. An aftershock sent her tumbling back against the ambulance. The vehicle skidded away from her and she did a comical little shuffle trying to catch up with it. The ambulance squealed as it slid sideways into a chain link fence on the opposite side of the lot. She leaned against the vehicle and gasped for breath.

Glass from the hospital towers, as well as from all the nearby buildings, exploded in a tremendous, shattering blast. Ouida dove under the ambulance, covering her head with her arms as the shrapnel rained down like hailstones onto the parking lot. Tiny hot sparks pelted her face and hands despite the relative safety underneath the ambulance. Her clothes, tattered and ruined from climbing out of the pit, offered little protection to her arms and the back of her neck, which was ablaze with tiny pinpricks of glass.

Sudden awful silence hung in the air as the window glass finally quit falling. A long, low howl from the emergency alert sirens across town pounded against the night. The siren picked up its tempo as it bayed. Ouida clapped her hands to her ears, tears spilling down her cheeks as she gazed up into the greenish-black sky.

Movement from the hospital doors attracted her attention. Personnel, hospital staff and patients who could walk vacated the building. Seconds later a low wall of blood disgorged into the parking lot, knocking slower patients off their feet. Others did their best to scramble out of the way. Bawling, Ouida scrambled out from under the ambulance then ran two blocks down the street in ankle-deep matted clots of blood and gore.

Ouida wailed in desperation and despair as she fled into the night. She did this despite herself, knowing she'd have to abandon her mother to the wrath of the blood-drenched hospital. She was unable to rescue her and knew that her mother wouldn't come even if she tried.

-4-

"Forget the instruments, the revival is here," Pa Neidi commanded his family as he hoisted his youngest up onto his hip. Ma and Dougie followed Pa past the jubilant congregation while the twins, now closer than ever, held hands as they scuttled behind their parents. Quickly they exited out of the side door.

Pa paused and looked back into the sanctuary. He openly laughed at the congregation and their leader who was so enraptured that they hadn't noticed they had slipped out, nor did they realize the church was rapidly filling with carbon monoxide. *Perfect*, he thought as he saw the angels appear. *Let the feast of the dead begin.*

Thomas, consumed with the unholy spirit, turned around and stared at the back wall. "She's here," he shouted. "The Whore of Babylon has come."

Neidi cackled and responded to Thomas's prophesy by slamming the door shut and locking it from the outside. Singing while gunfire played behind them, the Neidis marched into the rich, humid air and toward the marshes beyond the boat ramp.

-5-

Shotgun blasts kicked up large chunks of dirt and grass as Megan rushed toward the van. Her heart pounding, she plunged against the far side of the vehicle while bullets punctured and ricocheted off the metal finish on the passenger's side door. The garish light from the tree gouged out stark black shadows across the side of the church. Flames towered high into the sky. She found refuge in those shadows and moved as close to the van as she dared. The little pendant around her neck blazed, burning between her breasts. She ignored it.

An angel rose from the ground in front of her. Startled, she skidded to a stop, uttering a tiny shriek as the thing lunged at her. She turned to run away, but it grabbed her shirt and yanked hard. Megan toppled backwards, right into the arms of the beast. She could smell its rotting breath. She caught a sideways glimpse of rows of needle-thin teeth as it lurched for her neck.

Megan twisted, facing the creature and, either by instinct or by desperation, she would never truly know, she snatched the pendant and shoved it hard between the thing's prominent eyes. The angel wailed and went up in flames. Megan staggered back, gagging as the smell of scorched, rotting wood assailed her.

Two more angels arose and marched towards her, their eyes blazing, their jaws unhinged and showing off rows of metallic teeth. Megan ran, a loud whooshing roar rushing in her ears as she bolted toward the rear of the vehicle. The angels glided toward her. There were four or five now, lustful, hungry, gibbering between themselves as they approached. Megan thrust the amulet forward, making her think somewhat hysterically of an old Dracula movie where someone was fending off the Prince of Darkness with a crucifix. Light pulsed from the amulet. The angels tried to shield themselves from it, but went up into towers of bright white flame.

Megan scrambled back into the shadows. A bullet whizzed past her left shoulder. She could hear muffled swearing from her partner in the bushes. Ignoring Tim's pleas to return, she inspected the hose belching fumes into the window. Her heart plummeted as she looked inside the van, hoping, praying that Brody was still inside and at the same time terrified he might be hiding in the back with that awful hammer in his hands.

He was not.

Megan returned to the window and tugged at the hose. Instantly, she yanked her hands away, astonished at how it could be so hot. Yet it hadn't melted. But judging by the blistering, rubbery smell it wouldn't be long before it did.

Another gunshot blew grass and dirt across her right leg.

Too close, she thought as she snugged herself up tight while the deputies shot at the sniper in the woods. There was only one way to let in all the fresh air that she could, Megan thought. Calming her pounding heart, she crept back to the van, slid open the side panel door and slipped inside. Bullets pocked the van with metallic glee as she shoved the stick shift in reverse, engaged the clutch and floored the engine.

The AeroStar roared as it launched itself backwards into the church office. Wood and glass and cinder blocks shattered as the van rammed through the wall. A sudden avalanche of building facade crumbled on top of the van, causing it to rock violently from the impact. Megan was thrown against the steering wheel, the airbag rushing out to cushion her as she plummeted toward the windshield.

Megan lay stunned, her face pillowed in the dying remains of the airbag. *I have to get out*, her dimming mind warned her. *I have to help Brody.*

-6-

Mr. Jim slapped the gun out of the astonished man's hand. The weapon landed butt first onto the dash and discharged, neatly punching a hole into the rear tire well. The man swung. Jim blocked the intruder's punch and slammed the door open, pinning the man between the door and the side of the truck. Jim beat the man for a good five minutes before his rage dispersed. Not caring whether he killed the guy or not, Jim shut the truck door and backed away, letting the man fall onto the pavement.

-7-

Brody woke, groggy and confused. The church, once so loud with song and praise, was now silent. His tongue felt thick and dry and his head pounded. It was almost too heavy to lift and it took several tries before he rolled off his side and sat up. *They're all asleep,* Brody realized as he looked around. Supplicants were stretched out in the pews. Some were hunched over, clutching Bibles or hymnals, while others, like himself, were sprawled in the aisles.

And the angels were gone.

He groaned and held his head, which was now much too

clear. Flecks of light blazed inside his thick, pounding head as he moved. He pushed his palms into his eyes. "Where am I and what's happening?" Vague fear pierced him. "What am I doing here?" he wondered aloud. "And where's Megan?"

Adrenaline swept through him, clean and cold.

Megan, he thought. *There was something about Megan. But what was it? The last thing I remember was that we had... A fight,* he recalled. *But I don't remember what it was about or why I was so angry.*

"Daddy?" He heard the strained and distant plea. He raised his head. Nausea jolted his stomach. He was encircled by globs of greenish-white mist. He could almost make out the faces of children inside the vapor. Almost. But then the image faded until there was nothing left but a thin remote voice. "Daddy?" the mist whispered. "Don't you love us any more? Don't you want to be with us anymore?"

Brody closed his eyes. The sparks became more vibrant as his head pounded. "Get away from me," he muttered.

"Daddy?"

"Go away." He turned his head, mentally begging the room, the over bright room, to stop its crazy tilting. "Go away. I ain't your Daddy."

-8-

"The way of the cross leads home," Mr. Jim Balfour bellowed as his white extended cab roared up the driveway, then bounced and danced across the now-vacant church parking lot. "The way of the cross leads home." He jumped the parking lot's curb, singing as the truck rocketed through the tent. The king cab dragged it like slain ghost. He laughed as it tore loose from the windshield and billowed into the air as it flew away.

Jim shouted as he floored the accelerator and drove full tilt across the cemetery, the truck crushing headstones as he went. He hit one of the larger stones as he approached the tree and the king cab launched its front two wheels into the air. The truck slammed down hard on all four wheels. Jim's head smacked against the roof as he fought to regain control of the vehicle. Ignoring the pain, Jim swung the truck in a mad arc around the little fenced-in portion of the graveyard. The truck purred like a well-fed tiger as Mr. Jim shoved the vehicle into reverse and rammed the tail gate against the tree.

Mr. Jim was thrown forward, his forehead striking the airbag deployed by the steering wheel. He rested, momentarily stunned, as the tree shrieked and writhed, smashing its limbs down hard on the truck. The passenger's side of the roof caved in. The branches tore the metal apart, struggling to reach inside the cab.

In one quick fluid move, Jim opened the door and tumbled out. He rolled onto the ground, leaning behind the truck bed. He was close to the Hanging Tree now, as close as he had been since last spring when Pa and Dougie introduced him to the thing that lived inside it. He glanced at the tree, which was now too bright to stare at for long, and realized there was an almost radioactive glow filling the cracks around the roots.

Mr. Jim reached into the truck bed, and hearing a loud buzz breeze past his ear, he ducked behind the tire well. "You know the end is coming, don't you?" he asked it. "You thought tonight was your night, but it's not. There'll be no revival for your sorry ass, not now, not ever."

The tree limbs twitched. The trunk groaned and thrummed deeply. The light underneath the exposed roots pulsed.

He heard another gunshot, followed by a report from the sheriff's weapon. Red-gold light from the .45 blasted in the darkness beyond the tree line. There was a heavy thud, a wayward blast from a shotgun, and Mr. Jim grinned. *Another redneck bites the dust,* he thought.

He turned to the tree. "You're next," he said. The tree swayed in a nonexistent breeze as he rummaged around in his truck for the come along and logging chain he used during the monsoon season to pull out wayward vehicles stuck in the mud.

The tree thrummed, moaned and swayed. The limbs slammed against the ground as he ran the chain around the gnarled blackened trunk.

"Close but no cigar," he laughed as he made it to the back of the truck. "You ain't getting hold of me again. Oh hell no."

The ground vibrated as if a high voltage current passed through it.

"Where did the Neidis go? Are they off in hiding? And your angels too. I don't see them no more. Got too much going on to keep all the illusions going?" he shouted over the angry thrum. "It's all parlor tricks. You ain't God and there's no second coming. Not for you anyway," Jim shouted.

The throbbing, followed by a high-pitched shriek, reached a climax and the earth shook. Mr. Jim landed face first onto the charred earth, his fingers digging deep onto the ravaged soil. The ground cracked open. The world shook itself like a wet dog. Corpses, some recent, but others long dead, rose from their graves. As they stepped onto the ground, their bodies fell in deep, rotting clumps as their spirits continued their journey toward the tree. Jim felt his bladder loosen when he saw old Charlie Estille walk past, shed his decayed and mangled husk and glide toward the tree. Charlie joined A.J. Jones along with rest of the graveyard denizens as they circled the swaying creature in the form of a tree. They stood whispering, chanting and swaying with their ghostly arms outstretched.

They're waiting, Jim realized. *They're waiting for something, but what?*

Chapter Thirty

-1-

Trembling and bruised, Megan eased herself out of the dead van and stumbled out into the churchyard. From there she could see the white extended cab truck parked and idling, waiting faithfully for its master as the tall lanky man tied off the chain and furiously worked at the come along. The earth rolled out from under her. Megan lay in the grass and watched, shocked, as the graves split open. She crossed herself, closed her eyes and uttered a prayer to Saint Lazarus.

Megan opened her eyes and saw the man had also fallen. She moved quickly toward the tree. She was naturally afraid of being shot and even more afraid of the tree itself. Yet she was compelled to go toward to the blazing green column surrounded by ghosts. Seeing her, the specters uttered a dreadful cry.

Megan watched in horror as the tree swept its branches down, engulfing the fallen man. The tree raised itself up like a child standing tip-toe. Then in a quick twist, it hurled the bloodied pulp of what remained of Mr. Jim Balfour against the truck's tailgate. She clasped her hands to her mouth.

Tim shouted. Megan turned just in time to see Thomas float out of the church. He drifted over the rubble and hovered inches from the ground, his eyes gold-green, the pupils bursting red as he leered at her. His huge, gruesome mouth overflowed with ghastly green light. He stretched out his arms and rushed toward her. The toes of his shoes dug a thin trench in the ground as he approached.

Megan screamed. She turned and ran toward the king cab. She slammed into the driver's side of the truck, then yanked open the door. The deployed airbag bulged outward and she

280

sobbed as she did a desperate half assed job of shoving it aside. Just as she was about to climb into the cab, something cold and horrible grabbed her by the back of her neck and yanked her down hard.

Thomas hauled her to her feet. Megan struggled to get away, but the thing formerly known as James Thomas shoved her hard against the truck cab. She sagged, dizzy, her mouth smashed and bloody. Thomas spun her around smartly and shoved his face against hers. He was so close she could smell the rotten sweetness of decaying tree bark, hear his gurgling rattle as he clamped his mouth down on hers, and then sucked.

Megan felt the universe give way. Her soul ripped and shredded as he tore her loose from the inside out. She slumped backwards, drained, empty. She was devoid of substance while something truly dark and terrible filled her. *Hail Mary, Mother of God,* she prayed.

A sudden scorching sensation blazed between her breasts. The scent of sandalwood, once so faint she hadn't noticed it, now filled the air around her with rich blue smoke. She reached up between the compressed flesh between herself and Thomas and ripped the pendant from her neck. She shoved it against his ear. Thomas jerked away, growling and swearing only to clamp his mouth down this time much harder on hers.

There was a sudden, loud explosion. Thomas reeled backwards. She slumped against the truck, dazed and gasping for breath as the light shot through his eyes, nose, mouth and through the hole in the back of his skull where Lonnie Cox had shot him. Thomas blew apart in a brilliant blaze of light. The tree screamed and writhed in agony. Megan sagged against the truck, choked and gagged as her soul settled back into its spiritual moorings.

"Move aside," Lonnie said gently. "It's just about over." Megan sagged against Billy who carried her away from the truck while Lonnie got into the cab. There was a moment of grinding uncertain gears. Then he floored the engine.

Again, the tree shrieked, squirmed and thrashed. Like a rotten tooth being yanked from a decayed skull, the tree uprooted, unplugging the unholy light deep beneath the earth. She watched as the ghosts who encircled the tree began to step into the crater.

Megan gasped for breath, feeling the life return to her body, but her soul felt tainted somehow, and deep down she knew she'd never be the same again. *Never mind about that now*, she thought. *I have to do what I came here for.* Standing, swaying despite the returning strength to her legs, she gripped the amulet that found its way back into her hand. Slowly, she made her way toward the tower of light.

"Wait a minute," Billy shouted as he ran to catch up with her. He took her by the elbow and tried to guide her back toward the church.

'No," she said, shocked at how hoarse she'd become. "No, no, I can't. I have to do this first."

"Do what?" Billy asked, confused.

"It has to go into the hole," she explained as she showed him the amulet. "I have to do it, nobody else."

Billy pursed his lips and then nodded. "I'll help you." Holding her around the waist, he guided her toward the flames that shot at least three hundred feet in the air.

She stood, regarding the tree. *It puts out light but it's not hot. It's cold, like water from an artesian well.* Megan held the amulet in her right hand. "Saint Jude, Patron Saint of Hopeless Causes, Holy Mary, Mother of God, guide my hand," she prayed. She held her breath. Then, with her remaining strength, she tossed the spinning orb into the flames.

Billy and Megan stumbled away from the tower of light as it blasted from the hole. Tim left his refuge behind the shrubs and ran toward them, meeting them near the parking lot just as Megan collapsed into his arms.

"Look," she gasped. Her was voice hoarse, as if her throat had been scrubbed out with sandpaper. "Look at the woods."

The men turned their attention from the tower of light blazing from the crater to the thick greenish-white mist that formed in the woods and spilled down into the parking lot.

"There must be hundreds of them," Lonnie said, awed.

The processional of the dead marched past, chanting as they rose from the mist. There were men, women, children. People on horseback of every size and age. Young people riding along in a cotton wagon. An elderly freedman clucked to a pair of spectral mules as the wagon passed by. A little boy of about five or six waved at her. She raised her hand timidly.

"Are we really seeing this?" Billy whispered as the leading edge of the procession entered the glowing abyss and shot up into the towering flames.

Instantly, the light changed from green to a brilliant bluish-white. Megan and the men shielded their eyes as the processional stepped into the glare. Megan's heart ached for the spirits who became one with the light as they flashed like fireflies toward Heaven.

At last, Thomas, now dressed in antiquated preacher's garb, smiled and waved goodbye as he, along with his wife and daughter, stepped into the light.

As the last of the spirits entered the netherworld, the ground trembled. The tombstones in the cemetery crumbled to dust as the church roof collapsed. The extended cab slid into the hole, the headlights blazing an astonished yellow as it disappeared into the depths. Several coffins disturbed by the tremors were unearthed and toppled onto the ground like a gruesome toy box.

Megan moaned, tears streaming down her face. Lonnie and Billy, too disoriented by the tremors, were unable to get into the church before the remainder roof collapsed with a horrendous crash.

"Let me go," Megan cried as the tilted building sagged and then eased itself onto the ground. "Let me go, damn you," she croaked as Billy Wong grabbed her. She pounded her fists against his broad uniformed chest. "My husband is in there." She tried to pull away but she was too weak and the ground wouldn't stop its crazy dance. *It's too late*, she thought. *I lost Brody. I lost my Brody. I lost my sweet Brody...*

-2-

For the last time that month, rescue vehicles and curious bystanders appeared on the site of the now destroyed First Light Church of Prophecy. The tree, now a ruined, charred husk, lay next to the smoldering hole that, after nearly two hours of squealing and writhing, finally snuffed out.

Megan sat on the silver-grated foot guard on the fire truck. Despite the summer heat, she shivered beneath a blanket and watched as shell-shocked looking firefighters and rescue workers sifted through the ruined remains of the church. Ouida

Spruell hugged the younger woman close.

Slowly, Thomas's "faithful" were extracted from the rubble. Some of them were carried immediately to the waiting ambulances. Others walked out on their own, looking stunned and confused as oxygen masks were applied to their faces. Only a few were carried out in body bags.

"I'm sure they'll find him shortly," Ouida said, trying to sound confident.

"I'm glad you're here," Megan whispered. "I'm so scared. What am I going to do without him?"

"I was lost and I was found too," Ouida replied. "If it hadn't been for Tim's brother spotting me on the road an hour ago, I don't know what I would have done."

"You're so lucky to have Tim," Megan said. "If it weren't for him I'd be dead right now."

"Well, I'm glad that didn't happen," Ouida said. "Now let's not lose faith that your own husband will be joining you soon."

"He went crazy, totally out of his mind over that tree."

"Well, I've been told that once that devil's tree was uprooted, folks who were tempted by it returned to normal. I'm sure you husband will be as well."

Megan waited. The hours passed. Someone, sometime during the night, placed a cup of coffee in her hand. She sipped it slowly, feeling recharged by the heat and caffeine. Ouida stayed and comforted her new friend as the wait stretched on until the moon faded from the sky and the reddish-tinge from the sunlight obscured the early violet of dawn.

There was a sudden cheering from the remains of the old church. Megan blinked, trying to look past her tears as she recognized the unsteady lope of her husband's gait as he and two emergency workers passed from the dust-strewn ruins. "Brody," she shouted, overjoyed as she tossed aside both Styrofoam cup and blanket. She raced across the lawn and into her husband's embrace.

"Megan," Brody moaned as he held her tight. "My God," he whispered, his voice choked with emotion. He wept into her soft hair. "What in the world have you been rolling in?" he whispered in her ear.

Megan snuggled in his warm embrace and then laughed. "It's going to be all right now," she said, and meant it.

"Everything's going to be all right."

"We need to get you to Texarkana," the paramedic said to Brody. "The hospital there can get you checked out."

"I'll be right behind you," Megan said as Brody separated from her and was assisted into the ambulance. He waved and then the doors closed. The ambulance picked its way through the wreckage-strewn parking lot and disappeared down the road.

Megan, crying and laughing at the same time, met the Spruells who swept her away in their spare car toward Texarkana, and toward the newborn dawn.

Epilogue

"We sure hate to see you go," Ouida said as she helped Megan place the last box of kitchen utensils in the moving truck. "After all, we were just getting to know each other."

"I'm sad too," Megan said. She put the box down, turned and looked out of the square entrance and at her husband who was helping Tim navigate the refrigerator down the makeshift porch ramp. "We thought about it, but after everything that's happened, we decided to move. The memories and all—"

"I understand," Ouida said, gazing over her young friend's shoulder to observe her mother. Cora-Lee was sitting on the swing, covered in a bright afghan. She was having an animated conversation with an invisible friend. Ouida sighed. Her mother never recovered from the delusion of seeing Davy. *She sees him now, even after everything that's happened,* Ouida thought. *She still sees and talks to him.*

"Will she recover?" Megan asked, sensing Ouida's thoughts.

Ouida sighed. "The doctor says it's Alzheimer's. She's probably had a mild form of it for a while, but after everything that's happened, it just brought it to the surface."

"I'm so sorry," Megan said.

"Now, tell me. What about that man of yours? Has he recovered from what's happened?"

"I don't know," Megan said. "I think he has. He seems like the same happy guy I know and love. Although I know he feels guilty about all the things he said to me and what he tried to do to me. Poor Brody, he just can't seem to stop apologizing."

"He wasn't responsible," Ouida said. "Satan had hold of

286

him."

"Yes, that's what our priest said during our counseling sessions. He thinks that it would be best if we made a fresh start somewhere else. Somewhere far away where he won't be reminded of what we'd been through."

"I understand that. In some ways I wish Tim and I could grab the kids and get away from here too."

"Yeah."

"Ain't it peculiar," Ouida said confidentially, "that we're the only ones who seem to remember exactly what happened?"

"I haven't thought about it," Megan confessed. "My only concern is for Brody. I guess I hadn't been paying much attention."

"But what about your priest? Does he still remember?"

Megan pursed her lips. "He did at first, but the last time we talked he was abrupt. Told us that leaving the bayou was for the best. For everyone."

"I see. And you're going through with it?"

Megan laughed. "It would be hard to back out now."

"So where are you going?" Ouida asked as she adjusted two more boxes into neat cubbies.

"Bandera," Megan replied as she helped shift larger boxes so the extra space could accommodate the quickly approaching refrigerator. "We're using my studio money for the move as well as taking out some cash from our retirement for a down payment on a house. Brody's got a job at one of the CPA firms there and as soon as this old house sells, we'll be set again financially. It'll be a hardship at first, but we've been through worse."

"And there'll be lots less mosquitoes," Ouida said, laughing as she slapped one of the insects away from her face.

Megan returned the laugh, and then both women shouted with good-natured humor as the men rolled the refrigerator into the van.

-2-

Lonnie Cox and Billy Wong vacated their office early in the day to meet at their favorite park bench for lunch. They both sat and watched as life paraded around them. It was so good to sit in the heat, munching sandwiches with everything returning to normal.

"The eggheads up at the university said it was an earthquake," Lonnie said around a wad of tuna salad.

"Earthquake my ass," Billy said. "They weren't here and they didn't see what we saw last month."

"I know, but the official report is that Mercer's Bayou was the epicenter of an earthquake and that's what blew out all the windows in town as well as collapsing the church."

"Bullshit, how do they explain the blood running in the streets?"

"The lab reports say it wasn't blood at all but red sediment from the flood plains."

"Even more bullshit."

"Well, that's what everyone believes, and I think that's for the best. Everyone whom I spoke to who touched those flyers has no memory of what happened."

"None?"

"No, it's like someone wiped a hard drive with a magnet."

"And you think this is a good thing?"

Lonnie shifted uncomfortably on his concrete bench. "Do you want to remember what happened?"

Billy stared down into his lunch sack, extracted a fried pie and said, "No I suppose not."

"So I think we should just let sleeping dogs—"

"Lie, yeah, I get it."

"So right now, let's enjoy the fact that everything is going back to normal."

"Fine by me, but I do have a question for you."

"Okay, what?"

"What about the Neidis? They were there that night. Think we ought to run them in?"

"Run them in for what?" Lonnie asked. "They said they had left the church during the revival. Several witnesses say that they saw them leave right after the services were over." Lonnie shrugged. "They heard the gunshots out in the cemetery and decided to get out for the kids' sake. Suppose I can't blame them."

"And Wallace? He's not going to be charged?"

"Nope," Lonnie said as he dug through a bag of chips. "The DA doesn't remember what happened. So there was no crime. You, me, the Wallaces and the Spruells are the only ones who seem to know what's going on."

"That'll change in time too, I'm sure," Billy said with a faraway look in his eyes. "Even now their memories of what happened are fading, just like mine did. And yours. Don't tell me you still remember it all?"

Lonnie frowned. "I kept a log. That's how I'm keeping up."

"And the others?"

"I think they're letting nature take its course. In the morning, the earthquake story is going to sound plausible. In a week, everyone will agree that's what happened. In a month, no one will remember that there was even a preacher down on the bayou this summer."

"And what about the people who died? And what about the folks who left Mercer's before the end came?"

Lonnie laughed. "I don't have the answers to all the questions. But I suspect that the memories of those who left will fade too, and they'll think that, maybe sometime in the fall, I suppose, that they chose to leave for whatever reason or another. But those who died? It was just a series of tragic accidents, nothing else."

Billy laughed and shook his head. "You're full of answers today, ain't you?"

Lonnie shrugged. "Just speculation. There's an equal chance that Mercer's will become something like the incident at Roswell's where everyone knows a ship crashed there but nobody will own up to it."

"That sounds more plausible," Billy laughed. He gazed at the lake, the cool blue waters rippling as two men fished from a bass boat. Somewhere on shore, the sound of two teenagers in a brawl broke echoed down the shoreline.

"Yeah, I really am having trouble remembering," he confessed. "Where did all that graffiti around town come from?"

"Local thugs, I suppose."

"I want to remember what happened. It's important to keep it."

"Then just jot it down," Lonnie said. "That's what I've done. Leave it to future generations to decide."

Billy waved a celery stick in his partner's direction. "Now that sounds like a plan."

-3-

"Come help us rebuild our church," Pa Neidi called to the passing men and women who avoided the off-key band playing a strained form of bluegrass in the parking lot of the Super Target store. Pa hawked for collections while the men from the Victory in Jesus Mission for Lost Souls, as well as from the local Armory, carried buckets as they stood at the intersection, collecting funds as the stop lights held the traffic prisoner.

"Come help us rebuild the little church on the bayou. Come save the oldest church on Mercer's Bayou."

"Jesus loves you," the twins said in unison as a passerby dropped a wad of one dollar bills into the bucket by their bare feet.

"Hey, I'll pay you if you'll just quit playing," a man grumbled as he walked past.

"Jesus loves you anyway," Ma Neidi retorted as she ignored her youngest son as he slid the man's wallet out of his pocket.

"And God bless you for your contribution. Praise God. Praise Jesus... Bless you Lord."

-4-

Dougie Neidi drove his ATV into the old gray barn where his father once stored bales of hay. But now, newer technology created enormous round bails that wouldn't fit into the aged barn any more. Now the hay barn was kept as storage...and for other things.

Dougie turned off his four-wheeler, entered an old tack room and took out five ten-gallon plastic buckets he retrieved from a restaurant trash dumpster. Then he went back and pulled out the bags of potting soil, another bag of potash, a bottle of phosphorous and gardening equipment. He heaved down two gallons of water and then, when everything was ready, he moved to the back of his four-wheeler and extracted a toe sack filled with something that squirmed and groaned.

Dougie sang to himself. He put on a pair of leather gloves and then pulled heavy welding gloves over them. He added potting soil, phosphorus and potash to the buckets. A rooster crowed and he looked up, seeing the evening sun was declining behind the tree line. He smiled. *Just enough time left,* he thought.

He extracted a box labeled Uncle Severna's Rooting Extract from the collection of oddities clumped around his knees. Picking up the yellow carton with a ludicrous looking man grinning from the label, he decapitated the box. Holding his breath, Dougie opened the toe sack and extracted one of the writhing limbs from the Cold Hanging Tree. "God love you," he said sarcastically, "but I know better than to touch you, no siree. It won't do to die before the miracle is made."

He dunked an end of the limb into the rooting extract. Pulling it out, the powdery substance clung six inches up the stick. "Just right," Dougie grinned as he shoved the limb down into the soil. "It's a good thing folks are starting to forget," he told the rooted twigs. "If folks knew what I was up to, we'd all be lynched."

About the Author

To learn more about Patricia Snodgrass, please visit http://bluedelirium.bravehost.com. Send an email to Patricia Snodgrass at valhall13@yahoo.com.

In space, no one can hear you scream...
but don't let that stop you.

Tethers
© 2006 Sara Reinke

Survivor Kathryn Emmente must decide who is friend and who is foe when her cargo vessel, the Daedalus, explodes under mysterious circumstances. Many among her crew are killed and the rest are left helpless and stranded on a terra-farming colony moon of Jupiter called X-1226. They have no means of communicating with Earth or even the nearest stellar platform for aid.

Kat soon learns that the detonations aboard the Daedalus and the deaths of her fellow crewmates may not have been as accidental or incidental as they first appeared. She begins to suspect that one among the survivors may be operating on a hidden, sinister agenda—and that she and her young daughter, Jerica, could be the next victims.

Warning, this title contains the following: violence, strong language, sexual situations.

Available now in ebook and print from Samhain Publishing.

"Something's leaking in there, all right." Eric had stripped down to his underwear and sat on an examination table, while Frank leaned over his injured leg. "You've got some pretty extensive edema developing around your ankle and into your calf, and here around your knee, too." He glanced grimly at Eric. "And if you're pissing blood, that means it's already affecting your kidneys. I'm going to draw up some blood work, check your liver enzyme levels, too. That's my biggest concern right now. Stopping this before you go into liver or renal failure."

"Stop it how?" Eric asked.

Frank pressed his hands gently along Eric's knee and lower leg. "I don't know. But I'm going to try. This is real skin, right? Cloned tissue custom-developed for the prosthetic?"

Eric nodded.

"It's fed through a capillary system that ties into your bloodstream," Frank said. "The upper layers of underlying tissue, too, the muscles. That's how the lubricants from everything underneath, all of the mechanized parts, are getting into your system."

He glanced up at Eric. "They did a beautiful job of this." He patted Eric's leg. "Damn near a work of art. I may not have the right mechanical tools to get down in there, but I have scalpels. I can cut it open, try to figure out what's wrong once I'm inside."

He turned to a nearby cabinet and squatted, rifling through the contents. "I think I saw some surgical drains around here yesterday. Maybe I can rig up something with those so we can keep whatever's leaking out of your bloodstream."

Eric felt a glimmer of hope. "You think that will work?"

"At least until help gets here," Frank replied. "I'm hoping, anyway."

Eric forked his fingers through his hair. "I've been so fucking scared," he admitted shakily. "I thought I was going to die."

"In my line of work, that's only a last resort." Frank glanced at him and winked. "I think I can set everything up for surgery by lunch time. I'll find some way to distract Kat, don't worry. I'm going to give you something for the pain, in the meanwhile."

"No." Eric sat up.

"We've got plenty here," Frank said. "And there's no need for you to suffer."

"I can't." Eric was ashamed to tell Frank about his addiction; humiliated that Frank would discover he'd already been pilfering the compound's supplies. "I just...after the crash, when I lost my leg..." He looked down at his lap. "I got hooked on morphine. It took me years to get clean. It hasn't been that long ago, and I..."

Franklin opened the cabinet where the morphine was stored. If he noticed any missing, he didn't say anything. "You know what the difference between a junkie and a patient is, Eric?" He took a vial out. "A patient *needs* the drug. A junkie just *wants* it."

"Frank, I can't," Eric said, staring at the bottle of morphine.

Frank smiled at him. He opened a drawer and pulled out a fresh syringe. "Suffering is for martyrs and third-world countries. And while at the moment, this compound seems pretty damn close to that..." He winked at Eric again. "...it's not."

Frank set the morphine and the needle down. Eric jumped like he'd just placed a live rattlesnake next to him, and the doctor smiled.

"I'm your friend, Eric. You can trust me. I won't say anything to Kat. This'll stay between us. You're hurting. This can help you. *I* can help you—if you let me. That's my job."

"All right." Eric hung his head. He tried to tell himself that Frank was right; he wasn't going to use morphine because he wanted to. He needed to. *For Kat.*

Frank used a blood pressure cuff to cut off the circulation in Eric's arm. "How does that feel?" he asked, as he drew the needle out.

The effects were again almost instantaneous. Eric closed his eyes. "It feels great," he said, and he laughed. "Jesus Christ."

"Lay back, relax." Frank helped Eric lie down. "Ride with it. It's okay."

CREAT
cheap
FUN

Discover eBooks!

THE FASTEST WAY TO GET THE HOTTEST NAMES

Get your favorite authors on your favorite reader, long before they're
out in print! Ebooks from Samhain go wherever you go, and work with
whatever you carry—Palm, PDF, Mobi, and more.

Samhain
publishing
LTD

WWW.SAMHAINPUBLISHING.COM

Printed in the United States
142985LV00006B/1/P

9 781605 041698